Gather Yourselves
Together

Gather Yourselves Together

PHILIP K. DICK

Copyright © The Estate of Philip K. Dick 1994
Afterword Copyright © Dwight Brown 1994

The right of Philip K. Dick to be identified as the author
of this work has been asserted by him in accordance with
the Copyright, Designs and Patents Act 1988.

This edition first published in Great Britain in 2014
by Gollancz
An imprint of the Orion Publishing Group
Orion House, 5 Upper St Martin's Lane, London WC2H 9EA
An Hachette UK Company

3 5 7 9 10 8 6 4

A CIP catalogue record for this book is available
from the British Library

ISBN 978 0 575 13254 2

Printed in Great Britain by Clays Ltd, Elcograf S.p.A.

The Orion Publishing Group's policy is to use papers that
are natural, renewable and recyclable products and made
from wood grown in sustainable forests. The logging and
manufacturing processes are expected to conform to the
environmental regulations of the country of origin.

www.orionbooks.co.uk
www.gollancz.co.uk

1

IT WAS EARLY summer, and the day was almost over. It had been warm during the afternoon, but now the sun had set and the evening cold was beginning to come in. Carl Fitter walked down the front stairs of the men's dormitory, carrying a heavy suitcase and a small package tied with brown cord.

He paused at the foot of the stairs, stairs of rough wood, painted with grey porch paint that had chipped and peeled with age. They had been painted long before Carl had come to work for the Company. He looked back up. The door at the top was sliding shut slowly. As he watched, it closed tight with a bang. He put his suitcase down and made certain that his wallet was buttoned into his pocket in such a way that it could not possibly fall out.

"That's the last time I'll ever be going down those stairs," he murmured. "The last time. It'll be good to see the United States again, after so long."

The shades behind the windows had been pulled down. The curtains were gone. Boxed up somewhere. He was not the last person to leave the building; there was still the final locking up to do. But that would be done by the workmen, who would see to it that the windows and doors were tightly boarded, protecting the building until the new owners arrived.

"How miserable it looks. Not that it was ever such an inspiring sight."

He picked up his suitcase and continued down the walk. Clouds covered the setting sun, and only its last rays could be seen. The air, as it often does that time of evening, seemed full of little things; a layer of particles coming into existence for the night. He reached the road and stopped.

In front of him men and women were assembled around two Company cars. There was a large pile of luggage and boxes, and a workman was stacking them in the back of the two cars. Carl made out Ed Forester standing with a piece of paper in his hand. He walked over to him.

Forester raised his head. "Carl! What's the matter? I don't see your name down here."

"What?" Carl looked over his shoulder at the list. He could not make out any of the names in the evening gloom.

"This is a list of the people going with me. But I can't find your name here. You see it? Most people spot their own names right away."

"I don't see it."

"What did they tell you at the office?"

Carl looked vaguely around at the people standing about, and at the people already inside the two cars.

"I said, what did they tell you at the office?"

Carl shook his head slowly. He set down his things and carried the list over under one of the car headlights. He studied the list silently. His name was really not on it. He turned it over, but there was nothing on the back, only the Company letterhead. He gave the list back.

"Is this the last group?" he asked.

"Yes, except for the truckload of workmen. The truck will be leaving tomorrow or the next day." Forester paused. "Of course, it's possible — "

"What's possible?"

Forester rubbed his nose thoughtfully. "Carl, maybe you're one of those who's supposed to stay behind, until *they* get here. Why don't you go over to the office and see if you can find the main traffic sheet?"

"But I thought the people had been notified who — "

"Oh, well." Forester shrugged. "Don't you know the Company by this time?"

"But I don't want to stay here! I've already written home. My stuff is all packed. I'm all ready to go."

"It's only for a week or so. Go on over to the office and see. I'll hold the cars up for a few minutes. Hurry back if you're supposed to leave with us. Otherwise, wave to me from the porch."

Carl began to gather up his things again. "I can't understand it. I'm all packed. There certainly must be some mistake about this."

"It's six o'clock, Mister Forester," the workman called. "We're all loaded up."

"Good." Forester looked at his watch.

"Am I supposed to get in now?" one of the women asked.

"Get in. We have to catch up with the main group at the other side of the mountains. So we have to leave right on time."

"Goodbye, Forester." Carl put out his hand. "I'll run over to the office and see what the story is."

"We won't drive off until you come back, or we see you wave. Good luck."

Carl hurried off along the gravel path, into the gloom, toward the office building.

Forester watched him go up the stairs and through the door. After a few minutes he began to get impatient. The cars were loaded and the people were beginning to become uncomfortable and restless.

"Get your motors started," he said to the first driver. "We'll be taking off in a second."

He got inside the other car and slid behind the driver's seat. He turned to the people in the back seat.

"Did any of you notice somebody wave from the office?" They all shook their heads. "Damn him. I wish he'd do something. We can't sit here forever."

"Wait!" a woman said. "There's someone on the porch now. It's hard to see."

Forester peered out. Was Carl coming? Or was he waving? "He's waving." Forester spread himself out behind the wheel, making himself comfortable.

The other car started up and came abreast. It passed down along the road, its headlights blazing. Forester blinked and pushed his foot down on the starter.

"Poor kid," he murmured. The car moved under him. "It's going to be a long week."

He caught up with the other car.

Standing on the office porch, Carl watched the two cars drive slowly down the road away from the buildings, through the metal gates and out onto the main highway. It was very quiet, except for the sound of workmen somewhere, a long way off, nailing and pounding in the darkness.

2

"IT DOESN'T MATTER a bit to me," Barbara Mahler said. "I'm just a Company minion. I might as well stay here another week."

"It might even be over a week. It might be two weeks. We don't know when they're coming."

"So it's two weeks. Three, even. I've been here two years. I don't even remember what the United States looks like."

Verne could not tell if she were being sarcastic. The girl was standing at the window looking out at the machinery beyond. In the darkening fog of early evening the machinery looked like columns and pillars of ancient buildings that had been ruined by some natural catastrophe, so that nothing remained but these massive and useless supports. They were sprawled hither and yon, some one way, some another. Meaningless, sightless constructions from which everything valuable had already been removed and packed up in crates, stored away somewhere.

Dimly, the figures of two workmen appeared and passed by the window carrying some metal sections between them. They struggled silently, and disappeared into the darkness.

Barbara turned away. "What season is it?"

"Where?"

"In the United States. What time of year?"

"I don't know. Fall? Summer? No, it's summer here. What does it matter? Is it important?"

"I suppose not. Did you know there are people in the United States who voluntarily live in San Francisco?"

"Why not?"

"The fog." She gestured toward the window.

Verne nodded. "It bothers you? I'm surprised. You wouldn't be happier if it went away."

"I wouldn't?"

"I doubt it. You know what it looks like around here, behind the fog? The city dump. Or someone's old back yard. This is the back yard of the world. There's junk stacked up here going back—I don't know. The Company's been around a long time." He reached up and clicked on the overhead light. The office filled with a pale yellow glow.

"It's leaving now."

"It's leaving *here*. But it's arriving someplace else."

"Really?"

"You're a funny person. It's hard to tell what's going on in your mind. Maybe you're not thinking at all. At least, not like I conceive it. Women are like that."

"Oh, yes." Barbara walked away from the window. "I'll tell you what's on my mind. It's not our staying that bothers me."

"What, then?"

"It's their going. All of them pulling out."

"What else can they do?"

"They could put up some kind of a fight."

"Four hundred fifty million people are a lot to have to fight. Anyhow, let's face it. This whole region is Chinese. It doesn't belong to us. We have no legal claim to it. They've voided all contracts of this kind, all over China. As soon as the Revolution was over our goose was cooked. Everybody knew they'd throw out all the foreign business firms. Except maybe the Russians.

Our days have been numbered since the fall of Shanghai. A lot of other companies are doing just what we're doing."

"I suppose."

"We're lucky. We're far enough south to get across the mountains into India. That means we'll at least get out. Some of them in the north haven't been so lucky." Verne waved at the calendar on the wall. "1949 is going to go down on the books as a bad year for business. At least, in this part of the world."

"The people in Washington could do something."

"Maybe. I doubt it. It's the times. Trends in the great ebb and flow of history. Asia is no place for Western business firms to be hanging around. Anybody with half an eye could see this coming years ago. This stuff was brewing in 1900."

"What happened then?"

"The Boxer Rebellion. The same as this. The start. We won that. But it's been only a question of time. Let the yuks take over. The Company will have to chalk it up to profit and loss, whether it wants to or not."

"Anyhow, we'll be going back home."

"It'll be good to be out of here. You can feel it in the air. The tension. It'll be good to get out of it. We're too damn tired to keep this sort of thing going for long. It's too much of a drain. We're *personae* non *gratae*. Guests at the wrong party. Somebody else's party. We're not wanted. Can't you feel them all looking at us? We're in the wrong place."

"Is that how you feel?"

"That's how we all feel, out here. We're worn out. Our professional smile is beginning to wear a little thin. It's time we started edging toward the door."

"I don't like to get pushed."

"It's our own fault. We're being pushed because we stayed too long. We should have left fifty years ago."

Barbara nodded absently. She was not listening to what

Verne was saying. She was wandering around the office. "You know, it looks terrible without the curtains."

"The curtains?"

"They're gone. They took them down. Didn't you notice?" The office was shabby and bleak. The plaster walls were stained and scarred.

"I never noticed." Verne grinned. "Don't you remember? I never notice things like that."

Barbara turned her back to him and gazed out the window again. Outside, as the fog settled down from above, the great columns dissolved and grew even more vague and indistinct in the gloom.

"Don't you want to talk?" Verne said.

She did not answer.

"The last two cars are leaving about now. Want to go down and say goodbye to the lucky ones?"

Barbara shook her head. "No. I'm going over to the woman's dorm and start getting my room back in shape. They just now told me I was staying."

"They picked our names at random," Verne said. "Just luck. Or divine intervention. We stay — they go. Isn't it nice, you and I together? And one other person. I wonder who. Probably some lumphead."

Barbara went outside, down the porch steps.

Barbara walked slowly up the path to the dormitory building and stopped. A small group of workmen were putting a chain on the front door, with a large padlock.

"Hold on!" she said. "You can put your lock someplace else. This is an exception."

"We were only supposed to leave the office building and part of one of the men's dorms open," a workman said.

"Well, I'm not staying in the men's dorm I'm staying here."

"We were told —"

"I don't care what you were told. This is my place. I'm staying *here*."

The workmen considered, grouping together.

"Okay," the foreman said. They took the lock and chain back off again. "How's that?"

"What about the windows? Are you going to take the boards off?"

The workmen gathered their tools up. "Maybe one of your men can do it. We have a schedule. We have to get out of here this evening."

"I thought you were going to work through tomorrow."

The men laughed. "Are you kidding? There are yuks all around. We don't want to be here when they move in."

"You don't like them?"

"They smell like sheep."

"That's what they say about us. Oh, the hell with it. Go on, take off."

The workmen disappeared down the path.

"Yuks couldn't be any worse." Barbara went up the steps, inside the great, stark building. Once, it had been clean and white. Now it was grey; water had dripped down from the roof and formed long brown stains on the walls. The window frames were rusty, under the newly nailed boards.

"But it's what I have in place of a home. The god damn dirty old place."

She looked around, feeling for the light switch in the darkness. Her fingers touched it and she flicked it down. The hall lights came on. Barbara shook her head. The walls were covered with splotches of old scotch tape, from endless posters and notices. One notice alone remained.

NO SMOKING WITHOUT AUTHORIZED PERMIT

"Says you" had been pencilled underneath.

Barbara went on, up to the second floor. The doors leading off the hall were locked. She came to her own door, getting her key from her purse. She unlocked the door and went inside the room, crossing to the lamp. The lamp came on. The room was empty and dismal.

"My poor little room," Barbara said. Nothing remained but the iron bed, Company property, and the wood end table with its lamp. The painted floor showed an outline, where the rug had been. Not so much as a single spot of color had been left.

Barbara sat down on the bed. The springs creaked under her weight. She took a cigarette from her purse and lit it. For a time she sat smoking. But the barren room was too depressing. She got to her feet and walked restlessly back and forth.

"Christ."

At last she went back downstairs. She passed out into the darkness, down the steps, onto the path. By lighting matches she managed to find her way to the place where the baggage had been collected and stacked, by the side of the road. Most of it was gone. The great mound had shrunk to a tiny stack, a few wood crates and three suitcases. She found her own suitcase and pulled it away from the others. It was damp with mildew. And heavy.

She carried it back along the path, all the way to the women's dorm.

On the porch she stopped to catch her breath, resting the suitcase beside her. How dark the night was! Pitch black. Nothing stirred. They had all left, even the workmen. Cleared out as fast as they could. Everything was deserted, without sign of life.

It did not seem possible. The Company had always been alive with activity, all night long. The furnaces, the glowing slag, men working, trucks moving around. Gouges and scoops — But not now. There was only silence. Darkness and silence. Far up above her a few stars shone, faint and remote through the fog. A wind blew, moving among the trees by the side of the building.

She picked up her suitcase and carried it inside, into the gloomy hall, up the stairs to her own room. There, she lit another cigarette and sat down on the bed. Presently she unsnapped the suitcase. She took her clothing out, a robe, slippers, pajamas. Then her cold cream, deodorant, cologne, bottles and tubes. Nail polish. Soap. Her tooth brush. She laid them in a row on the table by the bed.

At the bottom of the suitcase she found her Silex coffee maker and a little brown paper package of coffee, tied with a rubber band. And some sugar and paper cups.

It was a damn good thing she had thought to pack the coffee and things in the suitcase, instead of letting the workmen crate them up. She plugged in the Silex and went down the hall to the bathroom to get water. She put the water and coffee into the Silex.

Then she changed, removing her clothing. She put on the bathrobe and slippers. She found a towel. A good warm bath and then to bed; that would help. Tomorrow things would seem brighter. At night, with all her things crated up, the world silent and deserted around her — No wonder she felt depressed.

Had she ever felt worse? The stained, bare walls reflected the stark light of the lamp bulb. No pictures. No rug. Just the iron bed, the dirty table, the long row of bottles and jars and tubes. And her underwear, lying at the end of the bed. God!

The coffee rushed up into the top. It would soon be ready. She unplugged it. What a way to live. Would it be like this for a whole week? Two weeks?

She poured a cup of coffee, adding a little sugar. Two weeks, perhaps. And with Verne. Of all the people in the world — It was a plot. Fate, as people used to call it.

Fate. She sipped the hot coffee, sitting on the bed in her bathrobe. What a hell of a situation! How was she going to stand it? Why did it have to be *him,* of all the people they might have picked!

It didn't seem possible. She looked around at the room. Could things be worse? The room was cold, barren. The cold was seeping around her, past the wool of the robe, chilling her. But the coffee made her feel a little better. Presently she began to feel sleepy. Her head ached dully. Her eyes were dry, tired.

She put the cup down on the floor and lay back, her head resting against the plaster wall. The springs groaned protestingly under her. She loosened her robe.

She was tired, tired and miserable. A week or two, living like this. And with *him* around. She closed her eyes. Her thoughts began to wander. She relaxed, her head sinking down. The pressure of the wall against her neck faded. The scratchy feel of the robe next to her skin began to recede.

She thought back, to other times. Other places.

Presently her cigarette ceased to glow. She had stubbed it out. Her cup of coffee grew cold.

Lying on the little iron bed she thought back, her mind wandering. The barren room around her dissolved and grew dim. The heap of underwear, the bottles and jars, the bleak walls, everything wavered.

She relaxed into her memories.

It was Castle she remembered. They had gone into the bars barefoot, in dirty pants and shirts. The bars had wood chairs and there were wood mugs on the tables. With no shoes they could feel sand on the floor under their feet. Most of the bars served fish dinners. Those bars had a fish smell about them.

Nobody seemed to mind if they were all sloppy and dirty, laughing and holding onto each other. She, Penny, and Felix. When it was warm enough in the evening they swam in the ocean without any clothes on. Sometimes they swam almost all night, and lay in bed the next day, too lazy to get up.

Felix and Penny were engaged. It had been decided that after their vacation, before school started in the fall, the two of them would get married. They would live in Boston, of course. Felix would go on with his post-graduate work in engineering, and Penny would continue to work at the library, at least until he got his degree.

Felix was tall and blond, with a small mustache. His eyes were always bright and button-shiny, and he looked down at people, his hands in his pockets or wrapped around a load of books. His skin was sunny and healthy; he was very good natured. Barbara liked him, but he got on her nerves. He tripped on things; he swung his arms when he talked. She found it hard to take him seriously.

Penny, plump and wearing a heavy canvas shirt, smoking a cigarette, was warm and attractive. She laughed, with a hearty, man-style deep bellow. She never wore lipstick, and when they came to Castle she brought only two pairs of shoes, both low heeled. And men's pants.

As for Barbara Mahler, at twenty, she found herself facing a world that was quite different from anything she had known in Boston. She faced it with a mixture of shyness and sullen reserve. When they were with people she sat off in a corner, holding a drink, impressing people as aloof and untouchable. If a man approached her she cut him down with a few well-chosen words. Actually, she was frightened. She was especially frightened of the very men she sent off, yet at the same time she wanted very much to talk to them.

At twenty, her hair was cut in a tight bob, even all the way around. It was brown and thick, with heavy wide strands. Like the Botticelli cherubs that one sees. Her nose was large and Roman, giving her face a strong hardness, but with a kind of young boy youthfulness. A combination of female austerity and masculine immaturity. To many she seemed more like an immature boy than a woman.

She was slender, then, with nice arms and legs. She wore a brass bracelet on her wrist; her only jewelry.

Sitting in the corner watching the group of people talking and laughing made her feel alone. She did not like to mix with them, and if she were forced to she spoke roughly and slowly, a few words at a time. Many years later she realized they all thought she was tough and hard. The men who tried to pick her up never repeated it.

She wrote to her family every week, especially to her younger brother, her favorite. Bobby was seventeen. He had dropped out of school to marry a silly, selfish girl who had been working as a secretary, and who had quit her job the same week that they were married. He had never returned to school, to the family's bitter dismay. Of all of them, Barbara was perhaps the only one who still wrote kindly and personally to the boy. And he appreciated the warm letters from his older sister.

Castle was a resort town up the coast from Boston. It was very small, and only a few people went there. But it had a lovely bay. In the winter time fishermen and shopkeepers lived in Castle, and perhaps one or two professional men who looked after them. But when spring came and the snow melted the tourists began to appear. Soon the real inhabitants were lost in a crowd of young people up from Boston. They rented cabins on the beach. They pitched tents, stayed in cars and in trailers, or in sleeping bags. As the summer came on, new faces appeared among them, old faces vanished. Finally it was fall, and they were gone.

Now, in July, Penny and Felix and Barbara lay in the warm sand, smoking and talking, enjoying the fish smells, the archaic streets and houses, the old wood that had been washed up from the sea around them. Ocean and wind, the smell of fish and salt and ancient timbers. But the last days of their vacation were on them. They would soon be going back to Boston.

Penny and Felix would be married. A new life was starting for them. But what of Barbara?

They had two cabins, next to each other. In the first one were Penny and Barbara; Felix had the other. After the first few nights Barbara woke up to find Penny gone. She was alone in the bed; the covers were tossed back on Penny's side. She was not in the bathroom. She had gone out.

Barbara lay in the bed, fully awake, thinking and looking out through the part of the window visible past the shade. There were stars out, bigger than the stars she saw from her Boston window, upstairs in the family home.

It was a warm night. Silence lay all around her. She felt strange, lying alone in the big bed, in the unfamiliar cabin. As if she were in a train, lost someplace in the world, moving through the night without any idea of direction. Past vacant fields, houses bolted up, stores closed for the night, signs turned off. Deserted streets and silence everywhere, without life or movement.

She thought about Penny. When would she be back? Of course she was with Felix. Penny was twenty-three, and they had been engaged for a long time. A vague unhappiness settled over Barbara. She pushed the covers from her and lay naked, thinking about Penny and Felix. The darkness was warm against her bare skin.

Finally she turned over and went to sleep.

In the later nights, when Penny was gone so often, Barbara had plenty of time to think about herself and what direction she was moving in.

She was young, younger than any of the other people she had

gone around with in Boston. Here, in Castle, they knew no one very well. Without Penny and Felix she was all alone. She was dependent on them. Her crowd was not here.

They were jazz enthusiasts, all of them. Not the jazz of the ballroom radio shows, the popular dance bands for high school proms. Their jazz was the real jazz, the jazz of the South, of New Orleans, the riverboats, the jazz that had moved up the river to Chicago. In Chicago it had become real music; in the hands of great musicians it had become an art.

Listening to the cornet of Beiderbecke, dead now, the rasp of Louis Armstrong, they found a raw, brutal and sophisticated music that seemed to move as they were moving. If the music were blind and lost, so were they also. They clung to this music, in the small places where it was played and heard, the cafés, the dim little Negro bars. There were records, the names, the sacred names. Bix. Tram. The hard, rough voice of Ma Rainey. Places and names. Sounds.

This was Barbara's crowd, but they were not here in Castle. They were back in Boston. Here she was with a new group which she did not understand; She felt no desire, when she watched them talking, to join in with them. A kind of heavy stupor settled over her; she moved away, to the back of the room, sitting quietly alone. By herself she watched. A spectator, perched on the arm of a chair, or leaning against a door. She seemed to be ready to leave at any moment, disdainfully, haughtily; in reality she struggled with the rising tide of terror, and the desire to fell in disorderly panic.

Lying in the darkness alone, night after night, looking past the shade at the great stars, she thought about herself. She thought: what will I be in a year? Will I be alive? Will I be in Boston? Will I be living this way?

The prospect of living as she was now, filled her with a cold despair. If she had to spend her life alone, sitting at the edge of rooms, watching the others, then it did not matter what happened to her. She might as well give herself to anything that came along, any cross-tide that might tear her loose and carry her off.

She thought again of Penny and Felix lying in bed together. She imagined the sweating, panting exhaustion of love. The periods of quiet. The blood. Restlessly, she kicked the covers back. She got out of bed and sat looking into the darkness. At twenty, her mind and body were a battleground for some internal fever that was working itself slowly to the surface. The symptoms were long in coming. The waves of intense longing and desire were still indistinct and wave-like, rolling around inside her like a heavy fluid.

She got up from the chair and paced back and forth. After a while Penny came inside quietly. She saw Barbara and stopped at the door.

"Hello, honey. I was out walking along the beach."

"I know," Barbara said. "How was it?"

"Fine."

Barbara got back into bed. "Coming?"

Penny came over and slid in beside her. Barbara felt her body, heavy and solid, almost like a man's body. She gasped suddenly, tense. But Penny was already asleep. Barbara lay back, staring up at the darkness, her mouth open a little, her hands clenched at her sides.

The next day was the beginning of their last day at Castle. Because they did not have as much money as when they had come, it was decided they would try to hitchhike back.

"Lots of people are driving down the coast, right now," Felix said. "An endless stream of shiny cars."

Barbara pointed out that it might mean they would have to separate; no car would want to pick up three people. Even two was a lot. The best would be to go singly, but of course, that would be no fun. They let the matter ride for a while. More urgently, there was a final party for them which some friends who were remaining were giving.

Penny and Felix went to the party together. Barbara was to come along after them, since she wanted to write home once more before leaving. She wrote to her mother and to her father. Then she wrote a short note to Bobby.

"Bobby, sometimes I envy you, being married. I hope you and Judy are happy. Maybe I'll get a chance to come and visit you later in the fall."

She looked at what she had written and then taking a new sheet of paper wrote:

"Maybe I'll have a chance to come visit you two and see how married life is. It must have *some* advantages."

She wrote some more, and then sealed the note in an envelope and put postage stamps on the three letters. After a time she went to the closet and began to bring out clothes she wanted to wear to the party. She put out a dark green skirt on the bed, and a light neutral blouse. She dressed carefully, heels and nylons. She combed her hair down into place and fastened it back with a silver clasp.

Over the skirt and blouse she slipped on a suede leather jacket. Putting the letters in the jacket pocket she went out into the warm night, locking the door.

At the party, sitting on the arm of a big couch, watching the people talking and laughing, she realized she would really be sorry to leave Castle. To her, Boston, with stale air, familiar streets and hills, the same old faces, the high school, the movie theaters, would be the same old life again, exactly as before.

She would have to go back and take things up just as before. Without change. Except that now she would be more alone than ever; Penny and Felix would be married and off by themselves.

She shut her eyes. The murmur of the room rolled around her. How could she face it?

While she was thinking about it a man came over to her. He was a small man, older than most of them, with a pipe and a grey rumpled suit.

"You're not drinking. Can I bring you anything? Scotch and water?" He had a glass in his hand.

Barbara shook her head. "No thanks."

"*Nothing?*"

"No."

"You wouldn't mind holding my drink for a second, would you?" He held his glass out to her, and she took it slowly. The man went off, and in a moment he came back with another glass. He grinned, his eyes dancing behind horn-rimmed glasses. She thought: what an odd little face, so thin and wrinkled. Like a little prune.

"I'll keep this one," he said. "It's fuller."

She started to get angry. But then she laughed, because he was grinning at her, watching her.

"All right," she said. "Give me the drink."

They exchanged drinks. Barbara sipped a little. The liquor was cold and biting. She wrinkled her nose. The man had not gone away. He was still standing beside her, at the end of the couch.

"My name's Verne Tildon," the man said.

3

AT LAST CARL left the porch and went slowly back inside the office. He put his suitcase and package down, deep in thought, oblivious to his surroundings. The office was barren, in the glare of the overhead light. The curtains and small furnishings were all gone; only a table and two chairs and a metal file cabinet were left. The bare plaster wall was marred by two screw holes where the pencil sharpener had been. A notice was still tacked on the wall.

NO SMOKING WITHOUT AUTHORIZED PERMIT

Suddenly he noticed there was another person in the room. Verne was sitting at the table, watching him through his horn-rimmed glasses.

"Hello," Carl said. "You still here?"

"You look upset."

"They didn't consider it important enough to let me know about it. About staying. That's what gets me the most. If I had known I could have let my family know in time. This way, they'll — "

"Oh, your family." Verne got up and clapped the young man on the shoulder. The solid flesh hardly budged. "Don't worry. They won't care whether you come back."

Carl gave up. "What the heck. Anyhow, it's only for a week." His usual good spirits were returning.

"A week! You should live so long."

"What do you mean?"

"A week. More like two."

"They said we could go — "

"When the yuks come. But the yuks may take their time getting here. The Oriental mind is inscrutable. It requires centuries to reach a decision."

"Well, it doesn't matter. Lord, it's dreary in here with everything gone!" Carl took off his coat and took it to the closet. He stopped, the door half open.

"What's the matter?" Verne came over. Inside the closet, piled high to the ceiling, were cardboard boxes full of dusty ledgers and file cards, account books and papers. All tied with string, crushed together in a heap, ready to fall any moment.

Carl slammed the door. "I give up. I thought they were going to take that."

"Why should they? It's not worth anything. The files of a unit that's gone bust. That's all they are. Records of a short, brief flame of economic passion."

"Not so short. A good many years."

"A good many years indeed," Verne agreed. "And in view of that fact, a week or so shouldn't make any difference."

Carl picked up the traffic notification paper from the table and scanned it again. "Who is this? This woman, Barbara Mahler. Do you know her?"

"A little."

"I thought you knew all the women here."

"I've heard the name. That's all."

"What's she like?"

"Nothing in particular."

Suddenly there was a deep roar outside the window A heavy

truck was starting up. As they watched, a load of workmen drove by, down the road, along the rim of the Company property and out through the gate. Then the truck was lost into the darkness. They could still hear its rumble for a time after it had disappeared, going away down the highway.

"What was that?" Carl said nervously.

"The workmen. I didn't think they'd finish up so fast. I guess they were in a hurry to get out of here."

"You mean there's just the three of us left?"

Verne nodded.

"Good Lord. Already. Things happen fast." Carl moved around the office. "Just us. Where is this Barbara Mahler? I'd like to meet her and see what she's like."

"She was around here earlier. She'll turn up, before the week's over. She has plenty of time."

Carl fidgeted. He paced restlessly, rubbing his hands together. "Lord, it's bleak in here."

"I guess so." Verne sat down at the table again.

"You wouldn't mind if I went and looked around for her, would you?" Carl asked.

"Why?"

"I'm curious to see what she's like."

Verne sighed. "Go ahead, if you want."

"Thanks." Carl took hold of the doorknob. "After all, we'll be seeing a lot of each other, the next couple of weeks." He opened the door and went outside, onto the dark porch.

"Goodbye," Verne said listlessly. He listened to Carl's footsteps die away down the gravel path.

Barbara Mahler. Well, he wasn't curious. He knew what she looked like. And a lot more besides. Verne lit a cigarette, putting his feet up on the table. Barbara — what an irony. Of all the people in the world! He grinned wryly. It almost seemed intentional. The next week was going to be interesting. How would she act? Could she keep pretending that—

But of course, it *had* been a long time. Maybe she had really forgotten.

When had he first met her? It was in Castle, sometime or other. Years, years ago. Castle. His thoughts began to drift. What an irony! She had been at some kind of a party. He had met her at a party. Sitting on a chair. No: a couch.

Sitting on a couch. And he had got her a drink.

Verne Tildon looked down at the girl sitting on the end of the couch. He was trying to understand her, to fix firmly in his mind what kind of person she was. She seemed like — What was her name? Vivian. Only Vivian had longer hair, and smoother. This girl's hair was hard and short and heavy. Like a pelt. It was hard cut, like a little helmet. He felt himself smiling at her, and presently he saw her set expression fade, and she smiled back.

"My name is Barbara Mahler," she said.

He considered the name. Jewish? German? "That's the same as the composer. Do you spell it the same way?"

"What?"

"Gustav Mahler. Or hadn't you been told?"

"I didn't know." There was a pause.

"Well, what *do* you know?" And he laughed out loud. The girl looked down at the floor. He could not tell if she were angry or embarrassed or what. With him, a person who had known many girls, who had, in fact, approached many under just such circumstances, the first few moments decided the issue. Either the girl liked him or she did not. If she did not he went away. He was too old to worry about it.

To Verne, life was a short affair. No long drawn-out eternity stretched away ahead of him. What he got he expected to get within a span of time so definite that he could fairly well see the end of it. He did not imagine that the kind of life he appreciated was going to continue forever. Looking down at the silent girl he waited, prepared for the next move, a sign telling him whether to go on off again or to stay. At the far end of the room a girl with long blonde hair had just arrived and was gazing around her. Slender, with large eyes and full breasts, this girl stood waiting. He looked down at Barbara again.

"You must think I'm awfully stupid," she murmured.

Verne laughed again. "You don't mind if I sit down, do you? You weren't planning to occupy any more of this couch than you are at present, were you?"

She shook her head. He thought; what kind of a girl are you, young woman? You seem pretty tough. And he thought: but that's not all. Not by any means.

He sat down, balancing the glass on his knee. His legs sprawled out loosely. Barbara's hand played slowly with a piece of thread that stuck up from the arm of the couch. He watched. Neither of them spoke. Verne knew how hard it was to tell what was going on in a woman's mind, what might come in the next moment. He had learned to force himself quickly in and almost bluntly push and shove. He either lost out right away or he was accepted. He had given up trying to match the complicated workings of a woman's mind.

"Do you know these people here?" Barbara said.

"A few. I don't live here in Castle, of course. I come from New York. I'm just up for a little while to get away from things. I have to go back."

"From New York? What do you do?"

"I'm an announcer. I even have a jazz program. *Potluck Party*. Haven't you ever heard of it?"

"I'm from Boston. *Potluck Party*? What kind of jazz is it?"

"Musicians' jazz. Progressive stuff. Not that doodle-de-dop-

dop business, but real jazz experiments. Rayburn, Shearing. Brubeck."

"No New Orleans or Chicago?"

"A little; we do get calls for it. Jazz is an evolving thing — don't forget that. Guys can't go on writing and playing something after it's dead. New Orleans and Chicago jazz were both products of specific environments. Chicago came out of the depression and the honky-tonk; that's gone. Jazz reflects the times, just like any music. A man can't any more honestly play Chicago jazz today than could Darius Milhaud write like Mozart."

Barbara's face began to struggle. "But don't you think men like Ory or Bunk Johnson — "

"They were good. In their time. And Bach was a good composer. But that doesn't mean everyone should keep on trying to write like Bach. What I say is — "

But then he stopped, grinning.

"Maybe we shouldn't talk about jazz. I can see that we won't agree."

"But no," Barbara said. "Go on. You have your own program? What time is it?"

"Thursday night at nine o'clock. Usually I use records and transcriptions. Sometimes I have a live group. The last I had was a quintet. Earl Peterson's Quintet. You know them?"

"No."

"It's progressive, but soft. Some people think it sounds like Debussy."

"I don't know too much about the classics."

"I hate that word," Verne said. "It smells of dust and museums. Anyhow, you wouldn't call Debussy classic, would you? How about Henry Cowell? Or Charles Ives?"

He could see that she did not know what he was talking about. He was beginning to get her typed in his mind. He felt better. To him, there were not individual women, each to be understood. There were kinds of women, types. Once he had figured out what type a particular woman was, the process of dealing with her was much easier.

"Listen to what they're playing now," he said suddenly. The couples who had been dancing had stopped and were sitting around the phonograph, listening.

Barbara listened. After a few minutes she turned to Verne. "All I can make out is a lot of banging sounds."

Some people, disturbed by her voice, turned to glare at her. She glared back.

"Be careful," Verne whispered. "They pray in front of that. It's a kind of little idol."

"What is it?"

"The Bartok Concerto for Two Pianos and Percussion. It takes time to get used to. Like blue cheese."

"I enjoy some of Beethoven's symphonies. . . ."

After the piece came to an end Penny and Felix came over. They greeted Verne.

"Do you and Barbara know each other?" Penny said.

"We just met. Over the sound of cymbals and drums."

"I don't like that Bartok thing," Felix said. "I see no purpose in it. I don't care what they say."

"How come all you people know each other?" Barbara demanded. "Everyone knows everyone except me."

"It's your own fault," Penny said. "You always go off by yourself, and then you complain about being left out. We met Verne when we first came here. I thought you were along. You probably stayed behind to write home."

"Can I get anyone a drink?" Felix asked.

"Not me," Penny said. "If I drink any more I'll pass out. Somebody ought to tell Tom to make them weaker. We still have two hours to go."

There was a stir among the people. A man was going from person to person collecting money.

"What's this for?" Felix said.

"We're running short of booze, fellow," the man said. "Pitch in like a good boy."

Felix dropped in a clatter of change. Verne gave the man a bill. The man went off.

"If I'd known it was going to cost us money I wouldn't have come," Felix said bitterly. "We have damn near not enough to get back as it is."

"Are you people leaving?" Verne asked.

"We have to get back to Boston. This is almost our last day. We're so broke we've got to hitchhike."

"That means we'll probably have to break up and go separately," Penny said. "I don't like the idea. What I want to do is wire home and demand bus fare."

"I could drive *one* of you down," Verne said thoughtfully. "I have to go back myself on Wednesday. But I only have the coupe, and three is all we could get into it. Myself, this fellow I've already promised, and someone else."

Penny nudged Barbara. "This would be a hell of a good deal for you, kid. Then Felix and I could take the bus with what we have. What do you say?"

"Well, let's not rush into things," Barbara said loudly. "Let's take it easy."

"Okay. It was just an idea. Don't get mad."

"Anyhow, my offer holds good," Verne said.

To Verne, the two weeks at Castle, if nothing else, were at least a temporary escape from a bad situation. It would all begin again when he got back to New York; but for the moment he could forget about everything.

The Woolly Wildcats had opened at the Walker Club early in January. At the time, busy with his program and trying to prepare a book on the history of jazz at the same time, he had no particular interest in them.

"They're really good," Don Field said to him. Don came around to the station to lend them jazz records from his collection or to make cuts on their professional recording equipment. Don Field drooped. He always wore clean, tasteful clothes, carefully pressed and in the proper style, but underneath them his whole being drooped. It gave him a wilted, worn-out look, as if he were just out of bed. A person for whom all activity was exhausting.

"They're good," Don said again. "Aren't you even interested?" His hoarse voice raised a little. "What's the matter? Aren't you interested in jazz anymore? You're too busy writing about it to listen?"

"I'm interested. I just don't have any time. It must be nice living on unemployment insurance, all the time."

"Not all the time."

"You are right now."

Don shrugged. "Anyhow, if you're interested, you ought to go and have a listen. You might get them on your show. Give it a little life."

"What's your connection with them?"

"None."

"Oh?"

"Well, my friend Buck McLean is first cornet. But it's purely a friendly interest. I have no other connection. I go every night to listen and enjoy myself. Also, the girlfriend likes it."

Verne glanced at Don, sallow-faced, drooping himself over the end of the table. "What's she like? Do I know her?"

"No," Don said. He went out the door, closing it noisily after him. Verne heard him clomping down the hall.

Eventually he found time to take in several new combos, including the Woolly Wildcats. The Walker Club had once been owned by a stripteaser of considerable fame, but recently it had dropped slowly down the social scale until now it was just another hangout for jazz cultists.

As soon as he entered the Club he saw Don, and a few more of his kind, besides. The Woolly Wildcats were playing fast and loud, "Emperor Norton's Hunch." He saw McLean puffing away behind his cornet, his cheeks bulging out. A little cluster of admirers hung around the stand.

Verne sat down at a table and played listlessly with some wax from the candle. When the waitress started toward him he waved her off. Presently he got up, and going over to the bar bought himself a scotch and water. He carried it back and sat down at the table again.

When the Wildcats finished Don Field came over to Verne's table. And with him was his new girlfriend. She was tall and thin, with long black hair. Sandals and a red shirt. Some sort of jacket buttoned around her throat. She was taller than he, Verne realized, when he stood up to say hello. He invited them to sit down for a few minutes.

"What do you think of them?" Don rumbled.

Verne shrugged. "It's a band."

"What?" Don said hoarsely.

The waitress came over. "What did you wish?"

"Hello, Susan," Don said. "I want a half order of red beans and rice, with a side of garlic bread." He turned to the girl. "What do you want, Teddy?"

"Coffee."

He looked at Verne. Verne tapped his drink.

"That's all," Don said to the waitress. "And a cup of coffee for me, too. My father here is paying for this."

The waitress disappeared. Verne studied the girl critically.

Her hair was dyed. He could see that; it was too dead, too lusterless. She was restless, bird-like. Her finger tips tapped continually against the table. Her thin hands were strong and determined. He glanced up at her face and found himself looking into two bright eyes. They sparkled and seemed to be enjoying some private amusement of their own. He looked away.

"Come on," Don said. "Let's admit they are about the best one-beat band around."

"Wood blocks. Banjo. Strictly rick-i-tic."

Don's great sullen face clouded. "All you crews want is this bop —" he began, but the girl put her hand on his arm suddenly, leaning toward him.

"Come on, darling. Let's not get excited about it."

Don subsided into silent gloom. The red beans and rice came. Don began to tear hunks of garlic bread loose and scoop up the beans with them. *Like some peasant of the Middle Ages,* Verne thought. He sipped his drink.

Presently Teddy leaned over toward him. "To get back to the problem of jazz. Do I receive the impression that you don't personally enjoy the Dixieland-style jazz?"

Verne shrugged. "It had its place."

He was watching her closely. If she was a bird, she was a dangerous kind of bird. A bird of prey. He found he disliked talking with her. She was pushing, searching. He did not like women who did that.

"Is this the first time you've been here?" he asked, changing the subject. "Miss —"

"Teddy."

"Teddy?"

"No, I've been here many times before. I like it here. And I especially enjoy the music."

He smiled. "Oh? That's nice."

She smiled back. Don ate, immersed in the problems of consumption. Once in a while he looked up, chewing, his great face blank and expressionless.

"I understand you have a jazz program," Teddy said. "What's the name of it?"

"*Potluck Party*. Thursday evening at nine."

"What kind of music do you play?"

"Progressive jazz, mostly. Brubeck. Bostic."

"I don't know much about them."

"You should. Some day people will sit around in dark places reviving them. Like you do Ory and Johnson."

"Do you write your own programs out in advance, or do you do it ad lib?"

"It varies." He uncovered his watch. "Well," he said, getting up slowly, finishing the last of his drink, "I guess I'm going to have to be getting on. You staying? I can drive you someplace, if you want."

Don looked up from his food. "See you later, dad."

"I'm sorry you have to leave so soon," Teddy said, the fixed smile still on her face. "I hope we'll see you again some time."

"Thanks. Goodbye."

He left.

The following Thursday he did his program. After it was over he chatted a while with the board man and then went to get his coat. As he walked through the waiting room outside the control booth he saw — from the corner of his eye — that someone had got up suddenly from one of the deep chairs and was coming quickly up behind him.

He turned. It was the girl, Teddy. She smiled at him. She wore a short bright outfit, brilliant with color. Her hair was tied into two braids, a ribbon in each. "Hello," she said merrily.

Watching her, Verne got out his pipe and began to put tobacco in it. He was trying to understand her, and he could not.

Her eyes were bright, matching the hard little smile on her lips. He thought: home guidance counselors and lady receptionists smile like that.

"Hello," he said. "What can I do for you?"

"I enjoyed watching your program. I haven't seen anyone do a program in years."

She had watched through the heavy glass soundproof window between the waiting room and the control room.

"Thanks." He put on his coat, sucking on the unlit pipe. She never took her eyes off him.

"Do you want a match?"

Verne got out his lighter. He wondered how old she was. Twenty-two? Eighteen? Thirty? It was impossible to tell. Her skin was white and thin, startling against her hair. What a hideous outfit she had on! It was like glaring plumage. It was not tasteless; it was simply outlandish. Like parts of different outfits stitched together.

"Do you want a ride?" Verne said. "Or are you staying here? Where's Don?"

"I came down alone. Yes, I'd love a ride. It looks as if it was going to rain."

"Oh?" He started down the hall, lighting his pipe, cupping it in his hands. Teddy followed. He passed through the heavy door, out of the building, stopping long enough to hold the door open for her. They walked down the short gravel path to his coupe.

"Well?" Verne said as they drove along. "Where do you want to go? Where do you live?"

"What time is it?"

He looked at his watch. "Ten-thirty."

"That's so early!"

"Is it?"

"Don't you think so?"

He was silent for a moment. "It depends on what time you have to get up."

"How about you?"

"How about me what?"

"What time do you have to get up?"

"Tomorrow's my day off," Verne said slowly. "I probably won't be getting up before eleven."

She was watching him, waiting for him to continue. He kept his eyes on the road, gripping the wheel. He was beginning to feel badgered. "Do you want to go by the Walker Club?" he said finally.

She laughed. "Not very much."

"Where, then?"

"Wherever you want."

They drove in silence. At last they came to a well-lit intersection. Verne turned. They drove along a short distance and then came to a stop at the curb. The car was in front of the Lazy Wren Club.

"Do we get out here?" Teddy asked.

Verne nodded. They got out and went inside, passing down a flight of dark stairs. The place was filled with people. They were almost all Negroes. Packed in tight against each other, they were watching a three-piece group playing on a small bandstand. The Club was shabby and old-fashioned. Drab and smoky, and very hot.

A thin bald Negro pushed his way up to them. He smiled widely. "Hello, Mister Tildon." He nodded to Teddy. "I'm very glad to welcome you folks here tonight."

"Frank, this is Teddy."

"I'm quite happy to meet you, Miss Teddy. This is the first time you've been here?"

"Yes. Verne has said some awfully nice things about . . . about the band."

Frank smiled more. "He likes our music, I think."

"Do you want to sit at the bar or at a table?" Verne said to Teddy.

"A table."

"I think I have one for you." Frank pushed a way for them through the people, to a table almost at the edge of the bandstand. "How is this, Mister Tildon?"

"All right. Bring us a couple of scotch and waters."

Frank left. Teddy began to struggle with her coat. Verne helped her fold it over the back of a chair. They sat down, facing each other across the table.

"It's awfully warm in here," Teddy said. She watched the three men playing. Their music was quiet, and very strange. It seemed to start off in one direction, only to wander away the next moment on a completely different path. The music seemed to be lost, bewildered, but calm, with a faith that everything would turn out all right in the end. And so it did — suddenly, with a few neatly turned chords. Everyone relaxed, and a mute, appreciative murmur rushed through the room.

Teddy turned to Verne, eyes shining. "I liked it."

"It's better than 'Ace in the Hole,' at least."

They stayed, listening to the music and drinking for several hours. Teddy was quiet, paying close attention to the sounds from the bandstand. Finally, when the three men were taking a break, she turned suddenly to Verne.

"Verne, do you want to take me home? I'm getting so tired!"

They got up, and he helped her put on her coat. He paid the bill and they went upstairs and outside. The air was cold and brittle.

Teddy took a deep breath. "What a sensation."

They got into the car and began to drive. Verne was silent. Presently he slowed down. "Maybe you better tell me which direction to go. I don't know where you live."

"Can't we drive around? The air is so good."

"If you like air, roll down the window."

She rolled it down and leaned out, her mouth half open, the wind blowing her braids up.

At last she expressed a desire to go home. He took her there and let her off in front of the apartment building, driving away with a feeling of mixed annoyance and curiosity. He wanted to categorize women; this one was hard to figure out. She seemed after something. A sort of determination gripped her. But for what? She had gone around with Don Field. What could she have found in him?

He considered the matter for a while, and then gave it up. It was not worth the trouble. He snapped the car radio on and caught an all-night concert. They were playing the Beethoven *A Major* Quartet. Listening to the music, he drove slowly home.

The following evening as he was entering his apartment building the manager suddenly came out and stopped him.

"Can I speak to you, Mister Tildon?"

Verne eyed him. "Sure. What is it? The rent can't be due again already."

"A young woman came here today, looking for you. I told her you weren't in, but she insisted on going upstairs to your apartment. She was very persuasive. She got me to let her in. I had never seen this girl before —"

"You let her in?"

"As you know, it's against the policy of the owners to allow someone into a tenant's apartment, but her condition was such that I —"

Verne went quickly upstairs. His door was unlocked, stand-

ing half open. He switched on the light. In the living room he
found a woman's purse on the floor. A coat and hat on the sofa.

He hurried into the bedroom. Lying on the bed was Teddy.
She was snoring dully. Her clothes were rumpled and messy. He
walked over and bent down.

"Drunk as an owl." She did not stir.

If he thought this was something—

4

CARL WALKED QUICKLY away from the office, through the gloomy darkness, toward the women's dormitory. The Company grounds were deserted and silent. It made him feel strangely sad. He increased his pace. At last he came to the great square building where Barbara Mahler was supposed to be.

He stopped, peering up, his hands on his hips. The stark side of the dormitory building showed no light, no sign of habitation. He stood for a while, letting the cold wind blow around him. Was nobody there? A shade began to flap, lost and dismal in the darkness. Everything was desolate. Most of the windows were boarded up.

Carl shivered. He began to walk along the path, still gazing up at the building hopefully. Suddenly he stopped. A faint streak of light glowed, half way along. He halted. The light came again, yellow, a slender strip in the expanse of darkness.

Presently he made his way to the porch steps that led up into the building. For a moment he hesitated, a sudden shyness overpowering him. Maybe it would be better for Verne to get her; Verne had known her, once. Maybe she wouldn't like to see a strange person coming around. He tried to think what she might be like. Had he ever seen her? Perhaps. In passing.

He reached the porch. The air was cold around him. There

was no sound. Everything was still. What would she say? What would she be like? Would she be glad to see him? Would she like him?

He entered the building and began to climb the stairs slowly, up to the second floor.

The second floor was dimly lit by a few light-bulbs, spaced far apart along the corridor. Could anyone really be nearby? He felt so completely alone, standing at the end of the hall, by the stairs, looking down the long gloomy passage with its shadows and closed doors, the walls stained and pitted.

But presently, as he stood listening and waiting, he heard a faint sound. The sound of a board creaking, not too far away. Perhaps half the length of the corridor.

He picked up a little courage and began to walk slowly along, listening and peering, looking for — for what? A sign of some sort. A sound, or a light. Something to tell him where he would find *her*. What would she be like? Would she be pretty? How pretty?

He stopped suddenly, by one of the doors. He held his breath, his head cocked on one side. Someone was on the other side of the door. He could hear someone moving around. A board creaked. Rustling sounds, clothes. A squeak, as if something were moved. And then the unmistakable sound of bed springs groaning and sagging.

Carl waited by the door. Now he could see a lean crack of light underneath it, shining from the other side, from inside the room. He raised his hand, starting to knock, but then he changed his mind. He withdrew his hand, putting it into his pocket.

It would be just the three of them, for heaven knew how long. Just the three of them eating together, talking together, being together. The three of them and no one else. Suppose his coming here this way got things off on the wrong foot? Wouldn't it be better to go back and get Verne to come and fetch her? Wouldn't that be less awkward? They knew each other; at least, a little. They had seen each other before.

But perhaps he had seen her, too. He might have seen her, talked to her, without knowing her name.

He thought back. There had been so many women working for the Company in the time he had been there. It could be any one of them. She might even be old. As old as Verne. A thin, middle-aged spinster. With glasses and grey hair.

Or she might be one of the little girls just out of high school, bright red lips, fuzzy sweater, clattering heels. A strange giddiness moved through Carl. She might be sweet and smiling, with warm dark eyes, soft hair — and the rest.

Carl searched his pockets until he found his comb. He combed his hair into place carefully, as best he could without a mirror. He straightened his tie, brushing down his coat. He took a deep breath, his heart beating rapidly inside him. All at once he was gasping for air, nervous and excited. The palms of his hands were moist.

Suddenly the door opened. Carl blinked in the light. A woman was standing, framed in the doorway. A towel over her shoulder. Short and square in a dark bathrobe, slippers around her feet. Hands full of jars.

"Jesus!" the woman exclaimed.

"I —" Carl muttered.

"Who the hell are you? What are you doing out there?" She dumped her armload down on a chair inside the room. Carl caught a glimpse of a small room, a bed, a table, a lamp, some women's clothing —

"I came to see you. I'm the other person. You and Verne and I. We're the three who're staying."

The woman said nothing.

"I was just about to knock." His voice sounded feeble, apologetic. Doomed. "It's the truth!"

Abruptly she laughed. "All right. You sure scared me. I was going down the hall for a bath. I thought everyone was gone."

"Everyone but us three."

"Come here so I can see what you look like." She moved to one side, pushing the door back. "Come inside. Do you want some coffee?"

"Coffee?" Carl went into the room. On the table was a little round Silex coffee maker, half full of black coffee. Steam drifted from the lip. A package of sugar, a spoon, paper cups, some hairpins, a ring —

"What's your name?" the woman said.

"Carl Fitter."

"I think I've seen you around."

"I think I've seen you." Carl studied her out of the corner of his eye. Barbara Mahler was standing with her hands in the pockets of her robe. She was small and chunky, with thick brown hair. Attractive. Her skin was smooth and clear. She was, perhaps, twenty-five. But there was a stern hardness in her face that made her look older. A reserve. Almost dignity.

"My name's Barbara Mahler."

"I know. Verne told me."

"Oh, yes. Verne."

"Do you know him?"

She nodded.

Carl walked around the room. "It's so barren!"

"I have to get my things back out. I was packed. Everything's crated up."

"Maybe we can give you a hand."

"Fine." She lit a cigarette and stood by the door, her arms folded.

"Did — did you want to come over to the office later on to-night? We should see about dinner. And maybe we could have a conference. The three of us."

"A conference?"

"To decided what we're going to do while we're here." He gestured vaguely. "To consider things."

"What things?"

"Oh, there are always things to consider."

"Enough for all three of us?"

"Certainly. First of all, we have to make sure there's food. Secondly, we want to make sure that the gas and water are still turned on. Then, we — "

Barbara laughed. "Okay. I get the idea." She put her cigarette out. "You go outside in the hall and I'll change. I can take my bath later."

"I don't want to interrupt you."

"That's all right." She moved away from the door. "Go on outside. I'll put on something else."

Carl went out into the hall. Barbara closed the door after him. He waited, in the half-darkness. The hall was very cold and unfriendly. The room, for all its bareness, was at least more cheerful than the naked bulbs, the dark stained walls. The vague gloom.

He shivered and wandered around. After what seemed like an endless time he heard her stirring beyond the door. The door opened and she stepped out. Now she had put on brown slacks and a red checkered shirt. Her hair was held back by some kind of clasp.

"Let's go!" she said. "Do you have a flashlight?"

"No."

"We can use matches."

They left the dormitory, crossing through the night darkness, along the paths, between the buildings, back to the office.

They climbed the steps. Carl pushed the door open for Barbara and they entered.

Verne was sitting at the table, deep in thought. At the sound of the door opening he leaped up, blinking.

"I found her," Carl said.

"You surprised me." Verne sat down at the table again. "My mind was wandering. A long way off."

"We're going to help her unpack," Carl said. "All her stuff is crated up. Her room looks terrible. We'll have to help her make it livable again."

"I can imagine," Verne said.

Carl sat down beside Verne, motioning Barbara to join them. "This is the first time we've all three been together," he said. "Let's consider our situation and see what we're up against."

"Christ," Verne murmured.

"For example, Verne and I will be living in the men's dormitory, very close to the office." He turned toward Barbara. "But you'll be all the way over in the women's dorm. We should work out some sort of way to get hold of each other in case something sudden should happen."

"Like what?"

"I don't know. Maybe some yuks might come and — "

"They won't give us any trouble. All they're interested in is the property."

Carl picked up the traffic notification paper. There was a directive attached to it. "What's this?"

"The original order." Verne took it from him.

"I'd like to read it. I never saw it."

"I'll read it aloud." Verne adjusted his glasses. "I've been pondering it, off and on. 'This is to inform Henry G. Osborne, the general manager of the Second Station of the American Metals Development Company, that to facilitate the transfer of Company Land and Property and all other Real Assets to the new owners, it is deemed advisable that three company employees remain on the premises of the Second Station during the transfer period, until such time as certified representatives of the new owners appear to take possession of their property. These three persons should be picked in such a way as to represent the Company and all it stands for and believes in, and it is important that they, as the last members of the Company, should adequately express those things for which the Company has stood in the past and for which it will continue to stand in the future, as long as it shall exist.'"

They were silent.

"That's all," Verne said, tossing the paper down.

"Osborne picked us at random. He opened the card file and pulled three cards out."

"What a way to do it."

"Can you suggest a better way?"

"Forget it," Barbara said. "It's all over with now. We've been chosen; we might as well make the best of it. Let's go down and see about something to eat."

"That's the real issue," Carl agreed.

They walked slowly through the dark toward the commissary, guided by the crunching of gravel underfoot.

"We better look up some flashlights," Verne said.

Barbara lit a match. They were very close to the commissary building. The front door was boarded over.

"Well," Carl said. "I guess we're going to need tools just to get in. Where can we find a hammer?"

"Aren't there *any* workmen left?" Barbara said.

"They're gone. It's just us three."

"It certainly didn't take them long to get off."

"There's no use standing around here," Verne said. "Carl, go back to the office and look around for some tools. Look in the closet and around the washroom."

"I'll go with him," Barbara said. "I'll light the way for him."

"Go ahead," Verne said. "I don't need any light to stand here. Anyhow, I'm getting used to the dark."

They went off. He watched the glow of her match until it winked out, disappearing in the gloom.

For a time he stood listening to the faint sounds of night. Then he became restless. He searched his pockets and finally found his lighter. By its light he made his way up to the commissary door. He pulled aimlessly on the wood boards, but they were too tightly nailed. He walked around the side of the building. It was a long low structure, with a narrow path leading from the main entrance back to the kitchen.

He found the kitchen unlocked. They had not boarded it up. He entered the building and snapped on the lights.

Everything was neat and orderly. The dishes were stacked up and put away on the shelves. The floor was swept. The garbage cans were empty and washed out. He approached the row of refrigerators. They were still turned on. He opened the first. It was full of food; sides of meat, packs of vegetables and fruits, cartons of ice cream and milk.

He opened the hatch to the huge storage rooms. And gaped in amazement. Piled high to the ceiling were hundreds of drums of food; fruits, vegetables, preserved meats, juices, everything imaginable. Sacks of grain, wheat and rice. Flour. Nuts, dried raisins and apricots. All left, all forgotten.

"Good God," he murmured. "They left everything."

The yuks were getting the works. They were getting everything. The Company had given up and gone off. It was no longer interested; it was tired. It did not care any more. Once, it had guarded these things carefully. Men had counted each can, each package, each ounce of food. Countless forms and records had been made out for the bookkeepers. Armed guards had patrolled the periphery of the grounds. Wire had been strung up, complex burglar alarms and bells.

The Company had protected its land and property with jealous cunning. Through centuries its craft and power had grown, breeding and multiplying. But now it no longer cared. It had gone off, turned everything over to someone else. Someone to come, who was not tired. Who was not exhausted.

The Company had been failing. For a long time it had been going downhill, secretly, quietly. Deep in its heart it was losing, dying. And in this last great fatigue, this final moment when the last threads of energy ran out of the withering Stations, those few men who stayed behind, who remained after the others had left, were rich. They had everything; men for centuries had dreamed of owning what these three now had. It was all theirs. The land, the buildings, the stores, the records — this whole Station belonged to them.

They had inherited it, the work of previous generations of workers, men behind desks, men in the mines, in factories. The work and the wealth from the work. The three who remained owned this, this heap that was the total remains of the Company Station. They had not built it, or done much to help produce it; but it was theirs all the same. They were the only ones left to have it, in the dim short days that remained before the new owners arrived. Before it became a part of that new world, that world which just a little while before had not even been entered on the Company's list of potential competitors.

Verne gazed at the food, and he thought of the other buildings, the stores and property abandoned to them, left behind. He could hardly believe it. The Company had worked so long to acquire all this; could it really leave it behind for others to find? For strangers to take?

But meanwhile, it was a stroke of luck for the three of them.

After they had eaten all they could, after they had slept in all the beds, bathed in all the tubs, listened to all the radios, taken out of boxes and crates anything they desired, they would disappear, too, like the others. After a little while there would be nothing left of them, either. They would join the others.

But right now there was at least a week ahead of them. Later, the yuks would come with crowbars and hammers and open up the doors and windows. Maybe they would tear down the buildings. Maybe they would make them even bigger, or change them so that no one would recognize them. They might do many things.

But right now he was not thinking of this. He was thinking of the week ahead.

Presently he heard the sound of footsteps. Carl and Barbara came into the kitchen, carrying a hammer. They stopped short when they saw all the food.

"I guess that answers that question." Barbara went into the store room; they heard her moving cans and drums around. "What do you think of these for dinner?" She came out, loaded down with canned chicken, canned peas, cranberry sauce, and a rum pudding.

"There's milk in the refrigerator," Verne said. "And frozen vegetables and meat. Tons of it."

"Put the cans back!" Carl exclaimed, looking into the first refrigerator compartment. "Forget them. Look at all this frozen stuff! Let's have that, instead."

"What a break," Barbara murmured. "It's strange. I've worked for the Company two years and I've never seen food like this. They must have held it back."

Carl rummaged through the drawers under the great sink. "Look!" He held up two long flashlights, snapping them on. They worked perfectly. "What do you say?"

"Let's take a look around outside before we eat," Barbara said. "Let's make sure there's no one else here."

"Come on!" Carl handed Verne one of the flashlights. "We'll go and explore. We can eat afterwards."

Verne accepted the flashlight silently.

"I'll go along with Barbara one way, and you go the other. We'll make a complete circuit of the property and meet back here."

"What a waste of time," Verne murmured.

"We ought to know for sure. There might be somebody left. Some old workman, some old Swede, working away in a deserted building."

"Okay." Verne wandered toward the door.

"Shout if you find anything," Carl said.

Verne made his way along the gravel path, flashing his light listlessly from side to side. The light caught a tree, then a row of shrubs, then finally a great granite building, one of the administration buildings. The windows were nailed over. The door was chained. In the fog it seemed forlorn and dismal.

He went on. Now he was coming to abandoned piles of machinery. Massive columns reared up into the fog and were lost. In the darkness it seemed as if they had been thrown there in no particular order, left behind, emptied out of some vast, cosmic bag. Or perhaps they were the beginnings of some new, never finished structures that had been given up, left to rust and corrode in the mists.

But more, these columns seemed like the ruins of some very ancient city. Verne stood at the foot of one of the towers, gazing up. Perhaps it had supported the corner of some Coliseum, or a long-forgotten Parthenon. Would tourists come later to look? Would the new owners stand and stare and wonder what his world had been like, what the people who had left these hulks might have been?

His people. His world. Verne moved on. These ruins were his ruins. The remains of the Company. He came to the fence that marked the edge of the property. Beyond, even with the flashlight, he could see nothing but rolling fog and darkness. Was there anything out there? What would come from the fog and darkness? Would it be good?

They were out there. The new owners who would soon be coming to claim their new possessions.

Verne turned away. He walked slowly back toward the commissary, flashing his light aimlessly over the ruins and towers. The commissary was silent; the others had not finished their tour.

He went inside and sat down to wait. After a long time he heard them clattering up the stairs, talking and laughing together.

"What did you find?" Carl said. "Anyone?"

"No."

"Nothing, either," Barbara said. "Let's eat. And then we can get my stuff uncrated. So I can go to bed."

"Sure." Verne got to his feet. "Let's start."

"I'm really hungry!" Carl said. "Really hungry."

5

VERNE WOKE UP. He was lying in bed, feeling the sunlight shining on him. If he opened his eyes it would blind him. He turned the other way and the red haze became black. He yawned. The covers were twisted around him. He opened one eye a little to see the clock.

The clock wasn't there. He was facing a bare wall, the paint peeling, stained and cracking with dirt and age. For a moment he felt startled. He sat quickly up. Across the room Carl was still asleep. His blond head was hidden under the covers; only his hand and arm, hanging over the side of the bed, were visible. Verne reached around on the floor and found his glasses. He fitted them into place and got slowly out of bed.

It was only eight o'clock. He went over and sat by his clothes, heaped across an unused bed, rubbing his hands together and yawning. The day was warm and bright. Out the window he could see the trees and carefully arranged shrubs that grew in front of the men's dorm. A long way off a blue bird was hopping among some weeds, growing up beside a heap of rusting slag. Presently he picked up his clothing and began to dress.

Eight o'clock was too early! He had wakened from years of habit; but there was no need, any longer. There was nothing to get to, nothing to begin. It was all behind him, in the past. He let go of his shirt, dropping it. Why was he up? What for? There was nothing to do.

He padded back to his bed and slid into it, pulling the blankets up over him. Carl stirred a little in his sleep. Verne watched him. How long he was! His feet and head stuck out at both ends of the bed. He smiled.

Gazing at the youth sprawled out on the bed, snoring faintly, Verne thought again of Teddy. The smile faded. That night he had come into the apartment; he had found her there, lying on his bed, passed out. Messy and asleep.

He let his mind wander back to the scene.

Her shoes had been kicked off. Her skirt was up around her waist, showing her thin, white legs. She had rolled her stockings down; they were wrinkled and sagging.

Verne went back and bolted the door to the hall. He returned to the bedroom. She had turned over, so that her face was away from him. He could still hear her dull breathing. What had the manager thought? Had he known she was drunk? Maybe he thought she was sick.

Why had she come to his place?

He sat down on the edge of the bed. It was hard to connect her with Don Field. Don was so square, so out of the course of things. He plodded along between one meaningless activity and another, hunting down a certain old Genet record of the New Orleans Rhythm Kings, reading a forgotten science-fiction serial in an old Air Wonder Stories magazine, patronizing some hum-drum cafe because it was off the beaten path and served some peculiar sauce. Everything he did was cultish, set aside.

But this girl looked as if she flowed in the main stream of things. Perhaps she had just picked up Don for a passing moment. It was hard to tell. He had never heard Don mention her before.

Watching, waiting for her to wake up, Verne lit a cigarette.

In the life of Verne Tildon there had been much trouble. That is true of most small men. A little man is aware of things a large man can ignore. Like colors beyond the end of the spectrum, invisible to the ordinary eye, certain things were major realities to Verne that another man would not even have noticed.

He had grown up in Washington, D.C. Most of his early life had been spent in the bleak snow-covered streets and vacant lots of the little town of Jackson Heights, just outside of the city proper. In the winter he and his brother went sledding. When they had to stay indoors they played duets on the piano together. He remembered nothing about the piano, later in life. Finally he had switched to the oboe, which he played in the high school orchestra.

Later he gave up that, too. Playing in the high school orchestra made him look silly. He was practicing in the afternoon when he could have been walking uptown with the other kids, and on some days he had to wear the gaudy red and gold uniform of the school that made him look like a ticket taker in a theater. After school he was very much alone. When he had finished practicing he ran up to the music store and listened to records.

At that age he talked with a slight stutter, in a nervous, excited way. It made him shy with people.

His brother graduated from college and left the family home. They got letters from him once in a while. Verne read a lot, and for a while he thought he would go on to college, too. But at nineteen, when he finished high school, his father convinced him that it would not be too bad a thing if he earned a little money working for a while. The family had carried the burden for too long; some help was needed. He got a job in the book-keeping end of a big department store, typing up monthly statements and emptying the waste baskets.

At nineteen, a boy who still stuttered and who occasionally blew a few notes on his oboe, he met a girl his own age who was enough interested in books and music so that there seemed to be something between them, for a time. She was blonde and tall, with hair like corn silk. Her people came from the Middle West. She had blue eyes and a soft, thoughtful voice. The two of them walked and read and went to Sunday concerts. And considered their lives together.

One rainy night, when his family was away at the movies, Verne and the girl went upstairs to his room, and with many giggles and heart-beats, many murmurs and fears and nervous glances out the window, they pulled the shades down and crept into the little wooden bed he had slept in since he was a baby. There, in the room with his postage stamps, his model airplanes and maps, his oboe standing up silently in the corner, all the things from his so recently discarded childhood, Verne and the girl lay huddled together, heart against heart, knee against knee, shaking and holding onto each other.

Outside the rain poured down. Cars slithered past. The room was silent, except for their own sounds. At first the girl was withdrawn, nervous and cold. But then, just as everything seemed to have come to an end, and he was starting to think about getting up again, something strange came over her, something he did not understand. All at once her rigid body relaxed, the coldness fled. He was pulled back, dragged abruptly against a scalding belly that strained and quivered with such violence that only the eventual return of the family and the sudden scramble to dress was sufficiently distracting to save him.

He escaped. His father drove her home; Verne and the girl were silent all the way. After that their relationship gradually fell off.

He continued to work at the bookkeeping office. The idea of the university became dimmer and dimmer. When he was twenty-one he met another girl. This one was tall and dark and quiet. Her treasure was sold dearly; he found himself married, all at once, living in a one-room apartment, watching her string bras and underpants across the bathroom, smelling the starch and iron in the kitchen, and the eternal mechanical presence of pin curls next to him on the pillow.

The marriage lasted only a few months. Sometime between it and the Second World War — he never knew just when — the last memory of college faded from his mind, to be lost and forgotten forever. When the reed broke he put his oboe away in the closet. The stutter had disappeared, and he had grown a small dark mustache. But his hands shook when he lit a cigarette; there was still a too-quick nervous motion about him.

Liquor helped that. Liquor allowed him to laugh at things that normally shut him up tight for days. He found himself beginning to get an edge on men; they were no match for his rapid tongue, his developing razor wit. A hard chilliness was slipping into him, into his speech. It carried him a long way; it was good to have.

When the War came he joined the army. He was too small and light to be much good; but they didn't like to lose a man whose mind worked so fast He finished out the war teaching others to do the things he couldn't.

The mustache disappeared, and he learned just how much he could drink before there was no turning back. His hair began to thin. It became soft and wispy. He put on horn-rimmed glasses and discovered French cuffs. The kind of music he had once played on his oboe was almost forgotten. Somehow, in the rarified classical strata, he felt more cut off and alone than usual; he was more separated than before, from the things he wanted. What did he want? He was not sure. He did not intend to let anything stand in his way, but he did not know in which direction that way might be found.

But a man can face the knowledge that he has not found his rut, his depth, his way and people, only so long. Then he stops worrying about it. Verne married again. This girl was plump and competent; she had been secretary to very important people. In her, he saw the drive and direction that he, himself, seemed still to lack. She knew exactly what she wanted: a husband, a home, a kitchen, furniture, clothes. She moved in a tight little circle, as hard and brittle as the red polish on her neatly-trimmed nails.

Whatever there was left in Verne of his memory of books and music, model airplanes and his ticket seller's bright uniform soon disappeared. With Anne, music and books and ideas were real enough, but they existed only as a means to something else. He found himself listening to things as background music that had, at one time, been intimate parts of his life.

One night he got up from the expensive couch in the graciously furnished living room, turned off the immense television set, and headed for the nearest bar.

Sometime, during the hazy, indistinct days that followed, he was rolled, left to lie in the freezing gutters of Washington in deep winter, and booked at the city jail. They let him go the next day. He wandered around, his hands in his pockets, watching the children sledding in the snow.

With his second marriage over, he gathered up what things were his and set off for New York. The taste that he had had for music had spoiled. He began to sit long hours in dark bars, tapping with a fifty cent piece, watching the people and listening to the sour, bitter music from the little Negro and mixed combos. His knowledge of jazz eventually became of use to him. He got a job with a small station, turning over jazz records in the early hours of morning; after a year or so he had his own program.

He had begun to slide into a kind of existence that seemed to fit. Why? He did not know. He was too small a man to drink as much as he did; there were many mornings when he could scarcely drag himself out of bed. His friends were stooped, pre-occupied cultists, occasional natty homosexuals, hard-voiced Lesbians. Smoke and sour sounds, half-dollars and endless commercials. Once he stopped, staring into the mirror, rubbing the yellow, hanging flesh of his neck. The tiny hairs stuck out like pin feathers; his eyes gazed blindly back at him. He was like some runt of a chicken, some plucked and charred creature that had been hung from a hook, drying slowly, corroding through the years. A wrinkled, dried-up runt of a bird . . .

But then he shaved, washed, put on a clean shirt, drank some orange juice, shined his shoes, and it was all forgotten. He put on his coat and went to work.

Teddy stirred. Verne snapped back, glancing down at her. He put his cigarette out and stood up, stiff and cold. He went over and pulled down the shades and turned on the lamp.

Presently the girl rolled over toward him. He could see her teeth, small and even, her long mouth, much too long for such a lank face. Suddenly she opened her eyes. She blinked, gazing at him fixedly, unwinking. Then she began to struggle to a sitting position.

"Jesus." She shuddered, gagging. "Christ."

"How do you feel?"

"How long have I been lying here?"

"It's about seven-thirty."

"That late? Help me up like a dear, won't you?"

She got up unsteadily. Verne took her arm. She pulled her stockings up and smoothed her skirt. Then she went into the bathroom.

Verne lit another cigarette and waited.

At last she came out and picked up her shoes. She put them on, sitting at the foot of the bed.

"Do you want to take me home?" she said.

"Now?"

"Would you?"

"Sure." He brought her the coat and purse she had left in the living room. Her hair was shaggy and disarrayed. Her clothes were messy and crumpled. When he went by her to let her into the hall he got a whiff of a sour, unhealthy odor: perspiration and urine and liquor.

They went downstairs silently and got into the car.

As they drove along the road Teddy said little. She stared out the window at the passing lights and signs, the window rolled down. Several times Verne started to speak, but gave it up and remained silent. They reached her place and he drew the car over to the curb.

Teddy pushed the door open and got out. Suddenly she stopped. "Verne, do you want to see what my apartment looks like? You've never seen it."

"Not particularly," he said slowly. "It's late."

"Suit yourself." She hesitated. "It's not so late."

"It is for me."

She turned and moved slowly away from the car, across the sidewalk toward the building. Verne got out. He rolled up the windows and locked the doors. Teddy stood waiting for him.

"You changed your mind?"

"Just for a few minutes." Verne gazed off down the dark

street. The houses were tall and close together, uniform in appearance and unattractive. At the bottom of a hill was the beginnings of a commercial district, a dank, ratty cluster of grocery stores, hardware stores, Italian bakeries, a boarded-up candy shop. The wind blew a newspaper along, against a gaunt telephone pole.

"Coming?" Teddy said, from the steps.

They went up to her floor. She opened her apartment door and turned on the light, walking quickly through the room. The place was in disorder. On a low table were two half-empty whiskey bottles and ashtrays spilling over with cigarette stubs. Clothes were strewn over everything, the chairs, the lamp, the bookcase, even the floor. He went slowly inside.

"I'll change," Teddy called, going into the bedroom. He caught a glimpse of an unmade bed, open dresser drawers, more clothes. On the wall over the bed was a big photograph, a thin nude girl, lank and bony, with little breasts like pears. He moved in to look at it. Teddy disappeared into the bathroom. "I'll be right out."

The picture was of her.

Verne moved back into the living room. One wall was a bright blue, a solid dark sheet. She had painted the apartment herself. On the walls were prints, Modigliani, Kandinsky, Hieronymus Bosch. A phonograph and records, jazz and chamber music. Mobiles, three of them.

He eased himself slowly onto the couch, crossing his legs. After a while Teddy came into the room and stood by the door, leaning against it, her arms folded.

"Want anything to drink?" she said.

"Nothing. I'm about to leave." Verne got his pipe out and poured tobacco into it. He lit up silently.

"What do you think of the place?"

"It's all right. Those are nice mats." He got up and went over to some Chinese mats, hanging down the side of the wall. From where he stood he could see into the kitchen. The sideboard was covered with dirty dishes, cups and glasses. He wandered away, hands in his pockets.

"It's cold in here. Maybe it's the colors." He fingered the burlap drapes.

Teddy watched him without expression. She had put on a scarlet wrapper, fastened with a knotted cord. And slippers. She lit a cigarette and smoked, long and austere in her flamboyant silk robe. Her face was haggard; she looked more like a bird than ever, her nose like a beak, her eyes' black and sunken. She walked toward the couch.

"I did the painting. The walls."

"I thought you did."

Verne sat down again, on a chair by the door. Teddy sprawled out on the couch, one foot up, waving her toes back and forth. Neither spoke.

"It's getting late," Teddy said finally.

Verne stood up. "I know. Well, it's been nice."

"You're going?"

"I'll see you."

"Thanks for coming."

He went to the door, taking hold of the knob. Teddy was still sprawled out, long and bony, her hair dark and lusterless, damp hanks against her neck.

"You look pretty washed out," Verne said.

Teddy smiled. "Look, baby. You've been a dear. Now run along. I'll see you again soon."

He laughed. "All right."

He went downstairs slowly, out onto the street. The air was cold and full of vitality. There was no sound at all except for a dim murmur that came from the entrance of a bar, at the foot of the hill.

He got into his car and drove away.

Don Field came stumping around to the station, when Verne was off his shift the next day. He carried a magazine under his arm; he had on dark glasses and a sports shirt.

"Greetings," Verne said, as they walked away from the station building, toward his car. "How goes it?"

"Medium. You?"

"All right." Verne got into the car. Don stood outside. "Do you want a ride?"

Don thought for a moment. He got slowly inside. "Okay," he said resignedly.

They drove along with the other cars, going home from work.

"Nice evening," Verne said.

"Uh-huh." There was a long silence. At last Don cleared his throat. "What did you think of Teddy?"

"Seemed intelligent."

"Uh-huh."

Verne looked at him out of the corner of his eye. "Why do you ask?"

"No reason. I'm getting kind of tired of having her around. They're all the same, after a while."

"Going to let her go, eh?" He thought, *You great arrogant gargoyle!*

"Well, of course, I hate to give up a good thing. But I have been toying with the idea." He fooled with the cover of the magazine he was carrying. "It costs money."

"Well, do what you want. You're old enough now."

"You going to eat at home?"

"Why?"

"Just wondering. I thought maybe I'd stop down at Jamison's for a French dinner."

"That's nice."

"You don't want to come along?"

"No thanks." He added: "But I'll be glad to drive you there and let you off."

He let Don off in front of the restaurant and then went on. After a few minutes driving he found himself in his own neighborhood. He drew up in front of his apartment building and turned the motor off. Sitting in the car he lit his pipe and began to smoke.

He did not want to go upstairs just yet. It was still early; not even seven. He had come off work and driven Don to the restaurant, and that was all. Now he was in front of his own building. In a moment he would go upstairs, enter the apartment, take off his hat and coat, and begin preparing himself something to eat.

And after that?

Outside the car a few people hurried along in the semi-darkness. Dark, similar lumps that moved quickly past his car and out of sight. One shape turned in at a doorway. A flash of warm yellow light revealed a middle-aged woman with an armload of groceries. For a moment she stood framed in the light. Verne saw into a living room. A man sitting in a deep chair with a newspaper. A boy playing on the rug. He could almost smell the warm air that drifted out, to be dissipated by the cold night.

He thought about it. He and his brother had sat on the rug like that, playing. Sometimes they went into the piano room and played duets together until dinner was ready. In the early evening, with the sun just down and the sky still brighter than the earth, in the warm piano room filled up by the massive old piano, with the stacks of music tossed everywhere, he and his brother played silly things by Grieg and MacDowell and Cui. Suddenly there would be their mother, filling up the doorway with her bulk, telling them dinner was on the table.

More people hurried past. Some newspapers blown by the wind rolled by in a heap and swept up against a mail box. Were there drops of rain beginning to show on the pavement? At the corner, the Italian who owned the little grocery came out with a bent metal rod and began to roll up his awning, slowly, with great elaborate turns.

Verne put out his pipe and switched the motor back on. He drove down the street and around the corner. He drove aimlessly, not paying any particular attention to the houses and cars that filled up the darkness.

When he saw a neon sign Club Twenty-One he pulled over to the curb and stopped. He rolled up his windows and got out. The night air was cold; a mist pressed against him, carried by the wind. He slammed the car door and walked across the sidewalk to the club, pushing the heavy plush doors open with his shoulder.

In the dim light he saw a long row of glasses and black onyx, and tall red columns of distorted light, wavery and subtle, that surrounded the mirror behind the bar. The rows of half-transparent glasses broke up the red light; it seemed as if the light came from inside each glass. The light slithered around the bar, appearing everywhere, mixing with the green coming from a Gold Glow neon sign in the window. On the left, in deep chairs around a table, three men and a woman were sitting. Their table was a litter of bottles and cigarette stubs. The other tables were vacant.

Verne walked over to the bar and sat down. The bartender put down his rag and turned toward him.

"Scotch and water. No ice."

The bartender nodded and went away. Verne sat, hearing the

thud of the counters at the shuffleboard table at the back. A little way down the bar two men were talking loudly.

"So if this god damn nag could have got in—"

"Listen! I told you if a horse could get its ass over the wire long enough—"

"Will you let me finish? I want to say—"

"I thought you were finished."

"I wasn't. You know I wasn't. Don't shit me."

"Sixty-five cents, mister," the bartender said. He put a small glass on the bar in front of Verne. Verne took a dollar bill and gave it to the bartender.

He drank the liquor slowly. As he drank he stared into the thousands of rows of bottles behind the bar. They were dully lit by the same red light, now more intense as it issued past the bottles, coming from behind them and around them, spreading out in a wave of motion.

It had become quiet. The two men stopped talking and put their coats on. They passed Verne, walking out through the heavy doors and disappearing beyond. The man playing shuffleboard gave up and came over to the bar to sit down. In the dim light his face was a dark shadow. He sat with his chin in his hands, not moving or looking to either side. Verne looked past him and saw other men sitting, gazing ahead of them, silent, lost in thought.

His mind began to wander. He thought about how he used to practice the oboe. He would sit in his room, holding the strange, cold instrument, blowing into it hour after hour. In the corner the radio played softly.

He could remember many details of his room in the family house. How long ago it was. He had owned a little table-top phonograph and some cheap records, part of a newspaper offer. The Dvorak *New World Symphony*. The Beethoven *Fifth*. Some

Strauss waltzes. He played the records until they began to turn white. He used cactus needles because when they got dull he could sharpen them, again and again.

He had a paper route. He used his mother's charge account at a department store to buy Heinrick van Loon's History of the World and Diseases of the Mind by Professor Benjamin Stoddard. At the end of the month he had scarcely any money left over, once he paid her back. He had owned a mimeograph machine. He put out a little newspaper that he sold to the neighbors for three cents.

In the silence of the bar a man coughed. He moved on his stool. There were no other noises. The men sat looking straight ahead of them, at the rows of glasses, at the red light that ran up and around the massive mirror. Their reflections gazed back, dim, hunched, unmoving. The minutes passed, and no one moved. Slowly, an uncomfortable tension built up around them. A sharp, painful pressure.

Suddenly the bartender came to life. He walked along the wood planking to the other end of the bar. The doors opened and a man and woman came in front the street, laughing and breathing loudly. They sat down at a table.

Verne finished his drink and pulled his coat around him. He got up and walked outside onto the sidewalk, his hands in his pockets. The air was cold. The street was deserted. There was no one in sight.

He got in his car and drove back slowly to his apartment. He felt listless and dull. Did he want to go home? But if he did not, where should he go instead? He parked the car and got out. He walked up the stairs, his shoes making no sound in the dull grey carpet. The hall was deserted. At the far end a deep red light glowed.

FIRE EXIT

Above him a small globe sunk in the plaster of the ceiling shed enough illumination for him to find his key. He pushed the key into the lock and opened the door.

Looking into the dark apartment, grey and still in the dim light, he felt a cold and unhappy chill move up and settle in his heart. Suddenly his jaws opened. His head began to shake. He caught himself against the door and held on tight, his teeth chattering and his eyes wide. The fit moved quickly through him and was gone.

He breathed a shaky sigh of relief, running his fingers through his hair. Had it been tiredness? Cold? He did not know. He turned around and went out of the apartment, pulling the door shut behind him.

It did not take him long to find Teddy's place. He remembered the bar on the corner, and the tall, unpainted signboard that was across the street. He parked his car and got out. Looking up toward her window he could see no sign of light. He moved a little way down the sidewalk, but still he could make out nothing. Nevertheless, he knew she was inside. How did he know? He did not bother to wonder. He made sure the doors to his car were locked and then going up the short flight of steps, he rang the girl's door buzzer.

The door clicked. He pushed it open and went inside. He had expected her to come out in the hall, but above him her door remained shut. He climbed the stairs and stood for a moment outside her door, his hand raised to knock. A crack of brilliance showed under the door, and muffled and far away he could hear voices.

At last he knocked. The voices stopped. He felt sweat rise to the surface of his hands and forehead. There was the sound of someone moving around, and in a moment the door was pulled violently open. Teddy, in a white shirt and women's jeans, stared at him in amazement.

"Really, this is too much!" Behind her several women were sitting around the living room. The phonograph was on loud, some deep New Orleans blues.

"May I come in?"

"Darling, please do."

He followed her inside. Three women, in men's pants and shirts, looked calmly up at him.

"Verne, this is Bobby, and Bert, and Terry."

They nodded, without speaking.

Verne turned to Teddy. "I just thought I'd drop by. Maybe I better come back later. I don't want—".

"Give me your coat." She walked into the bedroom; he followed.

"We can talk some other time," Verne said.

"These are just girls from the building. You're not breaking anything up." She hung up his coat. "They won't stay long."

"I don't want to—"

"Don't worry." She took his arm as they went back, leading him. Her fingers were hard and strong. When they entered the living room they found the three women on their feet, standing near the door to the hall.

"We have to go. We'll be back." They opened the door. "Glad to have met you, mister."

"Don't leave on my account," Verne murmured. They closed the door behind them. "I'm sorry I drove them out."

"That's all right." Teddy began picking up the glasses around the room. "What do you want to drink? How would some John Jamison go?"

"John Jamison would go fine." He sat down on the couch. The phonograph was still playing blues. He recognized Bessie

Smith's harsh, deep voice. He leaned back, his head against the couch. The room was warm, and smelled of women. Presently Teddy returned with two glasses. She put one by him and sat down on the floor, by the phonograph.

"Thanks," Verne said, lifting the glass. The glass was cool and moist. He swallowed, shutting his eyes. The liquor scorched his throat and lungs; it was incredibly alive. If there were ever a water of life, this was it.

He sighed.

"How is it?"

"Fine." Presently he said: "Were you surprised to see me?"

"No. Not very. You didn't have any trouble finding the place, did you?"

"I found it all right." He looked around the room. It had been cleaned up. The clothes and bottles were gone. The ashtrays had been emptied. "Your room looks better, this time."

"You didn't think much of it before."

Verne smiled crookedly. "I didn't think much of anything that evening."

"Don't think I'm going to apologize."

"Forget it." They were silent, listening to the music. Presently the records came to an end.

"What do you want to hear now? Anything?"

Verne set his drink down and went over to the record cabinet. Squatting down on his haunches he examined the backs of the albums, turning his head on an angle.

"How about the Bach *Flute and Strings?*" He drew out the album. "I haven't heard that in a long time."

"Put it on."

He placed the records carefully on the turntable. In a few moments the measured tones of the solemn little dances began to fill the room. Verne returned to his place, beside his drink. "Nice. Real nice."

"How long have you known Don?" Teddy said.

"A couple of years, I guess. Why?"

"Just wondering."

"I don't see much of him. He comes into the station once in a while. He tries to get me to play more Dixieland on the program."

"I see."

"What do you think of him?"

"I think he's an intellectual simp."

Verne laughed. "Well, you don't have to go around with him."

"No, I don't."

"Why do you, then?"

She shrugged. "Don's a nice boy. In some ways."

"He looks as if he were rotting away from some sort of fungus."

"Don knows some interesting places. You learn from each person you meet."

"What did you ever learn from him? All about mouldie-fygg jass?"

"He's quite an authority on New Orleans jazz."

"If that means anything. Well, let's forget it."

They listened to the Suite. "This part is so beautiful," Teddy said. "Do you remember what Huxley said about it in *Point Counter Point?* I liked that passage."

"About the guts of a cat? The violins? That was when the old scientist was coming down the stairs, down to the party. Where they were playing this."

"Music figured a lot in the book."

Verne listened to the music. Gradually it absorbed his attention. Some of the loneliness he had felt earlier began to seep back. He pulled himself up on the couch, rubbing his eyes.

"What's the matter?" Teddy said.

"Nothing. Thinking about the book." He lifted his glass, but it was empty. He held the empty glass up to the light, turning it slowly.

"The book was about death," Teddy said.

Verne got up and went over to the bookcase. He turned his back to hear, reading the titles of the books. After a time Teddy came over and stood beside him.

"I see you like Eliot," Verne said. "Great man, for a neo-fascist." He slid a slender book out. "What the hell is this? 'Murder in the Cathedral.'"

"It's a play about Thomas Becket."

Verne put it back. "You have a lot of Jung. All the neo-fascists. *Integration of the Personality*."

"He's a nice old man. He goes for long walks in the snow. What's wrong with you, all of a sudden?"

Verne turned around suddenly. "Well, young lady. Let's go someplace. Where would you like to go? Or do you want to go anywhere? Or shall I leave and go home?"

Teddy laughed. "Let's just talk. I'm tired of going around to dark little places. Okay?"

Verne sat down on the couch. "I know what you mean."

6

VERNE SAW DON Field the following day. Don looked more morose than ever. He plodded up to Verne as he was leaving the station after work.

"Well," Verne said. "It's you again. You're getting to be a familiar sight around this time of day."

"Where were you last night?" Don said hoarsely.

"Last night? Why?"

"You weren't home. I called you."

"What do you care where I was last night?"

"I wondered."

Verne unlocked his car door. "You can keep on wondering." He drove off. Through the rear view mirror he could see Don standing on the curb, watching sadly after him, his armload of records and books sagging.

That evening, Verne mentioned to Teddy that he had seen Don. She said nothing. They were going down to the Morning After Club to hear Muggsy Spanier.

"Spanier," Verne said. "One of the greatest jazz men alive. It's an experience."

"I've heard his records."

"That's not the same. You don't get the bite of the music from a record. The feel. Wait and see."

Did she enjoy the evening? She seemed to. On the way home she leaned against him, humming to herself. She appeared quite happy and content; her eyes were bright and held that same merry gleam he had first noticed that night in the Walker Club.

At the corner of the block near her apartment Teddy suddenly put her hand on his arm. "Verne, park here for a second. I'll be right back."

She got out and trotted up to a liquor store. It was just closing; the man had already turned the signs off and emptied the register. Teddy banged on the door, waving. The man shuffled over and unlocked it. Teddy went inside. A few moments later she came out with a paper bag.

She hopped in the car. "This is on me."

They drove up along the curb to her place. As they got out Verne began to check the doors and windows of the car to make sure they were locked.

Teddy laughed, standing on the sidewalk. "You're so earnest. No one's going to run off with your car!"

Verne grunted. "I suppose not. But it makes me feel better. Let's go."

He followed her up the stairs. She strode along, holding onto the banister, a pace ahead of him. At the top she halted, waiting for him to catch up.

Under her door was a slip of white paper, pushed half way inside. She picked it up and read it.

"It's from Don." She passed it to him. He read it and handed it back. Teddy put the note in her pocket and they went on inside. The living room light was on, a feeble glow hidden behind the table. It left the room dark and mysterious. He could smell things in the air. The perfumes and odors of women, the faint hanging scent of liquor and cigarettes. And when he went to hang up his coat in the closet, another smell. Almost an animal smell.

"Do you have a pet?"

"I had a cat, but she was run over. Her back was broken. I saw it out the window."

"I'm sorry."

"It's hard to keep a cat when you have only an apartment. Box of newspapers in the kitchen, furniture all clawed up. Come sit down."

He sat down. Teddy disappeared into the kitchen, humming as she went. He heard things being opened.

Now, sitting by himself in the living room, hearing the sound of the girl bustling around in the kitchen, he began to feel the first faint stirrings of a profound peace and contentment. He allowed his body to relax; his mind sank into a kind of half-sleep. A cloud of soft darkness moved over him, mixed with the smells of the room.

In the blanket of woman smells, the smells of perfumes and deodorants and female bodies, he found himself going to sleep. From a great distance he realized that Teddy had come back into the room and was standing in the doorway, gazing silently at him. Presently he struggled a little and managed to become awake.

He smiled at her. He had taken his glasses off and put them into his pocket. He loosened his tie, lying with his head against the rough fabric of the couch.

Teddy crossed the room noiselessly, growing and expanding until she stood before him. She put down a tray and then seated herself beside him. He did not look up. He was content. The warmth, the smells hovered over him. He was falling asleep again, and it was a long way to fall. Down and down he plummeted. The world noises, the coldness, the bright lights, everything rushed away from him.

Teddy's small hard fingers were against his face. He sighed. The pressure of her hands was increasing. Like the force of a coiled up spring the energy was coming out of her, moving through her arms and hands, into him. Surges of power, a flowing, overwhelming force. The demands of desire. He sighed again. Of bodily need.

The smells, the warmth, the room and the girl next to him, all blended and merged together. He ceased to know where one began, the other ended. Everything in and around him was rising to the surface, flowing out. A tide, a vast drumming tide was washing him away. He closed his eyes.

Without resistance, he allowed himself to be lost into it.

He ached. His body felt seared and blistered; he winced to the touch. Dazed, his mind struggled to collect itself. He was scattered, strewn everywhere, all over. Fragments and particles. He gasped, breathing like an animal that had come out of some desperate battle.

"Are you all right?" Teddy said.

He looked at her. The lean nose. Loose, hanging hair. Moist strands of black, glued together, dripping with perspiration. Her eyes gleamed, close to his.

Verne pulled away. He was laid open, unconcealed. He turned to one side, away from her. The couch lifted; she had risen up, onto the arm.

"I'm all right." His head ached. His glasses had fallen out of his pocket, onto the floor. He picked them up and put them on. After a while he sat up.

On the arm of the couch Teddy quietly fastened her clothes, pulling her dress together. She said nothing.

"What time is it?" Verne murmured.

"About three." She was watching him. "Are you all right? Do you feel all right?"

Could she tell how far she had been pushed away? He felt cold; everything in the room had receded from him. His stomach growled. His mouth tasted sour. He found the tray and ate a cracker smeared with Liederkranz. Presently he tried some of the drink she had fixed for him, but it choked, charring his wind pipe. He put the glass down.

"I'm sorry. I'll be all right."

He got out his pipe and began to light it. Teddy moved back beside him, drawing toward the end of the couch. He stared at her indifferently. Her face was thin; her body was underdeveloped and plain, like a boy's. He looked down at her feet. They were long and flat, like a bird's. A crane's. Teddy twisted her bony shoulders together, turning her head suddenly away.

"It's cold in here," Verne said.

She did not answer. Verne gazed around the room. He crossed his legs. A measure of vitality was beginning to come slowly back into him. It made the objects of the room seem less dead, remote. They were regaining their life, their color. What had happened a few minutes before had emptied them, sucked the meaning out of them, out of everything around him, all things in the room, wherever he looked. But now the meaning, the usual glow, was seeping back in, draining slowly back into place.

The room was becoming warm again. Verne smoked, his legs crossed, feeling a little better.

He turned to Teddy. "Maybe I should go home."

She turned quickly. Her eyes were shining. "Do you want to go? Is that what you want?"

He removed his pipe slowly. "It's late. I have the early shift tomorrow." He glanced away; it was not so.

"I'm sorry. You — you wouldn't want to stay here? It's not very far from the station."

"I have to shave." He plucked at his sleeve. "I need a change."

Teddy was silent. "I'm sorry."

"Sorry? Why?"

"I don't know. I do know!" She gazed at him appealingly. "You're disappointed. I wasn't — I wasn't enough." She bit her lip, her eyes blind with pain.

Verne shifted. "No. It certainly isn't that."

She continued to look at him.

"No, don't think it was that." He got to his feet. "It's late. I'm tired. You know."

"I'll walk downstairs with you."

"Good."

Teddy went to get her coat. She came back at once, gaunt and forlorn, her coat around her shoulders.

Verne took her arm awkwardly. "Ready?"

She nodded.

"Let's go." They went outside, into the empty hall. They walked down the steps slowly, neither of them speaking. The air outside was thin and crisp.

Verne stood for a moment on the porch, talking a deep breath. The streets were dark and silent. Far off, blocks away, a city street sweeper nosed along, gathering up papers and debris.

"Well, good night, Teddy," Verne said.

"Good night."

He walked down and across the sidewalk to his car. Teddy stood on the porch, watching him unlock the door. He slid in behind the wheel.

"I'll call you tomorrow on the phone."

She nodded.

He drove off.

The telephone was ringing. He opened his eyes. Everything in the room was running back and forth.

"Christ!"

He dragged himself out of bed, onto his feet, catching hold of the wall. He scooped up the phone, sitting down in the chair beside it.

"Hello?" He pushed his hair back out of his face with his fingers. His hands were shaky.

"This is Teddy." Her voice was emotionless. It said nothing, only words. He looked at the clock across the room, but he could not read it without his glasses. Bright sunlight was falling in, streaming through the window.

"What time is it?"

"Nine-thirty."

"I was asleep." After a moment he said: "I was going to call you later on."

"Yes."

He felt around for his glasses. They were in his coat, over the back of the chair by the bed. The sun blinded him; he squinted, rubbing his eyes. He yawned.

Teddy's voice came again, thin and expressionless. "Don wants me to go out this evening. I didn't know what to do. Should I go with him?"

"Don? Where? To where?"

"The Walker Club."

"Oh." He said nothing for a while. He could feel her holding tightly to the phone at the other end. He tried to think what to say. He was beginning to get adjusted to the sunlight. He closed his eyes and settled against the back of the chair, propping the receiver between his neck and shoulder. Time passed.

"Do you want to go?" he said finally.

"I don't know."

"Where are you now? At home?"

"In a drug store. I couldn't sleep. I've been walking around."

"What drug store?"

She did not answer.

"What drug store? Is it far from here?"

"No."

He considered. "I could drive over and pick you up."

"Could you?" She gave him the address.

"Do you want to wait there?"

"I'll wait."

"All right?"

"Yes, I'll wait here."

He hung up. After a while he went in the bathroom and took a shower. He shaved and dressed and listened to the news on the radio. Finally he put his coat on and went outside to the car. He had to be at work at noon. There was about two hours to go.

He found her standing in front of the drug store, leaning against the side of the building. He pushed the car door open and she made her way out to him.

"Greetings," he said, starting up the car.

"Hello."

"How are you today?"

"I'm fine." She turned toward him. "Sorry to wake you up so early."

He could not read her expression. He grunted. "It doesn't matter."

"What time do you have to go to work?"

"About noon."

"Then we have some time, then."

"I guess so." He edged into the traffic.

"Verne — What's wrong?"

"I'm worried about my program. I haven't got it ready for next Thursday. I was thinking about it."

"We can drive for a while, can't we?"

"Sure." He looked at his watch. "But I have to stop and eat someplace. I haven't had breakfast."

They drove in silence.

Teddy stirred. "Verne — You're not upset about last night, are you?"

"What do you mean?"

"You seem so — so aloof, all of a sudden. So pulled back. Withdrawn and silent."

"Sorry."

"I'd like to know why. Can't you tell me?"

"I told you. My damn program."

"Is that really it?" He could feel her watching him intently, looking at his face. "It isn't because of last night?"

"Why last night?"

"I think last night you were — disgusted."

Verne snorted. "For God's sake." He stopped for a red light. "No, it's not that. Having a deadline every week grinds me down. The constant pressure. Sometimes I go into a whingding of some kind. It has nothing to do with you. It's been going on for years."

"You're very nervous. I can tell by the way you move your hands. You're under a lot of tension."

Verne thought about it for a while. "It's a strange thing. About eleven o'clock in the morning I start feeling as if there were something settling down over my shoulders. Some sort of pressure. Like a heavy weight. It bends me over."

"Do you know why?"

"It's a weight like a glove. As if I had the weight of the world on my shoulders. Responsibility. To my job, I suppose. It wears me out."

"You try too hard."

"This is a competitive world!"

"Are you afraid of not succeeding?"

He scowled and relapsed into silence.

"I'm sorry," Teddy said.

"Well, don't worry about last night. It's funny the way women relate everything to themselves. Everything that happens; insult or compliment."

They drove aimlessly along.

"Are we going any place in particular?" Teddy asked. "Or are we just driving?"

"Just driving."

"That's fine."

"You said Don wanted you to go out with him tonight. Are you going to? Have you decided?"

"I don't know. What do you think? I thought maybe you and I—"

"Do you want to?"

"No. But—you and I couldn't do something, could we?"

"I have the late shift. I won't be off until after midnight."

"Do they make you work that long?"

"It's split. A break in the afternoon."

"Later in the week could—"

"We can probably work something out."

She nodded.

"Don't feel hurt," Verne said.

"I'm not hurt."

They drove for a long time without saying much of anything to each other. At last Verne took the car into Teddy's neighborhood. Presently he brought it to a stop in front of her apartment building. An old Negro was soaping down the front steps with a brush and a wash bucket.

Teddy looked up at the building, through the window of the car. "Well, I guess we're here."

"I'll give you a call later on."

"Thanks." She opened the door and got out.

"What do you think you'll do tonight? About Don. Maybe it would be a good idea to go along with it for a while more. You don't want to hit him over the head all at once."

"I suppose not. Well, I'll think it over. Thanks for driving me."

"I'll see you." Verne slammed the door shut and drove off. Through his rear view mirror he could see her walking slowly up the stairs of her building, past the Negro. Then a truck turned in behind him, and he saw nothing but the heavy, expressionless face of the driver, gazing impassively ahead.

Very late that night after he had come home from work there was a knock on the door.

"Who is it?"

A muffled male voice sounded outside, but he could not make out any words. He opened the door. It was Don.

"Isn't this sort of late for you to be out?"

Don came into the room. He dropped into a low chair, sighing. "Thought I'd stop and say hello."

"So I see." Verne sat down across from him. "Nothing special on your mind."

"No."

"What did you do this evening?"

"Went to hear the Woolly Wildcats."

"You and your girl?"

Don nodded.

"She likes it, eh?"

"Teddy's a good girl. She responds."

"That's nice."

"What have you been doing recently? You haven't been at

home. I'm sorry you blew up at me the other day. I was just wondering."

"That's all right. I haven't been doing anything special."

The telephone rang. Verne did not move.

"Aren't you going to answer it?" Don rumbled.

Verne got to his feet and went over slowly. He picked up the receiver. "Hello."

"Verne, this is Teddy. Can I talk to you? Don brought me home a little while ago. You're not in bed yet, are you? Could we —"

"I'll call you back. I'll call you in a few minutes. I have company."

There was silence. Then the phone clicked.

Verne hung up and walked back to his chair.

"Who was it?" Don demanded. "Anyone I know?"

"No."

"What's the matter?"

"Nothing."

"You sure are in a tizzy these days."

"That's too bad."

Don fidgeted with the books he was carrying. Neither of them spoke. Finally Don got to his feet and moved toward the door. "Well, I guess there's no use hanging around here. I'll come back when you feel better."

"I feel all right. I'll let you out."

He opened the door. Don plodded out into the hall and he closed the door after him. As soon as he heard him leave the building he phoned Teddy.

"I'm sorry. Don was here. I couldn't talk with him sitting right in front of me."

"Oh. I didn't understand. I thought —"

"You were wrong." He felt irritable.

"Verne, don't be angry. I didn't know. I'm sorry I didn't understand. I'm sorry I hung up that way."

"Well, forget it. What did you want?"

"Oh, Verne —" She moved away from the phone. Presently she went on in a low, thin voice: "I just wanted to see if you were still up. Could we talk? Could you come over? I could take a taxi to your place, if you're too tired."

It took him a while to answer. "Well. . . . It's hard to know what to say. I'm tired, of course. I feel like I've been hanging on the cross. But I want to see you. That goes without saying."

There was silence. "Perhaps it would be better if we got together tomorrow night instead."

"We'd have more time. It's pretty late."

"Yes. It's pretty late."

He could hear her twisting and turning, trying to know what to do. At last her voice came again, uncertain and hesitant.

"Well, we'll make it tomorrow night. If it's all right. You do want to come over, don't you? You haven't begun to — change your mind, have you?"

"No. I'll be over. About seven."

She said goodbye and hung up. Verne went to bed. He fell asleep right away.

The next day he telephoned her from the station, before he left to go home. It was about five o'clock in the afternoon. She sounded brighter.

"Did you sleep all right last night?" he said.

"Yes. I feel much better today." Her voice was calm. Firm.

"What time shall I come over? Seven?"

"Verne, I'll come over to your place. If it's all right."

"My place? If you want. But it's a mess."

"I don't care."

"What time shall I pick you up?"

"I'll come by taxi. You go on home and I'll be over later on. I have some things to do and I don't know how long it will take. Okay?"

"Sure." He hung up.

She did not come until almost nine. Restlessly, he paced around his room, deep in thought. There was no question any longer. Don could have her back. He was wasting his time; the thing had gone far enough.

While he was thinking the bell rang. He crossed quickly to the door and opened it.

"Hello," Teddy said merrily. She stood in the doorway, dressed in a dark suit, a coat over one arm. And in the other hand holding a suitcase. He gaped at the suitcase. "Can I come in?"

She entered the room, putting the suitcase down. Verne closed the door behind her. "Well," he murmured. "It certainly doesn't take you long when you've made up your mind."

"Come, darling, and help me unpack." She held her coat out. "Where does this go?"

"In the closet."

He showed her where the closet was. There was a cold, clammy feeling in his chest; a heavy weight seemed to drag him down. He followed her into the bedroom. She set the suitcase on the bed and snapped it open. From it she took an armload of dresses and laid them out on the bed. Slips, bras, underpants, nylons —

"Do you want to fix me a drawer to put some of the small things into?" Teddy said.

"Sure. I'll go along with it." He took his stuff out of the top dresser drawer, wadding everything into the bottom. "Is that enough?"

"I don't need very much. I brought only the things I'll need right away."

She put some clothing and small packages and boxes into the drawer. Most of the dresses went into the closet. Presently she was through.

"Where shall I put the suitcase?"

"I'll take it." He lugged it into the closet and pushed it to the back. Then he turned to face her. "Now what?"

Teddy smiled back at him without speaking.

"I wonder what the manager will say."

"Don't worry. In these big buildings they don't care, as long as you don't bother the other people."

"I see," Verne murmured.

Teddy laughed. "I'm not telling you anything you don't know. I'm hungry! Can we eat? Have you eaten?"

"I've eaten, but I'll fix you something." He moved toward the kitchen.

"Don't be silly. I'll fix it myself. We might as well get started right."

Verne studied her. "I almost believe you're serious about this."

"Almost?" She trotted into the kitchen and began opening cupboards and drawers, looking to see what he had.

After she had eaten they sat around the living room. Verne was in a turmoil. He kept looking at the girl and wondering what was going on in her mind. Was this real? Was it actually happening? He took out his pipe, but there was no tobacco for it. He searched his pockets for a while and then gave up. He went to the kitchen and drank a little soda and water instead.

When he came back Teddy had an announcement.

"I told Don this afternoon. Are you glad?"

"You told him what?"

"Verne —" She came over to him, smiling, her eyes bright. Hard, able fingers closed over his arm. "He was very upset. I told him to go read a science-fiction story!" She rocked merrily back and forth on her heels.

Verne said nothing.

A little after eleven o'clock while he was looking through some old programs he noticed that she had left the room. She was no place in sight, in the living room or in the kitchen.

"Teddy?"

There was a noise from the bedroom. "I'm in here." After a moment she said: "Verne, will you do me a favor?"

"What is it?"

"Will you pull down the shades?"

He went around the living room, pulling the shades down. He went back to looking over his old programs. All at once Teddy came running into the room. Out of the corner of his eye he could see her, standing in the middle of the rug behind him. He put down his pen and swung around.

His jaw dropped. She was naked. Bony and white, she stood smiling at him, her little breasts bobbing up and down, her hands on her hips, her feet a little apart.

"Darling, don't you think we should go to bed? I have to get up early tomorrow. I have to go all the way across town to Manhattan."

Verne got to his feet. He walked all around her, staring in amazement at her thin body. She turned to face him. In the bedroom the bedspread and sheets had been pulled back. "You're really serious," he murmured. He shook his head. "Well, this takes the cake."

Her smile froze. She said nothing, but her lean loins tensed, muscles standing out like cords.

"It's impossible. It really is." Inside him the cold clammy

weight grew. As if a net were around him, a great damp curtain, pulling him down. She had taken off all her clothes. He could see them piled up on a chair by the bed. Even her shoes. Everything. It was grotesque. He shut his eyes.

"Verne —"

"Let's face it! For Christ's sake." He pushed his glasses up, rubbing his eyes. "I'll be damned if —"

He stopped. Across her face an expression of wild terror had flitted, so crude and stark that it startled him into silence. For a moment she blinked, her eyes burning. Then abruptly it was gone. Her mouth set in a narrow line. Her eyes filmed over. She turned without a word and walked into the bedroom.

A moment later she came back with a heavy coat pulled around her. She pushed past him toward the front door. He caught her by the shoulder. She jumped away from him, and he stepped between her and the door. Her body was hard and tense. She stood a little way off, breathing shallowly and watching him.

"Teddy, for God's sake, let's —"

She rushed into the kitchen. He followed her, grabbing her arm. She snatched up a can opener from the drawer; he pulled it quickly away. Her fingers were like metal claws.

"Stop it." He held onto her arm. "Look — you couldn't possibly stay here. It isn't possible. They'd throw us out in twenty-four hours. He could feel her thin arm through the coat sleeve. "Do you understand? It's not my fault. I can't do anything about it."

Suddenly she relaxed. Everything seemed to run out of her. He let go of her arm slowly. "Of course," she said. "That's true. I guess we'll have to think of something else."

"That's right." He patted her shoulder. "Let's go back in the living room and sit down. Okay? We can talk it over calmly."

He led her back, over to the couch.

"I ought to put on something else." She plucked at the coat.

"All right." They went into the bedroom. Teddy unfastened her coat and hung it up in the closet. She dressed slowly, silently. He watched her, sitting on the bed. At last she was through.

"Finished?"

"All done."

He got up and went over to her. "Let's go out and have a drink. Then we can drive around for a while. You leave the rest of your stuff here tonight and we'll work out something tomorrow morning. We'll figure out something. Okay? Now — where do you want to go?"

"It doesn't matter. Wherever you say."

"We'll go across the street. It's a nice quiet little bar. We can talk there."

She nodded.

But on the sidewalk she stopped.

"What's the matter?"

"I think I'd rather go right home. I don't feel too well."

"Whatever you want."

"Can we walk?"

"Walk? All that way?"

"It's not far."

"All right. We can always call a taxi when we get tired."

They walked slowly along. The streets were silent and lonely. Above, the sky was overcast. Only a few stars were visible. One huge cloud, as large as a continent, hung across the horizon. It was moving, swelling larger and larger, spreading its opaque greyness over the whole world. One by one, the stars winked off and disappeared.

Verne looked away. Beside him, Teddy strode along, her hands in the pockets of her coat, saying nothing. Her head was up; she was breathing deeply, her mouth half open. Drawing the air into her lungs, the cold, damp air.

"It's a nice night," she said.

"Yes."

"I'm glad we're walking." She slipped her arm through his. "Do you mind?"

"No."

"Do you know what I've decided?"

He glanced at her. "What?"

Teddy kicked a stone from the sidewalk. It rolled into the gutter. "You're right about your apartment, of course. I remember how he looked at me — the manager. I should have realized. But that's all over with." She turned toward Verne, smiling. "Anyhow, it's better to start fresh."

"Fresh?"

"In a new place. Where you've never been before. Where you can paint and clean. Put up drapes, pictures. Start all over. Do you stay in one place very long? The same place gets stale, after a while."

Verne said nothing.

"We'll find a place with a yard. I want to plant some herbs. I've always wanted an herb garden. You can do wonderful things with herbs. And I can get Sheshahgen back again."

"What's that?"

"My cat."

"Your cat! You said — "

"This is a different cat. I gave her to some friends. They'll give her back again."

Verne was dazed. He shook his head. "I don't get it. You're giving up your apartment? Why? Don't you intend to — "

Teddy smiled. "I've already told the landlady. I told her this morning. Verne — there's so many things we can do! Have you ever painted an apartment? Have you? Do you know how it smells, late at night, the wet smell of the paint? You turn on the stove for coffee. The smell of the paint mixing with the coffee smell. The gas. The bright overhead light."

They walked on. Above them the last star had been absorbed, swallowed by the vastness of the grey continent that swelled across the sky. How could it be? How could great flaming suns, thousands of miles in diameter, burning masses bigger than the earth, be eaten up and absorbed by something so small, so un-important as a cloud? Everything was disappearing, vanishing. All around him the world was fading into the grey mists, the hodge-podge of stars, and trash, and tree branches, newspa-pers, the little things that roll around in the wind.

And himself.

He would be swept along with the rest; he had no power to stop the motion of these things. He glanced at the girl striding along beside him. Was it possible that things could be devoured by something so weak, so thin and small, so gaunt?

Had he always been so helpless? Was this the way it would always be? Was there nothing else for him?

They stopped at a corner for a street light. No one was in sight. The wet streets stretched out in all directions, dark and barren. Suddenly Verne tensed. He pulled back, away from the girl.

"What is it?" Teddy said. "Why did you stop?"

"Listen."

She listened. "I don't hear anything."

He moved down the sidewalk, straining to hear. A sound — a faint, familiar sound. A sound he had not heard for a long time. Someone was playing a musical instrument. But he could not tell where.

He came to a house and stood listening, his head to one side. Then he went back farther, past the house, until he stood by a fence, a lattice fence overgrown with ivy. Light was coming through the fence, where the holes were not filled up with the leaves and stems of ivy. He bent down, peering through the fence, cupping his hands.

On the other side a boy was sitting in the middle of a garden, on a wooden stool, playing an oboe. He stared intently ahead, his eyes fixed on a music stand. Above his head an electric light bulb hung. Nothing else seemed to exist for him. Only the cold instrument in his hands, the music in front of him. Nothing else.

All at once he stopped and turned his head. He looked past Verne, off into the distance, his instrument in his lap. Then he lifted it up again and began to play as before.

Down at the end of the block Teddy was calling angrily. Verne stepped back onto the sidewalk and made his way slowly toward her, his hands in his pockets.

"What happened? Why did you go back?"

"A high school boy. Practicing on his oboe."

Teddy shrugged.

They walked on.

Verne was still gazing at Carl when the young man began to wake up. He turned slowly in the bed, stretching and opening his eyes. He blinked at Verne.

"How long have you been awake?"

"Not very long," Verne murmured.

Carl sat up. "What kind of a day is it?" He pulled back the shade above his bed and peered out. The sky was bright blue. The sun shone down everywhere. Off in the distance they could see the machines of the Company, tall columns, rising up like abandoned towers.

"I guess it's time to get up," Carl said. He struggled out of his covers and onto his feet He smiled cheerily at Verne; his blond hair hung down over his face. He pushed it back out of the way.

"Let's go eat breakfast." Carl was all excitement. "Just think

—we can have anything we want! We can have turkey and creamed peas and plum pudding with brandy sauce."

"Is that what you want for breakfast?"

"No, but we could have it. Just think—everything here is ours. Maybe we're not so bad off, after all. We're like kings. We're wealthy. Emperors!"

"It's not so much. You'll get tired of it before the end of the week."

"Do you think so? Well, we'll see."

Verne nodded absently. He was trying to adjust to the present. The past was still with him very much.

They washed and shaved and dressed. Together they walked down the path toward the commissary.

"Do you think Barbara will be there already?" Carl asked.

"I don't know."

"She certainly seems to be a nice person. Don't you think so? But I get the impression that at some time she suffered a great deal."

Verne laughed out loud.

"Wait! Don't laugh. I can tell quite a lot about people, more than you'd think. It's the way she holds herself, and talks. And the words she uses. There's something in her face. Maybe we'll find out, before we leave."

Verne scowled. "Christ's sake."

"What's wrong?"

"Nothing." Verne seemed sunk in irritable gloom. He gazed down at the path, his hands pushed into his pockets.

"Sorry," Carl murmured. They walked in silence the rest of the way. The commissary was deserted. There was no one there. They wandered around inside.

"Well?" Verne said.

Carl looked sad. "I thought maybe she'd already be here,

cooking breakfast for us. Waffles and ham and orange juice. Or something like that."

"Cook it yourself."

"I'm not very good at cooking. Anyhow, it's not the same when you have to cook it yourself."

"All I want is a cup of coffee." Verne sat down at the table.

Suddenly Carl brightened. "Maybe one of us could run over and wake her up. She's probably still asleep."

Verne grunted. "Probably."

"Do you want to?"

"Why me?"

"You know her." Carl waited hopefully.

"Do it yourself. It won't hurt you. Haven't you ever got a woman out of bed? It's time you learned."

Carl's ears turned red. He moved toward the door. "I'll go over. I guess it's all right."

"It's all right. You don't have to go inside. Just rap on the door. Of course, if she invites you in, that's another thing."

"Goodbye." Carl pushed the door open.

Verne watched him go sourly. After a time he got up and went over to the sink. He fixed himself a glass of baking soda and warm water.

Making a face, he drank it down.

7

BARBARA MAHLER LAY in bed half asleep. From an open window the sun streamed across her body, across the bed covers, her pajamas, onto the floor. Suddenly she threw the covers back, away from her. She stretched out, her legs wide apart, her arms at her sides.

The warmth of the sun made her sleepy. It was a good feeling. She sighed, twisting a little in the bed to get all of herself under the warm rays. After a bit she sat up and slipped off the top of her pajamas. She tossed it onto the chair and lay back again, her mouth open, her eyes shut.

The thick beams of the sun pulsed against her shoulders and breasts. She could feel the heat moving across her body like a living thing. It had a strange touch, the sunlight on her naked body. It filled her with excitement. Inside her, something seemed to stir, responding to the sun.

She wondered how it felt to have a life inside her, down in her belly. How would an unborn child feel, crawling and expanding, moving, twisting, reaching out? A living child, breathing, moving toward the light. Like a plant. Plants did that. What was it called? Photo-tropism. Something like that. She opened her eyes and looked up at the sun, but the light blinded her. She turned her head away.

Perhaps people were like plants. Perhaps they were phototropic. That might explain the sun goddesses. Perhaps there was something of the sun goddess in her. She turned back, leaning toward the light, twisting up to meet it. Outside the level land of the Company grounds stretched out in all directions. She could see no motion, no movement of any kind. She gazed at the buildings, the towers, the silent heaps of rusting metal and slag. The world was deserted. All mankind had fled. She was alone.

Barbara stood up on the bed, swaying from side to side as the springs gave under her feet. Reaching down to her waist she unfastened the pajama bottoms and let them slide down to her ankles. Standing naked in the warmth she raised her arms above her. Was that what they did? Was that it? She tried to remember what she knew about the Aztecs. Or was it the Incas? Some South American tribe. And they tore out the hearts of people and cast them up to the sun.

She smiled. That was too much. She could not do that; she could not give her heart up to the sun, even if she wanted to. It was impossible. The sun would have to be satisfied with something else. She put her hands under her breasts and lifted them up, up toward the sun. She would present her breasts to the sun instead. What would happen? Would the sun accept them? Would the sun make her breasts grow and expand? They might swell and expand, and finally burst like ripe seed pods. She looked down at them. They had not changed. They were still full and round, the breasts of a mature woman.

She laughed. They were large enough as it was. She stepped down from the bed onto the floor.

After she had dressed she walked downstairs and outside onto the front porch. She stood for a moment and then started down the steps, onto the path. Soon she was walking toward the commissary.

After a few minutes she saw a figure coming toward her, walking from the opposite direction. It was Carl. She could see his blond hair shining in the sunlight.

"Hello, Miss Mahler!" Carl called.

She waited for him, stopping. "Hello." He came up to her, grinning from ear to ear. How old was he? Not more than twenty or twenty-one. She thought: he must be coming to get me. In another minute he would have gone along the path to the dormitory and seen me — standing at the window naked.

She blushed, her face turning scarlet. He was just a baby. What would he have thought?

It was a good thing she had not stayed there any longer.

"It's a nice day," Carl said.

"Yes. Very nice."

What would he have thought if he had seen her, standing there by the window? Would he have been ashamed? Of course. He would have run quickly away, his eyes shut tight. He would have run on and on. She was delighted, thinking of this, of the boy running away, his face red and burning. She smiled.

"What is it?" Carl said, worried.

Barbara laughed outright. Carl was frowning at her, puzzled and a little alarmed. What a child he was! There was so little of that left in the world, a boy who ran and hid himself. Perhaps he would have to be taken by the hand, sometime.

"Are you all right?" Carl said.

"Oh, yes." Had she been that shy at twenty-one? No. At twenty-one she had already been at Castle, and then at New York. With Verne.

Looking at the blond boy standing uncertainly in front of her, Barbara began to think back. The memory of herself at twenty moved up and around her, slowly at first, then faster and faster.

It was a tide carrying her away from the present, rushing her back into the past.

Back to Castle. And Verne Tildon.

When Penny had suggested she ride back with Verne Tildon she was outraged. On the way back to the cabin she told her so.

"But after all," Penny said. "I don't see what you're so excited about. What could happen to you? I suppose you're afraid you'll get raped, or something."

Barbara raised her voice. "I don't want to hear about it. I'll get home all right without help from men I don't even know."

"You're just afraid you'll get raped. I wouldn't be surprised if you *wanted* to get raped. They say old maids are like that."

Barbara was furious. "Old maid! What do you mean! Just because you're getting married — "

"I'm just teasing you, honey." Penny put her arms around the girl. "My God, kid, you're only twenty. You're not even grown up, yet. You know what they'd call you? As far as they're concerned you're 'San Quentin Quail.' You're under the legal age. You're out of bounds. There's nothing to worry about."

"I wasn't worrying about that. I just don't like the idea of riding all the way back with strangers. It's so unfriendly. Why can't we all go back together?"

"You know, honey. We don't have enough money. And if we don't have money we can't go on the bus. We have enough for two bus fares but not three. Of course, you and Felix could go back on the bus and I could go with Tildon, or you and I could go back on the bus and Felix could go back with Tildon. Maybe that would be safest. Tildon doesn't look like the kind who would molest Felix. Anyhow, Felix would hit him over the head."

"I'd hate to see you and Felix separated. I know how much you want to go back together."

"Well, think it over for a while." Penny considered. "There's one thing you might do."

"What's that?"

"Why don't you get to know this Tildon fellow a little better? Maybe you might like him. He should be pretty interesting. He has some kind of a jazz program back in New York."

"He told me."

"Well, you're a jazz fan. Go over and visit him. It won't hurt you."

"I don't think I want to."

"You never want to do anything."

"Well, god damn it, do I always have to do what you want? Can't I not do things? Can't I just *be*?"

"Sure, honey." Penny took her arm. "Come on inside the cabin. It's time to turn in. And don't worry. Everything will turn out all right."

Barbara sat alone in the cabin. It was evening. Penny had gone; she and Felix had walked over to visit with some people.

Sitting alone in the cabin, with Lawrence's *Sons and Lovers* on her lap, she imagined that she was happy. Was she really? She put the book down on the bed and stood by the window, listening to the sound of the ocean. It was a familiar sound; she had lived near it all her life. It was like the wind or the rain; an eternal presence, a natural being that was always there.

But tonight the sound of the water made her feel restless. Why was it always there? Why was it eternal? Whatever happened to people, whatever happened to her — it made no difference to the ocean. Suppose she were some sort of little creature caught in the surf, pounded back and forth, beaten to death against the rocks. . . . Back and forth, up and down, until every bit of shell and bone had been broken and hammered to a pulp. Did that happen to the little sea things?

Sometimes she saw them, washed up on the beach in the morning. Was that how they died? She thought about it. Perhaps a little sea thing would not even be aware of the ocean, the movements of the tide.

While she was meditating Verne Tildon came up on the porch and knocked. She could not imagine who it was. She opened the door and he came into the cabin.

"Hello, Barbara. How are you?"

She regarded him uncertainly. "I remember now. You're Verne. What did you want? Penny and Felix are gone. They went over to see some people."

"Well, I wouldn't worry." He sat down on a hard chair and leaned back. He was so little and strange. How old would he be? Over thirty, certainly. Perhaps thirty-three or -four. His eyes, magnified by his glasses, blinked up at her owlishly.

"Why not worry?" she said.

Verne shrugged. "I can talk to you instead, if you don't mind. Do you mind?"

"No. I guess not."

"Then I'll talk to you. Well? What sort of a person are you, Miss Mahler? Barbara Mahler. Barbara. I always like to know what kind of person I'm talking to."

"I don't know what you mean."

Verne got up and came over toward her. He was studying her so intently. Like one of her professors back in school. What would this man be like as a teacher? He wore a rough, heavy coat and smoked a pipe. She tried to imagine him with a dog. No, he was not big enough. The dog would pull him along. She smiled, thinking of this.

One of his eyebrows went up. "Well, you're not so god damn serious after all."

She felt her cheeks grow red. "Let's cut that out." He was frankly appraising her, looking her up and down. "Stop it! What do you think I am? Something hanging up in a window for sale?"

"If you were, how much would it cost?" And he added, "Do you think I'd pay it?"

She did not understand. He seemed to be kidding her, but she could not tell. He was puzzling. A little dried-up wrinkled man with hornrimmed glasses.

"You're an elf," she said suddenly. "A strange little elf. Just like in my story book."

For a moment she thought she had hurt his feelings, because he seemed to scowl. But apparently she was wrong. He bowed deeply, with great solemnity. "Thank you."

As he bowed his face had come close to hers. She caught the smell of liquor. He was drunk! No, not drunk exactly. But he had been drinking. That was why he was so lively. Suddenly she felt afraid. She backed away.

"What's the matter? Do you think I'm going to put a hex on you? Turn you into a pumpkin?"

"No."

He walked around the little kitchen of the cabin, pulling open the cupboards. He peered inside them. "Got anything to drink?"

"To drink?"

His mouth fell open. "You mean you have never heard of such a thing?" He closed the cupboards. "Young woman, how old are you?"

He put his hands on his hips. The corners of his mouth twitched as he glared in mock astonishment.

"I'm twenty-four," Barbara murmured. "Why?"

"Twenty-four? Really? And you never heard there was something beside eating and sleeping and — " He broke off. "Maybe you never heard of that, either."

"Heard of what?" She was confused.

"Forget it." He came up and put his hand on her shoulder. "My dear young lady. Perhaps it is time some older, more experienced person, wise in the ways of the world, introduced you to a certain practice, the indulgence of which — in which — is the producer of the most gratifying results." He paused. "What I am saying is this. How about walking over to a bar with me and having a drink? I promise to pay for the drink in the event that you do not care to finish it. Assuming that I may have what is left, of course."

She did not know what to do. She thought about it, her heart beating. He was so strange. He was partly drunk, but she could not tell just how much. He considered her a child; she could see that. He was teasing her. How much older he was than Felix or Penny! This would be the first time she would be going out without them. It was not the same, going to a bar with them for a beer. This was different. She could not make up her mind.

"I'll have to think it over."

He leaped to attention. "All right! I'll come back in late October to find out what you decided."

"Wait a minute." She hesitated. "I can leave a note for Felix and Penny."

"Would that make you feel better?"

"I really should leave a note."

"All right. You go ahead. I'll be outside." He pushed the door open and went out on the porch. The door closed loudly behind him.

Barbara hurried around the room until she found a pencil and a scrap of paper. She wrote: "Penny — I have gone out with Verne Tildon. I'll be back later on. Don't worry about me."

She got a thumb tack and put the note up on the wall, over the bed. Then she took her coat and went outside. Verne was sitting on the porch steps, smoking his pipe. He glanced up.

"So you decided to come. Well, let's go."

Taking her arm, he led her down the road.

The first bar they came to was a small wood place with high stools and sawdust on the floor. The juke box was playing loudly; they could see a few people inside, drinking and sitting.

"How would this be?" Verne said.

"It looks all right."

They went in and sat down at a table. When the bartender came over Verne ordered two scotch and waters.

"I don't like scotch and water," Barbara said, after the man was gone.

"It's the only thing to drink. All those mixed drinks with sugar make you sick. Like pink ladies. You stick to a straight drink like scotch and water and you won't get sick afterwards."

"Are we going to drink that much?"

"What much?"

"That we might get sick."

"That's what I'm talking about," Verne said, trying to be patient. "That's why I want to stick to scotch and water. Isn't that right, Charlie?"

The bartender agreed, setting the drinks down on the table. Verne paid and the man left. Barbara lifted hers slowly and tasted it.

"That's good blended scotch," Verne said. "I saw what he was using. Walker's DeLuxe."

"It tastes more like gasoline," Barbara said, making a face. "Phooie." She put her glass down.

Verne drank deeply. He sighed. "That's it."

"What?"

"The breath of life."

"I guess you can develop a taste for it."

"So I've heard." Verne drank more. Barbara sat, listening to the jukebox and the sounds of the people all around them.

"This is a nice place. Sort of warm."

"Yes it is. Very nice." He seemed less talkative. He had calmed down; he did not make as much noise as before. He sat peering into his glass, turning it around and around, his glasses pushed up a little.

"What are you thinking about?" Barbara said.

"What?"

"What are you thinking about? You haven't said anything for a while."

"Oh, nothing. I was just moldering. It's strange to be here. I haven't been here very long. It was hard to get away. I almost didn't get here. I had to promise to go right back."

"Your job?"

He nodded. "That, too."

"How long have you been here?"

"Two weeks. Two weeks — And now it's over. Back to the old grind. And everything else."

"You're leaving? When?"

"Later tonight."

"So soon?"

"We're taking off tonight. Bill and I."

"Bill?"

"You haven't met him. He's the person I'm taking along. I still haven't found a third rider. Bill is an old friend. You might like him. Maybe we'll see him later on. He's around town someplace."

"What kind of person is he?"

"Plays piano in a band. Back in New York. Bill Herndon is his name. Maybe you've heard of him. Does a lot of arranging."

"No, but I don't —"

"This is progressive jazz."

"You told me you were interested in it."

There was silence. Verne finished his drink. He waved the bartender over. "Two more of the same."

Barbara started to protest but the bartender was already gone with what remained of her drink. "How do you know I want another? Maybe I've had enough."

"Everybody wants another. It's part of life."

"Maybe I don't want to drink any more."

"You're still sober, aren't you?"

"Is that what we're drinking for? To get drunk?"

"Oh, get off it!" He scowled at her. "Put your god damn soap box away."

Her heart thudded. She became quiet.

"Sorry." He removed his glasses and polished them. "You can leave any time you want." Without his glasses he looked like a little child. He peered up at her, nearsightedly. There were great circles around his eyes. Like rings.

"What is it?" Barbara said.

"I see you're still here."

"You don't have to be so nasty." She watched him put his glasses back on. His hands seemed to be shaky and nervous. The bartender brought the drinks and Verne paid for them.

He lifted his glass. "Here's to."

Verne drank quickly. Barbara took a swallow. This one did not seem to be so strong. She managed to drink almost as much as he did this time. She felt a faint glow of excitement begin to form inside her.

"It's not so bad," she said.

The sensations of the room increased. She found herself more aware of the warmth and the sounds of voices. She noticed the colors of the bar, the glasses, the wood. The lights of the jukebox. She leaned forward to speak, but before she could start she found Verne already talking.

". . . And there never was such a one again," he was saying slowly. What had he said? She had not heard the first part.

She started to ask him to repeat it. But all at once he was gone. She blinked. What had happened to him?

He was at the bar. He came slowly back to the table, carrying two glasses with great care. He set them down on the table with a bump.

"There," he said, sighing.

Barbara took her drink. "Thank you."

"Not at all."

She sipped her drink. It did not seem to have any taste at all. But it was cold. She liked that. The room was too warm. She concentrated on the coldness.

"How long?" Verne said.

Barbara rubbed her forehead. The room was so hot! She was having trouble breathing. "What?"

"How long have you been up here?"

She focused carefully on his face. The ashtray was filled with cigarette stubs. She shook her head wearily. Lord, for some fresh air! She stood up.

"What's the matter?" Verne said.

"It's so close."

"What?"

"The room." She was standing by the door. But Verne was between her and the door. A man and woman pushed past them, coming inside. Cold air blew around her.

"Be reasonable," Verne said. He raised his hand, finger extended admonishingly. She giggled, covering her face so he would not see. "What are you laughing at?"

"At you," Barbara said.

"Me?"

He helped her sit down. She was having trouble with the chair. "Thank you."

Verne's breath blew against her face. The room revolved slowly. She put her head in her hands and waited. When she looked up again the room had come to rest.

As she drank she talked.

"We came up, the three of us. It was —" She was not sure. "A few weeks ago. Felix and Penny and me."

"How did you come?"

"By bus. We have two cabins. I live in one. Felix and Penny live in the other." She felt sudden horror: what had she said? "Penny and I live in one, I mean. Together. I didn't mean that, what I said."

"Why not?"

"Because she doesn't go walking. I know." Barbara felt suddenly sad. "I know. I know." She wiped at her eyes. Her tongue was thick; her lips seemed frozen. Like when she had her tooth out, once. "I know."

Verne patted her hand. "It happens to the best people."

"Am I one of the best people?"

He nodded.

"Really?" She felt a little better. "But I know. She never tells me anything. But when she comes back she's warm all over. And the smell. I can tell. Like an animal. It's like animals. Pungent. Like — musk. All over her."

"The best people get to earth that way."

"Do they?"

"Didn't you know?"

"I guess I knew. Is it wrong to know things? Things like that? Does everybody know?"

"Yes. Everybody knows."

It was true, she realized. Everybody knew but her. She was

alone. She pulled back, away from the table. She was cut off. The noise, the sounds, the warmth of the room — it was beyond her. Away from her. Another world. She could not reach it.

"I want to be — to be together," she said.

"How do you mean?"

"Not like now. Not on the edge. Not like I was. Don't you remember?"

"I remember."

"I was sitting on the edge. So far off. By myself. But you came over."

"Yes."

"Why did you come over?"

Verne considered. "To meet you."

"Did you want to meet me?"

He nodded.

Barbara leaned forward. "Why?" She waited, tense. It was very important. She felt numb all over, waiting. "Why, Verne? Why?"

"You looked — nice."

She settled back in the chair. "I was glad you came over. It's a long way." She tried to explain. "I mean, for me. Perhaps not for you. But it seems so far to me. Penny and Felix are going to get married when we go back. Everything's arranged."

"That's nice."

"I know. Have you ever been married?"

He was scowling. "Yes."

"Why are you scowling?"

"No reason."

"Don't you like marriage?"

"It depends."

"I'm glad they're getting married. But I wish — If only — "

"What do you wish?"

"I — I don't know." She was silent for a long time. An age

passed, an immense measure of time. At last she stirred. She felt heavy all over. With a great effort she raised her eyes.

Verne was waiting for her to go on. He had moved his chair very close to hers, not on the other side of the table at all. She looked down. He was holding onto her hand. Suddenly tears rushed up into her eyes. She felt them running down her face, down her cheeks.

He wiped them away with his necktie. That made her smile. Verne smiled back.

"Don't let go," she said. "Please don't let go. Promise you won't."

"I won't."

He smiled more, a funny little wrinkled smile. Like a prune. She thought of a song, a record her father had played for her. The Prune Song.

"I've never heard it," Verne said.

Had she spoken out loud? It was hard to think. Now he was holding onto both her hands. She could feel him close by her.

"Do you understand?" she said. He was nodding, so apparently he did. It made her feel better. "I hope you do. It's all right for them. I hope it's wonderful. It will be wonderful, won't it?"

She sat in silence for a time, thinking about it. Again she felt terribly lonely and sad. She was all by herself. There was no one with her, no one nearby. Verne had gone again. She sipped at her glass, but there was nothing left but ice in it.

Suddenly Verne was back. He was talking, but not to her. To whom, then? She started to get up, but all at once the room leaped up and began to twist slowly. She caught hold of the edge of the table to steady it. Verne looked at her sleepily. He had turned his chair sideways and was sitting, his legs crossed, playing with his tie.

"I feel funny," Barbara said. Her voice sounded as if it were coming from somebody else.

". . . If we leave at one we'll never get across the highway approach . . ." Verne was saying. She blinked. Who was he talking to? To her?

She looked around, but her head felt heavy and refused to turn. There was another man sitting at the table. He was all in black, his suit, his hat, his clothes, even his skin. He was a Negro.

Her hand was touching something cold. She was setting down her glass. She did not remember picking it up. The Negro smiled and spoke. Who was he?

It was Bill. Verne was saying so.

Bill repeated something, over and over again, looking intently at her. She nodded. What was the matter with him? He got up and left. He came back again.

Her hand was cold. The glass, icy, drops of wet against her fingers. The glass was full. The glass was half empty. She was belching.

She caught herself and pulled herself upright in the chair, looking around to see if anyone had noticed. Verne was gone. She could see him on the other side of the room talking to some people, hanging over the back of a chair. His feet were up; his soles needed mending. He was like a little child. A dried-up little elf. Why was he so small? Bill was huge. He was black all over. But he was a Negro.

Now it was "Time On My Hands." She said, can't you play something else?

The man with the glasses said, what do you want to hear?

She was on her feet. The room was moving slowly along like a carpet unrolling. Or maybe one of those little red amusement carts. The bar swung over to her. She saw a woman with a big wide face. And two men. Bland, round, filling up in front of her. She tripped. Her hands were numb, aching with pain. One of them was going along her cheek, rubbing against her face.

She got up. Verne said something, over and over again. Everything murmured and buzzed around her.

Now it was cold. She was cold all over. It began with her feet and went up her legs, through her body and into her arms. She lifted her arm up slowly. A terrible wind caught it and pushed it back. There was a vibrating. Was it the ocean? The ocean made her restless. She could see nothing but darkness ahead of her. Something hard was pressing into her side. She felt for it. It seemed to be a rod of some kind.

She felt fear. The rod would not move. She tore at the rod. Her nails cracked and bent. Then a hand closed over hers. Someone spoke. She forgot the rod.

She was in a car. The car was moving. Wind roared about her; she was against the door. The voice was telling her that, warning her about something.

Then she was sitting at a counter, staring into a stack of pies. Each pie rested on a little wire rack. A man in a white costume opened a little door and took out one of the pies. It was an apple pie.

"With ice cream?"

"Just plain," Verne said.

"Just plain."

Everything was bright. Her head ached. Her whole body ached. She turned slowly. Verne was sitting on one side of her, wearing a heavy overcoat. She turned the other way. A large good-looking Negro was sitting, drinking a cup of coffee.

"Good morning, Miss Mahler."

She stared at him. How did he know her name? He was smiling broadly. He said something more, but she could not make out the words.

". . . Better, I hope," Verne murmured.

Barbara leaned forward and rested her head against the

counter. Something seemed to be gurgling through her, crawling around inside her body.

She got to her feet and stood by the stool with her knuckles against her face. The two men looked up at her, Bill with his coffee cup half lifted, Verne smoking a cigarette. Bill was watching her with a polite expression on his face. An expression of tolerance and understanding. And amusement.

"I'll — be back." She turned toward the counterman. He looked at her without expression.

"It's over to the left," Verne murmured.

She walked unsteadily across the room and pushed open the door. Then she was hanging over the washbowl, violently sick. The only thing she could think of was: Verne was wrong. I *am* being sick. I am.

Disgust at being sick filled her with misery. She pulled away from the bowl, drawing herself up. In the square mirror over the bowl she saw her reflection. The grey face of a young woman vomiting stared back at her. The eyes partly closed with fatigue. The hair dry and stiff. She felt tears come, and she shut her eyes tight, squeezing them shut.

The sight was blocked out. She felt better. After a time she ran water into the bowl, cleaning it slowly. She ran the water over her hands and wrists and then rubbed her eyes. The water was cold. Her left hand stung.

Barbara sat down on one of the toilets and wiped her eyes with her fingers. The tears trickled down, along her wrists. She tried to make them stop; she did not want to cry. If she were to cry things would be worse. She wanted to pull everything into her. She did not want to release anything. If only she could hold herself in, pull herself together, smaller and smaller . . .

She rubbed her face clean and brushed at her dress. It was stained and rumpled. There was a bitter taste in her mouth and her nose. She blew her nose on a bit of the toilet paper.

Presently she went unsteadily back, into the room again. Verne and Bill were gone. No one was at the counter. She gazed dully around. They were in a booth.

She sat down next to Verne and stared at the napkin in front of her. She picked it up, twisting it with her fingers. She could see Verne's wrist-watch, buried in the hair on his arm, at the end of his cuff. What time was it? Nine o'clock? It was after nine, almost ten.

She looked through the window at the street outside. Sun was shining down. Trees and people. A few cars parked. Stores. A couple moved along. Older people, well-dressed. She wondered where they were going.

The café was almost empty. The counterman was at the back, washing dishes, turned away from them. He was a huge man with broad shoulders. He was whistling; she wished he would stop.

She rubbed her face. Her skin was dry and rough. Her body felt sandy, as if sand had got into all her joints and was making them stick and grind. She did not want to move. Everything in her resisted motion.

"Verne," she said.

He turned toward her.

"Verne — what am I going to do?"

"Do?" His face wrinkled. "What do you mean? You'll feel better. Drink some of this coffee."

"Verne knows better than anyone how it feels," Bill purred in a deep voice. "Don't you, Verne?"

"Try something to eat. How about some mush? Or some soft boiled eggs?"

"I'm not hungry." Her voice was low and thick. "I don't feel well."

"Nothing? Not even some coffee?"

Her lips twisted. "I was sick in there."

"You were sick in the car, too. But not on anything important. It happens."

Barbara turned away.

"We should be taking off pretty soon," Verne said. "Bill would appreciate it. He has to get home by nightfall. We hadn't expected to stop this long, if we're going to make schedule we better start."

"Where are we?"

"Aberdeen."

She shook her head.

"A little place. Off the highway. About half way along. We drove all night. At least, Bill did."

"It was a good thing I was along," Bill purred.

Barbara turned her gaze on Verne. She had not realized he was so untidy. His tie was gone and his shirt was unbuttoned at the top. He had not shaved. His skin was dirty and splotched. There were countless little stiff hairs pushing through the skin of his jowls and neck. A green spot of color showed from his coat pocket. His tie. He had put it there.

"I guess you don't feel well either," she said.

"I'll live."

"Who wants more coffee, before we go?" Bill said. "Refills are free here, according to the menu."

The last of his words blurred off. Darkness and fatigue rolled over her. The room faded away.

They were walking across a lawn. Everything was dim. Indistinct. She could scarcely see. Verne was holding onto her arm. He was saying, don't trip.

A man loomed up out of the gloom. There was a building of some kind. The man said, right here. If you will, please.

She was reading something. Was it a telephone book? No, she was not reading it. She was holding it in her hands. The book was heavy. It began to slip away from her, faster and faster. Someone steadied it. Her hand was being moved, guided.

The woman was saying to her, and if you don't see what you need come over to the office and ask.

Verne and the woman went off. She was sitting down, waiting. Where had Bill gone? She tried speaking his name experimentally, but nothing happened. Everything was silent around her. Silent and unmoving.

She was on her feet. It was light only in some places; all the light was concentrated into tiny knobs. And between there was only darkness.

The darkness moved up and down. The lights were drifting past her, flowing back away from her.

Then it was light all around. And warm. There was warmth for the first time; she sucked it greedily in. The warmth and light were bringing her to life. She was coming back into existence again, faster and faster. Her insides churned; she was belching.

She stopped herself, putting her hands over her face. Presently she took her hands away, peering out.

Verne was sitting on a bed. On the floor beside him was a suitcase. The suitcase was open. Its contents were shirts and socks, ties. Things wrapped up. Verne was leaning over, doing something on the floor.

She blinked. There were newspapers on the floor around his feet. He was shining his shoes. His hands moved slowly back and forth. Right, left, right, left. He had a brush.

Suddenly he looked up at her. "Hello. How do you feel?"

"Not very well."

"Can I get you anything?"

"No." Presently she said: "Maybe some water."

He got up off the bed and padded out of the room. She heard water running. A moment later he came back with a plastic cup.

Through the door she saw a small bath room with a shower and washbowl. There were little green soap squares wrapped up on the washbowl.

She took the water. "Where are we?"

"Almost in New York. A little town outside the city. We didn't quite make it."

"Where's Bill?"

"We left him off, fifty miles back. He lives up that way."

"Oh." She was silent.

He touched her arm. "Are you all right?"

"I'm better. Is my purse here?"

He found it for her. She fumbled in it and found a bottle of aspirin. After she had taken two tablets she felt a little better.

"How about Penny and Felix?" she said. "Do they know where I am?"

"They know you went with us. We told them. Don't you remember?"

"No. I — I can't remember a lot of things."

"Well, if it makes you feel better, there's a few things I don't remember either."

She smiled wryly. After a while she got up and walked about the room. In one corner on a wood table was a radio with a coin slot and a plunger. "Twenty-five cents for an hour's listening," a sticker read.

She looked out the window. It was dark. She could see a concrete ledge; beyond the ledge were lights. They seemed to be far away.

"Are we up high?"

"Third floor. That's some sort of a town. A little place. I've been here once before, but I don't remember much about it. It was a long time ago."

One door led into the bathroom. She examined the other door. It had a latch on it; it led out into the hall. She did not feel so confused, now. Her head was beginning to clear. Except for the nausea she was almost all right. She touched her skirt; it was wrinkled and dirty. Stained. Suddenly she thought about her things.

"My clothes! They're — they're still back at Castle?"

"Penny said she'd have them shipped to Boston for you."

Barbara nodded. She watched Verne. He was sitting on the bed again. He had finished polishing his shoes and had put them off in the corner. He wiggled his toes; he had on bright red socks.

"What time is it?"

Verne examined his watch. "After midnight."

"Midnight — twenty-four hours."

"Yes. We did a lot of things. What do you remember?"

She rubbed her head. "Not very much."

She felt cold suddenly. She stared around at the room, at Verne sitting on the bed. He shifted uncomfortably. He had taken off his shirt and was sitting in his trousers and undershirt. His shoulders were narrow and small.

She gasped. She was dazed.

"What's wrong?" Verne murmured.

"We're — we're both staying here? Together?"

"That's the general idea." He laughed nervously. "It's not so serious. People do it every day."

She said nothing.

"Don't look at me that way!"

She closed her eyes. Her heart began to pound loudly. As if it were trying to talk. She moved away from Verne, over toward the window again.

Outside she could see the tiny lights, so far off, lost in the immense darkness of night. Were they really lights of some small town, as he had said? Or were they something else? Stars, perhaps. But they did not wink.

She turned around. Verne was watching her intently. He was so small and thin, sitting on the bed in his undershirt. She had not felt afraid before, but now she was beginning to become frightened. Verne's face was anxious. Suddenly she realized — he was terrified. He was afraid she was going to leave.

In spite of herself she smiled. She walked back toward the bed. Verne seemed to draw away from her.

"Well," she murmured.

"How do you mean that?"

"I don't know. Everything seems to be happening so fast. I have to get used to it."

He said nothing.

"I'm still a little afraid," she said presently. "But not as much as before."

"Afraid of me?"

"No. I don't know. I'm confused. I can't remember . . . I've forgotten so many things. I still feel sick. Did I do anything — anything silly? Dumb?"

"Nothing out of the ordinary." Verne pulled himself up. "In fact, we didn't realize you were — that you had been affected so much until this morning in the diner. Do you remember that?"

She nodded.

"You were sick in the car. You had sort of gone to sleep. Passed out. We couldn't tell very much. You came around pretty groggy."

"I remember."

"That's about all."

Barbara sat down on the edge of the bed. "Verne, I —" He reached for her hand but she pulled it quickly away. "Verne, I think I told you I was twenty-four. I'm not. I'm only twenty."

His eyebrow lifted. He gazed at her, his face round and owlish, his lips twitching.

"That makes a difference, doesn't it?"

"Sort of."

They sat for a long time, neither of them speaking. Finally Verne sighed and began to move about on the bed.

"Well?" he said. "What do you want to do?"

"It's not very safe, under the circumstances." She hesitated. "We crossed the state line, too, I think. Doesn't that mean something?"

He nodded. "Yes. It means something."

"What — what shall we do?"

There was silence. The room had begun to grow cold. The heater had been turned off. Barbara realized, all at once, that she was beginning to tremble. Her body was trembling all over. She gripped her hands together.

"Brrrrrrr," she murmured. "It's cold."

Verne nodded. He drooped, sagging in a little heap on the bed. His face was long and sad. Presently he removed his glasses and put them on the dresser.

Barbara leaped up. "Verne — "

"Yes?"

"I wish I knew how you felt."

"Felt?"

"About everything. About this. You know."

He started to speak, but then he seemed to change his mind. He rubbed his chin and swallowed. Finally he looked up. "It's hard to me to say in so many words."

"I suppose so." She hesitated. "It's hard for me, too. To know what to do without being sure."

"Sure of what?"

"I don't know." She paced slowly across the cold room, her arms folded. "I wish I could tell what you're thinking. How you feel. What this means to you."

She sat down again on the edge of the bed. Someplace, far off, a clock struck. Outside in the night, a long way away. A wind had come up. She could hear it moving against the window, rustling in the darkness.

She began to take off her shoes slowly, conscious of Verne's eyes on her. Her heart was thrashing inside her, beating in hard little strokes. She was terrified and excited at the same time. Stage fright. Like when she had to make a speech in school. How far away that seemed! She was shaking terribly. From cold and fatigue. And fright. She smiled at him.

"I can hardly breathe."

"Will you be all right?"

"I think so." She took off the other shoe and pushed it against the first. She was cold all over. Cold and clammy. Little beads of moisture clung to her body. Tiny icy drops against her neck and arms. But she was excited, shaking with awe and terror.

"Verne — would you do something for me? Would you turn off the light? Please?"

He reached up and pulled the light switch.

In the darkness she undressed, her hands awkward, her pulse racing. What would Penny think of her now? If they ever guessed — But of course they knew. They knew all about such things. She laughed out loud.

"What is it?" Verne's voice was very near her.

"Nothing." She felt for the bed in the darkness. Her fingers touched the covers. He moved away to make room for her. "Verne —"

"Yes?"

"I hope you'll be patient with me. I've never — I've never done anything like this before. Will you be patient and understand?"

"I will," he said.

8

It was late August.

"How much money do you have?" Penny said.

Barbara opened her purse and got out the coin purse. She showed Penny her money: three tens and a twenty and some ones rolled up with a rubber band.

"All right," Penny said, nodding.

"It's enough?"

"Yes. You already have your ticket?"

Barbara showed her the ticket. The first bus was already starting to leave. It pulled out, away from the station, moving along the road with a roar. Penny and Barbara stepped back, away from the curb. The driver of the second bus brought his bus up to the loading platform, and the small group of people began to pick up their suitcases and shuffle forward.

Penny took Barbara's hand. "Good luck, honey." She grabbed her around the waist and hugged her hard. "And remember! If you get into any trouble in New York call me and Felix. We'll come up there, if we have to."

"I better hurry," Barbara said. "He's going to pull out."

She caught hold of her little bag and ran to the door of the bus. The other people had all got on. The driver started up his motor, shifting gears. Barbara clambered up the steps and handed him the ticket. He punched it and gave it back to her. She pushed down the aisle to the rear. The bus began to move while she was still on her feet. She clung to a seat handle and lowered herself into the seat, still holding onto her bag.

An elderly man sitting next to the window put down his magazine. "Want me to put that up in the rack for you, miss?" he said.

She said no very quickly, and clung even more tightly to the bag. The old man returned to his magazine. Barbara sat holding onto the bag, looking out the window past the old man's glasses, at the streets moving by.

In New York she checked her bag at the depot. She found a telephone booth and called the radio station.

"I'm sorry, lady," the man said patiently. "I can't tell you that. It's not the policy of the station. I'm sure Mister Tildon wouldn't mind, but it's the policy of the station not to —"

"You can tell me when he broadcasts, can't you?"

"Certainly." She heard him moving some papers. "He'll be on the air tonight at nine o'clock. That's the starting time of his program."

"Will he be in the station before the program?"

"I don't know that."

She thanked him and hung up.

When the taxi let her off in front of the station it was almost eight-thirty. She hurried along the gravel path, looking around uncertainly. Was this really the place? She saw a small modern building, one story, with shrubs and grass around it. A tall wire tower rose in the air behind the building.

Barbara pushed open the door and went inside. She was in a large, well-lighted waiting room. There was no one around.

At the end of the room was a great window, and beyond the window she could see a man sitting before a board of dials and meters and switches. The man leaned back in his swivel chair, turning slowly from side to side. He was reading something in front of him. Every once in a while he pushed a sheet of paper away.

Barbara walked restlessly around the waiting room, her heart thudding. The room was painted in light pastels, blue and green. The ceiling was some kind of perforated fiber. The light came from recessed fluorescents.

She sat down in a deep modern metal and leather chair and watched the man talking. On the wall next to him was a big round clock and some photographs tacked up, a row of girl pictures, mostly breasts and shoulders. There was a tall file case of phonograph records in heavy covers. And two immense turntables next to each other, with long thin tone arms. The man who was talking noticed her and turned his chair around. He was an older man with curly light hair, a necktie and a jersey sweater. He studied her a moment and then swung around, away from her.

At the end of the waiting room a door opened. She jumped, suddenly tense. But it was only a big man in a blue pinstripe suit, walking with a young fellow in his shirt sleeves. They glanced at her and passed on through a door marked PRIVATE.

The clock in the control room read five minutes to nine. Her nervousness increased. She took off her coat and folded it over the back of the chair. She picked up a magazine but she could not bear to read it. Presently she got to her feet and walked around, her hands in the pockets of her suit.

The man in the control room put on a phonograph record. She could not hear it play but she could see it going around. He got up from his swivel chair and lit a cigarette. He nodded to her. She turned away. On the wall the hands of the clock were still moving. Had the person on the phone told her the truth? Was this the right night?

Suddenly it happened. She turned pale. Verne had come silently into the control room, beyond the window of glass. He did not see her. He put down an armload of records and removed his coat. He sat down in the swivel chair and pulled the microphone down to him. The other man bent down, resting his hand on Verne's shoulder. He said something to him. Verne turned quickly, looking through the window at her. He gaped, his mouth open foolishly. Like some sea thing in a glass tank, suddenly surprised.

He started to get up from the chair but the other man pointed to the clock. Verne nodded. He picked up a sheaf of papers and unclipped them, turning toward the control board again. The other man left the control room through a side door. A moment later he came into the waiting room.

"Hello," he said to Barbara.

"Hello."

"You're waiting to see Verne?"

She nodded.

"All right." He looked around. "Don't you want to hear the program?"

"Hear it?"

"I can turn on the wall speaker for you." He reached up to a box over the window and clicked a switch. The room filled suddenly with the sound of jazz music, a heavy beating Chicago orchestra.

"Thank you," Barbara murmured. The man went on outside, down the path away from the building.

Verne was talking. "Men like Bix Beiderbecke represented a tradition in jazz in which for the first time — "

She listened. His voice was low and harsh. He was very nervous, she realized. He was sitting with his back to her, facing the control board. On and on his voice droned. After a while he put on a record and the sound of his voice was replaced by Paul Whiteman's band. He got up from the board and came over toward the window.

Again he gaped at her, his hands stuffed into his pockets. His expression was impossible to read. His face moved, his eyebrows twitching, the corners of his mouth going up and down. Barbara went over close to the window. They were only a few inches apart.

Suddenly Verne turned and ran back to the board. He snatched up his papers and sat down, adjusting the long rod of the microphone.

" — Beiderbecke's contribution to the field of Chicago jazz is unfortunately rated too low because of his early and tragic — "

She went back to the chair and sat down. A group of people opened the street door and came in. They stared curiously through the window at the men talking. One of them, a girl about fourteen, began to giggle. She pounded a young boy with her on the arm. Their parents led them on out of the waiting room down the hall and around the corner. Barbara sat back in the chair and tried to relax.

At nine-thirty the door opened and a woman came quickly into the waiting room. She stopped, breathing hard, her slim body quivering. She gazed around her, eyes bright, her chest rising and falling, breathing almost like some kind of animal. She was tall and angular, with jet black hair falling down her shoulders in two heavy braids which widened at the ends into plump tufts. She shot a rapid, keen glance at Barbara and then padded over to the great window. With something small she tapped against the glass. It gave off a tiny clicking sound; probably a coin.

Verne looked up, startled. He and the woman stood gazing

at each other, the woman breathless and flushed, Verne expressionless and grim-faced. He nodded curtly to her and then returned to the board. The woman continued to watch him for a few minutes. Then she moved away from the window. She walked across the waiting room and sat down in a chair a little way from Barbara.

Barbara studied her out of the corner of her eye. What kind of person was this slender, oddly-dressed girl? Was she waiting for Verne? Would she leave soon? The woman did not appear to be going. She opened a small purse and took out a cigarette. What strange shoes she had on — they were woolly, furlike. Her legs were bare; she had no stockings on. Barbara began to wish she would go. The brightness of the woman's clothes disturbed her; she could not seem to ignore her, no matter how she sat. She picked up a magazine and turned the pages, but it did not help.

The woman was looking at her, now. Watching her silently, her shining black eyes fastened on her.

She leaned forward. "Say, darling. Do you have a match?"

Barbara's head jerked up. She shook her head dumbly and returned to the magazine. Her cheeks were turning scarlet; she could feel the blood rushing up. The woman was still looking at her. Why didn't she stop? How long was she going to sit, leaning toward her like that?

The woman got to her feet. She walked around the waiting room. After a while she wandered off down the corridor. Barbara heard her talking to someone. Presently she came back, skipping from side to side carelessly, her arms folded. She was humming under her breath, repeating one syllable over and over:

"La-la-la, lalalala, la. La-la-la — "

She spun around, one hand on her hip, her skirt sweeping out. Her cigarette jutted from her thin mouth, still unlit. How tough and cold she seemed. Except for her eyes. They were bright and hot, too bright. At last she sat down again. Her long fingers drummed on the arm of the chair, tapping in time with the music that came from the wall speaker. She was so much in motion. Agitated. Was she nervous? Or just restless?

Barbara made herself as small as she could in the chair and tried to concentrate on the magazine.

Time passed. She glanced up at the clock on the control room wall. It was almost ten. Did the program end at ten? Verne had not looked at either of them since he had first seen this girl. He knew her; that was certain. But how well did he know her? She was waiting for him. That was obvious. She was not going to go away.

At five minutes of ten the other announcer came back through the waiting room.

"Hello, Teddy," he said to the girl. Teddy — Was that her name? Has she heard Verne mention her? She could not remember; there was so much of the trip she did not remember. The girl seemed at home here in the station. She knew the announcer and he knew her. Did that mean she worked here? The announcer appeared in the control room, behind the glass. He put a hand on Verne's arm, leaning over him to see the script. The last record from Verne's stack was coming to an end.

"Well, that ties up another *Potluck Party* for tonight," Verne's voice came. "We'll be back again next week with more of the same. And remember: there's a fine combo playing right now at the Tied-Down Club. If you want to hear some first-rate creative experiments in the — "

He finished, and the theme came on, some progressive piece she did not know. The other announcer sat down at the board.

Verne gathered up his records and papers into a stack again. He put on his coat slowly, pausing at the control room door.

Then very carefully he put down the records and got his pipe out of his coat pocket. He filled it with tobacco from a leather pouch. His hands were shaking. She could see them shaking through the glass. He snapped on a lighter and lit his pipe. Then he returned the lighter to his pocket and picked up his load. He disappeared from the control room.

The girl Teddy got to her feet. Barbara's heart began to thump again. She was frightened. She put down the magazine and stood up, too. Her heart was beating so loudly that she could not get her breath. Teddy glanced at her and smiled, a thin little smile.

The door opened. Verne came slowly into the waiting room. He stopped and stood looking at the two of them.

"Hello," he said.

"That was a gorgeous program, ducky," Teddy said. "I loved it."

Verne looked at her and then at Barbara. She smiled uncertainly. Verne sucked slowly on his pipe, his face expressionless. After a while he removed his pipe.

"You people know each other?"

"No, darling," Teddy said. "What's her name? Don't you want to introduce her?"

"This is Barbara Mahler," Verne said. "Barbara, this is Teddy." He had finished. He clamped his teeth onto his pipe again.

"Hello, Barbara," Teddy said. Her voice was bright and merry. She rocked back and forth on her heels, her eyes sparkling. Barbara noticed.

"How long have you been here?" Verne said to Barbara. "In New York."

"Just — just today."

"Well," Teddy said, "where shall we go? Have you had dinner, Barbara? Maybe we ought to go someplace where we can eat. What do you say, Verne?"

Verne rallied a trifle. "That's a good idea," he said dolefully. Presently he added: "This happened once before in Springfield, Ohio."

Teddy laughed and took his arm. "Come on," she said to Barbara. "Get on the other side. Do you think all three of us can fit in his little Ford?"

"I think we can," Barbara said.

They left the building and walked down the gravel path through the darkness. Verne's car was parked close to the building. It had not been there when she arrived. They got into the car and slammed the doors.

"Where to?" Verne murmured. He looked at Barbara.

"I don't know any places in New York. Wherever you want to go is all right."

"How about Kahn's?" Teddy said. "It's still open, isn't it? Let's go there."

"All right," Verne said. "We'll go there."

Kahn's was a restaurant, down under the street level. They went down a flight of steps. It was not a fancy place. It seemed to be some sort of foreign restaurant. Each table had a red and white tablecloth over it, and a candle in the center. They sat down and Barbara picked up the menu. There were dishes like Shish-Kabob, and Borscht, and Pilaf with shrimps, and Yialandji Dolma. For dessert there was Baklava and Melomacarona. What kind of dishes were these?

The waiter came over, an old man with a big black mustache. Verne ordered and he went away.

Barbara watched Verne. She had not seen him for over a month. He looked the same. He did not seem to have changed much since he let her off a block from her house, that morning. He was staring down at the table in front of him. Teddy was watching Verne, too, watching everything he did. Her eyes were avid.

What kind of a relationship did they have? Had they — She turned the thought away. If only she had known before she came to New York! But perhaps it meant nothing. Perhaps it was just bad luck that the girl had come to the station the same night as herself. How could she tell?

If only she could talk to Verne alone!

Teddy was humming to herself again, moving her head back and forth. Why didn't she leave! If only she would get up and go! But there was no chance of it. Obviously, she was here to stay.

The waiter came with the food. He set the big metal tray down on the edge of the table and began to unload dishes of steaming food. His thick arm pushed past her, and she drew back.

The food was spicy and strange. She did not like it very well. She ate only a little. None of the three of them said very much. Verne was glum. He ate quickly with big bites that filled up his mouth, pushing the food down with hunks of breadsticks from the glass in the center of the table. Teddy ate with rapid, nervous vitality, her fork flashing back and forth.

Time passed. The waiter refilled their coffee cups. Barbara wondered what time the last bus left back to Boston. She should have noticed while she was at the depot. But she had been too excited to notice anything. What if she missed it? What if she had to stay in New York? She glanced at Verne. He had pushed his chair back from the table, crossing his legs. Could — could she stay with him? Or would she have to go to a hotel? Now she did not want to do either, actually. But she could not go back to Boston without talking to him, without having been able to see him alone for even a moment. If only Teddy would leave!

"Well?" Teddy said. "Where'll we go now?"

They went across the street to a little dark bar. There were few people in the bar. A group of Negro musicians were playing.

"Let's sit here," Teddy said. They took a table off in the corner, near the back.

Verne went up to the bar and brought back drinks for them.

"Did you come on the bus?" Teddy asked Barbara.

Barbara nodded.

"How was it?"

"All right."

"Where are you staying?"

Barbara hesitated. She managed not to look at Verne. "I—I guess I'll go back tonight. I thought I would stay with some friends, but they're not here. They went out of town."

"That's too bad."

"They didn't know I was coming."

Verne looked up at her. "How have you been?"

"Fine."

"Were your parents surprised to see you back so soon?"

"They were a little surprised."

"How are Penny and Felix?"

"They're fine. They're married now. They said to say hello to you."

He looked at her keenly. "They know you came up here?"

"Penny drove me down to the bus station."

"Where are you from?" Teddy asked.

"Boston."

"Boston? That's a nice town."

"Yes."

"Do you live there?"

"Yes."

"What do you do? Go to school?"

"I graduated this spring."

"What did you major in?"

"Political science. I thought of going into some kind of social work."

Teddy smiled. "That should be interesting. There are plenty of people to salvage all the time. You see them everywhere. Don't you, Verne?"

He nodded.

"I'm finished with my drink," Teddy said. "How about another?"

Verne stirred. "All right." He started to get to his feet.

"I'll call her over." Teddy waved to the waitress standing by the bar. "Sit down."

The waitress came over, collecting their glasses on a small tray." What'll it be?"

"Martini for me," Teddy said.

"Scotch and water."

They looked at Barbara. "I don't want any more. Nothing for me." She shook her head.

The drinks came. Verne finished his quickly. Barbara listened to the music in the background. It was getting late. How late? She could see no clock.

"What's the matter?" Teddy said.

"I was wondering about the last bus. I don't know when it leaves."

"You're really going back tonight?"

Barbara nodded.

Verne grunted. "It's a hell of a long way to come." He pushed his glasses up, rubbing his eyes.

"What do you mean by that?" Teddy said.

"I mean it's too bad she — she has to go right back. Can't you stay at a hotel?" He adjusted his glasses into place, regarding Barbara solemnly.

"I don't want to stay at a hotel."

"Why not?"

"I hate hotels."

Verne considered this. He finished his drink. After a time he looked up at Teddy. "Teddy, what do — "

"No chance," Teddy said firmly. She smiled at Barbara. "If I wasn't full up you could stay at my place. It's too bad we didn't know you were coming."

Verne got to his feet. He went over to the bar with his glass and sat down on a vacant stool. Presently he came back with the glass full.

"Refill." He sat down at his place. Barbara and Teddy watched him drain the glass. He set it back down with a sigh.

"Verne — " Barbara said.

He looked sleepily at her. "What is it?"

She hesitated. Both of them were watching her. Verne seemed to be staring right through her. His gaze was oblique, unfocused. As if he were seeing into another world, a world that lay someplace behind her.

She chose her words carefully, watching his face. "Verne, I wish I could talk to you before I go back."

He frowned. "What about?"

"I — I just want to talk to you. I came up here to see you." Her voice sounded forlorn.

"I'll go off," Teddy said merrily. She pushed her chair back, one hand on the table. "I'll go into the powder room and sit for a while."

There was silence.

"Don't go," Verne said.

Barbara's heart almost stopped beating. She bit her lips, tears spilling into her eyes. She turned her head away.

"I'll be glad to go," Teddy said happily. She eased herself back down in her seat again.

Verne said nothing. His body sagged. He was resting his arms on the table. His chin sank down slowly, until it disappeared into the sleeves of his coat.

"It never rains but it pours," he murmured.

"What?"

He shook his head. After a time he reached out his hand and took Teddy's unfinished drink. Teddy said nothing. Verne drank it slowly.

"Good," he said.

He removed his glasses and put them into his coat pocket. He seemed to be slowly coming apart. He put his head on his arms, closing his eyes. His body was limp, like straw. A limp bag of straw. Barbara watched him. She said nothing.

Finally Teddy stirred. "It's late."

"What time is it?" Barbara said.

"One-thirty."

Verne lifted his head. "That's not late."

"It's pretty late."

"No." Verne waved his arm. The waitress came over to the table. "Do you think it's late?" Verne said.

"We don't close for some time yet."

"Bring me another scotch and water." Verne looked around. "I guess that's all."

The waitress went off.

"Why don't you all join in? What's wrong?"

"Nothing's wrong," Teddy said.

Verne pulled himself up on his chair. He took out his glasses and fitted them into place. "Well, Barbara?" he said. "How do you like it in the Big City?"

"It's fine."

"Is this the first time you have had the pleasure of coming to our great city?"

"I've been here before."

"Good. Good. I'm glad to hear that. It's a fine thing to get out and see the world, isn't it?"

She nodded.

"One should travel. To the mountains. Up in the hills. A mountain stream. Trout. A campfire. Or to the ocean. I sometimes go up the coast." His voice was dull, indistinct. It faded off. "Up the coast. Where the great surf beats endlessly. The sea. I like the sea."

"I know," Barbara said.

Verne's eyebrow shot up. "Do you?" He nodded. "So. Well."

"Did you meet Verne at Castle?" Teddy said suddenly.

"Yes."

"Then you must be the girl that came back with him. I remember now. He did say she lived in Boston." Teddy studied her with interest "So you're the girl."

"Verne told you about me?"

"Oh, yes."

"What did he say?"

"Verne thinks a lot of you. He was very — shall I say, enthusiastic? He was very enthusiastic about you."

"Oh?" Barbara murmured.

"I think a lot of everyone," Verne said thickly.

"Sure you do, Verne," Teddy said. "That's what's so nice about him, Barbara. You'll find that out, if you should ever get to know him better. He's so thoughtful. He thinks so much of everyone. Everyone is his friend — he loves everybody."

Verne grunted.

"The whole world is one great, warm family to him. He feels everyone's his friend. He loves us all. He wants to spread his love around everywhere. Right, Verne?"

Verne did not answer. His eyes were shut. His head rested against his arms. He was breathing heavily. Teddy prodded him, watching him. He did not stir.

"Verne?" she said sharply.

There was no answer. Teddy leaned back in her chair. She lit a cigarette, taking Verne's lighter from his pocket. She sat for a time, blowing smoke across the table, around the empty glasses, around Verne.

Barbara sat tensely, twisting her hands together, knotting the arm of her sleeve.

"We owe for the last drink," Teddy said. She stubbed her cigarette out abruptly in the ashtray. Then she waved to the waitress.

The waitress came over.

"How much?"

"Sixty-five cents."

"Here's the money." Teddy took a bill from her purse and gave it to her. "Keep the change."

The waitress started to gather up the empty glasses on the table. Teddy waved her away.

Presently Teddy leaned over close to Verne. She peered intently at him. "Come on, ducky. Time to go home. Come on. Let's wake up."

Verne did not stir.

"Help me, dear," Teddy said to Barbara.

"What — what'll I do?"

Teddy stood up. "Take one arm. We'll get him up on his feet.

Sometimes he comes around when he's on his feet. Take his left arm."

Barbara went uncertainly around to the other side of the table. She tugged at Verne's arm. Verne pulled away.

"Come on," Teddy said patiently. "Time to go."

They got him up on his feet. Two men at the next table wanted to help but Teddy waved them off. Verne began to stir a little.

"Hold on," Teddy said. "Don't let go of him."

Barbara held onto his arm.

"Let's go, ducky," Teddy repeated. "Let's go the whole way, all the way to the door. Out to the car."

"Jesus," Verne said thickly. "Let go."

"Can you make it?"

"Yes."

They let go of him. He walked unsteadily across the room to the door without looking back. His feet shuffled; he bumped against a table. Teddy put on her coat quickly, gathering up her things.

"Let's go."

She and Barbara followed after him. When they got to the door Verne had already crossed the sidewalk to the car. He was trying to unlock the door, pulling the handle down dully. Teddy found the key in his coat pocket and unlocked it. She helped him inside. He tumbled onto the seat and lay, his arms outstretched, his head forward.

"Get in," Teddy said to Barbara. Barbara slunk silently into the car, beside Verne. Teddy walked around to the other side and got in behind the wheel. "Close your door. Pull it shut."

Barbara closed the door. Teddy turned the motor on. She let it run for a few minutes. Presently she let the car inch forward.

"Anyone coming?"

"No." The streets were deserted. The stores were closed up tight, their neon signs turned off. No one was in sight.

"What street is the bus depot on?"

Barbara faltered. "Why, I — "

"Don't you know?"

"I think it's at — "

"Never mind. I can find it."

Teddy started the car up. They drove slowly down the empty street. At a red light Teddy stopped. She got out her cigarettes. She offered the pack to Barbara but then pulled it away.

"That's right — you don't smoke."

After a while Barbara said: "Did — did Verne tell you very much about me?"

"Not much. How old are you?"

"Why?"

"I just wondered. It doesn't matter."

"I don't see why you asked," Barbara murmured.

Teddy surveyed her. "You better go back to Boston. And get started on your welfare work."

Barbara slunk down in the seat and did not answer.

They reached the bus depot. Teddy drove the car up to the curb. A couple of bus drivers were standing together, smoking and talking.

She rolled the window down. "Hey!"

One of them stepped over. "What do you want?"

"When does the bus leave for Boston?"

He looked at his watch. "About ten minutes."

"Thanks."

She rolled the window back up and drove on. After a minute or so she parked the car and turned off the motor. They sat in silence.

"You have your ticket money?" Teddy said.

Barbara nodded. She took a deep breath. "I — "

"You know where to catch it?"

On the seat between them Verne stirred. He grunted, moving a little. He lifted his head.

"Verne — " Barbara said. He groaned and turned over, his head in his arms, sinking down into a little bundle, a soft shapeless heap on the seat. She gazed down at him. His knees were pulled up, his shoulders pulled together. A little wadded-up bundle. The little tailor, his glasses falling off, hanging from one ear.

"Come on," Teddy said. "You'll miss your bus." She reached past Barbara and pushed the door open.

Barbara hesitated uncertainly. "Teddy, I — "

"Hurry up. Get out."

She slid from the seat onto the sidewalk. The pavement was cold. A wind blew about her.

"Good night," Teddy said. She slammed the car door. The motor came on. The car drove off, down the street, into the darkness. Barbara stood watching it until it disappeared and the sound died into silence.

Some people waiting for the bus observed her with interest, a sailor, a girl, a middle-aged man.

She walked slowly into the depot.

9

"WHAT'S THE MATTER?" Carl Fitter asked.

Barbara started, coming suddenly back to the present. She blinked. "What?"

"You were a million miles away." Carl waved around him. "It's too nice a day to miss! This is one of the nicest days I can remember. Don't you think so? There isn't even one cloud in the sky, unless you count that unimportant little puff over there."

They went along the path, toward the commissary. "It is nice," Barbara admitted.

"Look at the towers over there. Like birds of some kind, standing on one foot. They must be abandoned machinery. You usually don't notice them because of the fog. I'm glad the fog has lifted today. It's our day to celebrate."

"Celebrate what?"

"Full and complete possession of all the world."

"Really?"

"All the world, as far as we know it." He pointed at the mountains, beyond the Company property. "What do we know of them? They're not part of my world. Are they part of your world? Like the moon. You can see the moon, but it's not the same as living with it. How can you believe in something that's only a sort of painting someone has hung up in the sky? Actually, our world ends before those mountains begin. At the edge of the Company land."

"Do you believe that?"

Carl laughed, kicking some stones away. "Today I believe a lot of things. Sure, the world ends at that line. And we own every bit of it. It's ours."

"Why are you so happy? The weather?"

"Partly. And partly because in a way I'm glad to see all the people gone. Of course — " his face clouded. "Of course, I'll admit I wasn't so pleased when I first learned about it. I was just about to go. I had my suitcase under my arm and everything. They didn't tell me until I was practically getting into the car. It made me feel sort of bad."

"I can imagine."

"But that's all over now. Today I've forgotten it. It was yesterday, in the past. Over with."

"So it doesn't exist any more?"

"Of course not. How can something exist in the past? Things only exist in the present." Carl's face took on a glow of excitement. "Do you know Aristotle's theory of the actualization of objects? It's a concept of the gradual developing of things, our view of which — "

"Let's forget it," Barbara murmured.

"What?" Carl's glow darkened to a flush of embarrassment. "Of course. I'm sorry." His head sank down. He ran on a little way ahead.

But after a minute his good spirits returned.

"Just think!" he cried.

"Of what?"

"Of all our — our wealth."

"What wealth?"

"The food! The beds! We can sleep everywhere, anywhere,

even in the station manager's home. Most of his stuff is still here, I think. His books, his blankets, his library, his kitchen. It's all boarded up, but it's there. All we need is a hammer and crowbar. The yuks won't know if we take a few little things out. We have a whole week to do it — seven days. Maybe more!"

He danced, leaping up into the air. Finally he became winded and gradually calmed down.

"I'm sorry. I didn't mean to get carried away like that. I guess you must think I'm crazy."

Barbara had been walking along behind him. She smiled a little. "No. Not crazy. It is a nice day. I — I felt a little like that myself, earlier. When I first woke up and saw the sun streaming into the room."

Now they were both embarrassed. They walked on in silence, Carl ahead, Barbara plodding along behind. At last the commissary appeared ahead.

Carl turned around, stopping to wait for the girl to catch up with him. "Can I ask you something?"

"What is it?"

"Is Verne an old friend of yours?"

"Why do you want to know that?"

Carl hesitated. "Well, he seems to know you, and you seem to know him, but both of you freeze up when you're together. And neither of you'll say anything. Why? What's the matter? Don't you like each other? Did something — "

"I'd rather not talk about it," Barbara said, her voice gruff. "Okay?"

"See? That's what happens. But I know you're old friends. I can tell."

"I wouldn't say 'old friends.' We knew each other, for a while."

"Before you went to work for the Company?"

"Yes. I came out here without—without knowing that he was here. We were both surprised to see each other. Not that it matters. I haven't talked to him for years."

"You talked to him last night."

"I don't mean that."

"Where did you meet each other?"

"For Christ's sake! Can't we forget it? Don't you ever stop talking about things?"

Carl slunk away along the path. "Sorry."

She hurried and caught up with him. "We can talk about it some other time. Later on."

"I didn't mean to make you angry."

"No, I realize that."

Suddenly Carl pricked up his ears. His whole expression changed. "Hey! What do I smell? Do I smell somebody cooking something? Verne must have started!"

He ran up the commissary steps, two at a time. Barbara followed after him, feeling some of his excitement. They pushed the door open and went inside. Verne was at the stove, squatting down beside it, examining its works. The burners were discharging jets of blue flame. The temperature of the room was beginning to rise.

"Greetings," Verne murmured.

"What are you doing?"

Verne glanced up at Carl. "Taking a bath."

"I never realized how hot it gets in here with the stove going," Barbara said. "Those poor people! That old cook, the fat one. What a time she must have had."

Verne had put the big frying pan on the burners. The bottom was damp with smoking grease. Carl peered down at it with interest. "What's this for?" he asked.

"Pancakes."

"I wish we were going to have waffles." Carl found the sack of flour. "This is for waffles, too. Besides just pancakes." He waited hopefully.

"We don't have a waffle iron."

"Oh. I guess that's right. But I certainly like waffles. Pancakes are always the same."

"Help me set the table," Barbara said to him. She was getting dishes out of the cupboard.

"What shall I put on?"

"Those little bowls up there. I can't reach them."

Carl got the bowls down. "I never saw any bowls like these before. They must have been used by the staff. And a lot of this food. We never had a lot of this. Like this." He held up a package of frozen chicken from one of the refrigerators. "Did we ever have frozen chicken?"

"Once in a while," Barbara said. "Put the bowls on the table."

"All right."

The pancakes were ready. They sat down at the table and pre-pared to eat. Barbara brought the platter to the table and set it down.

"Butter?" she said.

"In the refrigerator," Verne said.

"I'll get it." Carl scrambled up, pushing his chair back. He returned with the butter. "There's tons of it. I never saw so much. We won't run out. And cottage cheese and sour milk and eggs and regular milk."

Verne punched a hole in the lid of the syrup can. Barbara distributed the pancakes to their plates. Now the coffee was ready. Carl brought it over from the stove, setting the pot down on a piece of cold tile.

"Let's go," Verne said.

They ate, enjoying the food. The window over the table was open, and fresh air blew around them.

"Look how much color there is in the food," Carl said. "The syrup looks like mahogany finish. Look at the butter! I've never seen butter so yellow. And the coffee is like —" He pondered.

"Mimeograph ink," Verne murmured.

For dessert they had frozen strawberries with cream, in the little bowls Carl had got down. Carl found some ice cream and brought it over to be used on the strawberries.

"None for me," Barbara said firmly.

"Why not?"

"I don't like things mixed together."

Carl put a little on his strawberries but not as much as he would have liked. Both Verne and Barbara seemed strangely silent, eating with great seriousness and preoccupation. He glanced from one to the other but they said nothing.

"Anybody want any more?" Carl asked.

They shook their heads.

Verne pushed his plate away. "That's all for me." He leaned back in his chair, pushing himself away from the table.

"There's still some ice cream left."

They shook their heads.

Carl sniffed the air, blowing through the window. "It's a wonderful day out, isn't it? It's a good omen. Our first day here. It makes it more like a real vacation, having all the sunlight."

"A vacation?"

"We don't have to do any work, do we? All we have to do is be here when the yuks come. We can do anything we want. A whole week to do as we please." Carl grinned at them happily. "I can't wait to get started."

"Get started what?"

"Finding things. Seeing what there is."

Verne grunted. He looked across the table at Barbara. She did not meet his gaze. She was staring down at the floor, deep in thought. What was she thinking about? What did she think of *this?*

He pushed his glasses up, rubbing his eyes and yawning. Could this really be? The two of them sitting like this, across from each other, after so many years. As if they had got out of the same bed. He lowered his glasses into place. It was unreal. Like finding an old album of snapshots and poring over them. Or like being dead and in the Great Beyond and having everything come back and swirl around, echoing and gibbering, made of grey dust.

Or like judgment day.

Verne shifted uncomfortably in his chair. Not a pleasant thought. And sheer phantasy, as well. But it was strange how people could come back after years of being outside your existence, come back and reappear; and fully three-dimensional, too. Suddenly no longer ghosts, vague shadows. Was there a cosmic law about it? A law that demanded events and people stay alive, retain existence, on and on, until some prearranged end could be brought about?

Verne smiled. It was only a chance thing, three names pulled out at random, his and Barbara's and Carl's. It meant nothing. He continued to study her, as she sat, staring down. Chance had recreated this, the two of them sitting at the same breakfast table, in the warm sunlight. As they had sat once before.

Once before. Only once. Something to do with her parents being home and expecting her. Had that really been true? The trip. The hotel, outside New York. He thought idly back. Their night together, and then breakfast the next morning. Almost like this.

But not quite. There had been no Carl around. It was not really the same at all. And Barbara had changed. She was different, very different. Even the few words he had spoken to her in the office had told him that. She was hard, hard and sour. Like him, in a way. Not an innocent bit of lonely fluff any longer. Not by a long shot.

When had he last seen her? She had come to New York. That was the last time he had really talked to her. He had seen her once or twice since she came to work for the Company, but never to talk. She had avoided him. Well, it hadn't mattered.

The day she came, a Thursday. . . . He was broadcasting at the station. That was before he lost his program. He warmed inwardly, thinking about his old show. What was it called? *Potluck Party*. The warmth turned to an ache. That had been a good time in his life. The program, his job at the station.

He thought about Teddy. It was because of her that he had left New York and gone to work for the Company. Her, and losing the program. Had she been responsible for him losing it? He had considered it a million times in the last four years. Had she done it?

He shrugged. It was all over now.

Teddy and Barbara had both come to the station, that night. They had gone out to a restaurant and then to a bar. They had sat around talking together. The last of the evening he could not remember. It was hazy, sloping off into dark shadow. Something to do with his car. They had gone someplace after the bar. Then he and Teddy were back at her apartment. And the evening was over.

Barbara had gone back to Boston. He wrote to her a few times, but she did not answer. After a while he had given up. There were too many fish in the sea. . . .

"What do you think, Verne?" Carl was saying.

Verne blinked. What had he said? "I didn't hear you."

"What's the matter with you two? You're both a million miles away. I said, what do you think of the idea of getting out and sizing up the situation? We should try to get some idea of what we

have here. We might begin some kind of exploration to deter-
mine —"

Verne gazed past Carl, out the window at the towers and silent factories. He had already begun to lose the thread of what
Carl was saying. He felt dull and listless. He yawned again, and
looked in the coffee pot to see if there were any more coffee to
drink.

"Well?" Carl said.

"Let's wait a while." There was no more coffee.

"All right," Carl said sadly. "I guess there's no hurry. It's just
a suggestion for what we might do when we *do* want to go out-
doors." He fidgeted around on his chair. "It's one of those days
when you really like to be out in the sun, isn't it? I can't see staying inside when the sky is blue and the air smells the way it
does. It seems as if something's going on out there. Something
we should know about. Be in on."

"Open another window," Verne murmured.

"It's not the same thing."

"Why do you have to go running out after it? Let the air come
in here. It'll come, if you wait long enough."

"It's like sitting on the shore and watching the ocean, instead
of going in. It's not the same at all."

Both Verne and Barbara turned in annoyance. Verne caught
her eye and he smiled. So she was thinking about it, too. She
looked quickly away, but he knew. He crossed his legs, relaxing.
She was thinking about those times the same way he was. For
some reason this awareness gave him pleasure.

"Maybe Carl's right," he said. "There's nothing like rolling
around in the ocean. The surf, the spray —"

Barbara said nothing. Verne let the matter drop. He was becoming sleepy; the warm sun was shining down on him, all over
him. Before long he took off his coat and tossed it in the corner.
He unfastened his cuffs and began to roll up his sleeves.

"It's hot," Barbara said.

The warmth of the sun was making perspiration come out on her face. Little warm drops standing on her forehead and neck, rolling slowly down into her collar. Verne felt it, too. The glare of the sun was working itself into high gear; it was only eleven o'clock and already the heat was too much. But noon it would be like a furnace. Maybe the fog wasn't so bad, after all.

"What's the matter?" Carl asked.

"It's hot."

"Hot? This isn't hot. Wait until you've lived down in the South for a while."

"I lived in the South," Verne said. "And this is hot. I don't like it."

"It's actually hotter in here, than outside," Carl said. "What you're feeling is the amount of moisture in the air. This room is very moist. The water from the sink evaporating, the — "

"I know," Verne said. He lapsed into sullen silence. The talk annoyed him. What did it matter? Why did they have to sit around and discuss everything? He tried to relax. What was it that made Carl turn everything around and around, studying, examining? Every idea, every thought was like a bug under a lens, to Carl.

But it wasn't really Carl that annoyed him; he knew that. Verne glanced up at Barbara. She had got to her feet and was gathering up the dishes. She had filled out, in four years. She was much heavier, solid. She had been rather light, before. But she was only twenty, in those days. He could see fine gold fuzz along her arms, as she lifted up the dishes. In the sunlight, her skin was a rich, mellow gold. Her arms were rounded. He watched her until she noticed him. Then he looked away.

"Give me a hand," Barbara said.

It was going to be awkward. There was no doubt of that. He could feel the tension in the room. She didn't like him looking at her. She didn't even like him around. He got to his feet, pushing his chair slowly against the table. Carl rose, too, and they stood uncertainly.

"Come on," Barbara said.

"Are we going to wash them?" Carl asked.

"Let them go." Verne walked over to the window and stood looking out, his hands in his pockets. There was momentary silence.

"All right." Barbara left the sink and sat down at the table again. She lit a cigarette. "It's all right by me."

Carl hesitated uncertainly. "Maybe I'll get at the exploring business. I'm eager to begin."

No one said anything.

"After all, everything is ours. To do with as we see fit. Our possessions. I want to start getting the lids off the packages." He laughed.

"Just like Christmas," Verne murmured.

Carl moved toward the door. At the door he stopped, waiting hopefully. "Isn't anyone coming along?"

"I've seen too many Christmases," Verne said.

Carl smiled at Barbara, appealing to her with his eyes. "It's a nice day out there. Grass and sky. Places to get into. What do you say?"

"There's plenty of time," Barbara said. "Take it easy. We have seven whole days."

Carl could not decide what to do. He was visibly torn between his desire to begin looking around and his desire to remain with them. If they would go along, the problem would be solved. But neither stirred.

His desire to start looking won out.

"I'll see you people later, then." He opened the door. "I really am surprised, though. I can't see why you want to just sit around and — and smoke."

"You can have first claim on everything," Verne said. "Consider yourself the worm finder."

"I'm going to see what's left in the manager's house. That's the first place."

"All right," Verne said.

Carl closed the door behind him. They heard him going slowly down the outside steps, onto the walk.

"He's a nice boy," Barbara said, after a while.

Verne nodded. He was thinking. Maybe he should leave, go back to the dorm or to the office. Barbara was considering it; he could tell. The last person was the one who got stuck with the psychological short end of the stick, and he didn't feel much like being that person. It would be better for him to walk out on her than to give her a chance to walk out on him.

He turned away from the window.

"How've you been?" Barbara said abruptly. Her voice was harsh and loud; the sound surprised both of them. "How've you been making out?"

"It depends on just what you mean," Verne said guardedly.

"I mean, how have you been?"

"Fine."

She was silent for a time. "How long has it been?" she said presently. "Three years? Four years?"

"Saw you last week," Verne said. "Don't you remember? Saw you last night, in the office."

"I don't mean that."

Of course she didn't mean that. As if he didn't know what she meant. "I see you're smoking, these days. As I recall, you didn't used to smoke. In the old days."

It was weird to be talking to a woman who was a formal, remote stranger — and yet who — He smiled. How terribly weird. A kind of mystery of existence. What was identity? Here she was, cold, remote, so formal that he almost found himself saying, "Miss Mahler" to her. But once, a few years before, he and she had spent an intimate time together. Been in bed together. It was a memory, but a very real memory. Was it really of her? Was it always the same person who looked out of two eyes? Perhaps it was a different person; perhaps a new person came each few years.

"No," Barbara said. "I didn't used to smoke."

"No, you didn't," Verne said. The old Barbara had not smoked. This Barbara, this Miss Mahler, did. How could it be the same person? No two things were the same ever. No two stones, mice, drops of water, snowflakes. What did they call it? Nominalism. Perhaps it applied to people, to the same person at different times. There was no *same* person. Miss Mahler sat quietly at the table, polite, hard, detached, remote. A stranger. A person he scarcely knew.

But the same Miss Mahler, or another Miss Mahler, had, four years ago, rushed giggling and laughing, one cold night, leaping into bed beside him, still warm and damp, giggling and burying herself against him, pushing, pressing—

Barbara glanced up at him, and flushed. Could she tell what he was thinking? She probably was thinking the same thing, or something similar. Some other event, some other moment of their time together.

"Let me have a cigarette," Verne said.

She put her pack on the table. He came over and took a cigarette out.

"Thanks." He lit it and sat down across from her. She said nothing. "Mind if I sit here?"

"No."

"All right." He made himself comfortable on the chair. "Good cigarette. Nice and fresh."

She said nothing. Wasn't she going to talk? Was she just going to sit?

Barbara looked up at him. Her eyes were calm and level, but there were two spots of high color in her cheeks. She was going to say something. He set himself, waiting.

"Maybe Carl was right," she said.

He frowned. "Right? What do you mean?"

"Maybe it is better outside than in here."

"You thinking about joining him?"

Barbara did not answer. She considered. "No," she said finally. "I don't think so. But I ought to."

Verne thought that over. Did it mean anything? Was it some sort of a carefully-thought out dig, pregnant with implication? He could not tell.

"Maybe so," he said vaguely, staring around the room. "Well, don't let me keep you here."

They were both silent. Neither of them moved. Verne watched her, his eyes half closed. She sat leaning back, indifferent to him, self-contained. But she was on edge, nervous. He could tell. She was very conscious of him. The way she had always been. That hadn't changed.

No, there was a lot still the same. She had grown up, filled out, got older and harder. But underneath there was the same person, the same girl he had known before.

He studied her critically. She had learned a lot, in four years. It showed. Once, there had been an aggressive fear, a stubborn fright that had made her back away from people like an hysterical child. Men had not been able to come near her — at least, none before him. She scared them away. But had they seen what he had seen they would have realized it was all bluff. A covering of gruffness that hid terror and an almost pathetic fear of being struck down. He had seen that; they had not.

Now she was calm, adult. Certain of herself. Once, she had quavered in fear, fear that she could be made a victim. But that was over with; she was no longer worried about that. Why? Per-

haps because she had been made a victim. What she had feared
had actually happened to her. How odd that a man does not understand that, at the time. He had not understood it, although
now, so much later, he could look back and see it. It had happened; she had lost her treasure. Her jewel. What she had shel-
tered and protected and crooned over was gone.

Well, there was no use worrying about it. She did not seem
to have been too badly ruined. She appeared to be all right. She
had survived, even prospered. She no longer cowered in fear.
But perhaps that was because she no longer had anything to
lose!

Verne smiled. That was absurd. Women didn't think of it that
way, not any more. Or did they? Something had changed her,
made her hard. The great moment had passed; now she could
stare around calmly. But her fear had been more than just a fear
of that, of losing her virginity. It had been a great fear, general,
unspecific, a fear of being hurt and humiliated. Everyone had it.
He had it himself. And his virginity had been gone a long time.

In any case, she seemed to have survived everything that had
happened. She was older and stronger. What they had done together — what he had done to her — had certainly done no harm.
In fact, it seemed to have done her good. It had brought her realism. That was it. Her experience had removed the phantasies,
the terrors. She had seen it for what it was: normal, natural,
much like any of the processes of life. It had matured her, made
her into a woman, not a child any more. She should thank him.

But even he could not take that seriously. Thank him? Verne
smiled and rubbed his chin, amused.

"Why are you smiling?" Barbara asked.

"No reason."

"None?"

"Just my good nature coming out."

Barbara nodded, serious and wise. She had never seemed to

have much of a sense of humor. Life was too grim, too deadly for that. Or perhaps she thought laughing and smiling were for children. A sign of youth, of being too young. Like Carl. His booming humor annoyed her; he knew that instantly. Poor Carl! Well, it was his own fault. He would have to learn not to leap around and laugh all the time. He would have to grow up, too. The way everyone did. It could not be prevented. Carl, Barbara, himself— everybody had to face it, sooner or later. The world. As it really was. Not as one might wish it were. As one hoped to find it.

"Well," Verne said, "I suppose we should do something today, before the day's over with."

"Yes."

How solemnly she agreed! As a good adult should. She had learned well; she had absorbed her lesson. . . .

"Do you think it's really too hot to go outside?" she said suddenly, looking up. She had been thinking. "I love the sun. But not when it's too hot. And dry. I hate it when it gets dry, and you squirm and bake."

"Hot and dry, hot and damp. It's all the same." He watched her. She was about to get up. "Don't go!" he said quickly. "Stay here."

"Why?"

"It's cool in here."

"Is it?"

"Cooler than out there."

"All right." She dropped her cigarette to the floor and ground it out. She lit another, slowly, carefully. Smoke drifted up into the beams of sunlight.

"This is close enough to nature."

"You know," Barbara said, "it seems very odd to be sitting here like this, after so many years."

Verne grunted, watchful. "Does it?"

"Don't you think so?"

"Oh, I don't know."

"How do you mean, you don't know?"

His gaze flickered. "I mean, there's nothing so terribly strange about it. We both work for the same Company. We've both been here for a long time."

"Perhaps I mean *strange* in a different way than you do." She did not amplify. "Perhaps that's it."

Verne considered, choosing his words carefully. "You don't think He had anything to do with it, do you?"

"Who?"

Verne pointed up with his finger.

Barbara smiled thinly. "You never can tell. They say He's everywhere, watching over His flock."

"Are you of His flock?"

"We all are."

"Not me," Verne said. "My soul is as black as sin. I've been thrown over the fence long these years."

Her expression changed. It almost said: *I know what you mean.* He was sorry he had spoken. It was so damn hard to tell what a woman was thinking. When he tried to figure out a woman's mind he left out factors and added false factors. It was a hopeless task for a man. Better to forget the mind and concentrate on the rest. But he *had* made a mistake. He had led with his chin, and much to fast.

"Verne," Barbara said.

"Yes?"

"Is there going to — to be any —"

"Any what?"

"Any friction."

"Between us, you mean? Between you and me?"

She nodded.

"I don't see why," Verne said.

"I hope not. I don't want to mix in any trouble. I'd rather just forget the whole thing."

"Don't worry about it." He grinned good-naturedly. "I don't see why there should be any trouble. I certainly have no ill-feeling toward you. I have a great deal of respect for you. Why should there be any friction? I can speak for my side. I assume you feel the same way."

There was silence. Barbara considered what he had said. "Well, I suppose you're right. Only — "

"Only what?"

"Only sometimes we don't really know our own minds. Sometimes we don't know until — until a thing actually comes along. Then it just happens." She went on: "One night I was sitting, reading a book. Through the window a whole lot of god damn moths flew in, between me and the page."

"So?"

"I killed every one of them. Perhaps fifty of them. All over the floor. Ten minutes before I would say I'd never do a thing like that. Do you see what I mean? Sometimes you don't know, not in advance. Not until it happens."

"Not until what happens?"

She shrugged. "Anything."

Verne hesitated, licking his lips. "You don't feel any ill-will toward me, do you?"

"No."

"Well, I'm glad of that." He let his breath out, sighing with relief. "That should settle the whole matter, shouldn't it? Where's the trouble going to come from?"

He got to his feet, holding out his hand.

"Now that we've settled that, how about another cigarette?"

"Sure." She passed the pack.

"Thanks." He took a cigarette and sat down again. He beamed cheerfully at her.

"Verne, you're still like I remember you. In many ways. In many, many ways."

"You remember me?"

"Oh, yes. I remember you, Verne."

He didn't know quite how to take that. "Well, I'm glad to hear it," he murmured, not so cheerfully.

"Are you?"

"Of course." He lit the cigarette nervously. "No one likes to be forgotten."

"No. That's true. No one likes to be forgotten. It's not a nice feeling."

Verne felt vaguely displeased. "Why do you say that? Is there some implication I'm supposed to perceive?"

"No."

He scowled. What was she brooding about? He didn't like it. He knew when something was being dug into *him*. He stood up again, pushing his chair back and moving away from the table.

"Where are you going? Outside in the sun?"

"No." He didn't know where, but not outside in the sun.

"Where, then?"

"I'll have to think about it."

"Stay here. It's nice and cool, as you said to me a little while ago."

"How the hell long can you sit at the table after you've eaten, just rocking back and forth in your chair? It gets me down, after the first hour."

"You sound like Carl."

"Do I?" He moved around the kitchen restlessly.

"What do you propose to do instead? I'm open to suggestion."

"I don't know. This is going to be a problem during the next week or so. Let's hope the yuks get here soon. The sooner the better."

"You sound angry."

"I'm not. Just bored. I hate to sit and do nothing at all."

"That comes of working all your life."

"I suppose so, but that's how I feel."

"We could divide the Company up into three parts and play blackjack. How would that be?"

"No good."

"You could go help Carl explore."

Verne laughed. "With a pirate map and a flashlight? No thanks. I'm not interested in buried treasure."

They both smiled at that. Some of the tension left the room.

"He enjoys it," Barbara said. "After all, was it so long ago that we would have been glad to go racing all around, exploring and getting into things — "

"Sitting behind all the big desks and putting on all the badges and pins."

"Carl can be any kind of an official he wants."

"We all can. We can all be important."

"Who gets to be manager of the station? I think we should let Carl be manager first."

"Why?"

"It means more to him. We can take turns after him. But let him start, for the first day or so."

"I think a big bonfire — " Verne murmured.

"Oh, no. There's some things we want to keep."

"Like what?"

"Well, I've always wanted to sleep in the manager's bed," Barbara said. "I hear the mattress is stuffed with duck feathers."

"Has that been your ambition?" Verne said, grinning.

Barbara smiled evenly back. "Not any more than yours."

"Have to get to the top some way."

"Top for you," Barbara said with hard humor. "But bottom for me."

"You *have* changed since I knew you."

"That was four years ago. I wasn't even of age, then."

"I remember that."

"I imagine you do."

"It was an inconvenience."

"Not so much, though. Was it?"

Verne could think of nothing to say. Barbara had got up from the table and was pushing her chair under. He watched apprehensively as she crossed the kitchen toward the door. "Now what?" he muttered.

She stopped at the door, studying him thoughtfully. "I tell you what," she said. "I have a proposition."

"What's the proposition?"

"Neither of us wants to sit here and rock. I still haven't got all my stuff uncrated yet. You can help me."

"Sounds like work."

"Take it or leave it." She opened the door.

"I'll take it," Verne said.

He followed after her quickly.

The halls of the dormitory building were cool and dark. They smelled of perspiration and baths and cigarettes. The two of them went upstairs to Barbara's floor. The door to her room was closed and locked. She took her key from her purse and unlocked it.

"Why locked?" Verne said.

"Habit." They went inside, Barbara leading the way. She had left the shade down and the room was not too warm. She opened all the windows.

"What a day," Verne said. "Getting hotter each minute. Maybe it's the fiery furnace."

"Maybe so."

With the windows open fresh air was sweeping into the

room. But the air was dry and hot. The room had taken on an amber cast, with all the shades down. In the amber dimness Barbara moved about, carrying things to the chest of drawers and into the closet.

"Can I sit down?" Verne said.

"Yes. You can sit and watch."

"When I'm needed, call me." He sat down on the edge of the bed. The bed groaned under him. "It doesn't like me. Listen to it. Like a thing in pain."

"Maybe it's trying to warn me," Barbara said.

Verne ignored her. He stretched out on the bed, making himself comfortable. His body felt heavy and tired. Sweat was running down his arms, inside his shirt, collecting in pools at his armpits. His neck was damp, his collar rubbed irritatingly. He unbuttoned his top shirt button and removed his tie.

"Mind?" he asked.

She paused, her arms full of clothes. "What?"

"I took off my tie."

She turned around and went on working. Verne sighed. He wanted to help, but he was much too dragged out by the mounting heat. On days like this, sitting at his desk, he always found himself falling asleep, sliding slowly into the typewriter, until his forehead came up hard against the keys and tab indicators. Then he would come awake with a start and return to the endless stacks of files and memos.

But now he could relax. There were no memos. It was all over with. All in the past. There would be no more forms, no more punch cards, files, tabs, endless papers. He had seen the dusty stacks in the closet of the office. The curtain had been rung down. He could relax.

But he was restless. And irritable. He stirred, moving around on the bed. He took out his handkerchief and wiped his neck.

There were drops of moisture on the inside of his glasses. He wiped them, too.

"Maybe the sun is expanding," he murmured.

"Yes, it is getting pretty steamy in here. Like a hothouse."

"I feel myself slowly taking root and growing fast to the ground. All desire to move around is gone."

"You don't intend to help me at all, then?"

"What can I do? You were supposed to let me know when I was needed."

"You could open this box. It's nailed shut. I don't even know how to start on it."

"Don't you?" He grinned, getting up from the bed with great effort. "Well, I suppose that's not too much to ask." He pulled himself together elaborately. "This would be a good day to lie under a bush in the shade. With the leaves blowing all around you. Where's a hammer?"

"Look around. There should be one with the boards and things. Carl got it for me last night."

Verne found a hammer and a screwdriver. He began to pull the nails out of the top of the box with the claw of the hammer. Presently the lid fell off. He stood it up against the wall in the corner of the room.

"There you are. Any other chores?"

"Already? My, but men are handy. You can go and lie down again, if you want."

Verne put the hammer down and walked back to the bed. Barbara came over with an armload of clothes.

"Move. The dresser is full."

"Move? Move where?"

"To the end of the bed. I have to put these somewhere until I get another dresser."

Verne pulled himself over and she dropped the stack of

dresses and skirts and slacks down beside him. "What a lot of stuff." They seemed to make him uneasy. He did not know why. "Women always have so much junk. What are you going to use all these for?"

"What do you care?"

"Just curious. We're only going to be here a week. You could have left most of them crated up."

"Psychological reasons." She shot him a quick glance. "That's the way women are. All types of women."

Verne grunted. "More?" She was bringing a second armload over to the bed. Verne moved nearer the end. "I can't give you much more room. Not without getting off completely. And I never do that."

"There's just a few more coming." Barbara laid the remainder of her dresses with the others. Some suits slid gradually to one side until they were resting partly off the bed. "Push those back, Verne. Will you?"

"Sure." He pushed the suits up again.

Barbara wiped her forehead with her sleeve. Her cheeks were red. She was perspiring, too. "That's enough for one day. The rest can wait." She sat down on the floor a little way from the bed. "God."

Verne gazed down at her, in her dark slacks and red checkered shirt. On the back of her neck he could see drops of perspiration, at the narrow line between her collar and her brown hair. In the closeness of the room, steamy with moisture, he could sense the faint tinge of musk, the mist of human presence that was rising from the woman's body, from her arms and shoulders and neck, just a few feet from him. A smell of sweet closeness mixed with the crisp smell of the checkered shirt.

"This is pleasant," Verne murmured, stretching out on the bed as best he could. He leaned his head against the wall for a moment and then rolled over so that he lay resting on a stack of her clothes. He watched her idly, her back, her brown hair caught in place with a clasp, her bare arms. Her arms fascinated him. They were so full and rich. Golden. With the little hairs on them. Alive.

"Yes," Barbara said.

"Yes? Yes what?"

"It's pleasant."

"Oh."

She had not turned toward him. She was staring off into space. What was she thinking about? In the silence of the room he could hear her breathing. He could see her chest and shoulders rising and falling. He watched dully. It was still too far from him, too remote and lost in the past to be potent. Except, perhaps, the golden arms.

But even those did not really bring him out of his lethargy. This, what he saw before him, had been passed through already, far back and long ago. He did not go over the same motions again and again with a woman. There was only one time when a man could look at a given woman for the first, original time, newly, freshly, seeing her particular shoulders and back as different from all other shoulders and backs, her hair as softer and sweeter than all other hair. And that was four years behind him, with this woman.

She was attractive; there was no doubt of that. But it was not the same as seeing her as something that lay ahead of him. She lay in the past — the pun was unconscious, but he smiled at it — and that was a fact which could not be overlooked.

He thought of the week, perhaps more, they would be spending, the three of them, before the yuks came and they returned to the United States. One week, seven days at the very least, sitting and lying, frittering and fretting, picking at food, bored and restless, waiting, watching, cursing because the sun was too hot, the fog too gloomy and cold. Like a man in a shower bath, spinning the knobs first one way, then another. Never satisfied.

Right now, the hot was turned too far up. But night time it would be the other way around. But either way, they were not going to like it. Carl, perhaps. But not either of them. What Carl did and thought was another matter. But Carl was not being considered. For them, for himself and for Barbara, things were not going to be right, not until they had got away, gone each along his own particular path, by himself. As long as they were together there was going to be friction. It was a question of how much. And the heat didn't help.

"Maybe I should open the door," Barbara said, all at once.

Verne started. It was uncanny, the way her thoughts paralleled his! He didn't like it. They had come too close in their life-views, their *Weltanschauungs*, much too close for comfort. Once, they had been far apart. But now they were thinking much along the same lines.

"Why the door?" Verne asked.

"Air comes in from the hall." She got to her feet and opened the door. Air came in, but it was warm and dry, no better than what they already had. It smelled of people coming from the bathroom, coming and going, endless times.

"Fine," Verne muttered. "Just right."

"Anyhow, it's not so stuffy. There's a current going out the window, through the room."

But Verne was not happy. He was restless and uncomfortable. He stirred fretfully. His skin felt prickly, a revolting sensation, damp, prickly skin.

"Is there a shower in this building? There must be."

"Just tubs."

Sadness and angry despair settled over Verne. His face darkened; his whole body seemed to curl up into a scowl. Barbara watched curiously, her arms folded.

"What's wrong?"

"No shower."

Barbara continued to study him, her face showing no emotion. "Here," she said suddenly. "I'll take pity on you." She picked up her suitcase from the floor and put it on the bed. She unsnapped it and brought out a bottle, carefully wrapped in a towel. Verne watched with interest as she removed the towel.

"I know that stuff," he said, and the prickling and restlessness went away from him. "That's the old doc's magic snake oil, all right."

"It sure is. And it's the last I have."

She took a plastic cup and went down the hall to the bathroom to fill it. She brought it back, carrying it carefully.

"Is it cold?" Verne asked.

"I let the tap run. It's cool, I think." She mixed whiskey into the cup, stirring it with the screwdriver. "I can't find the spoon."

"That's all right. I've stirred it with a lot of different things, and it always tastes the same afterwards."

"You first," Barbara said.

He took the cup and drank deeply. It was good, warm though it was. Good? It did not taste good. No use to pretend that. He did not drink it because of its taste. He drank it for other reasons. He drank it because of the way it made him feel. And he was too old to spend time analyzing that any more.

He handed the cup back, smacking his lips.

"You didn't leave much," Barbara said, sipping at what was left. "It doesn't matter. After all, you deserved something for all the work you did."

"I consider myself repaid in full."

The two of them sat for a while without speaking, Verne

stretched out on the bed as best he could, Barbara sitting on the floor again, sipping at the cup.

It still seemed odd to Verne, but not as odd as it had. He was beginning to become used to seeing her again; it was regaining its naturalness. Now the other part, the four years of not seeing her, was starting to fade and seem unreal. The sight of the woman, sitting on the floor in her red shirt and dark slacks, was becoming an accepted event, almost partaking of the familiar. Like a habit which had been forgotten, it was all sweeping back on his again, after only a short reacquaintance; the groove was there, and it needed only to be filled.

Of course, what filled the void, the emptiness, the space, was not exactly congruent with its earlier manifestation. Four years had changed Barbara Mahler. Before, she had been an almost-grown child, on the verge of adulthood, womanhood. He had come along and plucked her, just as she was ripe. Well, perhaps still a little green, but edible for all that. She had been like a fruit that was still a trifle hard and sour; not too soft and easy. Now she had grown up. Now she had become the adult. She had ripened. But the image was lost: she was harder and more sour now than she been before.

The allusion did not work; she was not a plant. She had, perhaps, been like some green fruit then, hard with the chill bitterness of an unripe apple, a little hard New England apple. But her hardness now was not a green hardness. It was the hardness of white stone.

She was turning to stone. It was the calcification of rock, the fossilization, the early bitter taste of death and age. The coldness of the tomb. The breath, the frightening breath of the dead. He could feel it, in the small room. Almost a clammy thing; perspiration that had frozen on her body. She had become rock from deep inside, working out toward the surface. It did not show yet; her skin was smooth and golden, with millions of tiny hairs lying close against, but the hardness was there, down deep inside, and coming nearer and nearer to the surface.

Only the little drops of cold sweat on her neck, on her lip, told. And the moist, clammy tinge in the air. And her voice. The way she talked. That told, too. It came from far inside, from the central vaults and dark places, the very core of her body.

"Want more?" Barbara said, tapping the cup.

"More? No. Not now."

He could understand this, what he saw. The cold wetness of death. He had a little of it, himself. Yes, he had it, too. Perhaps she had even got it from him. Perhaps it had come from him in the first place; and he, in his order, had got it from someone before. From Teddy. Or from one of the others. The girl, the girl in his room. The blue-eyed girl with hair like cornsilk. Perhaps it had come to him from her. She had burned him, scorched him, dried him out.

But it was different, with him. He smiled as he realized this. With him it was a sort of surface coating, a cold, sharp outer coat, a kind of hard shell, that had adhered to his skin. It was on the outside, and it was working in. His heart would freeze last. Hers had been first, the very opposite. And he would keep warming it, his heart, his whole body. The freeze would be slowed down, not stopped, but at least slowed . . . by what he had just now taken in. He could feel it; it was warm and good.

That was what he meant by good.

"God damn," Barbara said suddenly.

"What's the matter?"

"I'm getting like you, Verne. I feel as if my skin were rubbing against me. What'll we do?"

"The heat."

"As they always say. But what can we do?"

Verne reached down and patted her on the arm. "It'll be cold tonight. Then you'll wish it was warm."

"It's not so cold at night. I'm not bothered."

"Maybe you've been sleeping better than I have."

"I'm prettier than you."

Verne smiled. "You are. I admit it."

"Thank you."

"No. Don't thank me. You always were attractive, you know. I told you that. Once."

"Let's forget it."

"It's a fact."

"Let's forget it anyhow."

"All right." They became silent.

Barbara stirred finally. "You know," she said thoughtfully, "when I first realized it was you who would be staying here I felt quite hostile to the idea."

"Oh?"

"I had a very strong feeling when I came into the office and found it was you there. I almost tried to push back into one of the cars."

"Why?"

"I don't know. A general feeling. But you must know what it is. Your past is even longer than mine."

"I guess I know what you mean."

"It should turn out all right, though. We're both grown people. Adults. If we act like adults and not skulk around like children —"

"Whatever *adults* means."

She swung around to face him. She was serious. "I mean, there's no reason why we can't be polite to each other. Not start trading deep and subtle knives."

"Do we do that?" Verne said feebly.

"No. I think that part will be all right. But it goes deeper than — than that, than talk."

"Carl would be offended."

"Doubtless. Well, let's drop it."

"I think things are working out. Don't you?"

"Yes." She was silent for a time. Suddenly she leaped up. "God, this heat! It really makes you want to jump around."

"How about some more stuff?"

"Another drink? Do you want another?"

"I guess I could get it down."

"All right." She took the cup and disappeared down the hall with it.

"Is it cold?" Verne said, when she returned.

"A little colder than before. It's been running."

He raised an eyebrow. "So? You are growing up."

"I suppose."

She poured the whiskey into the cup and stirred it. Verne drank first again, and then she drank, finishing what remained. He watched her. She was standing in front of him, very close. Her nose was a trifle large, her teeth somewhat crooked. But that was not noticeable unless she smiled. She had a good figure, although she had become a trifle heavy. All in all, she was in good physical condition. Suddenly she gave him the empty cup.

He handed the cup back. "Why give it to me? I looked in, and it's empty."

"Fill it."

He got to his feet. "All right." He went down the hall to the bathroom. The water was still running in the bowl. He filled the cup halfway. Then he poured part of the water out. He returned with what he had left in it.

"Thanks." She put the cup down on the dresser. She was pacing around the room, her hands in her pockets.

"What's wrong?"

She stopped pacing. "Verne, you have to admit that in a way —" She broke off.

"In a way what?"

"I mean, there are some things the same, and some that are not the same."

"What things?"

"Let's face it. Four years was a long time ago. We've both changed, especially me. There's no chance in the world that we can have any kind of relationship again. I'm putting the cards on the table. That's the way it should be. Let's be honest. Nothing will work. Nothing at all. Like we had before or anything else."

She glared at him hostilely.

"Isn't that right?"

Verne smiled blandly. "I don't know. This is the first time I've thought about it. It seems to be your idea."

"That's a lot of bilge. You've thought about it steadily for the last twenty-four hours. But too much has changed. We might as well face it and then forget it."

"Well, we don't have to fight."

"No." She nodded. "No, we don't have to fight."

"It's too hot to fight."

"Yes. It's hot." She sat down on the bed. "I'm sorry I shouted." She looked steadily up at him. "You know, Verne, I was too young. You should have known it. You really grabbed it right off the tree."

"Tree?"

"The cherry tree."

"Oh." He looked a little downcast. "Sorry."

"You never should have done it."

He twisted. "It's a hard thing for another person to see. Especially a man. Especially at a time like that."

"I told you how young I was."

"Try to put yourself in my place! For God's sake. Once it had gone that far —"

"You should never have done it. It was wrong."

"I suppose so. But it doesn't seem to have — to have stunted your growth. Has it?"

"Stunted my growth?" She smiled a little. "I guess not. No, I suppose it hasn't. I never thought of it that way. Isn't that what cigarettes are said to do?"

They both smiled.

"Well, let's forget it," Barbara said at last. "It's off my chest, at least. Maybe you're right. Maybe it didn't do any lasting harm. I don't know. It's hard to know. So hard to tell."

"At the time you didn't seem to be in any pain about it. You almost enjoyed it." He grinned.

"Yes — After the first five minutes I enjoyed it. So that's that,"

"What'll we think about now that we've settled that?"

"We can think about getting me a second dresser." She put her hand on the piles of clothing on the bed beside her. She was still frowning a little; he could not tell exactly what about. "I think one more dresser will do it."

"All right," Verne said. "We'll think about that."

10

VERNE STRETCHED AND yawned. "Well, let's go get the dresser. Where is it?"

Barbara leaned back on the bed, against the wall behind her. "Easy. Not so fast, on a day like this."

"I feel active again. Heat is strange that way. First you feel dopey. You don't want to anything at all. Then all of a sudden you spring right up out of your chair. This is the moment for me. I've sprung up."

Barbara got slowly to her feet "All right. I think we'll find a dresser in one of the other rooms."

"They'll probably be locked."

But the room next to Barbara's was not locked. And there was a little white dresser just like hers right next to the bed. Each of them took an end of it, and in a moment they had lugged it into Barbara's room and set it by the other.

"That's that," Verne said. "Do the clothes go in any old way, or is there some ritual about it?"

"Maybe I should put the clothes away. Then I'll know where things are."

"All right."

Barbara opened the top drawer of the dresser. "Damn!" she

said. The drawer had razor blades and some adhesive tape and pieces of string and nails lying about on the dirty newspaper that had been used to line it.

Verne looked in the other drawers. They were all the same way.

"I'll have to repaper it and clean it out. Maybe even scrub it. Christ."

She went over and threw herself down on the bed. The bed sagged and groaned under her.

"Not a very strong bed," Verne said. "Not much good for entertainment, is it?"

"Strictly a chaste bed."

"Well, there's always the floor."

"Not unless it's swept."

Verne studied her intently. Was she kidding him, going along with the gag? Or — or something more? He tried to read her expression, but it was hopeless. A losing game, trying to read a woman's face. Finally he shrugged. He reached into his pocket and got out his pipe and tobacco. Barbara watched him filling the pipe without speaking. Her eyes were wide.

Verne glanced up as he was clicking his lighter. "My pipe. Won't go until I light it."

"I know. I remember your pipe. I remember it very well. You had it that time. At Castle."

"At Castle?"

"Yes."

Verne sat down gingerly on the bed beside her. She said nothing. He went on sucking at his pipe, trying to get it lit. "God damn hard thing to operate," he said between his teeth. At last the tobacco caught.

"I don't see why you smoke when it's so hot."

"This isn't for warmth. This is for comfort. It relaxes me."

"Probably makes you feel more like a man."

He shot her a sharp glance. "Why do you say a thing like that?"

"I don't know. Tobacco, pipes, cigarettes, all make me think of high school kids trying to grow up."

"You smoke, too. These days."

"Not a pipe."

"No." Verne was silent, smoking and thinking to himself. "Well, it might be. Freud, again."

"What might be?"

"Let it go, if you've forgotten." Verne leaned back, trying to make himself comfortable on the bed. He kicked his shoes off. The shoes fell to the floor with a loud crash.

"What's that for?" Barbara said.

"To make myself comfortable."

"Are you going to stay?"

Verne glanced at her. "That," he said, "depends on you."

Barbara reached over and picked up his shoes. She set them in his lap. "Put them back on."

"Really? But I'm more comfortable."

"I'm not."

There was silence. Verne watched her with mixed amusement and embarrassment. Barbara's face was dark and sullen. Finally she relaxed.

"All right. It doesn't matter." She tossed the shoes back on the floor. "Let them lie there, then."

"I don't think I know quite how to take this," Verne said, still smiling at her. But his hand, gripping the pipe, was tense and pressed tightly to the wooden bole. Barbara did not say anything. She was looking indifferently off through the open door into the hall. Verne continued to examine her face intently, watching her with an almost eager interest. He blew smoke slowly into the center of the room.

"Want me to close the door to the hall?"

Barbara turned. "What?"

"Want me to close the door? Is that what you were staring out there for?"

"My God, no. I was just thinking."

"About what?"

"Lots of things. As one does. I was thinking about Carl, for instance. I was wondering what sort of a boy he is."

"Seems nice," Verne said noncommittally. "Certainly big enough. Why?"

"I don't know. Last night I started down the hall to take a bath and there he was, standing outside the door, in the middle of the hall. Not making any kind of a sound. Just standing. It scared the hell out of me. As if he were some kind of — of ghost. A spectre. A great silent figure, watching me with that strange look he has. That look of detached contemplation. As if I were some sort of natural wonder, like a waterfall, or an insect."

"The whole world is one vast insect for Carl. I think that about sums him up."

"Does it? We're going to have to spend a whole week with him. I'd like to know — But he does seem to be all right."

"We could always push him into one of the septic tanks."

Barbara laughed. "Anyhow, he'll be busy exploring with his compass and map. He won't bother us much. And I think he's nice, Verne. I see nothing wrong with him. He leaps around and shouts a lot, but that's natural for his age. Don't you like him?"

"He's your subject. You brought him up. I have nothing to say."

"You know, it's an odd thing, I don't suppose I'm more than three years or so older than he is. But I feel like I'm not in his generation at all. Why? It's not the age, I guess. The actual years. It's more the attitude. When we were coming down he was skipping and jumping and dancing around, all ready to pull off his clothes and run naked over the hills. Then he smelled breakfast."

"You never felt that way?"

"No. It's too hot."

Verne would have been glad to drop the subject. His pipe had gone out; the tobacco had been used up. He knocked it against the wall and emptied the ashes into the ashtray on the table.

"That's not actually so," Barbara went on. "On the way down I was almost ready to go with him — for a moment. Run and dance, leap and roll. And early this morning when the sun came up, when I woke up — "

She stopped.

"Go on," Verne murmured.

"No. Anyhow, I was almost ready to follow him across the countryside. But then all of a sudden I felt like a fool. I froze up around it. For a moment I felt myself in sympathy with him, and then the next minute I was disgusted. At myself. As if I had been lured by — by marbles and hopscotch again."

"I get the picture."

"Maybe I shouldn't have said anything. I'm working it out in my mind. I didn't intend to talk about it. I started thinking out loud. The door to the hall made me think about Carl. The way he stood out there."

"All right. We'll forget it. I'm just as glad."

"Why?"

He shrugged. "It doesn't fascinate me to any unusual degree."

"Have you forgotten your own youth?"

"I don't see that it has anything to do with my youth."

"Easy, easy. Forget it." They were both silent for a time. Barbara rubbed her bare arms. "God, but it's miserable! Like a Finnish bath house."

"By six o'clock it'll all be gone."

Barbara looked at the clock. "Almost six hours. We'll die. At least, I will. I can't stand just sitting in the heat like this. I want to do something."

"A shower would be fine. But actually, it's not unusually hot. It's always like this in the summer. But we've been busy before, working at our jobs. We never had time to notice the heat. We had something to do. When you get right down to it, we're really bothered by not having anything to do. The heat is only incidental."

"Oh?"

"We're being paid to sit here and do nothing. So we feel all upset. First we stand up, then we sit down. We blame it on the heat, but it's really because we don't know what to do with ourselves."

"I suppose so."

"We're restless. Our work filled up most of our lives. Now that's gone. Behind us. We don't know what to do without it. We're too strongly involved with it; it's too much a part of us. Like old fire horses. We won't live long, now that the Company's dead."

"Carl's doing all right, running around outside."

"He's younger. There's a slim chance that he might live through this. You might, too. You're young. You might be able to adjust to this, the fall of our world, the old world. Want to go out and start exploring?"

"Too hot." She wiped her neck. In the amber half-light of the room he could see her twisting in an agony of discomfort. Suddenly she leaped up. "Let's do something!"

"I already have made my suggestion."

"What's that?"

"Take a shower."

"There's nothing but a big pot of a tub here."

"Then take a bath."

"Oh, hell! Who ever took a bath at noon? Anyhow, that's not what I want. I feel restless. As if there's something I should be doing. Something undone. Some kind of work or something uncompleted. You're right, I suppose. It comes of having sat at a desk for years."

"You must try to adjust. Realize that it's over. The old life is gone. Dead."

"I guess so."

"This is a moment of importance. The moment of decision. We've shed an old life, for the moment. We've just gotten out from a dying world. Now we stand at the brink, looking around us. Like those crabs that aren't always in the same shell."

"What kind of crab is that?"

"I don't know. I read about them, once. They chase around, getting into empty shells. After a while they get tired of one shell and go on to the next."

"That's us?"

"In a way. We've lost the old shell; it wore out. Now we have to find a new one. We have to live in *some* kind of shell. We can go in several directions."

"What are the directions?"

"One is back."

"Back?"

"To whatever we've always done. To what existed before. The *was*."

"What's the other directions?"

"I don't know. I haven't worked it all out yet. You wait a while and I'll have the rest."

Barbara laughed. "A hell of a place to stop." She stood in the middle of the room, first on one foot, then the other.

"I know. But that's the trouble. We're at a time of decision, and we don't know what the decision represents or what choices we have, or even where they lead. Our world is gone, our old world. We can turn and go with it, die with it. The crab can stay in his worn-out shell and perish. We've been fortunate, the three of us. We've been pushed out to the lip of the shell. We can stand and look around us. The others have already left, gone with the old. Soon we can follow them. Or we can find something else."

"And if we don't?"

"Well, if we don't we simply die with the rest. Our being picked out this way, the three of us, gives us a chance to escape. We become free agents for a moment. The cosmic process hangs poised. We can start it spinning in any direction we want. Like the figure in the Greek play. He looks around him. What is he going to do?"

"He always does the wrong thing. That's why it's a tragedy."

"He does the greater thing. That's why it's tragedy. What he does brings personal ruin on him, but it had to be done. Duty. He recognizes what's at stake and does what he should do. Just like a man plunging into a burning building. He does it because he feels he should. Even if he is burned up. The tragic figure does what he must, and is burned up. But burned or not, the thing must be done."

"Why does the right choice always have to bring destruction on the person? It isn't fair."

"Well, if it brought him fortune, it wouldn't be tragedy. It would be just sound business."

Barbara was silent. "Anyhow, it makes an interesting topic for discussion."

She wandered over to the doorway and stared out into the hall. The hall was dark and silent. All the way along it the doors were closed. Nothing moved. There was no sound. Except for the musty, clinging smells, the hall was empty.

"What do you see?" Verne said, from the bed.

"Silence and immobility."

"Is that good?"

"Yes."

"Why? Why good?"

She did not answer. She continued to stand at the door, leaning against the doorjamb, her hands in her pockets. Verne gazed at her, square and supple under her slacks and her heavy cloth shirt. Her golden arms.

"You look pretty good," he said.

"What?"

"You look all right."

She did not answer, but she shifted a little onto her other foot. Her body straightened out. Some of the supple lines melted and disappeared. She was standing rigid and stern, because of what he said.

"What's the matter?"

She turned around. "Nothing's the matter."

"You don't want me to tell you that you look nice?"

"No."

"Why not?"

"Because I don't! Do you understand? I don't want any more of that. None. None at all."

Verne was surprised. "But — "

"Anything but that. Don't invent nice things to say. I don't want to hear them."

"I'll be damned."

"No doubt." Her chin was up. "I have no doubt."

"Get off it," Verne said slowly. "I thought we made an agreement."

Barbara relaxed. "Sorry. I'm divided up into a whole lot of parts. I want this, then I do that."

"Forget it."

"It's the heat. And boredom. I keep thinking I want to do things. But as soon as I start to imagine walking downstairs and outside into the sun —"

"Why go outside? Let's do something here."

"Like what?"

"Oh, goodness. What, indeed!"

"For God's sake, Verne."

He grinned up at her.

She smiled a little. "The bed will fall apart. It's almost ready to collapse. That's one reason why I've followed the straight and narrow."

"Have you?"

"For a while." She sat down next to him. "You know, Verne, it's so strange how some things are the same, and some things are different."

"How so?"

"You know what I mean. Four years kills so much, but it doesn't kill everything. The real problem is trying to find out just exactly what it has killed and what is still alive. It's so hard to know. It's impossible to know. In advance, at least. What goes on, deep down in your mind? I wish I knew what was still alive in me. I wish I could find out."

"There's one thing that nothing kills. At least, not until the whole body perishes."

"Four years is a long time. But what the hell." She turned toward him. "Look at how different I am. It must be fascinating to see. I've changed a lot, haven't I?"

"You've grown from a young girl into a fully developed woman," Verne stated.

"Stop it." She colored. "That's what I don't want to hear. I told you."

"But it's the truth."

"I don't care. That's one thing that is not the same. It's off." Color rose into her cheeks.

"Really?"

Barbara got up quickly and walked around in a little circle. "Of course. It's gone. It's a matter of complete indifference to me. There's no feeling left. I have no feeling about it. Maybe at one time it mattered. But not any more."

"I'm not sure exactly what you mean. I get just a sort of general picture."

"That'll do." She crossed to the door and looked up and down the hall. "I'm going to leave the door open. No one will be coming along."

Verne gazed up, wonderingly. "What — what's the pitch?"

Barbara came back and stood grimly in front of him. "The bed really will collapse, you realize."

"Oh?"

"Yes." She rubbed her neck. "This god damn heat and boredom. Don't take any credit for yourself. It's enough to drive a person crazy, looking for something to do."

"Is — is that the way you look at it?"

"Partly. I can't stand just sitting here in the room. I'll be god damned if I'll go outside in the sun. So that doesn't leave much."

"Well, I never heard of it coming this way. Not in all my life. I don't know what to think."

"Better decide soon," Barbara said. "What you said about the moment of decision is true, right now. Do you want to, or don't you?" She gazed past him, suddenly thoughtful.

"What is it?"

"Maybe — maybe we'll find out, once and for all."

Verne go up from the bed. "My God. But where? I don't want the bed folding up at the crucial moment, with us inside it."

"It's not that bad." She smiled. "But we really can't use it. Look at it sagging."

They looked at it.

"Well, how about the floor?" Verne said. "We can put a sheet down or something. Either that or outside on the lawn. But it's too sunny there. Of course, if the bathtub is large enough —"

"Oh, stop it! It's not that funny."

"I thought you said you didn't care any more."

"I don't. But it's not like drinking a glass of water."

"Lenin said it was."

"Well, it isn't. Anyhow, what will we do?"

"Don't change your mind while I'm working it out." Verne looked around the room. "We could move the mattress onto the floor. That way it'll be soft, and there won't be any hazard. What do you say?"

"All right."

Barbara began carrying the clothes from the bed, over to the dressers. She heaped them in stacks until the bed was clear. Verne took hold of one end of the mattress and she took hold of the other. They laid the mattress and the bedding onto the floor.

Verne straightened up. "How's that? Almost as good as the bank of a stream."

"It's good enough." She wiped her neck. "This infernal god damn heat. Will it never go away?"

"You'll forget it in a few minutes. That's the virtue of this. You can be stabbed and roasted and murdered during, and you don't notice until after."

Barbara leaned against the wall and began to take her shoes and socks off. "Well? I hope you're going to do this, too. You must be at least that much of a gentleman."

Verne took off his shoes and socks slowly. Barbara unbuttoned her shirt and laid it on the dresser with the other clothes.

"What's holding you up?" she said.

"A man can't go to trusting extremes. He may be called on to leap out of the window. I'll leave the rest of my stuff on."

"Suit yourself. But if I'm going to do it I want the pleasure of getting out of these sticky clothes." She reached behind her, unhooking the bra. She put the bra with the shirt, in a heap on the dresser.

Verne contemplated her. "Nice."

"Come on. Let's hurry, for heaven's sake. I'm irritable enough to change my mind."

"Really?"

"Of course. Only I can't think of anything else to do. That's the trouble with this sort of thing. The heat reduces you to animal level. Basic things."

"Well, it's the original form of entertainment."

Barbara finished undressing, gathering up all her things and putting them on the dresser. "It feels a lot better this way. Maybe we ought to run around like this all week long. Until the yuks come."

"What would Carl think?" Verne said, testing the mattress with his foot. "He'd be struck blind."

"He'll learn. Now? Ready?" She examined the clock. "We have five hours before it starts to get cool. Can we string it out until evening?"

"There's a limit, even for Verne Tildon."

Barbara sat down on the bedding and gingerly made herself comfortable. "You know, down here it's cooler. I don't feel all prickly and gummy anymore." She rested her head on her arm, watching Verne. "Is there a moral there?"

"There's a moral in everything." Verne gazed down at her. "How about the door? You really want to leave it open?"

"Who would come along?"

"No one. But you have to give my conditionings a break. After all, I'm an old man and I've learned a way of doing things." He closed the door and then got down with her on the bedding.

"Doesn't this seem to be your way?"

"How do you mean?"

"I don't know. You don't find this objectionable, do you?" She gasped. "Be careful, damn it!"

"Objectionable? Oh, no." He added, "You know, you really have filled out in four years. Very nice."

"Thanks. It should cost you extra, since you're getting such a good deal."

"You have changed since last time."

"Sure," Barbara said. "But it's a cruel world."

"Odd," Verne said. "You'd think it would make you warmer, and instead it makes you feel sort of icy."

"I suppose. Anyhow, I don't feel so fretful and agonized anymore."

"What, then?"

"Nothing at all. Just leave me alone for a while." She closed her eyes. "When you close your eyes it's as dark as night. Verne, I think you and I must be different from the others. We like it dark and cold. We have the shades down. We resent the sunlight. There's something symbolic in that. And Carl goes rushing around outside."

"For a little while today you thought maybe you wanted to run in the sun."

"I would have gone ten feet and fallen over dead. Just let me lie here with my eyes shut. Don't jar me. I'm all relaxed and at ease. They ought to recommend this to neurotic patients. It does wonders."

"That's my theory. I've been following that advice for years."

"I know," Barbara said.

Verne looked down into her face, so close to his, but he could not read her expression. Her eyes were shut. He bent over a little and touched his lips to her forehead.

She frowned. "Cut that out! None of that."

"Really? This is strange. You don't want me to kiss you, but you don't mind the rest."

"I enjoy the rest. After all, it's been almost six months for me."

"Almost that long for me, too. Most of these girls who work for the Company are after your pelt to hang up on the wall."

"A battle. Between you losing your pelt and the girl losing her greatest pride."

"Once they get you under lock and key they can quit their job. That's the psychology of a working woman. To them, it's a way of getting out of the grind. But take college girls, on the other hand. It's a completely different proposition. Marriage would only interfere with their fun."

"Which is your attitude. And therefore you can strike up quite a business."

Verne agreed.

"Where do I fit into the picture? I don't seem to fall into any of your categories."

"That happens," Verne admitted. He was silent. After a moment he went on: "Well, are you ready to call it quits for today? We can carry on some other time."

"Don't be too sure. Next time I might not feel the same. Better take advantage while you have it. What time is it? I can't see the clock."

"Still four hours to go. We're doing as well as could be expected. Shall we — shall we go on?"

"For Christ's sake!" Barbara said angrily, stirring a little. "Come on."

"I guess a bird in the hand is worth two in the bush."

"Your other phrase is: The woods are full of them."

Verne nodded.

Presently he said, "Well, I'm sorry. But even if there's a month to go I'm finished." He waited for her to say something. She did not answer. She lay with her eyes shut, her chest rising and falling. "Are you all right?"

There was no response.

"What is it?" Verne said. Her face was strange, twisting oddly. The muscles around her mouth locked, hard and rigid. They began to work. "For God's sake, what's the matter? What is it?"

"Verne."

"Yes? What's wrong?"

"Verne, there's something wrong."

"What is it?"

"I don't know." She opened her eyes, wide and terrified, staring up at him. "Let me up."

He helped her to her feet. She stood shakily, pressing her fist against her cheek.

"What is it? Are you sick?"

She shook her head. "I don't know. Maybe it's — something psychological." She tried to smile. "I don't know."

"Nothing physical?"

"No." Her voice was a whisper.

"What did it feel like?"

"Verne, give me my clothes."

He handed her clothing to her, from the top of the dresser. She dressed quickly, her hands shaking. When she had finished she sat down on the bed springs and tied her shoes. She did not speak.

"Are you all right now?" Verne asked.

"Yes." Her face was pale and set, like frozen marble. All the color had drained out of her. Her arms were grey. He could see her teeth chattering. All across her forehead and lip were tiny beads of icy perspiration.

"For God's sake," Verne said, alarmed. "Will you tell me what it is?"

"Do you remember what you said?"

"What I said? When? What do you mean?"

"About — about the moment. The choice."

"Yes."

"Verne, something happened. Didn't you feel it?"

"I don't know what you mean."

She was looking at him. "You didn't feel it?"

"I felt cold. But it seemed good to me. Because of the heat. Do you mean that?"

"I don't mean that." She rubbed her forehead. "Something terrible happened. Something got in. Like in a dream. Drifting in, cold and made out of fog . . ."

They were both silent.

"It felt good at first," Verne said finally. "It had been so hot. I guess I didn't get it as strongly."

"It was waiting. Like the thing in the dream. It was waiting there, all around us. Waiting to get in."

Verne considered. "We didn't do anything wrong. People do it all the time. Even the best people get to earth that way."

"But something got in. Something that was waiting. Cold and dead. It — it got inside me."

"What was it?"

"I don't know." Barbara brushed at her eyes, wiping them. "I didn't know there was anything. It came near after — after we began. It was there all the time." She looked up at him tearfully. "It's always been there, waiting to — "

"For God's sake. That's foolish. This is only a guilt complex setting up. A personification of some mental guilt."

"But you felt it, too."

"No." But he *had* felt it! He licked his lips.

Barbara watched him. "You did. I can tell. Not as strong, but you did. In spite of what you say."

"All right," Verne said impatiently.

"Verne?"

"What."

"It was like a sentence. A curse. As if we're — doomed."

Verne grunted.

After a long time Barbara went on in a tight voice, "Maybe we better put the bedding back."

They lifted the bedding and put it down on the springs. Verne pushed it into place with his hands. The bed looked as it had before. "That's that," Verne said.

They sat down on the bed. Barbara was still pale and shaken. She shivered. "I'm cold. I'm cold all over. Cold and clammy. Like a — a leper. Like worms and wet tomb stones. The grave. Cold, damp stone."

She took his hand and put it against her face. He started, pulling back. Her skin was moist and frigid. He swallowed, rubbing his hands together. "A reaction. A psychological reaction."

"I feel so awful."

"I know."

They looked down at the floor. Neither of them spoke. At last Barbara turned and raised the shade. A flash of yellow sunlight poured into the room, blinding them. They blinked.

"That's better," Verne said.

"Verne, we never should have done it. That's what it was. We brought it on ourselves. We let it in by what we did. It was our own fault. We — we called it down."

"Why? People do it — "

"This was different."

"How?"

"We took up where we left off four years ago. It was wrong. You can't go back. And we did go back. Only it was worse than going back. Even worse than that."

"Why?"

"It was all the bad part and none of the good. It was as bad as it could be. It was the slopping part, the blood and the seeping over. Mechanical. And none of the feeling. There was nothing to make it into something. When I asked you to do it I thought I was being — I don't know. I don't know what I thought. I wanted to find out something. It was my fault." She looked up defensively. "But it was your fault, too."

"Nuts. There was nothing wrong with it."

"Wasn't there?"

"It's a perfectly natural act."

"Verne, we've gone on with what we started four years ago. We've taken it up again. Only it was all the bad parts we brought back. None of the good."

"You said that." He got up and walked around the room. "Perhaps. I did feel something. Something coming onto me. Like a hand catching. Settling over me."

She watched him silently.

Suddenly he stopped. "Well, actually, there's no real problem. If our psychological apparatuses won't allow us to be together, then we'll have to separate. The human mind is very complex. The unconscious sense of guilt — "

"Separate? How?"

"We won't — "

"We already have. And you told me once the time is passed, the moment of choice — "

"For Christ's sake! This is silly."

"Verne, does it mean we're going to have to keep living this way, all the rest of our lives? Around and around . . . Can't we break away? Will — will it always be like this? Like it is now?"

"We can separate any time we want."

"We separated four years ago. We were apart four years. It's too late. We've already done it. We've made our choice. It's happened to us already."

"Well, then if we're in the soup we're in the soup." Verne smiled wryly. "And what's so bad about it? There could be a lot worse ways to live."

Barbara twisted. "I'm so — so dirty! So contaminated. I want to be clean." She got up and crossed the room to the door.

"Where are you going?"

"I've got to get clean. I've got to try to wash it away."

"That's not very flattering," Verne murmured. "I didn't have to hit you over the head, you remember."

"It's my fault, then. It's all my fault." She shuddered. "God, I've become so dirty. So dirty and cold. I can't stand it."

"Like I said," Verne murmured. "We can stop any time. We can make this the last. Now we know. It's a bad idea. But it's settled. It won't happen again."

"It's not as easy as that. How can we stop? What can we do?"

"Quit seeing each other."

"All right." She sagged. "All right."

"I guess it'll be hard to do. At least, during the next week. But after that — "

"We didn't see each other for four years. And here we are."

"Well, something will break it. There's always a way out." He grinned, trying to be cheerful. "I'm not joking. It's true; don't you remember? The curse always is lifted, when the right thing is found."

Barbara smoothed her slacks aimlessly.

"Think of all the old stories," Verne said. "The old legends. Remember the *Ring of the Niebelungen*? The gods were cursed by having the gold. They grew old."

Barbara nodded.

"They got rid of the curse."

"How?"

Verne pondered. He picked his shoes up from the floor and began to put them on. "Siegfried saved them. Or almost saved them. At least, he was supposed to."

"Siegfried?"

"The guileless fool. The virgin. Completely uncorrupted . . . The innocent fool."

"Very interesting," Barbara said. She smiled tightly, rocking back and forth, her arms folded. Some color was beginning to come back into her arms and face. "It's not really too promising, though. Is it?"

"Why not?"

"Well, we have no Siegfried to save us. To make us clean again."

They were both silent.

There was a sound, from the hall outside. They glanced at each other.

"What was that?" Verne said.

Barbara raised her hand. "Listen."

They listened. Someone was coming uncertainly down the hall, cautious and timid. He came closer and closer, until he reached the door. He stopped outside, and they heard a faint breathing sound.

Verne and Barbara moved together, listening. For a time there was no sound at all. Then, at last, a faint voice came, distant and polite.

"Barbara? Verne? Are you in there?"

"For God's sake!" Barbara exclaimed. "It's only Carl." She gasped in relief. "Lord."

Verne opened the door. "You scared the hell out of us."

Carl looked around hesitantly. "Can I come in?" He came

slowly into the room, smiling at them. "I didn't mean to startle you."

"It's all right," Barbara murmured.

"I got worn out looking around. It's hot, all right. But I found some very interesting things. Very interesting. I thought you two might like to come with me. It's no fun exploring around alone."

Verne was watching Carl intently, rubbing his jaw. After a time he brought out his pipe and began to fill it slowly, still watching the boy.

"What do you say?" Carl said, looking around at them hopefully. "If you say it sounds silly I'll agree with you, but — "

"No. No, it's not silly. It's something different to do." Verne and Barbara looked at each other.

"The manager's house is full of things!" Carl said excitedly, unable to contain himself, now that he had got some response. "Nothing has been taken out. I didn't get inside, but I know. I saw through some boards nailed over one of the windows. Everything's there. All of it! *They* must be going to have their officers stay there."

"Maybe we should go along," Verne said. "It might be interesting."

"Come on!" Carl cried. "I'll lead the way!"

11

THE STATION MANAGER'S house was set apart from the rest of the buildings. It did not look like them at all. Once, it had been an old home in New England. The manager had noticed it during one of his business trips to the United States. He purchased it and had it shipped piece by piece all the way across the world, by boat, by pack train across mountains, finally assembled by workmen at the station. Now it stood, an old-fashioned American Colonial house, trim and white, its austere front rising up like some pale frosted cake, among refining plants and towering factory units and heaps of slag.

Around the house was a lawn and a border of flowers. At the edge of the lawn was a white picket fence and a tiny gate. Three trees, birch trees, grew at the side of the house. Under one was a bench, a plain wood bench.

Carl and Verne and Barbara stood at the fence, all of them a little awed.

"Just think," Carl said. "We can open the gate and walk across the lawn and go inside the house."

"If we can get the boards off," Verne said. He fingered the crowbar.

"Let's go," Carl said. "I'm anxious to get inside." He pushed the gate open.

"Don't be in so much of a hurry."

"I can't help it." Carl waited for them to catch up with him. "Just think — we could move in here, if we wanted to. We could move right in, live here for a whole week. Until they come. We could use his things, his kitchen, his chairs, his bed —"

"All right," Barbara said.

Suddenly Carl stopped.

"What's the matter?"

Carl looked around. "Maybe —"

"Maybe what?"

"You know, maybe this isn't such a good idea."

"Why not?"

"Well, maybe we shouldn't break in this way. I — I don't think we're supposed to. That's why they boarded it all up."

"It was your idea."

"I know." Carl hung his head. "But now that we're actually going to do it I'm not sure how I feel."

"Come on," Barbara said impatiently. "I'm kind of curious myself. I'd like to see how he lived. We heard so many different things."

Carl hesitated. "Should we do it?"

"Why not?"

"I don't know. I guess I'm just letting my conditioned responses get the better of me. But it's like breaking into a church. Where you're not supposed to be. Like soldiers, the German Army during the war. Breaking in and sleeping in front of the altar, stealing things, breaking and tramping around."

"The manager was no god of mine," Verne said. They had come to the porch. Verne walked up the wide steps and tapped with the end of the crowbar on the boards that were nailed across the door. "This is going to be hard."

"Then we're really going in?" Carl asked. "I never realized how well I'd learned all the Company rules and taboos. I thought with everyone leaving—"

"They hang on," Verne said. "Old superstitions." He took Carl by the arm and turned him around. "Look. Do you see all that?"

Carl was facing the great domain that was the land and property of the station. It lay stretched out before them, all the way to the foot of the mountains.

"See all that? Miles and miles of buildings and machinery, slag piles, pits, quarries. All deserted. No one there. No one at all. The buildings are empty. The factories, the miles of pits and excavations. You and I can do anything we want. We can go inside and wee-wee all over the floor, if we want. Rules and mores don't mean a thing anymore. There's no one here but us."

"There's nobody here to stop us," Barbara said.

"There was nobody to stop the German soldiers. That was the whole point. They could do what they wanted."

"But what does it matter?" Verne said. "The rules and codes were artificial. They were good only as long as they could be enforced. Now there's no one to enforce them. So they don't have any meaning. They were just conventions. Don't confuse them with innate moral laws. They were just rules, nothing more. Man made. They came, now they're gone again. The yuks will have their own rules."

"I suppose so."

"Well, forget about it. This was all your idea in the first place." Verne hooked the crowbar behind the top board and began to pull. "Here we go."

"Let me give you a hand."

The two pulled together. After a while they had the boards off the door and stacked up on the porch railing.

"Now," Verne said, pausing for breath. "Here comes the real question." He tried the door handle. "Locked."

"That's bad," Carl said.

"We'll try the back. If it's locked we'll break it down."

They went down the steps and around the side of the house. Along the path grew flowers and vegetables, plants of all kinds and descriptions, an amazing hodge-podge that stretched out in all directions. There were pansies, begonias, tulips, watermelon, carrots and rhubarb and orchids, all mixed in together without any order, planted wherever there seemed to be any space.

"How eclectic," Carl said.

"It's a mess," Barbara murmured. "Look at them all growing together like that!"

They came to the back door. Verne and Carl tore the boards loose and stacked them up.

"Here goes," Verne said. He tried the knob. The door was unlocked. He disappeared inside.

Carl turned to Barbara. "After you."

"Thanks." She went on in, Carl following excitedly behind. They were on the back porch where the laundry tubs were. Verne was not in sight.

"Where are you?" Carl called.

"I'm in here." Verne was in the kitchen. Barbara and Carl came after him. And stopped short in amazement.

"Good lord," Carl said.

The kitchen was filled with cooking equipment of all kinds. There was almost no space to walk. In one corner an immense gleaming stove jutted up from beside a refrigerator. Piled up on tables and on the floor were mixers, blenders, a waffle iron, an automatic toaster, countless white and silver shapes of all sizes and uses.

"A lot of this stuff hasn't even been opened," Verne said. "It's still crated up."

Along one side of the kitchen were packing crates and boards and nails and mounds of excelsior, wrapping paper and wire and heavy cord.

Carl picked up an object of chromium and steel, with an electric cord hanging from it. "What's this?"

Barbara looked at the label. "It's an electric egg dicer."

Verne kicked at one of the crates. "God knows what might be in here. More egg dicers?"

"Probably a lot of different things."

They left the kitchen and found themselves in the dining room. In the center of the room was a heavy oak table, covered with a fine-spun cloth. To one side was a cabinet with glass doors, mounted against the wall.

Barbara opened one of the doors. "Look at these."

Verne came over arid stood beside her. The cabinet was filled with dishes. Old dishes, their edges encrusted with gold like spider webs. Barbara brought out a crystal bottle and stopper, holding it up to the light.

"These must be worth a million dollars," she said.

"Hardly." Verne took one of the plates down and turned it around. "Early American. It's worth something. Maybe not that much, but a lot." He replaced the plate.

Carl came to the door. "Come in here!"

"What is it?"

Carl disappeared through a door. Verne shrugged. Barbara closed the cabinet and they followed after Carl. They found themselves in the library. Carl was gaping up and around him, his mouth open.

"Look!" he said. "Do you see?"

Verne rubbed his jaw. "Could he read them all?"

"Could anybody read them all?" Barbara said.

Books ran along the walls of the library, around them on all sides, up over their heads, higher and higher, as far as the eye could see. It made them dizzy to look up; the ceiling seemed hazy and indistinct, and a long way off. Verne reached up and plucked a volume at random from the shelf above his head. He handed it to Carl.

"Look at it," he murmured.

Carl opened the book. It was incredibly ancient, a medieval illuminated manuscript, the vellum yellow and cracking. He turned it around — it was heavy.

"Here, too," Verne murmured. There were more crates, big wood packing crates, bound with wire twisted into knots. Wisps of straw stuck out at the ends of the crates. Some had been partly opened. Books were packed inside, brand new books that had never been taken out of their packing.

"We get all this," Carl said, dazed.

"Not exactly. We get to use this, for a while. But not more than a little while. A week, maybe. Very little."

"We won't get very many of these read in a week," Barbara said.

Carl pulled some more books down and opened them. He put them back and gazed up. Some trick of the colors made the walls seem to fall back, farther and farther, the higher he looked. The number of books seemed to be growing, increasing as he watched. As if he were looking down the wrong end of the telescope. Faster and faster the walls of books fell away from him, until it seemed as if all the books in the world, each volume and pamphlet, each novel, each collection of stories, essay, study, everything man had put down on paper were collected here in this old-fashioned New England house, in one room.

"It makes me dizzy," Barbara said. "How do you get up to the top?"

"Some sort of ladder." Verne wandered out of the room. Carl and Barbara followed him.

"What's all this?" Carl asked. They had come into a workshop of some kind, filled with objects, machinery and models of some kind, specimens, exhibits, displays.

"A television set," Barbara said.

There were specimens of the phonograph, the telephone, rows of electric lights through all their stages of development, a power-driven saw, even a flush toilet. Most of the objects were piled helter-skelter, on top of each other, stacked here and there without order or design. Some were still crated up, pushed off to one side, crammed together in packing boxes.

"Inventions," Verne said. "Looks like Menlo Park."

Dust was already beginning to settle over all the crates and exhibits. The three of them stood looking around glumly, none of them speaking for a time.

"Just think," Carl said. "They spent years bringing all this stuff here and now it's abandoned. It's all left here, left behind. Forgotten."

"Maybe the yuks can use them."

"Probably burn them," Verne murmured.

"What a depressing sight," Carl said. "It gives me the creeps. Imagine what the people who invented and made all these things would say if they could see them lying here, piled on top of each other, no order, no meaning, completely abandoned."

Barbara began to root through one of the heaps.

"What are you looking for?"

"I don't know. Something I can use."

"What do you want?"

Barbara straightened up. "I have nothing in mind. There ought to be something here we can use. Look at it all. Tons of things. Every kind of thing."

"Let's go," Carl said. He moved toward the door.

"Don't you want to fill your pockets?"

"No. It — it reminds me of when I was a kid. I had a room full of things. Microscope, stamp album, maps, model steam engine. Like this. Everything strewn all around. There's something wrong with it."

"Well, we can't take anything back with us," Verne said. "These things don't really belong to us. But we could use them, during the time we have left."

"There's too many. Too much stuff. Let's forget it. Let's just let it go. It's dusty in here."

"It would make a nice bonfire. Especially all the books. What a blaze."

"We could tear out the last page of each book," Carl said. "Think of the power we three have. We could tear out the last pages, we could tinker with all this stuff so none of it would work. Then the yuks would never be able to use anything. Or understand anything. They'd give up. They'd finally have to throw this all way. What power we have."

"They'll probably throw it away anyhow," Verne said. "This stuff doesn't mean anything anymore. Except maybe as museum pieces. We have power over a lot of useless objects."

They went back through the library, into the dining room, into the kitchen.

In the kitchen Verne halted. "There's one thing I want to take a look at."

"What's that?"

"His phonograph records. I might find something good. It's worth a try."

Carl grinned. "So there's something that isn't just a museum piece."

"I'm going outside," Barbara said. "There's too much dust in here." She touched one of the half-opened crates. "Dust on them, and they're not even opened yet. This stuff is already decaying, and it's hardly been used."

Carl pushed the back door open. "Come on. Let's go." He stood by the door and Barbara came toward him.

"I'll see you later," Verne said. He disappeared back into the dining room.

Barbara and Carl stepped outside, down the back stairs, onto the path. The air was warm and full of smells of flowers and grass.

Carl took a deep breath. "Smells good."

Barbara bent down, examining a flower. "What's this?"

Carl did not know. "Looks like some sort of rose. Only it's so small."

Barbara picked the flower. "Well? What'll we do? Where'll we go?"

"We could sit on the grass."

Barbara smiled. "Could we?"

"Don't you like to sit on the grass? When the sun's warm, and the air's full of smells. I'm tired of running all over the place. I've done enough exploring."

"You were so excited about the manager's house. Now you're not interested in it at all."

"I know. But there's something depressing about it. All those things. All those books and inventions and plates and egg dicers. Everything, stacks and crates and heaps, all strewn around. All abandoned. I'd rather be outside."

Barbara studied his face. "You change your mind fast."

"There was something about it —"

"I know," Barbara said. "All right. Let's sit on the grass in the sun. I guess it won't do any harm."

"But is it wet?" Carl ran his hands through the grass. "Not any more. It's all dried out."

They sat down gingerly, stiff-backed. The grass was warm and dry under them.

Barbara sighed. "It makes me sleepy, the sun and the air."

"How did you sleep last night?"

"All right."

"It was certainly quiet last night. I never realized how many sounds and noises there were around here. The people, the machinery. Things coming and going. Trucks. But last night there was nothing. Only silence. It gave me a strange feeling. It was so — so unnatural. After so many years of hearing things it's hard to get used to this. I wonder if we will get used to it, ever. It's a big change for us. I wonder if this is one of those moments in history when people will look back, years later, and realize that the whole world hung in the balance. Civilization on trial. Like the fall of Rome. Or when they stopped the Turks at Vienna. Or when the Moors came up into Spain. Roland. Remember Roland? How they stopped the Moors? Or Stalingrad. The end of Germany. History hanging in the balance."

He glanced at Barbara. Barbara was gazing up at the sky. A few faint trails of mist had come up and were blowing slowly along, white streamers mixed with the blue.

"It's getting cooler," Barbara said.

"The fog."

"We'll sleep better tonight."

Carl considered this proposition. "Do you suppose that if a person got less and less sleep each night — say he started with the full eight hours, and then he slept just under eight hours, then just a little less than that — that after a long enough time he could do without sleep completely? Somebody ought to experiment along those lines. It might turn out to be a major contribution to science."

"I like to sleep," Barbara said.

"There's something to that, all right. We should never forget the positive value of sleep. You know, often we wish that things like death and sleep could be gotten rid of, but have you ever thought what it would be like to have to face the world all the time, not just three quarters of the time? Every hour of the day and night. During sleep the whole system is rejuvenated. Especially the brain. All the poisons that have accumulated during the waking hours are flushed out. Carried off by the blood. And if there were no sleep the peasants would have to work twenty-four hours a day instead of twelve. And if there were no death there would never be any escape for them."

"I suppose," Barbara said indifferently. She leaned back, stretching herself out on the grass, her eyes closed.

"Is that comfortable?" Carl asked.

"The sun's in my eyes. It looks all red."

"That's the blood in the capillaries of your eye lids. The sun is shining through them."

"Anyhow it's a beautiful red."

"Blood, fresh blood, is an amazing color. But as soon as it strikes the air it darkens and looks unhealthy. On the other hand, blood that has been exhausted of air turns a dark purple. It's blood coming from the lungs that's so fresh and red looking. Blood in the veins."

"Is that so."

"I guess it's not very important. Can I lay back down with you?"

"If you want."

Carl lay back on the grass, resting his head on his arm, a short distance from Barbara.

"You're interested in a lot of things," Barbara said.

"I guess I am."

"In a way I wish I had your enthusiasm. It's been a year since I read a whole book. I start reading, but I don't finish anything. I haven't done any real reading since I was in school. I used to read all the time, then. Books and books. Like the girl in the ad."

"The ad?"

"The girl without a date. In her room."

"Oh. That girl."

"But a friend tipped her off and everything changed. Toothpaste or mouthwash or deodorant. Or the right bra. I always thought that went a little more to the heart of things. The right bra. Those ads didn't mince around. The little profile ads on the back page of the newspaper."

"Books aren't really so important," Carl said. "I used to think so but I don't any more. I don't read as much as I used to. I'm getting out of the habit. For a while I was reading Proust. I read and read, but I never got through more than the first couple of books. I'd start a sentence and by the time it finished I'd have forgotten the beginning."

There was silence. "What part of the country do you come from?" Barbara murmured, after a time.

"Oh, we came originally from Denver. When I was about three we moved to California. My mother died while we were in California. I went to live with my grandparents. I moved around. I was living in St. Louis when I went to work for the Company. They moved me from the domestic branch over here. I applied for overseas work when I signed up."

"How long ago was that?"

"About five years ago. Good Lord. I've been working for the Company five years."

"How old were you when you started?"

"Eighteen. Almost nineteen."

"Why did you want to work for the Company?"

"The draft, partly. I was tired of school. I had been going to the university for a while. I wanted to get a job. And I wanted to get a job that would keep me out of military service. Sometimes I think I made a mistake, but at the time I really wanted to give up school and work."

"Why?"

"Well, I had been going to school so long. I was tired of being a school boy. I wanted to earn my own way. Support myself. Get out in the world."

"Don't you miss school?"

"I had already begun to lose faith in books."

"That early?"

"I lost faith in my books and my microscope and slides and Bunsen burner. My maps and notes and papers."

"Why?"

"Well, I was in a period of internal turmoil. I didn't know what I wanted to do. I had been interested in a lot of things, but they never turned into anything that was important. They never seemed to get out of the hobby stage. I found myself in a world that was made up of quite different things than my slides and notes and books. There didn't seem to be any connection between — between all the things in my room and what I ran into outside."

Barbara sat up. She took out her cigarettes and lit up. Carl watched her, turning his head on one side.

"How about you?" he said.

"Me?"

"Where did you come from?"

Barbara laughed. "From Boston."

"I thought you had a New England accent! I was right."

"It's not a New England accent. It's not anything. Damn

it — why do people always think they're so clever when they figure out where you come from?"

"I'm sorry."

"Boston people talk completely differently from me."

"I've never been in Boston. What's Boston like?"

"Like any other town, I suppose."

"What do you remember about it?"

"Not much. A few impressions." Barbara leaned back again, against the warm grass. She folded her arms, cigarette smoke drifting up. "When I think of Boston I remember the Common. I remember that first."

"The Boston Common?"

"It's like a park. A public park. When it was hot in the evenings, in the summer time, we used to go out and sleep on the grass. Like this. Warm and dry. With the sky full of endless stars."

"Was that the kind of weather you had there?"

"Not all the time." She laughed. "Sometimes we had the worst possible weather. One night I was walking home. I had a job as a waitress after school, in a one-arm beanery, near the campus. It was about midnight. All of a sudden it began to rain. Great sheets of rain, coming down, blowing along, trees bending, signs blown over. I started to run. I ran and ran until I came to the Common, all dark and soggy. I ran right across it. Finally I came to a wall of some sort. I hid under the edge of the wall, where the rain didn't come. Water was pouring down on all sides of me. Nobody was out. Nothing but rain. I got out my cigarettes and my matches. I was just beginning to smoke. I lit every match, all twenty, one after another. They were water logged, I guess. None of them lit. There was water dripping off me, my hair, my clothes. And no one around. Only the rain and the grass. And the wall behind me."

"That's what you remember about Boston?"

"Yes."

"Did you ever get home?"

"Finally."

Carl considered. "Strange how things like that will stick in your mind. Bits and fragments from your past. Snatches, like tunes. Phrases. A few words."

Barbara smiled. "Do you have a past, Carl?"

He nodded.

"How old are you? Twenty-three?"

"Yes. How did you know?"

"You were eighteen when you began to work for the Company. You said that was five years ago."

"Oh." Carl rubbed his chin.

"What's the matter?"

"I wondered if I looked twenty-three. Sometimes I think I look older, and then sometimes I'm sure I look just like some kid. When I go to shave in the morning I always get a sort of a shock. I think I'll see a kid of fourteen, with long shaggy hair and — and skin trouble."

"Do you want to be fourteen again?"

"No! I really don't. I'm glad it's behind me, all those years. My boyhood."

"You said you were interested in things, then."

"Yes. I had books, and drawings, and my microscope, and my electric motor, and the chemistry set. But there was a sort of unhealthiness about it. I was so much involved in things, running from one thing to another. Like ants running around a hot stove. Faster and faster. I had a whole roomful of things, boxes and piles and heaps. A desk of things, every drawer stuffed full. Maps on the walls. Rows of books. I stayed home from school all the time, to work on my things."

"Was that so bad?"

"There was something unhealthy about it. Inside my room — And outside, everything was different. Two worlds, my room full of things, and the things outside." Carl stared off into space, frowning. "It was hard for me to get across. Over to the outside things. There was something about them that didn't make sense. At least, the things in my room made sense. I knew what they were for. Why they existed and did what they did. But the things outside — "

"What happened outside?"

"I remember one thing. There was an old cat, a worn out old yellow tomcat that lived at the house behind us. All torn, ears cut, one eye missing, nothing left of his tail but the bone and a few patches of fur. He was old. Finally he got sick and lay out in the yard, their yard. The people who owned him never even went near him. He lay out in the long grass with the sagging porch swing and the beer bottles, with all the flies buzzing around him."

"I saw him out of the bathroom window, lying in the grass, gasping and dying. I went to the refrigerator and got some ground meat my mother was saving for supper. I took the meat out to him. The grass was long and wet. I remember how it felt under my feet, against my pants. It was hot — the sun was bright. I sat down on a board in the grass and pushed the food toward the cat. I was about nine years old, I think. I held out the food, but the cat was dead. For a long time I sat looking down at him. His one good eye stared sightlessly up at me. Flies crawled all over his skinny body, over his skin and fur, into his mouth. I would have dug a hole and buried him, but I didn't think of it. A boy of nine wouldn't know that. After a while I went back inside the house, and put the meat away."

They were silent. Barbara said nothing. A few birds came hopping across the lawn, past the garden of flowers, big dark birds, listening for worms. Carl watched them hopping by, cocking their heads, waiting, then going on. The birch trees by the side of the house swayed back and forth with the faint afternoon wind.

"It's too bad when people don't take care of their pets," Barbara said presently.

"Well, perhaps it was a good thing. At least, for me. It had quite an effect on me. I never really got over it. Seeing the cat there, in the wet grass."

"What kind of an effect?"

"It was the kind of thing that made me begin to lose interest in my hobbies. That made me see that something was wrong. I started moving away from all my hobbies and things. Once in a while I wish I had them back. Once in a while I find myself thinking about them. They filled up so much of my life. I could have gone on. Becoming a biologist. Something to do with microscopes and slides. Perhaps I should have. I dream about it. I dream about some old book store, with old adventure magazines piled up. Or a stamp store with rare stamps still on the old covers. I saved stamps and magazines. I had heaps of dusty things."

Carl closed his eyes, putting his arm across his face to blot out the sun. He sighed.

"It's nice," Barbara said.

"Yes, it's very warm and comfortable. The grass and the sun. Waiting for the new owners to come. Dozing and lying and waiting. While the grass grows around us. It's growing right now, while we're lying here. Up and up. Higher all the time." Carl's voice trailed off. "Up around us. Covering us."

"Why do you say that?"

"As if we had all died. All of us that are still here. The few still left. Stretched out calmly, with our arms folded across our chests. Waiting for the undertakers to come. That's them — the new owners. Our undertakers. Coming from over the hills. Soon we'll be able to hear the sound. The rumble of their — of their hearses. The distant rumble, coming closer and closer."

He yawned and became silent.

Barbara turned her head, gazing at Carl lying beside her, stretched out on the grass, his arm over his eyes, his mouth open. He looked very young. His skin was pale and clear. He was big. Six feet, probably. A lot bigger than most men she had known. But Carl wasn't a man. He was still a boy. A boy, thinking about his microscope and stamps and books.

But someday he would begin to get old, too. He would dry up and wither away like everyone else. What he said was true. They would all die, and their remains would be turned under the ground, under the damp ground. Under the grass. Where the sun didn't shine at all. Where it was cold and dark, and things moved around. Blind things, reaching and feeling. Cold clammy things that touched and felt. That oozed along.

Barbara sat up. Sweat trickled down the back of her neck. It was hot. A bright, hot day. She took a deep breath of the fresh air. It smelled good. It smelled of all the flowers and the birch trees. And the drying grass around them. She gazed down at the boy. He had taken his arm from his face. His heavy blond hair glistened in the sun. How smooth his skin was! Even his chin and neck. Did he really shave? Probably not very often. Barbara watched him for a long time without moving. He was big and young, very young. Still thinking about his childhood. He was like the day. Like the sunlight and the trees and the garden of flowers. He was blond and glistening and full of life. She could see perspiration glowing on his neck, above his shirt. He was warm from the sun; she was warm, too. She rubbed her arms, yawning sleepily.

Carl opened his eyes. "This is Mark Twain weather," he said. "Along the Mississippi. Catfish and rafts."

His eyes were blue. Warm, friendly blue.

"Makes you want to sleep."

"Then sleep."

"No." She drew back suddenly, away from him. "No thanks." For some reason she had thought of Verne, and the sagging cot in her room. The covers, the clothes. Verne and the cup of luke-warm whisky. "I've slept enough, in my time."

"You know, if a person computed the total hours spent in sleeping during his lifetime — "

"We already discussed that once, today."

"That's so. I guess we did. Sorry."

Barbara nodded.

"It's interesting, though," Carl said presently. "Interesting to think about. Sleep involves time. Time is the fundamental problem of philosophy." He waited hopefully, but Barbara said nothing. She had lit a second cigarette and was staring down at it, deep in meditation.

"What?" she said abruptly.

"I was just talking about time."

"Oh."

"What are you thinking about?"

"Nothing." She shook her head. "Nothing at all. Go on with what you were saying."

"I was just talking. You know, I've started an essay about this kind of thing. Time and change. Death, growth. Trying to sum up what I think. A sort of treatise."

She nodded.

"A summary of what I believe. A philosophical credo. I have it all wrapped up with brown paper and cord, to make sure nothing happens to it."

"Is it finished?"

"Almost. I have to get somebody to type it up for me. It's in longhand."

"What are you going to do with it?"

"I don't know. I'm not sure."

"Are you going to try to have it published?"

"Well, I could get it published, if I wanted. I know a woman that works for one of the big publishing places. But I don't think I'll do that." Carl plucked vaguely at a stalk of grass. "I think I'll just keep it around to look at, from time to time. It has no universal value. I may well be the only person who ever reads it."

"Maybe you could show it to me, sometime."

Carl brightened. "That's an interesting idea. I might read you parts of it. Not long parts, of course. A few sections here and there."

"That would be nice."

Carl warmed up. "You wouldn't mind, would you? If it bored you, we could stop instantly. Most of it is pretty dull, but you might be interested in some parts. I'll go over it and pick out the interesting parts. What do you say? Do you mind listening to some of it?"

"I'd like to." Barbara studied the boy thoughtfully. He was smiling at her, his eyes large and blue. Again she thought of him, standing timidly outside her door. Standing in the hall, gathering himself together to knock. Trying to get up enough courage to do what he wanted to do. Twice he had done that. The first night, while she was putting all her things away. And then again, while she and Verne were in the room together. Both times he had come, the big tall boy with his honest blue eyes, his blond hair. Siegfried . . . The innocent youth, come to redeem and save.

Carl's face was devoid of guile. His smile was warm and open, without secret meaning or intent. Now he wanted to read his essay to her. What did it mean? Anything beyond what he said it meant? No. Carl was as open and guileless as Christ Himself. If it were anybody else asking her — But she could not imagine him telling a lie. She could not imagine the great blond features screwed up into deceit.

"Yes, I'd like to," she said again.

"Fine."

Barbara got slowly to her feet, putting out her cigarette.

"Where are you going?"

"It's getting cold. I'm going in."

"Is it?" Carl scrambled up. "You're going inside already?"

"Want to walk along?"

"Sure. You're not — not mad at me, are you?"

"Mad? Why should I be mad?"

"I don't know. Do you mind listening to my essay? If you do, just say so."

"I don't mind."

"I don't want to impose on you."

"For Christ's sake!"

Carl shrank away, pain flushing across his face. Like a struck child. She was sorry instantly. She put out her hand, touching him on the shoulder.

"I'm sorry. I didn't mean to snarl. I have a lot on my mind. Things to worry about."

He blinked hopefully, regaining some of his lost joy. "I guess I talk too much."

Barbara put her arm through his. "Let's go. Come along. We'll get burned if we stay out any longer."

"That's right," Carl said. "It's hard to tell about that. The wind blows over you and gives you the false notion that you're not directly in the path of the sun's rays. You don't feel it, but all the time —"

He stopped, seeing that she wasn't listening. She was thinking again, far off in thought. Frowning a little. As if a bug were buzzing around her head, while she was trying to think. Carl became silent.

"Where shall we go?" Barbara said suddenly.

"Wherever you want."

"Let's go fix some coffee."

"All right."

"You can read to me tomorrow. How would that be? If it's a nice day. We'll sit outside and read."

"Fine." Carl beamed. "It's much more fun to read out in the sunlight, instead of inside. Reading inside has a kind of museum quality about it. Stuffy. Like dry dust."

Barbara walked across the grass, Carl following behind her. She felt vague annoyance; why did he have to worry everything to death? On and on he went, shaking each subject until there wasn't anything left in it.

But he was like a child. A big child that had never learned. She slowed down, waiting for him to catch up.

"The hills look nice," Carl said.

Already, he had forgotten. She sighed. Like some big overgrown child. "Yes, they look fine."

They walked along together. Carl put his hands in his pockets, kicking at rocks ahead of him. Neither of them said anything. Carl gazed around at the trees and the sky and the distant hills.

"If you find you don't enjoy it, after we start, all you have to do is just say so and I'll stop. I have a lot of good ideas, but that doesn't mean much. Everybody has good ideas. That doesn't mean another person would be interested."

"All right," Barbara said. "If I change my mind I'll tell you." She smiled a little. "Are you satisfied?"

"I don't want to impose on you," Carl said. He looked at her out of the corner of his eye.

Barbara nodded. "I get that impression."

12

"WHERE IS HE?" Barbara said. Verne was sitting on the edge of his bed, cleaning his pipe with a match and a strip of toilet paper.

"Where is who?"

"Carl. How many people are there here?"

Verne looked up at her, standing in the doorway. "He's shaving. Down at the bathroom. Why?"

Barbara came into the room. It was morning, a clear bright morning. Sunlight danced through the windows into the room, over the cots and chairs, the piles of clothing and neckties and men's shoes. "We're going hiking," Barbara said.

"Hiking? What's that a euphemism for?"

"We're going up in the hills and he's going to read his manuscript to me. Didn't he say anything about it? Wasn't he jumping up and down and telling about it sixty times?"

"No. He's been very quiet. What sort of manuscript? What's going on?"

"It's a philosophical treatise. A credo. All the many thoughts he's had about the universe and what makes it go."

"Does he know what makes it go? I'm beginning to get interested. Am I invited?"

"Not by me. Anyhow, you wouldn't enjoy it. We're going to sit and discuss and watch the wind blowing through the trees and the clouds crossing the sky."

Verne gave her an inscrutable glance. "Really? Is that so? Nothing else?"

"Stop fishing around. Of course nothing else."

"All right. I gather, however, that you're taking an interest in our young man."

"Our?"

"Don't you remember what we were saying — when was it? Yesterday. Or have you forgotten already?"

"We said a lot."

"About him. About the young blond-haired boy with blue eyes and an empty head."

"We said that?"

Verne studied her. "No. Not exactly. But something along those lines. Something about a youth, a virgin youth coming along. I guess you're all over your spell. You have certainly recovered quickly. No residue? Nothing left of all your fright? I can't believe you've completely forgotten."

"No. No, I haven't completely forgotten."

"Is that why you're going to hear his thesis? Because of yesterday? Because of what happened — to us?"

"Perhaps."

They stood looking at each other across the room. Distantly, down the hall, came the sound of water and somebody moving around. Somebody began to whistle.

"Since we're all going to have to live with each other I'd prefer to know him a little better." Barbara smiled at Verne. "I already know about you."

Verne shrugged. "It sounds like a good enough idea to me. Go ahead. I see nothing wrong with it. Except — "

"Except what?"

"If you're going to hang around him you should try to watch

your step. Sometimes you can rather foul up a naive person. The way you talk. You seem to have developed quite a brisk attitude toward childhood foolishness. If you want to get anywhere with Carl, don't be too harsh on him. He may tax your patience."

"So?"

"So watch out." Verne stood up, cocking his head on one side. "He'll be out in a minute. I see nothing wrong in your going around with him, but if you're not careful you can queer the whole thing right off the bat. As far as I'm concerned, I'd like to see something work out. After all, I have a stake in this, myself. Or so we seemed to believe the other day. In any case, remember this, when he starts rushing about, kicking his heels and jumping up in the air."

"I'm glad you approve of us. Thanks for all the benedictions."

"Not at all. Here he is."

Carl strode into the room, a shaving mug in one hand, a towel thrown over his shoulder. He was naked to the waist. At the sight of Barbara he stopped abruptly, his face turning red.

"Come in," Verne said. "It's just a friend."

"Hello," Carl murmured. "I was shaving."

"Then it's true," Barbara said.

"What's true?" Carl put down his mug and towel and slid into a sports shirt, buttoning it rapidly.

"That you shave."

Carl grinned sheepishly. "Why not?"

"I understand you're going up in the hills with this young lady," Verne said. "Why didn't you tell me about it? I feel left out."

"Sorry. I —"

"Am I invited? Can I come along? I wouldn't mind spending some time out of doors."

Confused, Carl glanced at Barbara. He twisted helplessly. "You want to come? I'm sorry I didn't say anything about it. I guess there's no reason why you can't come. Are you sure you want to come? It'll be very dull. If you want to come I guess it's all right. It's all right by me."

Verne pondered. "No. I have some work to do. I think I'll stick around here. You two young people go on alone. I'll be all right."

Barbara moved to the door. "Let's go. Let's get started before it heats up."

"It's going to be a wonderful day." Carl sat down on his cot and tied his shoes quickly. He bounced to his feet again. "Well, here we go. Goodbye, Verne. We'll see you later."

"Goodbye."

They went down the hall, downstairs, and out onto the porch. "You see?" Carl said. "Wonderful day. How could we ask for anything better?"

"Where's your manuscript?"

"My gosh. I forgot it. Wait." Carl went back into the building. "I'll run up and get it."

He clattered up the stairs. A few minutes later he returned, breathless and excited, holding a brown package under his arm.

"Is that it?" Barbara asked.

"That's it. Imagine forgetting it. I would have noticed, but not for a while."

"All right," Barbara said. "Let's head for the woods."

It took quite a long time to reach the woods. They left the Company property, passing beyond the strip that was the final marker, and began to climb. The woods were near the top of a long row of hills. Trees, crooked and bent, like ancient people too old to follow after the others who had left.

Carl and Barbara crossed a plowed strip and entered the first grove of trees, panting with exertion as they walked.

"Stop," Barbara gasped.

"Already?"

"I have to get my breath."

They stopped, turning to look back down. Below them, stretched out across the floor of the valley, was the Company, the towers and buildings, slag heaps, pits, open furnaces. Roads crossed here and there, roads and paths.

"How small it looks," Carl said. "From here it looks so small. I thought it was much larger. I guess it really isn't so much after all. I've never been outside of the grounds before, not since I first came. Now I'm standing on the outside again after years. It feels strange to look down at it from beyond."

"It does feel strange."

"Well, let's go." Carl started on, into the woods. "We have to find a place to sit down."

"Is it safe?" Barbara looked around them.

"Is what safe?"

"The woods. It looks so dark and hostile. Are there any animals or anything?"

Carl laughed. "Not any more. Company men went in and beat out everything, all the animals and snakes and birds they could find."

"Why?"

"I don't know. Company policy in a new location."

Barbara peered in between the trees. The woods were silent and dark. Nothing stirred. "I feel like Gretel. You're sure it's safe?"

"Come on." Carl went off first, leading the way, "I personally guarantee your safety."

He disappeared into the trees. Barbara followed slowly after him, her hands in the pockets of her slacks. She gazed up at the trees above her. At the masses of dark brush and weeds on all sides. Great roots twisted through the damp soil. Old roots. Bigger than the trees themselves.

"Coming?" Carl halted.

Barbara came up to him. "Yes."

"We better stay together."

"All right."

They tramped up the hill to the top. For a time they were on level ground. Then the hill sank abruptly, sliding down into a canyon below. Scrub plants grew in bunches at the bottom. The soil was dry and sandy. Carl and Barbara stood gazing down.

"Maybe we can read here. At the top." Barbara walked around, looking for a place. "How about over there under that tree?"

Carl stood with his hands on his hips, his brown paper package at his feet. "Isn't this something? We're at the top of the world. This is high. Do you know how high this is? We're on one of the highest plateaus in the world. This is old land." He waved his hand at the canyon and the hills beyond. "Very old land. This is the original continent. These hills have been weathered through millions of years."

"Oh?" Barbara sat down gingerly, at the foot of a great tree. She lit a cigarette.

Carl continued to stand. Hills and valleys, narrow canyons and flat stretches surrounded them on all sides, as far as the eye could see. In the distance, the mountains took on a bluish tint, an indistinct hue. The mountains went up, higher and higher. The highest were lost in the rolls of white clouds scattered across the sky.

"I feel like God," Carl announced.

"Why?"

"To be here. At the top of the world." He waved his whole arms, like a symphony conductor. "Look! I'm creating the world. Here it comes. Hold on tight."

His whole body moved as he swayed back and forth, as if he

were conducting some heavy masterpiece of the middle eighteenth century. He frowned, concentrating. He blond hair hung down, slapping against his forehead. Back and forth he swayed, eyes shut, jaw set.

Barbara watched silently, smoking and resting.

"Look! It's here!" Carl stepped back, throwing up his arms as if to protect himself. "Get back."

"What's here?"

"The world. I just made it. It's still hot. We'll have to wait for a while until it cools off." He came over to her, grinning down, his hands in his pockets. "Well? What do you think of it? Any suggestions?"

"For what?"

"Suggestions as to how it should be." He considered. "What'll I do with it? I have to put things on it. Men. I want human beings running around. No world's complete without people. Let's see." He folded his arms solemnly. "I wonder if there's anything better than men that's come along recently. Maybe there's something new. I better get hold of the monthly bulletins and study them."

Barbara shook her head.

"What's the matter?" Carl squatted down. His grin faded a little, shading into embarrassment. "Am I acting silly again?"

"No. It's all right."

"Wait." Carl went back to get his manuscript. "I left it behind again. You see? I forgot it. That shows something. It's very important, the way I keep leaving it behind me."

"What does it show?"

"It shows I don't really want it. It shows I want to get rid of it. It's a secret unconscious wish."

Barbara smiled. "Really?"

"It's true! I forget on purpose. That's what forgetting is. An unconscious act, getting rid of something you don't want. That's what Freud says."

He sat down beside her and began to unfasten the cord from around his package.

"You certainly have it all tied up," Barbara observed.

"I'm protecting it. It has to be safe from all harm. You see, if my unconscious wants me to get rid of it I have to fight all the harder *consciously* to protect it."

He folded the cord up and put it in his pocket. He removed the brown paper carefully.

"How does it look?" He held the package up.

"It looks fine."

"Well, that's half the battle." Carl slid the first few pages under. "Now the question arises as to just how it sounds."

He stroked the paper for a time, not saying anything but just sitting and holding his manuscript with his large, pale hands. Presently he reached up and pushed his hair back from his forehead.

"I'm ready," Barbara said. "Any time."

Carl nodded. "All right. It's quite a strange place here, isn't it? So silent. Not a sound. No one at all, anywhere around us. We might be the only two people left in the world. Like in those English doom stories that were popular in the thirties. Where the world has come to an end. Except for a young man and a young woman. No one else left but them. Civilization in ruins. Apes and bats running all over. Empty cities. And just the two of them, to rebuild the world."

"Do they?"

"Well, they have to get married first."

Barbara laughed.

"Why are you laughing?" Carl turned toward her.

"No reason."

"I used to read a lot of those stories. I have made a study of them. As near as I can tell, the first one of that type was written about nineteen-ten by George Allen England. It was a huge book called *Darkness and Dawn*. Nobody today remembers it."

"How did you come across it?"

"Oh, I found a copy in an old book store. That was a long time ago. When I was about thirteen. I don't remember very much about it. Except that the girl had long hair. And that — that their clothing had rotted away during all the years they were in suspended animation. And when she got up all her clothes fell away in pieces."

"Well, that's something to file away in your mind."

Carl nodded. "I guess so. Funny I remember that."

"Maybe sometime it'll turn out to be useful. A bit of information like that."

Carl gazed at her owlishly. Barbara smiled at him, her cigarette held loosely against her lips. She blew smoke lazily toward him. The smoke circled around him, dissolving in the air.

"Cigarette smoke looks so odd here," Carl said.

"Why?"

"We're so far from things like that. Cigarettes and radios and movies and bathtubs. All the things that go to make up our world." He gestured back the way they had come. "There it is down there. Our world. Like a little postage stamp, a little square behind us. And someday it'll be gone."

"I guess so."

"And soon. Only a few days. They'll be here in a few days. And that'll be the end."

"Why? Are they going to burn it all up?"

"It doesn't matter. For us, it's the end."

Barbara shook her head. "I don't understand."

"Whatever they do, it's the end for us. Because it won't be ours anymore. To do with as we want. It's only your world and my world as long as we have power over it. In a few days the power will pass from us into other hands. Then we'll leave. The three of us."

Barbara stubbed out her cigarette. "Do we have to talk about it? It depresses me."

"Why?"

"Well, it's so much like death."

Carl grunted. "It is, isn't it? But death is strange. You never know where it'll come from." He looked up at the sky. "For instance, a bird might drop half a clam shell down on us and kill one of us."

"Does that happen?"

"Once in a long while."

"Why would a bird be carrying a clam shell, for God's sake?" She lit a new cigarette.

"They take them up high to drop them on something. A stone, something hard. To break them open."

"We're a long way from the ocean."

"That's true. I guess it won't happen, then."

They were silent for a time, each of them deep in thought.

Finally Carl roused himself. He shuffled through the pages of his manuscript. "I guess I could start."

"Fine."

"I'll just read parts here and there. I don't want to bore you. It's all the philosophical notions I've picked up, from time to time. As soon as you're tired of hearing them, just nod to me and I'll stop."

"Okay."

Carl folded a leaf back, clearing his throat. He wiped his upper lip nervously. "Shall I start?"

"Yes, start."

Carl began to read, slowly, carefully, his voice low and intent.

. . .

After he had read for a long time he suddenly put the manuscript down and gazed over at Barbara.

Barbara stirred. "Go on."

"How does it seem to you?"

"Fine."

"I'm skipping quite a lot, of course. I mainly want to give you
the conclusions."

"So far it sounds fine."

"I'll read you some more, then."

Carl read on. Above them, great clouds drifted across the sky,
covering the sun. The air turned cold.

When Carl stopped to turn a page Barbara reached out and
touched his arm.

"What is it?" Carl blinked.

"I'm freezing."

"You are?"

"I sure am." She scrambled to her feet. "The fog's in."

Carl gaped up at her. "Are you *going*?"

"I think we should go back. We can read some more later on."
She held out her hand. "I'll help you up."

Carl was crestfallen. "I'm afraid you were bored."

"Bored, hell! I'm cold and damp, and I'm beginning to get
hungry."

"Hungry? Really?" He got up slowly, gathering together all
his papers and string and wrappers. Barbara caught hold of his
hand, pulling him toward her. "Thanks."

Her hand was firm and small. He could feel her hard nails
against his skin. He let go suddenly.

"What's the matter?" Barbara said.

"Nothing." Carl wrapped up his manuscript and tied the cord
around it. He pushed it under his arm and turned toward her.
"All finished."

Barbara began to brush bits of leaves and grass from her clothes. Carl watched. Presently he made a move to help, patting her gingerly with his big broad hand.

Barbara stopped, rigid.

"Did I hit you?" Carl said.

"No. I'm jumpy."

They looked at each other. Barbara smiled a little. Carl circled around her. "I'm sorry if I hit you."

"No. You didn't." She finished brushing herself off. "Come on. Back down to civilization."

Carl nodded, falling in beside her. They made their way back the direction they had come.

"I didn't hurt your feelings, did I?" Barbara asked.

"No."

She glanced at him. He was trudging along, his eyes on the ground, his face blank. Was he mad at her? Had she hurt his feelings? It was hard to tell; she knew so little about him.

"Watch your step," Carl murmured.

Dirt and leaves rained down the slope ahead of them, dislodged by Carl's huge shoes. He jumped down onto some big roots, helping her down beside him. He was strong. She could feel how strong he was. It was in his hands and arms. In his shoulders. She had felt it when he tried to brush her off. He had struck at her awkwardly, clumsily. Like some sort of big kindly animal. It was the strength of youth. Carl was very young.

But not really so young. Not much younger than she was. She had forgotten how young she was; she had thought for so long about her *age*, not her youth. Carl was not more than a few years younger than she. Not even that much. They were almost the same age. It was hard to believe, but it was so.

They were the same age, but their lives had not been the same. What kind of life had Carl lived? Books and stamps and microscope slides. A world of ideas. But that was not all. If it had been all, Carl would have gone on and become a biologist. He would still be peering through his microscope at his slides. No, there was more. He had lost faith in those things. Not completely, but somewhat. Enough so that he had given up his way of life. His roomful of stamps and books and maps and whatever else he had mentioned.

And in their place, what? What instead? What had he done? What had there been that he had not told her about? She watched him as he strode down, kicking dirt and leaves out of his way. It was hard to tell about him. Maybe he had done things he had not told her about. Things with women. But it was hard to imagine him with a woman. Very hard. It was not possible. He would have run away. She tried to picture him, the great blond boy, his cheeks red, his heart beating —

It could never happen. He would run off.

But she had been mistaken about another man. She had not understood him, and her misunderstanding had worked against her. This other man had appealed to her, too. But he had been very different from Carl. He had not been large; Verne was small and slender. And he was older, not younger than she. Verne was not some friendly, excited animal. He was crafty and cynical, behind his horn-rimmed glasses, with his pipe and his talk and his thin, nervous hands.

She had learned a lot from Verne. There was no getting around that. It had made her wary. She would never go to another man the way she had gone to Verne, naked and warm and blushing, ready to be taken. Taken so easily, as if it were nothing. It would never happen that way again. She was much too wary, now. No man would have her like that again.

But Carl wasn't a man. He was a boy, a huge, excited boy. It was not the same thing at all. Carl had come to a ledge and was waiting for her, looking up anxiously at her, his big face full of alarm. She smiled down at him, down at his warm blue eyes, so innocent and concerned.

"Thanks," she murmured.

It was not the same at all. She reached out, and Carl took hold of her hands. Barbara jumped down, gasping. She came to rest beside him, panting and flushed. They were getting to the bottom, down onto level ground again. Carl was still holding onto her hands, gripping her hands tightly with his own. She did not pull away.

"We're almost there," Carl said.

Barbara nodded. His hands felt good, wrapped all around her own. She stood quietly, head down a little, by the great blond boy. This was so different, so far removed from all the things that had come before. All the things that had happened to her. It was nice, the pressure of his hands, the cold wind moving through the trees and bushes around them. The silence. No one to bother them. They were completely alone.

Barbara closed her eyes. She felt her body relax. Her arms, her shoulders, her face muscles were beginning to loosen. Her whole frame seemed to be giving away. Like a heated candle it seemed to be melting down, dissolving, a sudden softness creeping through every part of her. What an odd feeling! Would her arms come off, her fingers drop off, now that there was no support, no form on which they could be fastened?

She felt shaky, unsteady on her feet. Inside her all her parts were oozing and thawing. Her organs, the organs of her body, must be bleeding. Blood must be running down them, dripping and dropping, forming puddles and pools, warm and thick. What an awful thought! But that was the way it felt. The melting of her insides continued. She thought of the old fairy story about the princess who had a heart of stone. A heart of rock, hard, heavy, lodged inside her like shot.

Her whole body was like this heart. And now it was dissolving back into blood and liquid, wavering and swimming into itself, murky and heated. Heated from underneath, like a caldron bubbling in some witch's cave.

"Are you all right?" Carl said. "You look so strange."

"I'm all right."

She thought how the sun had set fire to her that morning, when she had awakened and found her room warm and bright, rays of sunlight streaming across her, across her bed. Heat was good. It drove off the cold and wet. Cold and wet — She felt suddenly terrified. In cold and wet she might rust or freeze. She needed the sun. Something had to be there, shining around her, warming her, driving off the dampness. Something from outside. The internal fire was not enough. It did not stay long enough to melt everything.

Barbara set her lips. Already, she could feel her organs settling back into their cold shapes. The warmth in her was exhausted, worn out. It was leaving again, as quickly as it had come. The cold was seeping back.

She shuddered. "It's cold."

"Yes. We better go." Carl took his hands away.

"Wait."

He stopped, questioningly.

"Wait. For me." She stepped quickly down beside him, walking close by him. "The god damn wind."

"Oh."

Barbara rubbed her arms. "I'm freezing. When we get back we can fix coffee."

"All right."

"Carl, don't go so fast. Wait for me."

Carl slowed down, waiting for her to catch up with him. He was so big — he moved so quickly, crashing down the slope. She was afraid, of the cold wind, the rows of twisted, silent trees. There was no one around for miles. Only silent trees and wind and the fog coming down from the sky, blotting out the sun. Suppose Carl left her? Suppose they got separated? Suppose she were left behind?

"Damn it!" Barbara said. "I can't walk as fast as you can."

"Sorry."

She was breathing quickly, her face flushed. Carl glanced at her, puzzled. She was walking with her head down, stepping carefully. Was she angry at him again? What had he done this time? Carl shook his head. It was hard to tell, with her. Maybe he had read too long.

"We'll be down soon," he murmured.

She nodded.

"I guess we stayed up here too long. I lose track of time when I'm reading. That's a funny thing. The way time gets longer or shorter, depending on what you're doing. Like at the dentist's office. Every second seems like an hour."

He glanced at her but she said nothing.

"That's not just an illusion," he murmured. "As I recall, Einstein mentions it in his theory. About how time is elastic."

They walked in silence.

"Next time we won't have to stay so long." Carl gripped his package sadly against him. "I'm sorry I made you stay so long. I can see you're mad at me."

"I'm not mad."

"I can tell."

"How?"

"By the way you look."

"How do I look?"

"Your face is red and you're not saying anything. That means you're mad. Maybe I should throw the whole thing away. Maybe that would be best." Carl lifted up the brown package. "I think I'll throw it as far as I can. I used to be pretty good at discus throwing. In school I was second on our team."

He stopped, legs wide apart, body bent to one side, the package swinging back and forth. He closed one eye, his body tense. He took careful aim.

"Watch. I'm going to throw it over that group of trees. I used to be able to heave things that far."

"Are you sure you want to do it?"

Carl hesitated, wavering slightly. "Will you let me read some more of it to you?"

Barbara laughed. "Of course."

Broad smiles broke out all over Carl's face. "I guess I won't do it, then." He put the manuscript back under his arm. "I'll keep it a while longer."

"That's good."

"You're not mad at me any more. Your face isn't flushed with rage."

"Really?"

"I guess you've decided to forgive me." Carl was beginning to regain his enthusiasm. "I'm glad. I can't see why people stay mad. Quick to anger, quick to forgive. The Irish are that way. That's the only way to be. You should never allow emotion to cloud your rational mind for very long. It's impossible to make decisions when you're emotionally dominated. Emotion is like liquor or drugs. It distorts reality for you. You can't see clearly."

"Is that so?"

"Someday I'm going to make a study of things like that. The non-rational influences that overcome man."

Suddenly Barbara stopped. "Look."

"What? What is it?"

"It's Verne."

Somebody was coming across the plowed slope toward them, walking slowly across the brown soil. Verne gazed up at them through his glasses as he came nearer, his hands in his pockets, his pipe between his teeth.

"Greetings," he said, stopping.

Carl's joy faded. "Hello, Verne," he murmured.

"What you been doing? You're all over leaves and bits of grass." Verne brushed Carl's shoulder.

"We've been reading," Carl said.

"Well, well."

"Come on," Barbara said, continuing down the slope. "Let's go."

The two men followed her.

"You're going back with us?" Carl asked Verne.

"Might as well. Nothing else to do."

"What were you doing out here?"

"Just wandering around. Did you have a good time with your treatise?"

"All right."

"Good."

"We're going to fix something to eat."

Verne showed interest. "Really? Sounds interesting. What sort of something? I might come along."

"Come along if you want," Carl said indifferently.

"Thank you."

"I thought you said you had work to do."

"Oh, I finished that."

Carl said nothing for a while. At the bottom of the slope Barbara stopped and waited for him and Verne to catch up with her. She noticed that his joy had fled.

"Why the glum look?"

"No reason."

"I'll tell you what. Would you feel better if I fixed you some waffles?"

Carl brightened. "Sure. That would be fine."

"We don't have a waffle iron," Verne said sourly. "We already went through that, once."

The three of them went on, back toward the Company grounds.

13

By evening the fog had come in over all the world. Verne carried a big floor lamp from the manager's house over to the dorm. He plugged it in by his bed and clicked it on.

"That's a lot more cheery," Carl said. He went to the windows and pulled the shades down, one by one. The room filled with yellow light from the floor lamp.

Verne kicked off his shoes and stretched out on his bed, picking up a book. He found his place, adjusting his glasses and pushing the pillow behind him.

"I guess I'll go to bed," Carl said.

"Fine."

"I can't think of anything else to do." Carl sat down and untied his shoe laces. He unbuttoned his shirt and tossed it over a chair.

"Fine," Verne murmured.

Carl got his pajamas out. He finished undressing and began to put the pajamas on.

After a while Verne looked up from his book. "Have a good time today?"

"Sure."

Verne lowered his book. He contemplated Carl for a long time without speaking. It made Carl feel uneasy. He finished putting on his pajamas and moved aimlessly around the room, picking up things and laying them down.

"Sure I had a good time. It's nice to have someone to read my concepts to. I don't often get the chance."

"Everything go all right? Did she listen?"

"Of course." Carl lifted his bedcovers back. "I guess I'll go to bed. I'm tired. I think I'll lie in bed and meditate. I've noticed that you can think more clearly while you're laying in bed. Your mind is freer from strain."

He got into bed.

Verne continued to study him. Carl pulled up his covers around his chin. He lay on his back, gazing up at the ceiling above him.

"Are you meditating now?" Verne asked.

"I'm just beginning."

"How does it feel?"

"Very restful." Carl closed his eyes. "After I've meditated for a long time I drift slowly to sleep. There's no sudden break between meditation and sleep."

"I can believe that."

"You wouldn't mind moving your light around just a little, would you? It's easier to do this when there's not so much light."

Verne moved the lamp back.

"Thanks. That's a lot better." Carl took several deep breaths, trying to relax. But he did not seem to be able to relax. After a while he opened his eyes again. Verne had picked up his book and was reading.

How small Verne was. Small and thin. His wrists were nothing but bone. A little dried-up thing, sitting on the bed, reading silently.

"What's the book?" Carl asked presently.

"*Three Soldiers.* Dos Passos."

"Is it good?"

"It's all right. I've read it before."

"You're reading it again?" Carl sat up in bed. "How come?"

"I enjoy it."

"What's it about?"

"The First World War."

"It's a war novel?"

Verne sighed. He slid off the bed, getting slowly to his feet. "Here." He tossed the book over onto Carl's bed. "If you want to read it, go ahead. It isn't mine. I picked it up while I was in the manager's house."

Carl picked up the book and examined it. "I'd like to read it sometime."

"Fine."

Carl watched Verne, mildly astonished. Verne was getting ready to go to bed. He unfastened his shirt cuffs and removed his glasses.

"You're going to bed?"

"That's right."

"Because of me?"

Verne considered. "No. No, not because of you."

"Why, then?"

Verne grunted. He unbuttoned his shirt and tossed it over the back of a chair. For a time he stood scratching himself, yawning and blinking. He looked very odd without his glasses. There were circles around his eyes, wrinkles and lines. He gazed half-blindly ahead of him, as if he could barely see. His chest was small and thin, with almost no hair on it. He was scrawny.

Carl felt a pang of pity. "You know, you should get out in the sun more. You should exercise."

"Christ," Verne said, in the middle of a yawn. He set his jaw. After a moment he reached around and found his glasses. He fitted them back into place. "Maybe I don't want to go to bed after all."

"If you're not sure you can sleep then don't go to bed. That's what causes most insomnia. People going to bed just because they feel it's time to go to bed, when they don't really feel sleepy."

Verne nodded absently, looking around the room.

"You could tell me about Jackson Heights, Maryland," Carl asked.

"Why?"

"Didn't you tell me you came from there? I'd like to hear about it."

"Why do you want to know about it?"

"I'm always interested in places I've never been."

"You wouldn't be interested in Jackson Heights."

"How do you know?"

"No one is." Verne picked up his shirt and began to put it back on again.

"You're not going to bed?"

"No."

"What are you going to do?"

"I don't know. Walk around outside for a while."

"It's cold outside. Wait until daytime so you can get a tan. A good healthy tan wouldn't look bad on you. We could do something. Can you play chess? I have a pocket chess set."

"Oh?"

Carl sprang out of bed. "They're fun. The men all lock into place. You can close up the board and leave the men where they are. Then you can finish the game later on. I use it to work out chess problems. You see chess problems in all the newspapers."

He rummaged in his dresser drawer, looking for the little chess set.

"Never mind," Verne said wearily. "I'm going outside anyhow." He moved toward the door, rolling up his shirt sleeves.

Carl straightened up. "Verne — Can I ask you something?"

"What is it?"

"You're not mad because Barbara and I went up into the hills, are you?"

"Why should I be mad?"

"Well, you knew her in the past. You're old friends. And I hardly know her at all. And — " He hesitated, smiling. "And after all, I'm so much younger than either of you two."

"How old are you?"

"Twenty-three."

"That's about the same as Barbara."

"But she *seems* so much older. You and she have done so many things I don't know anything about."

"What sort of things?"

"I don't know. But I can tell by the way you two talk. You're old friends, and you lived in New York. And you have a lot in common. That's important. You have a great range of common experience. Things you've done and seen."

Verne considered, standing by the door to the hall. He twisted back and forth, frowning. "I don't know. It's hard to say. About Barbara. Maybe she is too old for you. It's a difficult question. You have to work it out for yourself. I can't work it out for you. But I think you're overrating her experience. I doubt if she's been around as much as you seem to think."

"It's terrible to be too young," Carl murmured.

"Is it?"

"I keep telling myself that eventually I'll be as old as everyone else, but by that time they'll be even older. I'll never catch up."

"You can also be too old," Verne said.

"I suppose so. I know some people feel that way. But that's certainly just an academic problem to me. When you're too young you feel left out. You haven't done any of the things other people have done. Every time you open your mouth you say something foolish. Like — like a kid."

Verne opened the door. "Well, don't worry about it."

Carl followed after him plaintively. "But look, Verne. I wish you'd tell me what you think. Am I too young for Barbara? If I am, then maybe I better forget about her."

"What exactly did you have in mind?"

"I don't know. I just meant our being together. Like today." Carl smiled his wide, honest smile. "I enjoy being with her. It's nice to have somebody to read to."

"You're not too young to read to her, for Christ's sake."

Carl was silent. "I wouldn't want to be with her if she were laughing at me," he murmured.

"I don't think she is."

"What do you think I should do?"

"Well, I wouldn't give up. At least, not for a little while. Try it out."

"You think it's all right, then?"

Verne took a deep breath, a weary breath. "I don't know. It's a deep problem. Only time will tell. Maybe one day we'll know."

"I went out during high school to dances, and there was a club I was in that had parties once in a while. But I never went around with girls much. I was always reading or doing that sort of thing. I was never very lucky with girls."

"I'll see you later." Part of Verne disappeared into the hall.

"When will you be back?"

"I don't know." Verne closed the door after him. He was alone in the gloomy hall. "I have no idea."

Barbara's light was visible, gleaming through the darkness above him as he mounted the stairs to the porch of the women's dorm building. He entered the dark corridor and climbed to the second floor. Barbara's door was partly open, down the hall ahead of him.

"Who's there?" Barbara stepped out into the hall.

"Me."

"For God's sake. What are you doing around here so late?" She had been brushing her hair. In one hand she held her brush, tapping it against her leg angrily. She had on dirty army pants and a bra. Her feet were bare.

"I got restless."

They stood looking at each other, Barbara tapping her brush, Verne plucking aimlessly at his shirt cuff. In the dim light from the lamp, shining out into the hall, the girl's bare arms and shoulders glowed and sparkled, each tiny hair distinct and alive.

"You just took a bath," Verne said. "You're still damp."

"Well?" She put her hands on her hips. Verne gazed down at her bare feet.

"Well what?"

"What do you want? Do you want to come in?"

"I suppose so. May I?"

"I don't know."

Verne scowled. "You don't know? That's a new one. Why not? What's the matter?"

There was silence.

"Why can't I come in?"

Barbara turned abruptly, going back into her room. "All right. Come on."

Verne followed after her. She closed the door to the hall. The room was tidy and neat. All the clothing had been put away. Prints were up on the walls. And there was even a vase of flowers on top of one of the dressers.

"Nice," Verne said. He sat down in a chair, crossing his legs. "Combing your hair?"

"Yes." Barbara sat down on the bed. She had fixed up a mirror. She began to brush again, moving the brush through her heavy dark hair, slowly and regularly.

"You have nice feet," Verne said presently.

"Thanks."

"I'm sorry to bother you."

"That's all right." Her voice was distant. Remote. She went on brushing, frowning into the mirror, her head on an angle.

"Have a good time today?"

She shot him a glance. "When?"

"Up in the hills."

"Not too bad. It got a little too cold and damp for me. The ground doesn't dry out completely."

"It will later on."

"We won't be here later on."

"That's true. But you did have fun?"

"Yes. I suppose you'd call it that."

Verne got up and wandered around the room. He stopped at the dresser, examining the vase of flowers. "What sort of flowers are these?"

"Roses."

"They're too small to be roses."

"Well, then I don't know."

There was silence. Barbara went on brushing her hair. Verne stooped down to see what books were in the bookcase. He pulled one out and thumbed through it.

"Ezra Pound. How are these?"

"*Personae*? Not bad. It was a gift."

"A gift."

"From Felix and Penny."

"Oh." Verne put the book back into place. "How are they? I haven't heard from them for a long time."

"They have a child. A boy."

"I knew that."

"Then you know as much as I do."

Verne smiled. "Thanks."

"Perhaps more." Barbara studied him. "What's on your mind? I can tell something's going on inside. You're restless. Jumpy."

"Am I?"

Barbara put down her brush. She turned to face him. "Has it got anything to do with our going up into the hills today?"

Verne was silent. He rubbed his chin thoughtfully. "I don't know. I really don't know."

"It does have something to do with it."

"Maybe so."

Barbara walked across the room to the closet and took down a jacket. She put it around her, fastening the cord into place. A long-sleeved jacket, pale yellow. She returned to the bed and seated herself. From her purse she took a cigarette and lit it slowly. "It was your idea, you know. You suggested it."

"I did?"

"You wanted to bring him in." She shook her head. "Sometimes I don't understand you. What *do* you want, Verne? First you say — "

"Let's not argue. I'm too tired."

Barbara leaned back, blowing smoke toward him in a great cloud. The smoke mixed with the light from the lamp. "It would be interesting to know what goes on inside all the nooks and crannies of your mind. I guess it would take a first-rate analyst to figure out what's the matter."

"There's nothing the matter. I just came over to spend a little time with you. That's all."

"Really?"

"Can't we sit and talk? Have we got to the point where we can't do that anymore?"

"We can talk for fifteen minutes." She looked at her watch. "Then I'm going to bed."

"You're pretty damn hostile, all of a sudden."

"Reaction to yesterday. I'll get over it. In time."

"That's good." Verne tried to make himself comfortable on the chair, drawing his feet under the chair, his arms folded. "Brrrrr. It's chilly in here."

"Is it?"

"You know, it's odd. All this. What you're doing. In a way I can take a detached interest. A sort of impersonal intellectual interest. The way Carl would."

"Interest in what?"

"In what you're doing. The way you're acting toward me. What you're doing right now."

"I wasn't aware I was doing anything."

"Your hostility. You blame me even more, don't you? More than you did before — before yesterday. And if it ever happens again you'll blame me just that much more. Every time it happens you'll go through the same business. You were done in. Robbed. It was all my idea. I made you do it. I held you down on the bed and unbuttoned your pants."

"Is that what I think?"

"Something like that. A period of time goes by, after it happens. After yesterday. You forget what really happened. That it was as much your idea as it was mine. You forget all that part. All you remember is that it did happen. Again. And you blame me. I can see it settling down over you like a shroud. A shroud of outrage. Frigid hostility toward me. But there's no use blaming me. It was your fault, too."

Barbara nodded. "I know."

"Do you?"

"Yes. I know. Now, does that settle it? Can we let the matter drop?"

Verne was nettled. "I suppose so." He cleared his throat. "What ever you want."

"I'd like to drop it."

"All right. We'll talk about something else. How much time do we have?"

Barbara looked at her watch. "About ten minutes."

"Good." Verne considered. "Let's talk about what you did today. You say you enjoyed yourself? You had fun?"

"Yes."

"What's his treatise all about?"

"Ethics. Something to do with morals. The power of reason. Free will. I dozed a little."

"Was it confused?"

"No. It was clear enough. But I got to thinking about other things."

"Is he going to read more to you?"

"Yes."

"Soon?"

Barbara did not answer.

"What's the matter?" Verne said.

"Why do you care if he's going to read more?"

Verne stood up. "I guess I'll leave. You can't keep from turning your guns on me, can you? You're full of resentment and it's me you want to fight."

Barbara shrugged. "Go if you want to go. You have about seven minutes left."

"I'll stay." He sat down heavily, sagging against the chair. For a time he sat, his legs crossed, picking at his sleeve. "Carl liked to read to you," he murmured after a while. "He says it means a lot to him."

"Good."

"He's beginning to like you. Before I came over here he wanted my advice."

"On what?"

"On whether you're too old for him."

"Old? Too old in what way?"

"He wasn't sure. He didn't know what way. Maybe he hasn't found out yet what ways exist."

"Maybe not."

"But he is beginning to get interested in you. In some vague manner. A kind of sense that you make a good companion to read to. Very general and nebulous. Nothing to do with sex. He's a strange kid. He's very alert in an intellectual way. There's nothing stupid or dumb about him. But in certain areas his mind doesn't seem to function. Dead spots. As if he didn't understand or hear."

"He's led a different life from us."

"Maybe that's it. He frisks around like a great big colt. I have the feeling you could shout and shout like hell at him and he'd never hear you."

"It would depend on what you were shouting."

"True. But you are going to let him read his stuff to you again?"

"Yes. You don't object do you? Yesterday you seemed to think — "

"No. I don't object. You go ahead, if that's what you want to do. It's probably the right thing. I'm not sure anymore. I guess we have to be saved somehow."

Barbara nodded.

Verne eyed her. "Is — is that it? Is that what all this is about? You want to try to shake me off and get away from — from everything I represent?"

Barbara did not answer. She sat smoking silently, staring off into the distance. Verne shifted uneasily.

"Say something, damn it! Answer me."

"That's part of it, I suppose."

"Then you want to call it quits between us?"

"I thought we had already decided that."

"Not in so many words."

"That was my impression. Isn't that what we were going to do? Yesterday—"

"We talked about it. Had we made up our minds?" Verne's voice was low and dry.

"I thought so."

"I see. Well, I guess maybe you're right. The whole thing is settled, then? You're going to wash off your sins in lamb blood." Verne got up and moved to the door. He stood by the door, lingering. "Remember one thing, though."

"What's that?"

"You have to slaughter the lamb to get the blood."

"That's so."

Verne shoved his hands in his pockets. "You know, Barbara, I think in a lot of ways you're taking the wrong attitude."

"Oh?"

"This sort of thing never works out. It's like what you do on New Year's Day. Resolutions. That all the wicked old habits are going to be kicked out the window. But after a couple of days there they are back again. Just as before. Resolutions don't work."

"What works, then?"

"I don't know. Genuine conversions, I suppose. I don't know much about that. But the Church says that works. Where the whole soul is lifted. Not just the soul's face."

"Maybe this is a conversion."

"You still look the same." He walked back toward her. "In fact, you look pretty good. Not half bad. Even in bare feet and dirty pants. And your jacket hanging out."

"It was your idea. You saw it before I did. That through him—"

"Christ. A story. A ghost story to scare us. The kind of thing you think up at night."

"We were scared, weren't we?" Barbara said softly. "We were both scared. Even you, Verne. You were scared, too. Along with me."

"That was yesterday." Verne grinned crookedly. "A whole day and a half ago. You're not still thinking about it, are you?"

"Yes."

"I advise you to forget it. I've changed my mind. You can ignore my previous suggestions. I've changed my mind about it."

"I haven't."

Verne laughed. He sat down on the bed beside her. "Carl is too big. He'll squash you to death. You won't live through it."

Barbara smiled stiffly.

"Do you want to have someone around like that? Running back and forth, knocking over things, talking all the time? Wait a while. Maybe somebody better will come along. Somebody even purer. More innocent. More virgin. Just wait. You don't want to pick up the first stick you see. The woods are big."

"And full. I remember that phrase."

Verne put his hand on her shoulder. "Wait until you see the dove fly up. Don't rush into this. You have a long life ahead of you."

Barbara did not answer. Verne put his arm around her, rubbing her neck. Her skin was warm and a little damp, above the collar of her jacket, where her dark hair ended. He rubbed slowly, pressing his fingers into her firm flesh. Barbara said nothing. She swayed a little with the motion of his fingers. In the ashtray her cigarette burned down. Smoke drifted into the lamp, circling slowly around the shade.

"It's nice in here," Verne murmured.

"Yes."

"You've made this room into something."

"Thank you."

"I remember that. It's been a long time, but I still remember that. How you changed that other room. In Castle. At that party. Do you remember? That was when I first saw you. You were sitting there, at the end of the room. All by yourself. All alone. But you did something to that room, too. The same way. You changed it. The way you've changed this room."

"I remember."

"That was a long time ago. So many things have happened since then."

Barbara nodded a little. "Yes."

Verne's fingers tightened against her neck. She was rigid and tense. He could feel her taut muscles under the skin. Like steel cables. "Relax. You're all wound up."

She relaxed a little.

"That's better. Don't be wound up. Is there anything wrong?"

"I guess not."

He rubbed her neck slowly, around and around. She leaned back, closing her eyes.

"Fine. Do you mind if I do this? You don't mind, do you? It's good for you."

"Is it?"

"Of course. Physical therapy. Doctor's recommend it. It's considered very soothing."

Barbara nodded. "Yes. It's soothing."

"Good. Then you don't mind?"

For a long time she did not answer. Verne watched her. The girl's eyes were still shut. She seemed to be a long way off. Far away from him. What was she thinking about? There was no way to tell by looking at her. He did not say anything. Her flesh felt good under his fingers. Warm and full. He touched her hair. Hard, dry hair. It was good, too. His fingers pressed against her muscles and tendons, into the warm flesh.

Barbara sighed.

"All right?" Verne said. He moved closer to her. The room was still. Neither of them spoke.

"Verne."

"What?"

"When you found out how young I was you should have let me go. It was wrong. I was too young."

"For God's sake! Can't you forget that ever?"

"Why didn't you let me go? Why did you go ahead with it? You knew and yet you went ahead."

"It didn't hurt you any. Did it?" He looked into her face. "It didn't hurt you. Not too much. How long ago that was. It seems strange to be sitting here talking about it. Another world. Another time stream. You were so mixed up in those days. A girl playing at being an adult. You were so scared of men. I could see that. You were shaking with fear. And it made you gruff. You chased men off by being gruff and harsh."

"Why did you come near me?"

"You were pretty. You looked very nice. You still do, Barbara." His fingers pressed against her neck, suddenly unmoving. "You still look very nice. That hasn't changed at all. Perhaps some things have changed. But not that. You're a grown woman, now. You're not a little girl playing games. Now you're grown up. You've come into bloom. Your hair. I can see it in your hair. Your eyes. Your whole face. Your body. It's there, everywhere in you. Do you know it? Do you realize it?"

She nodded.

"It's strange to see that come into existence since we were together before. It was there, in a way. Not like now. Not full, like this. Perhaps only the first trace. I saw a little of it, then. Traces here and there. But not what I see now. Not this."

He touched her cheek. Her shoulder. She moved under his

touch. He drew his fingers along the sleeve of her pale jacket. The fabric was sheer and strange, still cold from the closet. He pressed it against her arm. Through the fabric he could feel the warmth of her arm, through the coldness of the cloth. Warmth. He leaned toward her, looking into her face. Her eyes were still shut, closed tightly together. She breathed slowly, evenly, her mouth open.

He touched her throat, running his fingers over her bare flesh, where the folds of the jacket came together. She quivered, tensing under his fingers, the muscles moving.

"It's all right," Verne said.

She did not answer. He watched her silently. She said nothing. Presently he kissed her, tasting her hard mouth. She did not stir. He kissed again, feeling her lips, cold and hard, against his own. Her teeth.

"Barbara?"

She moved a little. He put his hands on her warm shoulders, drawing back a little. After a time she opened her eyes. "Yes?"

"How — how do you feel?"

She shook her head.

"I wish you'd say something." He waited. His hands pressed into her shoulders. He ran his fingers over her arms, over the pale fabric. Still she did not speak. He could feel her breasts against his arms, below his wrists. He moved his hands from her arms, covering her breasts with his fingers. Under his fingers her breasts rose and fell, again and again. Her heart. He could feel her heart beating, beneath the full cups of her breasts. His hands moved upward again, toward her neck. He pulled her toward him.

"Barbara — "

"Yes?"

"Isn't this all right? Is there anything wrong with this?"

He kissed her again, on the cheek. She looked up at him as he pulled away. Her eyes were bright. In the half-darkness of the room they gleamed, sparkling and dancing.

"Your eyes are so bright."

"Are they?"

Again he pressed his fingers into her neck, where her hair ended, above the collar of her jacket. Neither of them spoke. Time passed. Barbara sighed once, shifting a little on the bed.

"I wish I knew how you felt," Verne murmured.

"Don't you know?"

"No."

"It's strange that you don't know. I thought you knew so much about women."

"Well, not everything. How do you feel? Don't you want to tell me?"

"You've known so many. Done so much. It's very strange that you don't know. Yes, it's nice here, Verne. I worked a long time on this room. I'm glad you enjoy it."

Verne waited a while, watching the girl beside him. Barbara's face was expressionless. He could not read anything there. She stared ahead of her, into the distance. He could see her nostrils flare a little as she breathed. Under her long pale jacket her chest rose and fell.

"Real nice," he murmured.

Barbara stirred a little, reaching out to stub the remains of her cigarette against the side of the ashtray. She leaned forward, bending over her purse. Her warm neck slipped from between his fingers. Verne lowered his arm slowly.

Barbara lit a new cigarette, shifting on the bed and leaning back. She blew smoke past him, folding her arms. Verne reached out his hand toward her.

She shook her head. "No."

"No?"

"Don't."

Verne let the air out of his lungs. He said nothing. Beside him the girl smoked quietly to herself, so close to him that he could see the pores of her skin, the faint lines around her nose, the chipped edge of her thumb nail where her hand rested against her lip, against the white of her cigarette.

There was no sound. Outside the building a feeble wind rustled the trees, stirring the branches together. The room was cooling off. What heat there was had already begun to drain away, drifting out through the cracks in the walls, under the door, past the windows, out into the night. The night was full of fog. He had seen it as he made his way from the men's dorm. Wet fog, masses of it everywhere, over everything. Fog outside, silent fog.

Barbara looked at her wristwatch. "Time for bed."

"So soon?"

"Afraid so." Barbara stood up.

Verne got to his feet. "I guess it's time to go, then."

Barbara, her cigarette between her lips, bent over the bed, throwing the covers back. She smoothed down the sheets with her hand. The last wrinkle disappeared. The bed was smooth and even.

"I'll see you," Verne murmured. He wandered over to the door.

"All right." Barbara started to unfasten her long flowing jacket. But then she stopped.

"What is it?" Verne said.

"I'll wait until you're gone." Barbara stood with her fingers against the cord of her jacket, waiting.

"You don't have to make such a god damn big thing out of it!"

"I'm tired. Good night, Verne. I'll see you."

"You really mean it, then."

"Mean it?"

"About all this. About Carl. And me."

"It's the best thing."

Verne twisted. "But damn it — We've known each other a long time. This sort of thing never works. These New Year's Day resolutions. After a little while the old leaf slips back."

Barbara nodded.

"It's true," Verne murmured. He gazed across the room at the bed. "You don't think — just for old time's sake — "

"No."

Verne sagged. "All right." He opened the door and moved out into the hall. "Well, I'll see you."

"Good night."

Verne went slowly down the hall. Barbara waited a minute. Then she closed the door. She stood listening. She could hear him walking slowly downstairs, onto the front porch, then down the front steps onto the gravel path. The sounds died away. Everything was quiet.

She looked at her wristwatch, winding it thoughtfully. "That was more than fifteen minutes," she said half-aloud.

She unfastened her jacket and got ready for bed.

14

THE MORNING WAS warm and bright. But not too bright. And there was enough of a breeze to keep the heat down. The sky was clear of fog. It stretched out, blue and uniform, on and on. Forever. Without end.

Barbara walked aimlessly along the path, between the great towers and buildings of the Company. She walked with her hands behind her back, gazing around her. Today she had put on short pants, short corduroy pants, deep red in color. Sandals were on her feet. A bright scarf was around her neck, a swath of color above her gray blouse and wide leather belt.

She was all by herself. Carl had gone by her window, before she had even got up, whistling and skipping along. Headed off down the road, vanishing between the buildings, his whistle dying away in the distance. She had lifted the shade and watched him until he was out of sight. Then she had jumped out of bed and dressed quickly. She hurried down to the commissary as soon as she was finished. No one was there. Both Verne and Carl had eaten and gone. In the sink were dirty dishes, and bits of Verne's pipe ashes.

Barbara carefully washed the dishes and cleaned up the kitchen. That was all the chores she could think of. Her room was clean and swept. She had even picked some new flowers and thrown the little roses out.

Now she walked happily along, going nowhere in particular, taking deep breaths of the warm air, filling her lungs with the smell of the clean new day. The sun danced around her, from bits of mica in the path. From the roofs of buildings. From windows half-boarded up. From all sides sunlight danced and streamed.

She felt good. She increased her pace.

Presently, as she walked along, she realized that she was coming to the Company park. The park was in the center of the grounds. Here a wide lawn had been planted, paths laid, trees arranged, so that the appearance of nature was given among all the machinery, the excavations, all the refining and smelting processes that had gone on day and night. Barbara came to the lawn and stopped, gazing across it. It was a perfect lawn. No weeds grew in it, and at the far border flowers had been carefully planted in low rows, endless bright streamers of color, red and blue and orange and every other color there was.

She paused for a moment, hesitating. Then she hopped up onto the lawn and walked quickly across it. Some mounds of clover grew here and there. Bees buzzed around the clover, getting at the moisture inside. Barbara skirted around the mounds of clover, avoiding them. She came to the low rows of flowers and stepped over them. Beyond the flowers was a narrow path.

And beyond the path was the Company lake.

The lake was a basin of concrete, huge and round, set like a gigantic pie pan among the flowers, laid down and filled with warm water. The water sparkled blue in the sun, shimmering and dancing. Barbara crossed the narrow path to the very edge of the lake. She stepped up on the concrete rim, her hands on her hips, gazing across the lake to the other side. On the other side were trees, a grove of immense fir trees, planted in a careful straight line, each one of them trimmed exactly like the next.

It was nice, very nice. Even though it was somewhat artificial. Everything was so — so perfect. The lake was round, exactly round. The trees were in exact formation. Even the flowers had been planted with care, according to innate geometrical concepts. Clover had got into the grass, but except for that —

Yet, it was better than clanking machines and the smell of molten metals and slag. All day long the factories had clanked and whirred. The roar of the blast furnaces, the unnatural charring heat. Furnaces withered life. Machinery devoured and destroyed, scooped up and burned away everything. The little oasis was much better than that.

Barbara stood for a long time, gazing across the lake. A slight wind blew bringing a fine mist from the water, up into the air. The wind increased, and the mist moved across the water in a great sheet. It touched her, the sheet of fine mist, and she found it cool and exciting. She looked around to see if anyone were watching. How foolish! She was alone. She was as completely alone as the first person in the world. And she had this tiny bit of the Garden of Eden to herself. In front of her was the dancing lake, the surface moving with the wind. Above her was the sun and sky. Behind her the flowers and grass. She was surrounded by the garden. Cut off. Isolated completely from the rest of the world, if such existed.

Here she was free to do what she wished. There was no one to watch her, frowning and noticing. No one to scowl and be offended. To sneer and make fun of her. To know and remember what she had done. She could run. She could dance, the way Carl had danced, along the path in front of her. She had been ashamed to join him, then. But she could dance now. There was no one to see.

Barbara turned, gazing all around her, her heart beating with excitement. She could leap and run. She could destroy, if she wanted. She could dig up plants, trample the grass. She could push over the trees, break the flowers, scoop out the water, pick up the great pie plate and empty all the water out onto the ground. There was nothing she could not do. Nothing at all.

Barbara sat down on the concrete rim of the lake. The concrete was hot, baked by the sun. She could feel it through her clothes. She untied her sandals rapidly, her hands shaking. She placed the sandals carefully on the rim beside her and then dangled her feet, down into the blue water. The water was cold, much colder than she had thought it would be. She gave a little cry, shuddering and pulling back. But it was good.

Presently she slid off the rim and waded out into the water, kicking water high in the air. The water came back down in great drops, heavy and cool, splashing around her, into her hair, onto her blouse. It made her tremble from head to foot. She began to shake with an intense fever. The icy drops rolled down her bare arms. The water lapped against her legs. Where the water touched it was like the touch of chilly fire.

She splashed back to shore. Standing back on the concrete rim she gazed up at the sun and across the water. Before, she had imagined herself as a sun goddess, giving her heart to the sun. Here she could do even more than that. She could give her whole self, her entire self, not merely her heart. She could give all of herself to the sun, to the sun and the water and the black ground around her.

She could be absorbed into the ground, back into the soil, like the rain that collects in puddles and finally drains away, sucked down into the earth. She could dissolve herself. Part of her would turn into the trees. Part of her would enter the lake. Part the sky, the sun, the grass —

She would be lost here in this garden, where no one could see her or follow her or know her. She would be gone. She would run away, run so fast she would disappear and be gone, vanished into the garden. She would become a portion of the garden, and no one would know which portion was she and which was not.

Barbara unbuttoned her blouse and slipped out of it. She unfastened her belt and stepped out of her short pants, laying them carefully on the narrow path beside the rim of the lake. Quickly she reached up for the sun, stretching out her arms, standing on tiptoe. But the sun was too far. She reached down to the water, bending over. The water was not so far. It was quite near.

Barbara entered the water, moving out, away from the shore. The water came to her eagerly, lapping around her, at her knees and ankles. She unhooked her bra and tossed it back with her other clothes, beside the concrete rim. Then she stepped rapidly out of her pants. She wadded the little silk pants up and threw them back onto the path. Now she was naked, completely naked from head to foot. She ran through the cold water, splashing it against her thighs and hips, against her flat belly. She ran as far as she could and then, when the water was up to her waist, she dived into it, letting it cover her completely.

Barbara lay in the water, drifting and floating. She was losing herself into it. The water was taking her. She would be gone forever. She was melting away, merging with the landscape. She dropped her feet, standing up. The water reached to her breasts. She looked down at them. The sun had refused them, when they had been offered to him. But the water would accept them. She could feel the water pressing against them, asking for them. It was begging for her, for her whole body, and if the sun would not accept, then she was sorry for him; he had lost out, and for him it was too late.

She moved out farther, gasping for breath, shuddering and

splashing. The water was sucking at her breasts, nursing at them. It desired to have them. It was eager. It could not wait. It wanted her now, at once. It could not be put off.

She stretched herself out on the water and lay, floating and drifting, moving with the slight currents set in motion by the wind. Now she was giving herself, all of her, without reservation. She was giving herself to the water, and the vast blue water was taking her eagerly. The water desired her. It was flowing into her, lapping into her, coming into her ears and nose, into her eyes and mouth. She opened her mouth and torrents of water rushed in. The water was bursting wildly into her, filling her up, swelling into her body. The water wanted to get inside her. It was pushing in greedily — too greedily! It was lustful. It was destroying her.

"Stop —"

She gasped for breath, choking and panting. She struggled to her feet, her toes barely touching bottom. Terrified, she pushed toward shore, wading toward the far rim of concrete. The water sank down. Finally it was down to her waist. Water poured from her, splashing from her.

She stopped, coughing and retching. The water was bitter, strong. She shuddered, spitting water, dribbling water from her nose. Water dribbled down her face in a dark stream. Her hair, soaked and dripping, hung down in her face. She pushed it back. She was sick, sick and shaken. And frightened.

Barbara made her way to shore. What had she been doing? In another minute she might have drowned. She was all by herself; there would be no one around to save her. A few minutes more and it would have been over. She shook, gasping, pushing her hair back out of her eyes.

She reached the concrete rim and stepped shakily over it, onto the warm path. She made her way through the flowers and threw herself onto the grass. She was exhausted. She lay without moving, her eyes shut, feeling the warm ground under her, the firm earth.

Finally she sat up, some strength coming back into her. She got unsteadily to her feet and walked over to her clothes. She was still wet. Her hair was slimy and thick, heavy and shapeless with water. She tried to squeeze the water out of it. Bubbles came to the surface of her hair. She gave up and began to put her clothes on.

She dressed slowly, feeling the cloth cling to her wet skin. Above her, the sun was white and blinding. She blinked. Her head ached. When she had finished dressing she hurried away from the lake, through the flowers, across the grass. Away from the garden itself.

She came to the path and stopped, her chest rising and falling, gasping for breath. She had tried to give herself up to the earth and the sky and she had not succeeded. The sun had refused her; he was too distant and aloof. He had not wanted her. He had not been interested enough to come and possess her and carry her away. She had given herself to what was below, the water and the ground. The water had covered her and rushed greedily to take her. But it had been cruel and demanding, destructive. It cared only about itself, not about her. It would have filled her up and killed her. She would have been destroyed. The water in its lust to enter her would have broken her apart.

She had been too quick to approach it. She had made a mistake. She had not understood it correctly. It was dangerous to misunderstand. She had to be more careful. Much more careful. The next time she would know what she was giving herself to; she would not rush heedlessly forward, to be devoured and destroyed.

The next time she would be sure. The next one who took her

would not destroy her; she would make certain of that. It had happened too many times. It would not happen again.

Barbara looked back at the lake and the dark soil around the flowers and grass. She had come from such things, billions of years before. She had slid forth from the water and the sun and the ground as a microscopic jelly, and each generation she had been recreated from the microscopic jelly. But once having come into existence she could not go back.

This world, the machines, the chimneys, the heaps of slag, the hearths, the furnaces, the towers, the concrete buildings, the smell of molten metal, this world could not be escaped. She was part of it, and whether she liked it or not she had to remain with it. She could not go back.

If this world had been abandoned, if it were of no value or significance any longer, if it had been deserted to rust and rot, to be picked over by the new owners, then she must go along with it and rust and rot, too. And lie out among the other piles of useless and discarded objects, to be ridden over and crushed under by what was to come later, what ever it might be.

Barbara turned to go, away from the grass and the flowers and the great pie pan. But suddenly she stopped. She put her hand quickly up, shielding her eyes. Something had moved, something among the trees at the far side of the lake. A brief flicker. She continued to watch, feeling her wet hair dripping cold thick water down the back of her neck, inside her blouse. Had she been mistaken?

No. There it was again, a flash of white among the trees. As if a person had stepped for a moment out into the sun. As if the sun had shrunk his shirt.

Barbara walked carefully along the grass, circling the lake. The grass ended after a while and she entered the grove of fir trees. The ground was dry and hard, covered by a thin layer of leaves and cones and needles. She felt the leaves crunch under her sandals as she tip-toed quietly from tree to tree, holding her breath, trying not to make any noise.

A person was standing ahead of her, between two of the great trees, standing with his hands on his hips, gazing off across the lake. She knew who it was before she saw his face. That morning he had passed her window in the same white shirt, skipping and whistling along.

"What are you doing?" Barbara said sharply.

Carl turned slowly toward her. "Hello."

"For God's sake! What are you doing?"

Carl studied her evenly. "Was that you out in the water? I see you got to shore all right. I thought for a little while you were in some sort of trouble."

He did not seem embarrassed at all. Barbara felt confused. She shook her head, trying to clear it. "If I had drowned would you have pulled me out? Or would you just have stood here, watching?" Her voice was low. She was shaking all over. Carl had been watching all the time! It was impossible. And now he stood quite calmly, not at all embarrassed.

"I would have pulled you out," Carl said. He folded his arms. His sleeves were rolled up. His arms were big and bare, furred with reddish fur.

"I don't understand. What are you doing here?" She was nettled and puzzled. Her head ached. Down the back of her neck the slimy water still dripped. "Why were you watching me? What's the matter with you?"

Early that morning the sun had wakened Carl out of his usual deep sleep. He opened his eyes, blinking at the sunlight pouring through the window. He reached up and pulled the shade back. Sunlight burst into the room, streaming over everything, across his bed, across the floor, onto the dresser and the chair with Verne's clothes piled on it.

Verne stirred in his bed, opening his eyes. "For God's sake. Let the shade down." He turned over, pulling the covers up around him.

Carl was sitting up in bed, gazing out the window. He could see buildings and machinery, and gravel paths running here and there, back and forth between the buildings. Beyond the buildings were the hills, and the woods. And beyond that were the mountains, blue and cold.

"Will you let the shade down?" Verne muttered from under the covers.

"Sorry." Carl let the shade back in place. He slid out of the bed and onto the floor. The floor was warm where the sunlight had touched it. He began to dress, climbing into his clothes, whistling under his breath.

"What's going on?" Verne raised his head, peering out from under the covers. He felt around on the floor and found his glasses. "What the hell time is it?" He put his glasses on and examined the clock. "Seven-thirty! My God."

"It's a wonderful day."

Verne grunted, turning toward the wall.

"If you're going back to sleep you should take off your glasses," Carl said. "Otherwise they might break."

Verne did not answer.

Carl held out his hand. "Give them to me and I'll put them under the bed for you."

Presently Verne's hand came out, holding onto the glasses. Carl took them and laid them carefully on the floor.

"They're right by the bed. Just reach over when you want them. I'm going out for a stroll. I'll see you later."

He finished dressing and then trotted down the hall to the bathroom. He washed and cleaned vigorously, combing his blond hair back in place. Then he stood before the mirror, looking at his reflection.

"Well, Carl Fitter!" he said. "What do you have on your mind today?"

His image, blond and blue-eyed, stared back at him. It was the face of a boy, young and strong and full of great enthusiasm. But still a boy. Carl sighed. When would he look in the mirror and see a man's face? How long would it be? He rubbed his chin. What was lacking? Something was lacking. He had begun to shave; he had been shaving now for several years. His voice had deepened. It was even lower than Verne's. Verne's voice was squeaky.

Yet he was still a boy. For all his big shoulders, his good-natured smile, his booming voice. Carl's happiness faded. He gazed at his reflection forlornly, drooping sadly.

But after a while some of his spirits returned. He straightened up. Someday it would change. Someday it would be different. There would be a flash of fire, a burst of white flame from heaven, and there he would be, a man.

Carl walked down the stairs to the ground floor and outside onto the porch. He leaped from the porch onto the gravel path, scattering gravel into the grass and bushes that grew around the side of the building.

In the early morning sunlight the grass was still wet with tiny beads of moisture. They glinted up at him, like globes of crystal. Or perhaps they were drops of perspiration, sweated up from the ground during the night. But why should the ground labor during the dark hours? What kind of activity was in progress, when the sun had gone and the long shadows were over everything?

The activity of growth, of course. The beginnings of life, the first stirrings down in the soil. Tiny things pushing their way up. All this began in the darkness of the night, and when the sun came the plants were ready to break through the skin of the earth to come out into the heat and warmth. That was the way it was: life came into being in the dim darkness of night, and the ground perspired from the labor of it.

Carl walked gingerly along the gravel walk, feeling the small stones breaking under his shoes. Everything seemed wonderful on a day like this. The world was full of wild and exciting objects. What he crushed under his feet might be rough diamonds, diamonds that had not been stolen from the stone yet, diamonds that were still dark and coated with the dirt and grime in which they had lain for centuries.

A road of breaking diamonds, shattering under his shoes! He increased his pace, kicking the gravel as he went, sending waves of stones flying up into the air. There was mica in the gravel, and the sun caught the bits of mica and made them sparkle. Carl laughed in excited wonder. Maybe he was right. Maybe there were precious stones under him.

He entered the commissary. It was cool and deserted. No one had been there since dinner the night before. There was no sound except the tap-tapping of the water as it dripped in the sink. He opened the window above the table and gusts of fresh air came sweeping in, blowing the curtains back and forth. Carl took a deep breath, letting it out slowly.

He began to assemble a meal. What did he want? He looked in the refrigerators. There were so many things to choose from. What would it be? He considered. If he were going to do a lot of things he would need a big meal. What was he going to be doing?

Today he would wander around. He would go off and walk by himself, as far as he could, until he was too tired to walk any farther. He would be alone. Everyone was still sound asleep in bed. There was no time more exciting, no time more strange and wonderful than the early morning, when people were silent and asleep, and he had the great bright world all to himself. This time of morning, before the dew on the lawns dried up, before the bees began to come out, when his footsteps echoed among the buildings — this was his favorite time. Then, the world was entirely his personal property. There was no one to dispute his ownership, to try to inhabit it or take it away from him. Everyone was turned to stone, the people quiet and immobile in their beds, enchanted by magic. He only, could walk about and inspect the world, his land, his buildings, his silent stone people.

Thinking of this, Carl turned the fire on under the frying pan and began to lay strips of bacon into it. He got eggs and milk from the refrigerator, humming to himself as he worked.

When he had finished eating he carried the dishes to the sink and carefully stacked them up. Then he left the building, going back out of doors again. The day was still bright, but it was not so cool, now. Time had passed. It was later. Subtle changes were already coming over the day.

Carl started up the road, his hands in his pockets, whistling to himself. Presently he began to sing, not loudly, but in a deep low voice, like a concert baritone. It all had a strange effect on him, the warm motionless day, the unmoving buildings and trees and bushes. It made him foolish. But he did not care. He could be as foolish as he wanted. No one could stop him. And after all, it was his morning, his day, his world. Everything belonged to him. He glanced up at the women's dorm as he passed by it. The shades were all down. He smiled to himself. Barbara was asleep. Verne and Barbara. Sound asleep in their beds. And down below them, in the warm sunlight, he moved happily through his great warm world, completely alone.

He left the buildings behind him, whistling and skipping along. It was just as he was passing the last of the slag piles that he came across — *it*. He stopped, frozen. His whistle died on his lips. At first he did not know what it was. Was it something a person had dropped? It looked like a little bag, or a wallet, or something wrapped up.

He bent down. It was a bird, a red-breasted robin. The robin was lying on its side, its feet sticking out. It was stiff and rigid. Dead. And already, a line of busy ants were moving back and forth from it to the weeds.

Carl stood for a long time, staring down. The bird had died during the night. Sometime in the night, when the ground was generating new life, the already living had passed away, without any sound, without attracting any attention.

The bird might have been flying over the road. It must have sunk lower and lower, until at last it was hobbling across the ground, flying a few feet, then running and falling, until at last it had fluttered against the gravel in a bouncing heap. After a few feeble thrashings and struggles it had become inert, staring with its beady eyes, its chest rising and falling. And in the first hours of sunrise the bright eyes had dimmed over. The bird had died, quietly, by itself, with no one around to see.

This was what happened to all the things that came out of the wet earth, out of the filthy slime and mould. All things that lived, big and little. They appeared, struggling out of the sticky wetness. And then, after a time, they died.

Carl looked up at the day again, at the sunlight and the hills. It did not look the same, now, as it had looked a few moments before. Perhaps he saw it more clearly than he had, a moment ago. The sky, blue and pure, stretched out as far as the eye could see. But blood and feathers came from the sky. The sky was beautiful when he stood a long way off from it. But when he saw too closely, it was not pretty. It was ugly and bitter.

The sky was held together with tacks and gum and sticky tape. It cracked and was mended, cracked and was mended again. It crumbled and sagged, rotted and swayed in the wind, and like the sky in the children's story, part of it fell to earth.

Carl walked on slowly. He stepped off the road and climbed

a narrow dirt ridge. Soon he was going up the side of a grassy slope, breathing deeply and taking big steps. He stopped for a moment, turning to look back.

Already the Company and its property had become small, down below him. Shrunk, dwindling away. Carl sat down on a rock. The world was quiet and still around him. Nothing stirred. His world. His silent, personal world.

But he did not understand it. So how could it be his world? He had come out to smile at the flowers and grass. But he had found something more, something that he could not smile at. Something that was not pleasant at all. Something that he did not like nor understand nor want.

So it was not his world. If it were his world he would have made it differently. It had been put together wrong. Very much wrong. Put together in ways that he could not approve of.

The silent bird, lying in the road. It reminded him of something. His thoughts wandered. What did it remind him of? A strange feeling drifted through him. This had happened before. This very thing. He had gone out and found something terrible. Something that did not make sense. Something he could not explain or understand.

After a while he remembered. The cat. The dying old cat, with its broken ears, one eye gone, its body thin and dry with patches of loose hair. The cat and the bird. Other things. Flies buzzing around. Streams of ants. Things dying, disappearing silently, drifting away. With no one to watch or care.

He had never understood it, this thing that he found, in the great warm world. It had no meaning. No sense. Was there some purpose? Some reason?

When he understood the cat was dead he had gone back inside the house, walking slowly, deep in thought. Back inside, to his room, his things. His microscope. His stamps and maps and drawings and books. They had meaning. Purpose. Their existence had reason to it. He could look at them and understand them.

Carl sat on the hillside, thinking about his childhood. It was not so long ago. Not so very many years in the past. He could feel the memories rising up around him, seeping up on all sides of him. Sights, smells. Tastes. His past was very much with him. It was close, just below the surface. Waiting to come up. His room. His microscope. The drawings he had made.

He sat and remembered about them.

15

"CARL!" THE WOMAN called sharply.

And the little boy Carl ran into the room.

"Carl, I'm going to work. You might at least empty the garbage sometime today. You'll have all day to do it."

"I will," Carl said. He waited, hoping she would not ask him to do anything else.

"And don't you think you should work on some of your school work? When you do go back you'll be so behind you'll never catch up."

"All right," Carl said.

The woman put on her coat and hat. She took her sandwich, wrapped up in a paper bag with a rubber band around it. "Goodbye."

"Goodbye."

He watched her go up the front walk, up the concrete path, onto the sidewalk. Then she was gone. Carl ran into the kitchen. He pulled the little doors under the sink open, bending down to pick up the sack of garbage. He carried the dripping sack through the house, out the back door, onto the porch, carefully pushing the door open with his foot.

The day was warm and bright. He blinked in the sun, looking around him, taking deep breaths. A joy passed through him.

He had the whole day to do as he pleased. And there were many things he wanted to begin.

Carl took the garbage down the back steps, along the walk by the great lily plants, their leaves wet and green, spiders crawling over them. He dropped the sack into the garbage can. Then he ran back inside the house and slammed the door behind him.

He stood in the center of his room. His gaze took in the entire room and all the things around him. What should he begin first? There was the electric motor he was building out of paper clips and wire. But that could wait. On the desk among the litter of papers and books and pencils was his stamp album, and a teacup of stamps, soaking. He passed them by. They could wait, too.

Carl crossed to the desk. He pushed the magazines and books aside and pulled out a picture. It had been torn from a magazine, the picture of a girl, breasts and legs and red fingernails, smiling up at him in unnatural invitation. Carl stared at the picture, trapped. This. He would begin with this.

He reached into the top drawer of the desk and got out a piece of drawing paper and a heavy black pencil. He sat down carefully on the edge of the bed, holding the picture and paper and pencil in his hands. Sitting on the bed, with the sun shining on him through the burlap drapes, he began to copy the picture, his body hunched forward in absorbed interest, his eyes only a few inches from the paper. The pencil left greasy, smeared lines, and every few moments he rubbed feverishly at the lines, so that the drawing began to take on an ominous, cloudy appearance, almost as if it were coming out of some angry storm cloud.

At last Carl gave a groan of despair and crumpled up the paper. He threw it against the far wall. The ball of paper fell into the litter on the floor. Carl put the picture of the girl back on the desk, and the drawing pencil back into the dresser.

For a few minutes he sat on the bed, thinking. At the end of the bed was a book. He picked it up. *The Nature of the Atom*. He opened it and read, turning the pages very rapidly, his eyes intent on the lines of print. But after a while he found himself too restless to continue. He closed the book and put it down.

Carl went to the desk, shoving the books and papers aside. He drew out a square metal box. The box was cold in his hands. He ran his fingers over the surface. For a time he pretended not to know how to open it. His hands touched each inch and corner of it, pressing, feeling its texture, its hardness, its cold smoothness. Suddenly his fingers found the catch of the box, and the lid snapped open.

Carl lifted out the great microscope, metal and glass, its bright mirror flashing in the sunlight that filtered through the burlap drapes. A torrent of glass slides showered out of the box, falling down onto the bed. Carl placed the microscope carefully on the desk and began to gather up the slides, one by one, until they were all safely beside the parent engine.

Presently he selected one of the slides and pushed it onto the stage of the microscope. He tilted the shaft backward, pushing his eye against the eyepiece, staring down into the tube.

At first he saw only darkness, the black of night. He manipulated the mirrors, the adjustments of the machine. And presently an object appeared, swimming slowly along, rising and falling, coming at him and going away again.

What was it? It was the reflection of the blood of his eye, the movement of his own body fluids. It was a part of himself that he saw. Only a part of his own being, reflected back at him. He changed the setting of the lens.

And this time the light, maneuvered into the hollow tube by his deft manipulations, brought the specimen on the slide into view. Carl caught his breath. The transfixed interior of a cell wall gleamed up at him.

For an endless time he gazed down at it, the section of rat

liver, purple and ivory, a massive worm cut cleanly through, its vacant center revealed for all to see. His eye feasted on the pulpy puffed-up rat tissue. His eye took in every line and bulge of the fleshy ring, the doughnut magnified by the tube and lenses of the big microscope.

What was this, so small and far beyond ordinary sight? What had it meant to the rat, this single portion of its body, this bit of its physical self? Did the disembodied soul of the rat yearn for what lay here, for what rested on this slide, and on other slides, thousands of slides everywhere, viewed by cold and unsympathetic eyes, curious and objective, each beyond the possibility of any understanding, of knowing in any way what this pulpy ring might have once meant?

The ring, the section, was alive with import, full of sense and greatness. At least, for a little while. But at last Carl's attention wilted. Torpor filled his veins. His hands, resting expertly on the adjustments of the microscope, began to become heavy and clumsy.

Carl folded the microscope back into its box, into the felt and hair interior where it lived. He slotted the slides into place and snapped the lid tight, sliding the box over to the corner of the desk.

He sat for a time, regaining his energy. After a time he began to look about him, at all the things in the room. The phonograph records stacked up at the end of the bed. The little record player, with its cactus needles and sharpener lying on the turntable. His box of recipes, the metal file box with cards squashed together, bulging and out of order. His model airplanes, German planes of the First World War, two black wings, the stubby body. The huge still of the Kaiser.

His stamp album. The magnifying glass and the cup of stamps. Carl leaned toward the desk. He thrust his fingers into the cup, groping for the gummy squares of wet paper, bright bits peeling loose from the sections of cut envelope.

The battle maps on the wall caught his eye. The front lines were no longer correctly indicated; they were all out of place, left behind by the shudders of the war. Carl rushed to the map, shaking drops of sticky water in every direction. He grabbed up a pencil from the desk, snatching it from the top drawer.

But again he saw the picture, the picture of the girl, torn from the magazine. He stopped, standing by the desk, staring down at it. Presently he sat down on the bed. He took the picture and a fresh piece of drawing paper, drawing them to him, onto his lap.

He studied the picture. His eyes told him everything about the girl. He did not need useless touch to tell him what he needed to know. The texture of her skin. The feel of her hair. He needed nothing but sight to tell him everything. He had learned to follow and to understand through his eyes alone. He had seen them, what he saw now in the picture, walking along the street, sitting near him in the bus, leaning out the window of the house next door to hang up washing on the line. He had seen them many times.

Carl began to draw, slowly, carefully, his tongue pressed against the roof of his mouth, his fingers gripping the pencil. There was a bright, feverish color in his face, a high redness in his cheeks. He drew with forceful, nervous strokes, the muscles of his arm rigid and locked, as hard and unbending as the wood of the pencil. When he was displeased his face darkened and the bright color dimmed. He smeared the black lines on the paper with sudden anguish, rubbing his finger against the rough paper.

Slowly, from the heavy, greasy lines, the figure of the girl emerged, an image rising from the smudges of the charcoal and oil and lampblack. A flowing mass of blackness. That was the hair, streaming around the face. He drew the neck and shoulders, the arms.

The original, the print torn from the magazine, fell from his lap, skidding into the corner. He did not notice or care. This girl, emerging on his drawing paper, did not come from any magazine. She came from inside him, from his own body. From the plump, white body of the boy this embryonic woman was rising, brought forth by the charcoal, the paper, the rapid strokes. He was giving birth to this figure from his own body. And as he drew he watched it struggle out of him, gaining form and substance.

The figure fought with the inky cloud, its birth sack, the charcoal and lampblack, and the waters of birth drained down his arm in dirty streaks, smudges of grim, like the dust of the street, the soot of factories.

He finished the arms and began the torso. Blood beat inside him, rising in a pitch of excitement. He put down his pencil, shaking and trembling. He could not go on. It was too difficult, too demanding. The ecstatic agony of birth was too much. He could not let it emerge, not just yet. The pain was too great.

Carl sat, staring down at the picture, perspiration dripping down his face and arms. In the warm closeness of the room, with the sunlight pouring through the tightly closed windows, his sweating body gave off a strange musky smell. But he did not notice. He was too lost in concentration.

In the steamy, musky room the boy was much like a kind of plant, growing and expanding, white and soft, his fleshy arms reaching into everything, devouring, examining, possessing, digesting. But at the windows and doors of the room he stopped. He did not go beyond them.

He was a part of this room. He could not leave it. Outside the room the air was too cold, the ground too wet, the sun too bright. Outside the room the objects moved by him too quickly to be grasped or consumed or understood.

Like a plant, he fed only on things brought to him. He did not go and get them for himself. Living in this room he was a plant that fed on its own self, eating at its own body. What came forth from his own vitals, these lines and forms generated onto paper, were exciting and maddening. He was trapped, held tight.

Carl's fingers gripped the edges of the drawing paper. This picture, the head and shoulders of the girl, the tide of inky black hair, was something he wanted, that he had to have. It had worked itself out of his physical depths, and he wanted to pull himself after it, smother it with himself, cram it back inside him again. He bent forward, his face close to the paper, his lips brushing the dark lines, the swirls and currents, the motions of the girl's form, her hair and arms and shoulders, the shocking white that would be the rest of her body, someday. Finally.

But the effort was too much. He could not last it out. Carl collapsed back onto the bed with a sigh, and the picture fell once more to the floor, with the dust and litter.

Dust and spiderwebs. Tiny webs crossing the deep black lines, the hair and face and shoulders he had drawn. Dimly, from a long way off, he could still see the picture, the form that had emerged from him, the part that had come forth from his womb.

But he was exhausted. He could not stir toward it. He could not cram it back into him again. It lay on the dirty floor, such a long way from him, resting silently with the trash and spiderwebs and debris. He closed his eyes.

Untidily, the boy dozed on the bed.

Carl stirred, blinking. How clear the scenes and sights of his boyhood were! He stood up a moment, gazing down the hillside at the buildings and towers below. He took a deep breath, yawning and stretching.

Presently he sat down again. He relaxed, letting his mind wander, back into his youth, into his childhood. Back farther and farther, into the depths of his memories. Around him the memories moved and swelled, drifting and murmuring.

The procession of old women were coming along the path. It was snow all over. They were carrying white, but it was not snow. The first old woman staggered with the heavy sheet of rock, thin, paper-stuck, powdery, and dropped it at the edge of the path.

The sheet of rock fell and broke apart, each section falling away, brittle, old. Carl looked down the path of broken paper and rock.

"Because you jumped."

He had been angry. The old women lugged out the last pieces of rock. The great dark warm heap of chocolate flesh, the massive body that was Lulu the maid, was saying, and holding onto his arm: "But you had your tantrum in the mownin'. They is wrong. It was in the mownin'. Don' you see?"

He did see. Yet the ceiling *had* fallen, just as in Henny-penny. Only it was not the ceiling. It was the sky. He went to the store with Lulu.

Along the road the ice and snow had turned to slush, yellow and crusted. He reached his hands into it. And the mittens became stiff with cold, and his hands had no feeling.

"Are you a little boy or a little girl?" he asked the heap of brightly colored rags, huddled on the steps. He was skating back and forth across the tracks made by people along the sidewalk, feeling the ice and pavement under his feet.

"I'm a girl," the child said. It was evening. The sun went down. The air was dark. He could see the great white Merrit

House in the distance, and in front of it the path of rocks and paper. He skated and hobbled across the ground, slushy and frozen, the water striking him. At the top of the hill he stopped, looking back.

The bundle of rags raised itself up. "I have to go!" it sang. "I have to go." It turned and fled. Along the edge of the hill the child ran home, dancing, dashing, the rags flying.

Carl went inside. His mother was putting down the groceries on the table, getting out her key to see if there were any mail today.

He stood in the hall, gazing up at her.

The air was full of things. Carl had seen them come out of the trees. Each left a little body behind it when it emerged. The body was a tiny worn self, sitting on the branch of the tree. He pulled, and the little worn bit of shell case came away in his hand. He gathered them up all together, and presently he had a pile of them. They were not dead; they had no insides. It was strange.

Carl was at school. His mother had not found an apartment. It was dark, and the night air was full of the strange buzzy things that had come out of the trees. At the back door a woman was calling the children. Upstairs the two Donnic twins were being bathed. They slept in his room with him. They snored at night. Once under the bed he had run a piece of wood into his finger, under the nail. It was in the afternoon, and no one heard him. The room was always warm and stuffy, with the windows shut tight. He came out from under the bed crying.

Now, in the cold dark evening he looked up at the shadow of the building, and the figure of the woman by the back door. Far off in the distance there was a siren.

"Police!" little voices cried.

"Fire trucks! Fire trucks!"

Carl scampered over the grass. In the dimness the grass was black. He ran past the huge tent staked down at the corners. He ran along the hedge, across the plowed field, onto the bottom slope. He could not see the end of the slope. He ran and ran, down and down, until he came to the fence. The bushes had grown up against the wires of the fence and along the posts, and he had to push them aside, tugging at the thick stalks.

The slope dropped sharply on the other side of the fence. Below the slope, at the bottom, was a highway. He could see the lights of the highway going off into the distance. There were no houses as far as he could see. The highway went along and another highway cut across it. There was a sign of bright yellow where the two roads met, a strip of light in the vast darkness, the yawning immensity of night.

HANCOCK GASOLINE

Two tiny cars were drawn up at the side of the highway. He heard the sirens again, moving along the highway toward the hills. The hills were very far off, a black edge near the violet skyline.

Kneeling, peering through the bushes, he listened to the sirens fading away into the hills.

When he got up to go back, the air was heavy with night, cold and damp. He walked slowly, feeling his way along. He passed the plowed ground and came onto the grass. He ducked under the ropes of the tent and went up onto the driveway, brittle and crackly under his feet.

When he got to the door of the building the woman seized him by the arm. "Where have you been?" Her voice was shrill and sharp in the night air.

Carl pushed by her, murmuring. He went up the hall to the

stairs. His room was hot and unpleasant with steam and the smell of baths. The Donnic twins were asleep.

He sat down on the bed and untied his shoes.

When Carl was twelve years old he was allowed to go to summer camp. He was very excited about it. Jimmy Petio was going along with him.

"I'll drive you up," his mother said. "I'll drive both of you."

Carl twisted uncomfortably.

"What's the matter?"

"I—"

Mrs. Fitter put down the magazine she was reading, *The New Yorker*. "What's the matter?"

"I thought we might hitchhike."

Mrs. Fitter raised her magazine. "Now I've heard everything." She adjusted her glasses. "Twelve years old and they want to hitchhike."

Carl gazed out the window of the car. Mrs. Fitter drove up beside some trees and stopped. "Well, here we are." She pushed the door open. "Don't leave your sleeping bags behind."

Carl and Jimmy dragged their sleeping bags out of the back of the car. Carl kissed his mother goodbye. She slammed the car door and started up the motor.

"Gosh," Jimmy said.

The camp was immense and cool. Vast trees, their tops lost in a green tangle of branches, surrounded them. A bird squawked, flying far above, its cries echoing away.

A counselor approached them. "Fitter and Petio?"

They nodded.

"Your tent is down here. Come along with me."

Jimmy and Carl laid out their sleeping bags on the two cots a few feet from their weathered canvas tent. Beyond the tent rose a wall of earth and roots and vines. Black and green mixed together, damp, silent, awesome. In front of the tent was a slender trail, and just on the other side of the trail was the creek.

Carl went over to the edge of the trail and gazed down at the creek. The water was deep and dark. A few tree branches drifted slowly along. On the far side land rose up again, trees and brush. Dimly in the brush more tents could be seen.

"What's over there?" Carl asked.

"I don't know." Jimmy threw a stone into the creek. Ripples poured away, widening silently.

"It sure is quiet."

"Let's see where they all are."

They ran back along the trail, the way they had come. They came to the dining building and the sand bar where everyone was out swimming. Shouts and splashes echoed around them. On the far side of the creek was a high platform and a diving board. A few brown shapes basked in the sun. The sand bar was swarming with swimmers. Canoes, red and blue and orange, drifted up and down the creek.

A counselor with boys hanging from him made his way toward them. "Did you boys just come?"

"Yes."

"Put on your trunks and jump in."

They ran back to get their trunks. They changed quickly. A moment later they were pattering back along the trail, the wind blowing against their bare bodies, tiny stones cutting into their feet. Jimmy hopped expertly. Carl did the best he could.

"Come on!" Jimmy shouted.

"I'm coming!"

They reached the sandbar, past the redwood dining building. The sand was warm and dry under their feet. Jimmy leaped into the water. Carl ran to the edge, making his way through the brown glistening bodies curled up in the sun.

At the edge of the water he halted, looking around him. He stood gazing across the creek, at the platform on the other side.

Jimmy's head rose up in the water, spluttering and gasping. "What's the matter?"

Carl did not answer.

"What's eating you?"

Carl dived into the water. He swam around and came up to the surface. He paddled toward Jimmy. The water was icy. He gasped, goose-pimples breaking out all over him.

"It's freezing."

"It sure is."

They crawled up on the sandbar. Water ran down their faces, dripping from them. They struggled to breathe.

"I'm worn out," Jimmy muttered.

Carl was worn out, too. More by excitement than anything else. No one paid any attention to them. Most of the figures on the sandbar were asleep. A few splashed into the water from time to time. One boy struggled with another to get a huge green ball. Across the creek a lithe shape dived from the platform into the water.

"You just come?" a fellow said to them.

They nodded. "We just got here."

"How long you going to be here?"

"Two weeks."

"This the first time?"

"Yes."

"Nice place," the fellow said.

Carl gazed at the shapes splashing and shouting in the water. He was very quiet, saying nothing.

Jimmy punched him. "What's wrong?"

"Nothing."

"Homesick?"

"No." Carl looked up toward the platform on the other side. Figures lay in the sun. Beyond them a bank of black earth rose, twisted tree roots. A road, half way up the hillside. Along the skyline a distant row of firs.

"What, then?"

"I didn't know there were girls here. I thought it was just boys."

"They live across the creek," the fellow put in.

"Sure, we saw their tents," Jimmy said.

On the edge of the platform a girl sat resting. In the sunlight her body sparkled and glistened. She had taken off her cap. Her hair was long and dark. It fell around her neck and shoulders. She was staring down into the water, her face expressionless.

Carl watched her until Jimmy grabbed him and tried to roll him into the water.

"Let go!" Carl shouted. The water closed over him. He dragged himself out, spluttering and spitting, water pouring from his mouth and nose.

"You're mad," Jimmy said, noticing his expression.

Carl threw himself onto the sand. "No."

"Yes you are."

On the platform the girl had disappeared. Carl did not know where she had gone. He waited, but she did not come back. A girl came up the ladder from the water, onto the platform, but it was not her. It was someone else.

The sun crossed the sky. A cold wind whipped around them. The swimmers left the water.

"Time to go in," a counselor said. "Get cleaned up for dinner."

There was a dance. It was night. The tables in the redwood dining room had been cleared away to make room. A phonograph had been set up, records and a loudspeaker in the corner. Boys shuffled in, moving over to one side, lining up as far away from the girls as possible.

"I can't dance," Jimmy said.

"Too bad," said Carl.

"I didn't come to camp to do any dancing."

A lot of the boys were punching each other and shuffling around. In the center of the room was a big space, separating the boys from the girls. Mr. Fletcher, the man who ran the camp, got out in the middle, waving for silence.

"The first dance is girl's choice!" he announced, wiping his neck with a red handkerchief.

The music started from the phonograph. The boys slunk back against each other, moving toward the wall. A few girls came across the space toward them.

"What'll I do if some girl asks me to dance?" Jimmy muttered.

"Tell her you want to sit this dance out."

"What's that mean?"

"It means you don't know how to dance."

A skinny girl with yellow hair wandered around in front of them, looking for somebody to dance with. The boys edged sullenly away, watching her uneasily.

"Let's go," Jimmy whispered, tugging at Carl.

"Where?"

"Outside."

"We can't go outside. We're supposed to be in here dancing."

Jimmy said nothing. The girl had gone off with a little short fellow wearing a bow tie. "Whoever heard of a bow tie," Jimmy said.

In the warmth, the fellow's face was shiny with perspiration. Several couples were dancing slowly.

"Look at them."

Carl tried to see across the floor to the other side. Was — was *she* there? The girl with the dark hair. He looked and looked, but he could not see her.

"What are you staring at?" Jimmy demanded.

"Nothing."

"You see somebody?"

"No." It was true. He did not see her. More couples were on the floor. More girls had come across to ask boys to dance. Jimmy was getting more nervous.

"I'm going outside," Jimmy said.

"All right."

"Aren't you coming?"

"No."

"You — you turd." Jimmy punched him and then made his way over to the door and outside.

Carl was alone. Sadness filled him. The music roared through the room. Couples shuffled around him, back and forth. A low murmur of talk dinned against his ears. He wandered around aimlessly. At a table there was punch, served in paper cups. A woman gave him a cup. He went on, sipping it. The punch was warm and thick. It tasted of fruit, like stale pop.

When he got back to where he had been standing he saw her. His heart turned over inside him. She was dancing, in a long white dress with red flowers in her hair. She was laughing. He could see her teeth, little and even. Her skin was dark. She was Spanish or something. Her eyes were large and bright.

Gloom descended over Carl, a strange sweet gloom, like the punch in the paper cup. It made him ache all over. He moved to the edge of the circle of watching boys.

A plump girl grabbed his arm. "Dance? Dance?"

"Let go." He pulled away angrily. The plump girl ran off after someone else, laughing and shoving.

The music ended. Jimmy came back inside, slipping over beside Carl. "How was it?" he asked.

"How was what?"

"The dancing."

"I didn't dance."

"I never thought they'd have dancing at a camp," Jimmy said. "Who ever heard of dancing at a camp?"

It was very silent during the long nights, with everyone asleep and no light anywhere. Sometimes Carl woke up and lay listening, warm in his sleeping bag, only his head out. The night wind moved through the trees growing by the creek.

Carl lay listening. He could hear many scratching sounds in the darkness. Animals? One morning he had found a grey squirrel standing on his sleeping bag. The air was heavy with mist. No one was up. The squirrel stood upright, gray and rigid. Then he flowed off onto the ground, followed by his tail. The squirrel dipped and weaved across to a big redwood tree and scrambled up it.

Later, when the mists had faded, the kitchen people began to bang things around in the dining room. Lying in his sleeping bag, waiting for the breakfast gong to sound, Carl could hear their sound, echoing up the creek, a hollow sound, a distant drumming. A strange sound, mixing with the slowly drifting creek, the great silent trees, the leaves and earth.

Everything was so different from home. His regular life seemed unreal. A dream. His room, his microscope, his stamps. The pictures. Books, records, endless drawers and piles. The stuffy closed-up room. Here the air was thin and clear. He could see for miles, rising green hills and trees, higher and higher. The smell of the air, the trees, the moist ground. The way stones felt under his feet. The freezing water. The dry sand against him.

He paid a nickel to ride in a canoe, up the creek until he came to a bridge. The shore was covered with stones. Endless gray stones. He drifted with the stream, allowing the canoe to go where it wanted. He forgot that it was costing him a nickel an hour. He put the paddle down and lay stretched out, listening to the sound of the water, to the silence of the woods around him.

On and on the canoe went. The camp was a long way behind. He stirred. It was time to go back. He was entirely alone, for the first time in his life. There was no one at all. It was not like being alone in his room. There he was surrounded with things, a whole roomful of things. And beyond the room was the whole city, endless men and women, countless people. In the city no one was ever alone.

But here there was no one. He gazed at the steep banks that rose on both sides of him, tangled shrubbery, old roots, crumbling soil. The lines of trees, firs, redwoods, Cyprus, pine. A bird cried out, rushing away. A bluejay. So alone. It made him feel sad, but he enjoyed the sadness. The sweetness. . . . It was such a strange sadness. As if he were rushing away, faster and faster, in his canoe, down the stream between the steep banks. Leaving everyone behind him forever.

He picked up the paddle and turned the canoe. He paddled back.

At night he could hear the creek. He could not see it, but he knew it was there. The creek was very close to him, just beyond the trail and down the slope. Moving always, silently, carrying bits of bark and twigs and leaves along with it. Branches and leaves, all the way to the ocean.

Carl stared up at the dark sky. Above the redwoods a few stars winked. He could see the outlines of the trees, the columns rising up on all sides, supporting the sky. He thought about the girl, the girl with the dark hair. Would he ever see her again? The two weeks were going swiftly. Across the stream was her tent, someplace on the other side. She was there, beyond the water, sleeping silently.

He closed his eyes. When he opened them again the first feelers of gray mist were starting to settle down. It was morning. A vague, diffused light hung everywhere. The stars were gone. Carl shivered. It was very still and cold. In the cot next to him Jimmy grunted and turned over.

Carl lay watching. Mist blew around him. His face was moist. He could see the creek, now. The broad surface, like pale stone. And the bank on the other side rising up, the trees and roots and vines. The ancient twisted roots.

After a while he slipped out of his sleeping bag. He was trembling all over from the damp coldness. There was no sound. The world was utterly silent. He pulled his cotton pajamas around him and padded across the trail, down the slope, picking his way carefully. Nothing stirred. The mist eddied everywhere. He came to the bottom of the slope. There was the water, the flat opaque surface. It moved so slowly that it did not seem to move at all. But it was moving. A branch passed, a black dripping branch, cold and stark, its leaves hanging limp.

Carl sat down on the slope at the edge of the water. Time passed. He did not feel the cold. The mists began to go away a little. But there was no color anywhere. The sky, the water, the trees, everything was dull and flat. Gray. A world of ghosts, silent shapes.

He dozed. And when he opened his eyes *she* was standing on the other side of the stream. He was stiff all over, stiff and cold. She was looking at him. She did not speak. Carl and the girl gazed across the gray stream at each other.

A bird flashed through the trees. Faintly, down the creek, a metallic booming drifted. The kitchen people, starting breakfast. The girl stood between two trees, her hand against one, at the very edge of the water. She wore a kind of gray robe. Her hair was long and black. Her eyes were black. He could see her tiny white teeth. Her mouth was open a little. A cloud of moisture rose from her lips as she breathed.

Carl did not move. The trees, the girl, the water, everything blended together in the silent grayness. After a time he fell asleep again.

When he woke, Jimmy was kicking him in the small of the back.

"Get up!" Jimmy demanded, his voice shrill and far away.

Carl stirred. He could hardly move. His bones ached. He was stiff and numb.

"Get up!"

Carl got slowly to his feet. His head ached and rang. He could hardly see. He was terribly tired. Up the bank he climbed, trembling and shaking.

"What's the matter? You sick? Why were you sitting there? How long were you sitting there?"

He did not answer. He made his way to his cot and sat down. One of the counselors came striding along the trail. He halted. "Anything wrong?"

"He's sick," Jimmy said.

The counselor came over. "You sick, Fitter?"

Carl nodded.

"There's something wrong with him," Jimmy said.

He lay in the nurse's tent, in the big bed. The sheets were crisp and white. He was very tired. He wanted only to lie quietly.

The nurse came in. "How do you feel?"

"All right." It was early morning, about ten. He could see the sun, shining through the tent flap.

The nurse took his temperature. "Your mother will be up sometime today. Do you feel well enough for the trip back?"

Carl nodded.

"Have you had breakfast?"

"No."

"I'll have someone bring over your pancakes." The nurse went out of the tent, past the table of bottles.

Carl gazed out at the sunlight and the trees and vines. Soon he would be going home. His mother was coming. He was tired. He turned over on his side and closed his eyes.

A sound filtered into his sleep. He lifted his head a little. The room came into focus. Someone was standing by the bed, looking silently down at him. He stirred, turning over. Was it — His heart caught. Was it —

The woman moved closer. It was his mother. He lay back.

"What did you do, fall in the water?" his mother demanded.

He did not answer.

"Get your clothes on. We're going back to town. I can't understand why they'd let a child fall in the water and just sit and get sick."

"I didn't fall in." But she had gone out of the tent. He got slowly out of bed.

"Hurry up," her voice came. "Do you need help?"

"No," Carl said.

Carl's mother died while he was in junior high school. He went to live with his grandmother and grandfather. They were German. His grandfather worked for the Wonder Bread Company. He slept all day long down in the cellar, coming up late at night to go to work.

It was a huge old house that his grandparents had. In the front an ancient palm tree rose up, dirty and ugly. The front porch sagged. One of the side windows was broken. Carl had a room of his own, in the back of the house, where he could see the garden. The backyard was large. It was full of cats. At night he could hear them quarreling among themselves. The yard was wild and overgrown. The garden had not been tended for years. There were many plants out in the back. Bamboo, wisteria, jungle grass. At the far end berry bushes sagged with dripping blackberries.

Early in the summertime Carl liked to go outside and stand, smelling the berries rotting in the sun, a sweet hot smell, like flesh of a person near him. He liked to go and lie down in the jungle grass near the berry bushes, smelling them, feeling them close to him. The smell of the berries, the warm wind, the movement of the bamboo all came together and made him sense life so close and tangent that he could scarcely believe there was not someone in the yard with him.

He would become tired and go to sleep, lying in the grass. When he woke from sleep he always felt loggy and saturated with the smell and presence of the garden. He would struggle to his feet and go into the house to wash his face.

Looking in the cracked mirror in the high-ceilinged old bathroom, the walls yellow and peeling, Carl would wonder at his reflection, wonder where he was going and what would finally become of him, as he grew older. His mother was dead. His grandparents were quite old. Soon he would be out on his own, earning his own living, making his own way. Where would he go? Which direction would he take? Soon he would know.

He gazed and wondered.

16

WHEN CARL WAS in high school he joined the chess club and the debating team. He debated political questions with great zeal. There was one debate a week, held after school in one of the class rooms. Anyone who wanted to could come and listen. A few students came, and some of the teachers.

"You're a good debater, Carl," Mr. McPherson said to him one day. "When we debate against Lawrence High I want you on the team."

Carl swelled with pleasure. "No kidding?"

"What question do you want to take? The teams usually submit sample questions."

Carl considered. "I want to defend the Political Action Committee," he stated. The PAC was under attack that year. Sidney Hillman was on the hook from all sides.

Mr. McPherson raised an eyebrow. "Really? That's not my idea of a good subject. Why don't you take federal aid to schools? Wouldn't you rather tackle that?"

"No. I want to defend the PAC. I feel a labor union has the right to make itself heard. How else can the working class gain political representation? It's useless to expect the regular parties to represent labor. They're firmly in the hands of reactionary big city business men."

Mr. McPherson shook his head. "Well, we'll see," he murmured. He went off down the hall.

Carl had been a socialist for some time, ever since the middle of the tenth grade. He had attended a lecture on socialism by the Youth Socialist League at a neighborhood church. He contributed twenty-five cents and took home a handful of pamphlets. The pamphlets described the condition of the working masses. It was pretty awful.

"Look at this," Carl said to Bob Baily. They were sitting at a soda fountain. It was after school. Other high school kids sat around them, throwing paper wads at each other and playing the juke box.

"What is it?" Baily said.

Carl handed him a pamphlet, folded open. "Read it."

Baily read it, his lips moving. Presently he gave it back.

"What do you think?" Carl demanded.

"Interesting."

"Did you know things like that went on in this country?"

"I guess not."

"Strikers beaten, their wives terrorized. Children working fifteen hours a day." Carl told him about a book in which a child, working in a pork refining plant, had gradually lost his feet in the pools of corrosive acid lying everywhere on the cement floor, until at last there was nothing left below his ankles.

"Terrible," Baily said.

"Well?"

"Well what?"

"What are you going to do about it?"

Baily considered. He was a tall thin youth with glasses and red hair. He shook his head. "I don't know."

"Don't you want to get out in the streets?"

"Streets?"

"The barricades!" Carl shouted, his eyes flashing, his face alight.

Baily was puzzled. But by then their cokes had come and the matter was forgotten. Carl drank his coke, staring off into the distance.

"What are you thinking about?" Baily asked.

Carl stirred. "What?"

"What are you thinking about?"

Carl smiled a little. "Many things," he said.

Carl went to college only one year. It was election year. A friend of his, a graduate student doing work in the political science department, was running for the office of city councilman against the corrupt Democratic and Republican candidates. Earl Norris was running on his own. He did not go along with anybody, not even with the Progressive Party, which was controlled by Stalinists.

Carl helped him with his campaign. They argued with Progressives they knew and distributed leaflets in the downtown district of town.

One night, very late, they drove through town putting up campaign posters of Norris on telephone poles. Their old Ford drove silently along, without lights. When they came to a pole Carl leaped off, ran up to the curb and stapled the poster to the pole, and then ran back.

"How's it coming?" Norris whispered. He was behind the wheel.

"Fine."

At the next pole, as Carl was running back to the car, a police car slid up behind them.

"All right," the policeman said.

There was an old city law against using property of the city for campaign purposes. The telephone poles all belonged to the city. But when the judge learned that Norris was running on his own as a graduate student of the political science department he suspended sentence and let them go. It would have been thirty days.

Carl and Norris stood outside the police station in the bright sunlight. People flocked by, going to work.

"See how the reactionaries stifle the voice of the masses," Norris grumbled.

He did not win the election. The Republican candidate won, with the Democratic candidate next. Norris received almost no votes. But at least, the Progressives didn't get in.

"It's pretty hard to make yourself heard," Carl murmured.

"Someday it'll change," Norris said.

To stay out of military service Carl accepted a job with the American Metals Development Company, for overseas work. It was an indefinite assignment. And as long as he were with the Company he would be draft exempt.

The night before he was supposed to sail he felt a strange nostalgia begin to move around inside him. It began as he was walking back to his room after eating dinner uptown. He walked slowly, his hands in his pockets. It was a warm July night. Thousands of stars clustered overhead. Many people were out in the streets, walking along the sidewalks, men and women together, kids scampering around, high school boys in cars parked with their girls in drive-ins, eating hot dogs and ice cream.

Carl thought about himself and all the things that had happened to him. He thought about the early years of his life, when they had lived in the East where it was cold and the land was snow-covered in the winter. He thought of his mother working all day. He had been very much alone as a child, alone with his things, his stamps and books and thoughts.

Carl turned and walked back past the neon signs of the stores, back toward the campus. The campus was dark. All the buildings were silent and deserted, except the library. The university library was still open.

He thought of camp. The time he had gone away to summer camp. The redwoods. As he walked through the campus he thought of the stream, the silent trees, the cold water and bright sun. The campus was like that, dark and empty with trees rising up around him on all sides.

Carl came to the library building and stopped. The great marble building was ablaze with lights. Did he want to go inside? He walked around it. Grass was under his feet, moist green grass. He could see it in the light from the library windows. A group of college kids passed, girls and boys, laughing and talking together. After a time a silent couple came along, a boy and girl walking quietly together, holding hands in the darkness.

Carl thought of high school. The debate team. The Youth Socialist League. The speech he had made for socialism that time the principal was there.

His thoughts returned to camp. How wonderful it had been, before he got sick. He had never gone back. His mother had not let him. Now she was dead, killed in a street accident. His life had been much happier since her death. She had been so thin and hard. Pushing him all the time. Making him do things.

Now he was leaving the country. Going away to work in Asia. How long would he be gone? He did not know. A year, perhaps. Maybe many years. What would it be like? He did not know that, either. He did not know where he was going. He scarcely knew where he had come from. His past was dark, in shadow. A vague gloomy memory of sounds and shapes and smells. The redwoods. Grass at night. Neon signs. Snow. A slow moving creek. His old room full of stamps and microscope slides and pictures.

Carl went inside the library. The marble halls were bright with yellow light. He climbed the stairs to the main reading room. He did not have a card, but he could use the reference books.

For a while he sat in the reference room, reading the Cambridge *Ancient History* series. He read about Greece. The familiar passages, the wars, the battles. Alcibiades. Cleon. Pericles. He found the part about Thermopylæ and his heart warmed. The brave Spartans. . . .

He found somebody he knew, a friend studying for an exam. With his friend's card he took out Xenephon's *Anabasis* and sat reading it. The snow. All the hills. . . . They reminded him of his own life. That was what he retained of his life, the memory of snow and of streets, trees, silent water.

Carl closed the book and dropped it into the return slot. It was growing late. The library would be closing in a little while.

He left the building, walking down the great while halls, down the stairs, outside into the warm darkness. He took a deep breath of the night air. The air was sweet, heavy with the odor of flowers. There was a huge purple bush by the door. The air was full of its smell.

He walked down the path, away from the building. One by one the library lights winked off behind him. Other young men and women walked with him, some behind, some in front. They were quiet. A faint wind had come up. The wind rustled around Carl, carrying sounds to him. Snatches of conversation. The noise of footsteps. Men and women walking through the darkness away from the library.

He crossed a small bridge. His shoes echoed against the boards. A level grass meadow sloped away. Beyond it the neon signs of town glinted, red and yellow, deep orange and violet. A restaurant. A theater. A real estate place. A loan office. A cafe.

He stood at the end of the bridge, looking out across the grass

at the black buildings and neon signs rising up against the sky.
People passed him, students going home, books and papers under their arms.

Soon he would leave. Soon he would be a long way off. Maybe
he would never come back. Maybe he would never stand in
this spot again, see these trees, the grass, the outlines of the
buildings. Far off a car honked. Cars and busses. Traffic moving through the town. People on the sidewalks. In the cafés. The
theaters.

More students passed him. Carl pulled himself upright. He
crossed onto the grass. Ahead of him a girl cut across the grass,
walking quickly and silently. For a moment she was outlined
against the night sky. Slim, slim and supple. With long hair. In
the darkness her hair was black. He could see her face, the line
of her jaw, her nose, her forehead.

His heart jumped. He hurried, walking quickly up behind
her. Vague memories pulsed through him. A slim girl, dark,
with long black hair. He hurried, trembling a little, staying behind her.

The girl came to the edge of the grass, stepping down onto
the sidewalk. She crossed the street. Carl crossed after her. She
passed under a neon sign.

It was not the girl with the dark hair. In the light this girl's
hair was brown.

Carl slowed down. After a while he turned off to the right. It
was time to go home. He had to get up early the next morning.
The ship was sailing at eight o'clock.

The girl disappeared, lost from sight, into the night darkness.
Carl walked back to his room, his hands deep in his pockets.

Carl shook himself, standing up. He was stiff. How long had he
been sitting and thinking about himself? Down below him the
Company grounds stretched out, bringing him back to the pres-

ent. What a bad thing to do, sitting in the bright morning sunlight, going over his youth, again and again!

He was glad he had finished with it, got it all behind him. It was an unfortunate youth, a time of doubt and not knowing. A time of groping in ignorance. He looked up at the sun. What time was it? The sun had moved almost to the top of the sky. He had been sitting a long time.

Carl stretched, throwing out his big arms and opening his mouth. He made a great bellowing sound, twisting around, stamping his foot several times. Then he began to pick his way back down the slope again, solemn and full of thoughts, going over what he had been thinking of, all his memories, the little dead bird, the strangeness of his childhood.

Preoccupied with these thoughts he wandered at last to the artificial lake in the center of the Company property. He stopped by the lawn a moment and then crossed and entered the row of fir trees. He was about to come out on the edge of the water when he heard a sound. It was splashing, something in the lake, leaping around, throwing water in all directions.

Carl made his way quickly to the edge of the lake, his heart beating rapidly. Someone was in the water. The sun shone down, reflecting on the surface of the water with a brilliant glare of light. He shaded his eyes. The person in the water was thrashing around. He saw the glistening of a pale golden body, limbs slender and round. It was Barbara. She was in the water with nothing on, playing by herself. He started to back away, his face red.

But then he stopped and stood quietly by the trees. Could he be seen? Probably not. The mathematical chance was very slight. A curious boldness had come over him. He had been pondering the mysteries of life, the secrets of the dark universe, ever since early morning. Wasn't this part of the universe?

Wasn't this one of the hidden realities, held back, usually concealed from sight, an esoteric scene viewed only by a few? And if he were careful she wouldn't see him.

Carl stood watching the girl in the water. She was having quite an exciting time for herself. Water flew in all directions. Presently she began to make her way toward the shore. She climbed out of the water, up onto the concrete rim, dripping and struggling. Carl felt his heart begin to beat more quickly, and in spite of his deep inner calm a glow of redness crept up into his cheeks and ears. The lake was not wide. He could see the girl quite clearly as she clambered up on the opposite side.

This was the first time in his life he had seen a woman naked. It was like birth and death and marriage and becoming twenty-one. It was strange and important. And it would never come again.

He watched her, kneeling by the edge of the grass, wringing her hair out. For a moment his sight blurred, as if it were failing. He put his hands on his hips and took a deep breath, filling up his lungs. His vision danced before him, bits of red and specks leaping and darting about. On his skin perspiration slid slowly down. A rushing clamminess oozed under his shirt. His body was damp and cold.

But then the moment passed, and after it came a surge of hot blood, blood flowing to his heart, surging with white foam on it, racing through the hollows of his body, through his veins and arteries.

Kneeling on the bank, twisting her brown hair, the girl glistened wet and smooth in the sunlight. A million points of light glittered on her sleek skin. All the rare jewels, all the precious stones were there, too many ever to count, far beyond the diamonds of the path, the orbs of dew on the lawn. This was beyond what he had known before; this shone with a tawny richness that reduced the grass and the soil and the trees and hills to their proper place.

Nothing he had seen had such grace as her naked arms and shoulders. No colors he knew were as intense as the gold and white of her skin, fresh from the water. He saw her hands move. She was shaking her head, tilting her head on one side. She squeezed one last time and then threw her head back, looking up at the sky. Her brown hair, thick and heavy, fell back onto her neck. Her face, small and clearly lined, gazed up. She got to her feet slowly and stood.

Now he saw her completely, for the first time. She was not tall. She was much smaller than he had expected. It was not what he had expected at all. The pin-up pictures and drawings and calendars had misled him. They had pictured great women with immense legs, curved and long, massive breasts high in the air. This girl was not like that at all. She was small and rather heavy, not fat or dumpy, but rather short. Her body was not so different from the bodies he had seen among the boys in the school gym. Except that it was smoother, and the hips were wider. But she was not tall, and her legs were only legs, with knee caps and feet, feet resting firmly on the ground.

Her breasts amazed him. They did not jut out and up. They did not swell, pressing forward as the drawings had shown them. They hung down, and when she bent over they fell away from her. They bounced and swung when she picked up her clothes, bending over and reaching down to dress. They were not hard cups at all, but flesh like the rest of her, soft pale flesh. Like wineskins hanging on tent walls, in Middle East villages. Sacks, wobbling flesh sacks that must have got in her way every now and then.

She buttoned her short red pants and fastened her gray blouse around her. She sat down to tie her sandals. Now she looked the same as she always had, not white, bare, chunky. Her breasts were again curves under her blouse, not bulging wine-skins hanging down. In the close-fitting pants and blouse she looked taller and slimmer.

She finished dressing and then went off, across the lawn. He lost sight of her. She had disappeared. It was finished. He re-laxed. His blood subsided. His heart began to return to normal, the color draining out of his cheeks and ears. He sighed, letting out his breath.

Had it really happened? He felt dazed. In a way he was disap-pointed. She had been white and short, bulging here and there. With legs for walking and feet for standing. Her body was like all bodies, a physical creation, an instrument, a machine. It had come into the world the same way as other things, from the dust and wet slime. After a while it would wither and sag and crack and bend, and the tape and glue and tacks would give way to let it sink back down into the ground again, from which it had come.

It would break and wear out. It would fade and pass away, like the grass and the flowers, the great fir trees above him, like the hills and the earth itself. It was a part of the ordinary world, a material thing like other material things. Subject to the same laws. Acting in the same way.

He thought suddenly of his drawings, the pin-ups he had copied, all the notions and images that had crowded into his mind as he sat in his stuffy room with the sunlight shining through the drapes. He smiled. Well, at least he had gained a new understanding. He had lost all the cherished images and illusions, but he understood something now that had eluded him before. Bodies, his body, her body, all were about the same. All were part of the same world. There was nothing outside the world, no great realm of the phantom soul, the region of the sublime. There was only this — what he saw with his eyes. The trees and sun and water. He, Barbara, everyone and everything, were parts of this. There was nothing else.

And it was not as if his secret inner world, the spirit world that he had nourished so long, had suddenly come crashing down around him. There were no ruins and sad remains to pick over. Rather, all the dreams and notions he had held so long had abruptly winked out of existence. Vanished silently, like a soap bubble. Gone forever. As if they had never existed.

While he was thinking this Barbara came up behind him and stopped a few feet away.

"What are you doing?"

Carl turned slowly. "Hello."

"For God's sake! What are you *doing*?"

Carl studied her. Her hair was still wet and dripping. Her clothes were already beginning to stick to her in great dark patches. She looked angry.

"Was that you out in the water?" Carl murmured. "I see you got out all right. I thought for a little while you were in some sort of trouble."

She was standing very close to him, her damp blouse rising and falling. The gray cloth stuck to her wet skin. He could see the outline of her breasts, her nipples hard and dilated, quivering angrily. Her teeth were crooked and uneven, and her hair was thick. But she was pretty. She had lovely eyes, and her skin was smooth and clear. Wet and angry, she was still supple and attractive.

"If I had drowned would you have pulled me out?" She was trembling. Her teeth were chattering.

"I would have pulled you out," Carl said, folding his arms.

"I don't understand. What are you doing here?" Barbara shook her head. "Why were you watching me? What's the matter with you?"

Her voice trembled. He saw tears come up into her eyes. She looked so cold and miserable. . . . He felt sudden pity, and a little guilt.

"I'm sorry," he said. "Don't be mad."

She did not answer. She stood without speaking, staring down, wiping water from her neck.

"You better get inside. You should take a bath and dry yourself off. Get into dry clothes. Otherwise you probably will catch cold."

"Really?"

"Let's walk back to the dorm. Okay? We'll go back together."

"I don't care." She turned and started through the trees. Carl hesitated. Then he followed after her, deep in thought, not hurrying but keeping up with her. At the edge of the grove of trees, Barbara halted, waiting impatiently for him.

"Come on! Do you want me to catch cold?"

Carl smiled. "No."

"Then hurry."

He came up beside her. "If you walk in the sun and keep out of the shadows you should be all right. But a good hot bath would be a good thing."

They walked along together, neither of them saying anything.

"Are you mad because I saw you?" Carl asked.

Barbara did not answer.

17

WHILE EVERYONE ELSE was outside enjoying himself, Verne Tildon sat in the office at the typewriter, a sheet of soft yellow paper sticking up in front of him.

With one finger he tapped slowly, weighing each word carefully.

" . . . I, Verne Tildon, acting as Agent for the American Metals Development Company, during the period of actual transfer . . . "

He stopped typing and studied the paper. Then he went on.

" . . . to the new owners, for whose guarantee of adequate protection the Company is maintaining through my own self and two other responsible employees a constant watch over . . . "

He stopped, scowling. There was something wrong with the sentence. He took a second piece of yellow paper and scratched a few lines of words with his fountain pen. He read them over carefully, pondering. Then he got up from the desk and went over to the window. He opened the window and returned to his place before the typewriter.

He pulled the paper out of the typewriter and inserted a fresh sheet.

"I, Verne Tildon, representing the American Metals Development Company, have been given responsibility in the following matters to arrange and otherwise bring about in the best possible manner the main physical transfer of all holdings and real assets . . ''

Suddenly he leaped up. Somebody had come up on the porch. Strange light feet. Not Carl. Not Barbara. He listened, frozen. There was no sound, only silence. Maybe he had been mistaken.

The sound came again. Somebody was standing on the porch. The doorknob turned slowly. Verne's heart thudded. He glanced around the office. What the hell — no hammer, nothing. Where was Carl? Carl was big.

The door opened. A small man peered uncertainly inside, blinking and bobbing nervously. A thin Oriental face turned in Verne's direction.

"Hello," the Oriental said.

"Who are you?"

The man came in, shutting the door behind him. Verne did not move. The man was small and slender. It was hard to tell how old he was. Perhaps forty. He wore a faded uniform of the last war, cloth leggings and metal-soled boots. In his left hand was a small cap.

"Who am I?" the man echoed. His voice was dry and nasal, as if he had a cold. He reached into his coat and brought out an envelope. "You may examine these, if you wish. My papers."

Verne took the envelope and opened it. Cards and documents, written in Oriental characters, stamped and signed, with tiny photographs of the man, rows of numbers and seals.

"I can't read these."

"They are to inform you that we will be moving in here in a few days. I have come a little ahead of time to make sure everything is in order."

"You represent the new owners?"

"I represent the Chinese People's Political Consultative Conference. At this time the All-China People's Congress is not in convocation. Supreme power of the People's Republic of China is therefore vested at this time in the Chinese People's PCC."

"I see," Verne said. "In a few days? I thought we had more time than that. This comes as somewhat of a shock. Just a few days?"

"Two or three days. I came on ahead. If everything is in order the change can be made at once. We were not sure if you had been able to evacuate your personnel on time."

Verne hesitated. "Do you want to sit down?"

"Thank you." The little Chinese sat down by the desk, crossing his legs. He took out a package of Russian cigarettes and put one in his mouth.

Verne sat down across from him. He watched the Chinese light his cigarette. The matches did not seem to work. Several of them were needed before the cigarette was going.

"You speak American," Verne said. "Are there Americans around?"

"Oh, no. I learned American in Peoria. Ten years ago. I was there on a business trip."

Verne put out his hand. "My name is Tildon. Verne Tildon." They shook hands.

"Harry Liu."

Verne studied him. Harry Liu was pale and slight. His face was flat and expressionless. He was beginning to become bald. His hands were long and the fingers thin. On one finger was a heavy metal ring.

"You don't look like your name ought to be Harry."

Harry Liu smiled. "Use any name you wish, then."

"You're a soldier?"

"Oh, yes. For a long time. I have not been active for a number of years. On the Long March I injured my leg. It was a very long way."

"Yes. It was a long way. I remember."

"I wonder what Kafka would have thought about it. You recall his story, 'The Great Wall of China.' He told how the people in one part of China might be paying taxes to an emperor, long since dead, not knowing of the new emperor. The country is so large. . . . I walked most of the distance. Near the end I went on in one of the trucks, when my leg gave out."

Verne nodded. "I suppose historians will someday call that one of the turning points in history."

"It depends, I think, on what kind of historians exist in the future."

"But it did represent something. An end to something and the beginning of something else. Maybe the end of a cycle. As Toynbee or Vico would say."

"Yes, the cyclic historians."

"Some of them seem to think our time is going into a period like the Roman period. About the time of Christ. Or later. When the Empire began to retreat. When the *pax* was beginning to break up."

Harry Liu smiled. "Would you say, then, that you are the last of the Romans? I wonder what that would make us. It's an interesting analogy."

"Interesting?"

"It would seem to make us the first Christians."

Verne stood up. "Is there anything you want me to show you before you go? Any of the installations?"

"Yes. It might be a good idea. I'm supposed to see what condition the grounds are in."

Verne opened the door and walked out onto the porch. "I'll show you what you want to see."

Harry Liu joined him. "Fine."

They walked down the porch steps, onto the road. Verne saw

a little light bicycle parked a few yards down. He walked up to it. "This is yours?"

"Yes."

It was a Russian-built bike. Verne examined it. When he was finished he and Harry Liu walked down the road, away from the office.

"What do you want to see?" Verne said.

"Nothing in particular. The main question was whether you had removed your staff and closed down all the processing."

"We have."

"How many people remain here?"

"Three. Myself and two others. We're supposed to turn the ground over to you." Verne was deep in thought, scowling as he walked along.

"Is anything wrong?" Harry Liu asked.

"Your analogy. To the Romans."

"Not mine," Harry said. "I didn't create it."

"My analogy, then. That we're the last of the old world. The old Romans. And you're the new. The first Christians."

"Yes?"

"I'm wondering about the Dark Ages. That's what the Christians brought. Brutality, cruelty, force. The end of reason and freedom. Serfdom. The Middle Ages. The lowest ebb in history. Each person living on a tiny hunk of ground like an animal. Chained to it. No hope, no education. Just enough food and clothing to keep him alive. Slavery — under a different name."

"But that's not all."

"Oh?"

"There was the Church. Don't forget that. Was it really so dark? Look what the Church gave him, a chance for eternal life, a meaning for his existence. The Church explained why he was alive. And it gave him the key to salvation."

"It *promised* him salvation. Empty promises to keep people in line. They sucked the people dry. Worked them to death. Fairy tales, glitter and pomp to make up for their empty lives. Don't you remember what Lenin said?"

"'The opiate of the people.'" Harry Liu nodded. "I remember. God, the Holy Trinity, the Virgin Birth. It doesn't mean much to us today. But it meant a lot, then. I wonder if it was really so dark. The Dark Ages. We call them dark, but there was a spiritual activity there, a strong spiritual feeling. They didn't consider their times dark. The early Christians were willing to die for their Church, for what they believed."

"They were swindled."

"By our standards. But our emphasis is so much different. We have lost interest in their things. The idea of God. The hierarchy, physical and moral. The levels, earth to water to air to fire. The universe in which a moral God moved. In which there was a visible rise to purity from the gross earth below, to more pure water, to the heavens, and finally to God's realm, the fire beyond the heavens, the stars. And someday every man was taken up there, lifted and purified."

"Empty words."

"Perhaps. And perhaps the New Christians bring only empty words, too. Promises. Promises and a new Dark Age. Brutality and ignorance, and the end of reason. But our words have meaning for us, the way their words had a meaning for them. The Holy Trinity. Empty words — now. But not empty then."

Verne glanced at Harry Liu curiously. "Do you believe in God?"

"I? Oh, no. But it depends on what you mean by God. We took down the ikons and put up pictures of a man instead, and perhaps he is our god. Some of us may bow down in front of him, before his will, and it it said that he can do no wrong." Harry Liu considered. "So perhaps we have the Holy Trinity back again, in a new form. Old wine in new bottles. We have restored a lost age. And perhaps the brutality and ignorance, too."

Verne stopped to light his pipe. Harry Liu's eyes followed the flick of the lighter with interest.

"A pipe lighter," Verne said. "Quite a gadget." He passed it to the little Chinese.

Harry Liu studied it. "Yes. Much better than these." He tapped his box of Chinese matches in the pocket of his coat. "Only a few of them light." He held Verne's lighter out.

An impulse seized Verne. "Keep it."

"The lighter?"

"You can have it. I can get another easily. A present. From the old world to the new." He smiled grimly.

Harry slid the lighter into his coat. "Thank you." He was silent for a time. "The others. You said there were two others here."

"Yes. A woman and a young boy."

"Where are they?"

"Off someplace. Probably listening to his treatise on ethics. At least, that's what they say they do."

"Do you have doubts?"

"I don't know. Maybe they're reading. It doesn't matter."

"What are they like, the woman and the young boy?"

Verne shrugged. "Nothing unusual."

"Is the woman young? Is she attractive?"

"As a matter of fact she's a girl I had an affair with, years ago."

"Does the young boy know?"

"I doubt it. I doubt if she'd mention it. It wasn't too pleasant. She was very young at the time."

"And you were much older, of course."

"Of course."

"You and I are perhaps the same age," Harry Liu said thoughtfully. "We are getting old. I am getting bald and your hair is thinning. It was not like that when you and the girl had your affair, I assume."

"It had started."

"I wonder why an affair between a young woman and an older man should be unpleasant. In China such things are common. But they're not usually unpleasant."

"She wasn't even twenty. It was at a vacation resort in New England. She was staying with some college people. We met by accident. I drove her back down in my car. She didn't know what was happening. I took her to a motel and pushed her into bed. It's a good way to learn realism."

"Your society places such a value on realism. I noticed it when I was in Peoria."

"Don't you?"

Harry Liu set his lips. "What is wonderful about the real world? Atoms and void. I will tell you a very interesting fact. In our society, we older people are forbidden by law to destroy the fantasies of youth. In fact, we create fairy tales for them to believe."

"So I've heard. Your scientists are under the thumb of the politicians. They can't tell the truth about the world. And the artists the same way."

"That's so. Like the science of the Middle Ages. Our science and art are bent to social needs. Servants of our political planning."

"Slaves of your new religion. You approve?"

"I think so."

"You want a country of children? You want to keep them from growing up and learning the truth about things?"

Harry Liu smiled. "Are we doing that? Perhaps."

"It's vicious. What are you? A new Church with a new pope, ruling the people with an iron club, dictating to them, telling them what to think and do and believe — "

"Yes. We direct them now. And hope they will be able to direct themselves, someday. I and my group are almost gone, the group that knows our tales are fairy tales. Fantasies. Those who are coming will believe them and call them truth. They won't want to grow out of them. They will not even know there is such a thing as growing out of them. And I will not tell them, because I can't. It is the law. And it is a very wise law."

"You don't want them to know."

"It's for their own good. Atoms and void. . . . It is social realities that count. That must come first. All other truths must be bent. Art, science. We provide them with myths, wise myths. As the Church did. They are not literally so. But they are wise. They have meaning. They will help, when they are needed."

Verne and Harry Liu walked along in silence, neither of them speaking. At last they came to the huge heaps of slag, the quarries dug out of the ground, the miles of rubbish and scrap that had been discarded, voided by the great machines and factories.

"This is the end," Verne said, stopping. "There's nothing more from here on. We might as well go back."

They walked back.

"Well?" Verne said finally. "What are you going to do with it? It's all yours. What are you going to do?"

"I don't know. It's not for me to decide."

"Are you going to use it? Or break it all up?"

"Some things will be destroyed. We need parts, tools, materials. But everything will be reworked. We will have to change everything." Harry Liu kicked at a piece of rock in the road. "We'll cart off all the piles of rubbish. Tear down the towers. A lot of cleaning will have to be done. And then reworking, reforming. Changes everywhere."

"For good ends, I hope."

"Good? Good, beautiful, truthful. I wonder."

"You wonder?"

They had come to Harry Liu's bicycle. The little Chinese swung himself onto the saddle, lowering himself in place. "I wonder if such things are real. Remember what your famous judge said. Pilate. The judge in the Bible."

"Pontius Pilate."

"He said one very good thing. 'What is truth?'"

"But Christ said, 'I am the truth.'"

Harry glanced at him. He smiled, a thin hard smile. "'I am the truth.' Precisely."

Verne felt a cold chill. "So that's it."

Harry Liu moved off down the road, balancing himself expertly on the bike, a thin man, very small, in his faded uniform. Verne watched him as he grew smaller and smaller, bouncing up and down slightly, holding onto the handlebars with both hands, his face expressionless.

Verne turned to go. All at once he paused.

Harry Liu had halted the bike. Verne watched him, puzzled. Harry Liu groped in his coat pocket. He brought out something. Very carefully he dropped it onto the road and stepped on it, grinding the heel of his boot into it. The remains sparkled in the sunlight.

Verne's lighter.

Verne shuddered. "My God." He made his way back toward the office. When he looked again Harry Liu was gone. "My God." He shook his head, dazed. "So that's what it will be. . . . "

Carl and Barbara walked slowly along the paths. In the warm sunlight Barbara's hair was beginning to dry out. The stream of water that had been trickling down her neck had stopped.

Her clothing no longer clung to her. Some of her spirits began to flow back a little.

"How do you feel now?" Carl asked.

"All right."

"That's good." They continued in silence for a time. Presently they came to the women's dormitory. Carl stopped. He waited for Barbara to speak.

"Want to sit around while I change?" Barbara said, finally.

"I should go on and get something to eat. I've been up a long time. I'm hungry."

"If you want to wait I'll eat with you later."

Carl considered.

"Hurry up," Barbara said impatiently. "Make up your mind. I want to get inside and change."

"Lead the way."

They walked up the steps into the building. On the second floor Barbara opened the door to her room. They went inside.

"Not bad," Carl said, looking around. "Those are pretty flowers in the vase there." He wandered around the room, gazing at the prints on the walls and the books.

"I'll leave you," Barbara said.

"Yes, go ahead. I'll try not to be in the way." Carl was standing before the bookcase, his hands behind his back, his head tilted to one side, trying to read the titles of the books. Barbara went to the closet and took down her dark slacks. From the dresser she nabbed a white shirt.

"I'll be back soon." Barbara left the room. She hurried down the hall to the bathroom. In a moment hot water was running in the tub. She stripped off her damp clothes.

Soon she was sitting in the tub, letting the hot water pour around her. She sank down into the water as it rose higher and higher. Odd how warm water could take the dampness out of a person. She sighed with relief as the water filled up the tub, covering her more and more. There was no pleasure like a hot bath.

For a long time she lay stretched out in the tub, her hands resting on the rim. She was relaxed, at peace. After all, she had not been in real danger, If she had started to drown Carl would have saved her. Probably he would have waded out, picked her up, and carried her back to shore explaining the Archimedean principle of the displacement of volume and the loss of proportional weight of a body immersed in water. . . .

She laughed nervously. Would he have done that? It would be like him, lecturing and announcing in a booming voice. Maybe he would be too busy explaining to save her. Maybe he would stand over her as she drowned, lecturing and talking, on and on.

Barbara rubbed the bar of Ivory soap into foam, patting the foam against her arms and shoulders. She reached over and turned the taps off. The tub was full. She sank down, washing the soap foam from her. She pulled the plug out and stepped from the tub, onto the bath mat on the floor.

She dried herself, carefully and rapidly. When she was completely dry she put on her clean clothes, the dark slacks and crisp white shirt. Standing before the small mirror she brushed her hair over and over again, until she could feel it against her neck lying light and fluffy. Then she gathered up her old damp clothes and hurried up the hall to her room.

Carl was sitting on the bed reading a book.

"What is it?" Barbara said. "The book."

"Russell's *Outline of Western Philosophy*."

"How is it?" She hung up the towel in the closet.

"Interesting. I'd like to borrow it sometime."

"You can, if you want." Barbara sat down on the chair. "Cigarette?" She held out the package to Carl.

"No thanks. I don't smoke."

Barbara lit a cigarette and put the package on the table. She sat smoking, watching Carl as he turned the pages of the Russell book. Carl glanced up at her uneasily. After a while he put the book down on the bed, closing it.

"I guess I don't want to borrow it. I used to read a lot of philosophy, but not so much any more. I think when I'm through with my treatise I'll forget the whole business."

"What will you read, then?"

"Fiction. I haven't read much fiction. I've spent all my time with Kant and Spinoza."

"Was it wasted?"

"Not completely. Not more than the geometry you learn in high school."

"I'd call that wasted."

"Perhaps." He nodded. "I suppose so. There's more outside to see than in books."

"Do you feel that way?"

"Yes. That's why I walked around today. I got up very early, at seven-thirty."

"You passed by here. I heard you whistling."

"Did I wake you?"

"Yes."

"I'm sorry."

"It doesn't matter. It was a nice morning. I like to be out, too. That's why I was in the water."

"I was surprised to see you splashing around. I was walking back from the hill and I cut across the park. I didn't mean to spy on you."

There was silence.

"Are you angry about it?"

"I was. But it doesn't matter. After all, the park is a public place."

"I'm glad you're not mad any more." Carl smiled at her, his

big honest face beaming in relief. "You were mad for a while. I don't blame you. I shouldn't have been standing there watching. I knew I was doing something wrong. I knew I should have gone away. I realized it at the time. But I'm afraid I didn't. I just stood and watched you."

"I want to know why," Barbara said quietly.

Carl flushed, startled. "I didn't mean to watch. I — "

"You had no right to. You must never do that to another person."

Carl hung his head, crimson with humiliation. He muttered a few words and then subsided into choked silence.

"Don't ever do anything like that again. Not to anyone." Barbara stirred. "Everybody has his own world, his private world. Don't spy and ruin it."

"Did — did I do *that*?"

She looked quickly up. "That's what you wanted to do."

"No!"

"You invaded my world."

"No! I didn't mean to! You're wrong. It wasn't that at all."

"Okay." She nodded briefly. "Let's forget it."

She lit another cigarette and sat smoking rapidly, her hands pressed tightly into fists, not looking at Carl. Carl shifted unhappily. He swallowed a few times. At last he got to his feet.

Barbara glanced up. "What is it?"

"I think I'd better go."

"No. Sit down."

Carl sat down awkwardly, feeling for the bed behind him. Barbara continued to sit in silence, her eyes bright, staring into the distance, unseeing.

"I have to do some things," Carl muttered. "I have some letters to write. I — "

"You're going?"

"I really have to."

"Do you think you can come and go as you please?"

Carl did not understand. He shook his head, bewildered. "What do you mean?"

Barbara crushed her cigarette out. "You came and watched when you wanted. Now you're going. Do you think you can do that? Do you think people will always let you do that?"

"I —"

"You're growing up. You're getting to be a man. Someday you will be a man. Do you think you can do that when you're a man?"

"I don't know."

"You can't. You can't." She put her hand up, rubbing her eyes quickly. Carl slunk down in his chair. She was crying. Tears were running between her fingers, down her cheeks, falling silently onto her shirt, staining her starched white shirt.

"Can — can I do anything for you?" Carl murmured.

She shook her head. After a long time she jumped up and crossed the room to the dresser. She pulled a handkerchief from the drawer and turned her back to Carl, blowing her nose. She moved over to the window and stood, her arms folded, the handkerchief pressed in a tight ball between her fingers.

"Carl," she said.

"Yes?"

She turned around, smiling at him, her eyes dark and bright. "I'm sorry. Don't worry about it."

He nodded.

Barbara sat down on the bed, leaning back. She sighed, letting her breath out slowly. "It's too nice a day. It is nice, isn't it? The sun and everything."

"Yes."

"Why were you up so early today?"

"I wanted to get outside. I wanted to take a long walk and see how things were."

"Where did you go?"

"Oh, I wandered around. I went up on the hill and sat thinking. I thought for a long time. About my childhood. Then I came down. That was — that was when I saw you. I crossed the park and I saw you in the water."

"Yes. It was beautiful. The sun and the water. I know. Well, Carl?"

"Yes?"

She leaned toward him, looking intently into his face. They were very close together. Carl waited apprehensively, his hands on his knees. Barbara rocked back and forth, touching her hand to her cheek, her ear. He could see the rapid tension of her body, taut and nervous. Her eyes were dark and large.

"You go ahead and do whatever it is you have to get done," she said suddenly. "Run along and get it all finished."

Carl stood up quickly. "All right."

Barbara crossed to the door, opening it for him. "When will it be done?"

Carl faltered. "Done?"

"When will you be finished?"

He considered. He felt strange. His scalp and ears prickled. He licked his lips nervously. "I guess in a couple of hours."

Barbara examined her wristwatch, calculating to herself, her lips moving.

"Why?" Carl murmured.

"Why? Don't you remember?"

"No."

Barbara smiled. She swayed back and forth, her arms folded, her lips twisting. "You really don't? You don't remember? You left something unfinished. You have to finish. You started. And when you start something you have to go through with it. Didn't your mother tell you that?"

"What — what is it?"

"Your treatise. You haven't finished reading to me. Don't you remember? I'm surprised at you. I thought it meant so much to you."

Carl grinned doubtfully. "That's right. I was going to read the rest."

"Of course you were. I expect you to read the rest. I've been waiting."

"Have you?"

She nodded. "Yes."

Carl put his hands in his pockets. "There were several parts I wanted you to hear. That's right. I began to read, but I didn't get a chance to finish."

"When are you going to finish?"

Carl considered. "Well, I — "

"How about after dinner?"

"It'll be dark."

Barbara's eyes flickered. "That's so. It will be dark, won't it? I hadn't thought of that. It's a problem. Well, I think perhaps we can read inside where there's light."

"That's an idea."

"Then I'll expect you after dinner. About eight. All right? Don't forget to bring the manuscript with you. You'll be finished with your letters by then. That should give you plenty of time."

"About eight?" Carl moved out into the hall. He felt a little confused. "I guess that's all right."

Barbara closed the door slowly behind him. "I'll see you then. Okay?"

"Okay," Carl said. "About eight."

18

IT WAS EVENING. Carl stood at the top of the stairs, watching Verne climb slowly, his hand on the rail.

"Where have you been all day?"

Verne grunted. "Talking."

"Talking? To whom?"

Verne pushed past Carl, down the hall and into the room. He sat down on his bed with a sigh.

"We thought maybe something had happened to you when you didn't show up for dinner."

"I was thinking. I didn't feel like eating."

"Who were you talking to?"

"A man named Harry."

"You mean they left somebody here besides us?"

"No." Verne pushed up his glasses, rubbing his eyes. "Harry represents the Chinese People's PCC. Or as we call them, the new owners."

Carl's mouth fell open. "Then they've come."

"Yes. They've come. They'll be here any time now. We had a very interesting talk. It gave me something to think about. I've been thinking about it ever since."

"Is he still here?"

"No. He's gone again."

There was silence. Carl was at a loss for words. He opened and closed his mouth a few times. "Well, then we'll have to get ready to leave."

"That's right."

"What's wrong? You sound depressed."

Verne fitted his glasses in place. "I'm tired. Worn out. I guess I'll turn in and get some sleep."

"Gosh, we should do things. Take advantage of the time we have left."

"What do you want to do? Get drunk and fall downstairs?"

"Oh, no. Nothing like that." Carl picked up his brown package, gripping it tightly. "I've got everything all planned out. I'm going to finish reading my treatise."

"By yourself?"

"No. To Barbara." He peered at the clock. "At eight we're going to start. Maybe I can get all the rest of it finished."

Verne turned his head toward the window. The sun had set. The sky was dark violet. A few stars had already begun to come out. "Isn't it a little too dark to go up in the hills? Of course, it depends on what you're going to do."

"We're just going to read."

"For that it's too dark."

"But we're not going up in the hills." Carl beamed happily. "We're going to read in her room."

"Oh?"

"She has her room all fixed up with prints and flowers. It looks wonderful. You should take a look at it. It's quite attractive."

"I've seen it."

"Don't you think it looks fine?"

"Yes. It looks fine."

"What's the matter? You look strange."

"I told you I'm tired."

"Sorry." Carl laid down his package. He began to unbutton his shirt, humming under his breath. He put his shirt over the doorknob and took a clean blue sports-shirt from a hanger.

Verne watched him getting into the new shirt. He raised his eyebrows. "What the hell's that for?"

"This? I'm just changing my shirt." Carl finished buttoning it and went over to look in the mirror. "Maybe I should put on a tie. What do you think?"

"You don't need a tie to read."

"I want to look nice."

"Why?"

"I just want to. After all, a person should try to look his best." He sat down on a chair and rubbed at his shoes with the edge of his handkerchief.

Verne stirred, sitting up a little on the bed. He studied Carl for a time, his face expressionless. At last he got to his feet. "You look fine. Especially for reading a treatise. You have my blessings."

"Your blessings?"

Verne made his way over to the dresser. He pulled the bottom drawer open. "My blessings. I don't think I'll need them any more. I've been saving them. But what the hell. It isn't worth it."

He held up a bottle of John Jamison.

Carl stared at it.

"My blessings."

"No thanks," Carl said.

"What?"

"No thanks. Thanks anyway. I appreciate the gift. And I understand the spirit in which it's given. But you know I never drink."

Verne set the bottle down on the dresser. His face twisted. "You don't?"

"No."

"You belong to the Prohibition Party?"

"I'm just not interested."

"Don't you know anyone you might pour a little glassful for?"

Carl reddened slightly.

Verne put his hand on Carl's shoulder. "Your reaction comes as somewhat of a surprise. Is there some doubt in your mind as to just what's in this bottle? I'm trying to do you a favor, you know. If I had a box of candy I'd give you that. But I don't have a box of candy. Anyhow, I don't think much of candy. There's a poem to that effect. Liquor saves you a lot of intermediate steps. Candy is a waste of time."

"I'm not going over for that."

"For what?"

"For whatever you're talking about. To drink."

"That's not what I'm talking about."

"All right." Carl pulled away. "Maybe I like the intermediate steps. Did you think of that?"

Verne scowled. "Have it your way. I thought you might want some of the obstacles removed."

"I appreciate your help, but I don't want anything like that."

"You should appreciate it in the same sense as pouring anti-freeze into a motor. It does the same thing, only quicker. It's a lot easier to pour the anti-freeze in than to have to push the car twenty blocks to a garage."

"I don't know what you're talking about." Carl grabbed up his manuscript. "It's getting late. I think I'll go."

"Wait a minute."

"What for?"

"I want to talk to you."

Carl halted by the door. "I don't want to be late."

"You don't want to talk, do you? Why not? Are you afraid of what I'm going to say?"

"No."

"Then stick around and listen." Verne sat down on the bed again, leaning back against the wall. "Christ, I'm tired. This thing today almost finished me off."

"What thing?"

"The little yuk. Harry Liu. It's a hard thing to have to face. It's a blow."

Carl waited silently.

"I wish you had been there. You would have learned something. It would have shocked you. It gave me a lot to think about. I wish I could sleep. Maybe I'll feel better tomorrow."

"I'll go and you can go to bed."

"No. I want to talk to you. Before you leave. I think it might be a good idea."

"I'm waiting."

Verne nodded. "Fine." He lapsed into silence, plucking aimlessly at his collar.

"Go on." Carl was impatient. He could not see the clock where he was standing. Not being able to see the clock made him uneasy. "What do you want to say?"

"I don't know. I wish I had more time to work it out. You're going over there? To her?"

"To her room."

"Same thing. The trouble is, I've already made my big offer. The John Jamison. If you don't want that I don't know what to give you."

"Don't give me anything."

"I have to give you something. Even if it's just advice."

"Why?"

"Because you need something. You've got to be careful. Don't walk over there right away. Walk around outside for a while. Get things clear in your mind."

"My mind is clear."

"Do you know what you're getting into?"

"We're going to read."

"You don't believe that anymore than I do. I can tell when the time has come. It's come for you. You know it, too. That's why you changed your god damn shirt."

"I want to look nice."

"For what? I'm trying to talk to you, but it's hard. Maybe there's nothing I can say. I keep searching back in my mind for something. You know, women are very strange. It's difficult to tell about them. You have to proceed cautiously. But your problem is different from mine. Maybe it's not the same."

"My problem?"

"You're too young. And I'm too small. It's a funny thing. Seen through the bottom of a glass all people are the same height."

"So?"

"And the same age. It'll make it a lot easier for you. It's good whisky. The best there is. Take it along. Ask her if she wants some. She'll tell you."

"No thanks."

"You'll be going uphill all the way. It's a long climb. Especially the first time. You have to push over too many road blocks. They set them up." Verne's voice trailed off, sinking into a vague mumble. He sank down on the bed. "They set them up as you go along. As fast as you knock them down they set up another. It gets tiring when you get near the top. Too damn tiring. You want to have a little energy left. Otherwise, what the hell's it all for?"

He was silent, staring blankly ahead.

"But that's not all."

Carl waited, his hand on the door, gripping his manuscript. Verne was silent a long time, deep in his thoughts. At last he roused himself.

"That's not all. There's more to it. Women are complex. You

never really understand them. Be careful when you're around them. I wish you had more time. I could tell you a few stories. You know, when I was your age an interesting thing happened to me. Sometime I'll have to tell you about it. I was nineteen."

"I'm older than that."

"I was working for Wineberg's Department Store. In the bookkeeping department. I met a little girl, tall and blonde. Blue eyes. Soft hair. God, what a lovely little bitch she was. Ellen something. I don't even remember. It was a long time ago. She was my first. Up in my room. I was shaking like a leaf. I could hardly move. It was raining. I remember that. The rain was coming down outside. Pouring rain. Cold. Gray. And us in the bed, warm like toast. It went on and on. Us, and the rain outside. Forever."

Verne closed his eyes.

"Well?" Carl said.

Verne stirred. He raised his head, blinking.

"Go on."

Verne pulled himself up. "You sure you don't want the John Jamison? It's good stuff. It'll keep you warm."

"No."

"You're making a mistake. It casts a glow over things. A lovely glow. Things get soft. Plastic. Not rigid. You can bend them."

Verne slipped back down again.

"I'm tired. You go on. Have a good time. I wish you luck. Who knows? You might make out all right. After some ground work. She might be a good place for you to start." Verne yawned, sagging. "As I recall she wasn't too much trouble. Some are. It varies." His voice died away.

"Goodbye," Carl said. He went out into the hall. The door closed behind him.

Verne lay on the bed. Outside, Carl's footsteps died away.

There was silence. At last Verne struggled up, pulling himself awake. He yawned again.

"Christ." He got to his feet and walked over to the dresser. He stood swaying back and forth, scratching his groin. Finally he belched. "Christ. Well, my intentions were good."

He took the John Jamison down from the dresser. Presently he went down the hall to the bathroom to get a glass.

Carl walked very slowly along, his manuscript under his arm, feeling his way through the darkness. For a little while he thought about the things Verne had said. But after a bit all thoughts seemed to leave his mind.

He gazed up at the sky. Ahead of him the dim outline of a building moved, swinging to one side as he walked toward it. His mind was empty. He clutched his manuscript tightly. How strange! He tried to think of what Verne had been saying, but nothing came. He was relaxed. His mind lay in sleep. The violet sky, the ground under him, the vast dim outlines, all were exciting and full of mystery. They made it hard to concentrate.

He halted, catching his breath. Then he went on, increasing his pace more and more.

His shoe touched something. He was there, at the foot of the steps. Above him, the great wood building cut off the sky, blotting out a section of the violet dusk.

Carl stood for a time. The air was thin and cool. It blew around him, stirring some trees along the side of the dormitory. He could hear the branches of the trees, rubbing together in the darkness. There was no other sound. Only the wind and the trees.

Carl started up the steps. He climbed one at a time, holding onto the railing, going very slowly and quietly. Almost solemnly. As if he were part of some procession. The first person in a religious line, slow-moving, solemn and serious. With his manuscript gripped tightly under his arm like an offering.

On the porch he stopped. He rested. Why should it all seem so solemn to him? Why was he making such an important thing of it? He was only doing what he had done before, carrying his manuscript over to read to Barbara.

But the feeling remained. Perhaps it was what Verne had said. He had made everything seem so important and grim. But this was not grimness that he felt, not now. Not hardness, not that at all. It was awe, the hushed awe of the church. As if he were entering the temple.

The temple. Carl gazed up at the building. And he, carrying his offering. A procession winding its way slowly to the temple, with solemn steps. The offering held tightly, a sacred thing.

But that made him smile. His brown-paper and string bundle, a sacred thing? There was nothing holy about his treatise. It was much too calm, too intellectual, to be a religious object. It was not enough alive.

But there was life, somewhere around him, in the night. The stars, coming out above him. They were alive. The wind and the trees. And dimly, half way up the steep side of the building, a thin line of yellow light. The outline of Barbara's window. And, of course, he, too, was alive. At least, in some sense or other.

Carl entered the building. He made his way up the stairs to the second floor. Yes, he was alive. Especially of late. Since he had stood that moment, in the hot sun, gazing across the water at the girl. Since then especially, he had been alive. But why that had mattered he did not know. It was a mystery, in part.

He came to Barbara's door and rapped.

The door opened. "Come in," Barbara said.

Carl hesitated. "All right."

"Come on!"

He went inside slowly. Barbara closed the door after him. Carl stood shyly in the center of the room, looking around him. "Your room looks wonderful."

"Thanks." Barbara rustled past him. Her face and hair shone, reflecting the light from the lamp in the corner. As if she had been carefully brushed. She had on a flower-print blouse and dark slacks. And sandals. Carl glanced at her again and again as she moved about the room, fixing things here and there.

"Yes, it looks wonderful."

"Put your book down."

"All right." He set his manuscript down on the table by the bed. Barbara had fixed the room up with many colors and fabrics. The room was rich and warm. Carl sat down gingerly on the edge of the bed. "I can't get over how it looks. The drapes. The prints. All the flowers."

Barbara was at the window. She ran her finger over the glass. "It's cold outside, isn't it?" The glass was wet with collected moisture. She pulled the shades down.

"Yes. It's cold." Carl unwrapped his manuscript. He laid the brown paper and string on the floor. Barbara seemed very quiet and withdrawn. She was not saying much. "I won't leave these wrappings around. I'll take them with me when I leave. I don't want to spoil your room."

"It's not so wonderful." Barbara sat down across from him, in a chair.

"I think it looks fine."

"Thank you." She nodded curtly.

Carl leaned back on the bed, arranging his papers. The bedsprings squeaked under him. He made a face.

"Don't mind that. They always do that."

"All right." He made himself comfortable. "Shall I begin?"

"Already?"

He blinked. "Well, I —"

Suddenly Barbara leaped up. She swept two small glasses from the dresser and set them on the table by the bed. From the corner of the room she brought out a bottle of wine and uncorked it.

"What's that?" Carl asked.

"Burgundy."

"Oh."

"Don't you like burgundy?"

"I —" Carl hesitated.

Barbara lowered the bottle. "What's wrong?"

Carl did not know. He searched his mind, but he found everything confused, unclear. "I'm sorry. I guess I would like a little. Thank you very much."

Barbara poured the two glasses full and recorked the bottle. She gave Carl his glass.

Carl sipped. "It's good."

"Yes. It's good wine." Barbara sat down again. The two of them sat silently, sipping from their glasses, neither of them speaking. At last Carl stirred.

"Well, I guess I'll go ahead."

"Fine."

"You — you don't mind listening, do you? I don't want to impose. There isn't very much left."

"Of course I want you to read. I asked you to bring it. You're funny, Carl."

Carl picked up his papers. The room was partly in shadow. Only the small lamp was on. It made the colors and textures of the drapes and prints seem deep and full. The room was lovely, but it was hard for him to see his pages. Barbara was sitting almost in darkness. Her eyes were large and dark. She was lovely, too.

Carl smiled at her. "Here goes."

Barbara leaned back in her chair, crossing her legs. She rested her hands in her lap. Carl felt his heart begin to beat a little faster. And to his surprise he found his voice low and husky, as he began to read the first page of the remaining sections of the treatise.

After he had read a while he noticed that Barbara seemed restless. He lowered the pages.

"What is it?"

Barbara stood up. "I can hardly hear you. Wait." She crossed the room and sat down beside him on the bed. The bedsprings creaked. Carl felt the bed sag.

"Not very strong, is it?" he muttered in confusion. He edged away from her. "I'm sorry my voice is so dry."

"It's all right. Go on." Barbara stretched out on the bed, resting her shoulders against the wall. Carl glanced at her. Then he went on with the treatise.

Barbara, listening to the sound of Carl's voice, felt herself slowly passing into sleep. She rested her body against the wall, hearing the low, intense murmur coming out of him as he sat bent over his manuscript, the pages on his lap. His words were losing their meaning, blending and fading together. But it did not matter.

She watched him sleepily as he read. Carl's face was serious, absorbed, his lips moving. His pages meant so much to him. He had worked on them so hard. His hands were clasped tightly around the page he was reading, as if he were afraid something would happen to it, as if it might blow away and become lost any moment.

"Does it mean so much to you?" she said suddenly.

Carl started. "What?" He lowered the page.

"Does your paper mean so much to you? You're holding it so tightly."

Carl noticed his hands. "I am, aren't I?"

"I didn't mean for you to stop. Go on."

"No. I'll rest my voice for a moment." He laid the paper with the others on his lap. She saw how careful he was to handle them loosely, now. Carelessly.

"I didn't mean to criticize you. I only wondered why. I wondered what was going on in your mind."

Carl tried to think what was going on in his mind, but he did not seem to know. "Why?" he asked.

"I like you, I suppose."

"Do you?"

"Yes. Which is strange. I don't usually like people. I've always been remote from people. Off to my self. As long as I can remember."

Carl nodded.

"Carl, what was your mother like?"

"My mother? Oh, I don't know how to answer that. She was very business-like. I didn't like her. She had some sort of job in personnel work. Job interview work. I always think of her looking up over her desk with her glasses on, business forms in her hands. And a sharp new pencil and eraser."

"She's not alive?"

"She was killed in an accident when I was quite young."

"I think you told me. I'm sorry."

"I never missed her. I lived with my grandparents until I was old enough to work. It was my father that I loved. He played golf and wore an old cap. He had an old Model T Ford. We used to go out into the woods and have picnics. Maybe that's why I like the woods so much. He died when I was only six. It's funny. I haven't thought of him in years. I remember his voice. He had a big booming voice. He was huge. He towered over me."

"Did you have many girlfriends in high school?"

Carl's answer came slowly. "Not exactly. I went out a few times. But I was wrapped up in my books and that sort of thing."

"Did you have a crush on a certain girl?"

Carl flushed. "No."

"Don't you want to talk about it?"

He did not answer. His face was red.

"I'm sorry." Barbara touched his arm. "I didn't mean to pry. I want to know about you. I want to know the things that have happened to you. You don't mind, do you? Would you rather not talk to me?"

"Sometimes it's hard for me to talk to — to a woman."

Barbara smiled. "I won't make you talk. Do you want to go on?"

"Go on?"

"Reading. Your treatise."

Carl snatched it up. "Yes, I'll read some more." He found his place quickly. "I'll go on."

Barbara lay back again, against the wall. The room was warm and quiet. She closed her eyes. "It is comfortable. It's nice to lie here and listen to you read. You have a nice reading voice. It's pleasant to listen to. It makes me feel relaxed. I've been very taut, the last few days."

"Thank you." Carl cleared his throat. He went on, reading slowly and carefully, not looking at the girl beside him, but keeping his eyes on the page he held.

Again she was becoming sleepy. She tried to concentrate, but she could not make head nor tail of what he was reading.

What did it all mean? Ideas, words, carefully prepared sentences. She was going faster and faster to sleep. Her eyelids were like stones. She was slipping down farther each moment, her body lifeless, unresponding. She was powerless to help herself.

Carl glanced out of the corner of his eye at the girl. The sight of her, lying so close to him, gave him a sense of importance. He was glad to read to her. She was the first person who had heard his treatise. He was happy. Barbara liked him. She had said so. It was a long time since a girl had told him that. Had any girl ever told him that? He tried to think, but he could not remember. Perhaps this was the first time.

Carl read on and on, happily, contented to sit with the pages in his hands, aware of the room, the textures and colors in the half-darkness, the unmoving girl on the bed so near to him. It was very pleasant. Barbara was right. He felt relaxed, too. It was a good feeling. Warmth and the soft colors in the room.

After a while he set the manuscript down and took a deep breath. He was finished. He had read all the good parts to her. The reading was over. He turned toward her.

Barbara was asleep. She lay, partly against the wall, her hands limp in her lap, her body sagging, her head to one side. Her mouth was open slightly. Her chest rose and fell under her flowered blouse.

Carl was astonished. Dismay flooded over him. He stared at her. She did not stir.

"My gosh!" Carl exclaimed. "My good gosh!"

19

BARBARA STIRRED AND turned a little in her sleep. Carl gazed down at her. How could it be? How could she fall asleep? It did not seem possible.

Deep sorrow rolled over Carl. A tide of misery and despair. The silence of the room made him want to shout out loud. He gathered up his papers numbly and pushed them onto the table.

Barbara lay outstretched on the bed, one arm across her chest. She was pretty. Carl's unhappiness ebbed slightly. He studied her. What a strange face she had. There was nothing cute about it. The features were stiff, the nose a trifle too large, the teeth crooked and uneven. But her hair was thick and deeply colored. And her skin was clear and smooth. In her blouse and slacks she seemed quite slim. The heaviness that he had seen in that moment, as he stood watching her across the lake, was completely gone. She was supple and lithe, like a sleeping animal. Her inert body was full, rounded and filled out.

She was close. He could touch her if he wanted.

He fixed his gaze on her hand, resting only inches from him. Her fingers were white and tapered. Her nails a light red. A small hand. It was really a woman's hand that he saw. Strange. The hand seemed quite different from his own. Perhaps hands were more a key than anything else. The narrow wrist. Smooth skin.

Many times in his youth he had imagined this moment, when he would be sitting with a woman beside him. He could touch her. He could touch any part of her that he wished. Again, as in the early morning hours, he was a king, and this was one of his stone subjects, one of his enchanted people who had fallen into eternal sleep. As he had walked in the morning he had known the buildings belonged to him. They were silent and empty, and his footsteps had echoed hollowly as he passed them. They were his. The hills had been deserted, too. They also belonged to him.

It was the same way now. Beside him the girl lay, sleeping silently. She belonged to him. She had become his, to do with as he wished. It had been a long struggle to reach this point. He had never been this close to a woman before, close enough to see her chest rising and falling, close enough to hear the sound of her breathing. He leaned over her. He could touch her hair if he wanted to. He could let the strands of dark brown fall between his fingers.

She was enchanted, turned to stone, but not a hard and rigid stone. She was soft to the touch. He could see that. When he was a boy he had played with plastic oil clay, kneading and mashing the clay with his hands, making it warm and pliable. The Bible said that man was made from the clay of the ground. But this girl was made from soft clay, the soft warm clay that melted and bent in his hands, forming itself into shapes and forms that he wished, the soft oil clay that was never dry, never hard to the touch.

The clay of the ground from which man had come was a dry clay, nothing like this at all. He could almost feel the softness of her face. His fingers were only a little distance away. Carl trembled. It had been a long way for him, to come this far. Many years. His heart was pounding. Perspiration rose on his neck.

He had come so far. He was so close, so very close! He reached out his hand toward her, toward the soft silent face. She was only inches from him, from his touch. His fingers hovered above her cheek. So near —

He touched her.

Carl let out a deep shuddering breath. He had been holding his breath without realizing it. He gazed down in speechless wonder at the sight of his hand against the girl's face. Her skin was warm, warm and smooth. Even a little moist. The room was warm; there was a soft glow across her features, a moist sheen. Perspiration. There was perspiration on both of them. On his neck, under his arms. On her face.

His fingers moved toward her temple. And for the first time he touched her hair. It gave him a shock, a sudden surge that rushed up his spine, chilling him. How strange her hair felt! The countless strands.

Carl bent down. She was deep in sleep. He watched her breast rise and fall, under her flowered blouse. In the dim light the red of the flowers had deepened almost to black. Black flowers, great awesome orchids of purple and black. He could see that her blouse was silk. Through the fabric he could make out the line of straps. Her slip. And her — her bra. That was what it was called. He gazed at the line of her bra, rising and falling evenly.

He studied her neck. Her ears. The strange way her lips were parted, as she breathed. Her eyelashes. What a vast and complex mystery a woman was! There were so many things to take in, to consider and meditate over. Already he had seen enough to occupy his mind for days to come. So many strange and almost mystical things.

Mystical — that was the word for it. He caught his breath. He had felt that way outside. All the way, through the darkness, a feeling of religious awe. The temple, the offering. The solemn procession. And this —

His hands became rigid. His body tensed. He did not even breathe. The silent girl, lying asleep on the bed. Here was where the spirit was. He could feel it all around her. The aura. A radiation that seemed to pulse from every part of her.

He drew back and sat, not touching her at all, but only watching. A vigil. The idea captivated him. He was keeping a vigil over her. The Guardian. He was a protector. One who watched, endlessly, beside the holy fire. Beside the fire burning around the sacred couch, on which the sleeping goddess lay.

Carl sat, feeling the warmth from her, the glow of life that lay over her, rising from her. Time passed. He did not move. He could only sit and watch. He was rigid, silent, held spellbound by the sight, the sleeping woman before him. The holy fire surrounding her like an invisible cloud.

And then, slowly, almost invisibly, another idea crept into his mind. As he sat, watching the sleeping girl, a thought came to him that completely staggered him. It drove everything else out of his mind. It came soundlessly, inexorably. He could not tell from where it came. All at once it was there, within his mind. And there was nothing else.

He was amazed. Sweat broke out on his face, on his hands and neck. He began to shake. He licked his lips again and again. Down inside his shirt his heart began to thud loudly, painfully. Where had the thought come from? Why? He gazed down at the sleeping girl, at her half-parted lips. The orchids of her blouse seemed to have darkened even more. Her skin was light in contrast, a pale, glowing hue, rich and warm.

Carl leaned down. Would she wake up? Perhaps she would. But the idea could not be put down. It could not be denied, not now. Now it was too late. It had come. There was no turning back. It controlled him. It acted through him. He was a puppet. Even if she woke —

He bent over her, twisting to one side, toward the wall. His head dropped, lower and lower. And behold —

He peeked down the front of her blouse.

Barbara opened her eyes. Carl pulled himself up quickly. He flushed with embarrassment. The girl sat up slowly, blinking and rubbing her eyes. She looked around, at him, at the room.

"What — what did you say?" Her voice was thick with sleep. "I heard something. Did I — I didn't fall asleep, did I?"

"Just for a moment," Carl muttered.

"*Did I?*"

"Yes."

"Oh, Carl." She was silent. "I'm so sorry. I'm so terribly sorry."

Carl looked away in confusion. He said nothing. Did she know? Had she seen? He shut the memory out of his mind. Shame flooded up into his cheeks, burning them scarlet. He stood up quickly, taking out his handkerchief and blowing his nose.

On the bed, Barbara watched him, pulling herself up nervously. "Please forgive me, Carl. I didn't mean to fall asleep. I was listening."

He nodded, putting his handkerchief away.

"Will you forgive me?"

"Of course. It doesn't matter."

"It does." She stood up beside him. "Here, do you want some more of your wine?"

"No." Carl wandered around the room, not looking directly at her.

"Had — had you finished reading?"

"Yes."

"Would you read the last part again?"

Carl waved his hand impatiently. "It's not worth reading again."

"Don't be mean to me, Carl."

But he meant it. The treatise seemed remote to him, a thing far away. He did not care about it. He had forgotten that it existed. A strange, vague restlessness moved through him, making him walk about. He could not stay still. What was it? Shame? Guilt? He did not know. Whatever it was, he had never felt it before. Not that he could remember.

"What's wrong?" Barbara asked softly.

"Nothing."

"I can tell something's wrong."

"No." He went on pacing. What was it? Suddenly he turned toward her. She had sat down again, on the edge of the bed. The sight of her, her soft features, the bright silk of her blouse, made a rush of color climb to his cheeks again.

"You're still angry, aren't you?" Barbara said.

"No."

"What, then?"

"Nothing!" He went to the window and pulled the shade back. He stood looking out. After a time he became aware of Barbara standing silently behind him, standing very close to him. He could almost feel her breath against his neck.

"Carl?"

"Yes?"

"Will you ever forgive me? I didn't mean to fall asleep."

Carl smiled a little. The treatise. It was a good thing she hadn't — hadn't seen him. She thought he was angry at her for falling asleep. "Forget it."

He went back to looking out the window. The sky was full of stars, tiny bright stars. The sight of them made him feel more restful. They were so cold, so cold and remote. Like bits of distant ice.

He became calmer. The color drained from his cheeks. The flush of shame was gone, or whatever it had been. What *had* it been? Maybe he would never know. It was awful not to understand. What had happened to him? Why had he done such a thing? It was incredible! It was beyond belief. Incomprehensible.

He turned abruptly away from the window.

"I wish I could make you feel better," Barbara said. "Won't you tell me what it is?"

"Forget it."

"The wine didn't make you sick, did it?"

"No."

"Do you want some more?" She picked his glass up. "I'll pour you some more."

"No. No more wine." He had to get hold of himself. Gather himself together. He had to think. That was it. He had to think. Restore his reason. He had lost his reason for a while.

Carl sat down on the bed, picking up his papers from the table. He began to wrap the brown paper around them rapidly. Barbara watched him tie the string hurriedly into place, his hands trembling.

"Are you leaving?"

"I think I should." He got up, moving toward the door. "I'll see you tomorrow. At breakfast."

"But why?"

Carl shook his head. He was dazed. All he could think of was getting away. The sooner the better. Leave, get away. Where no one would see him. He had to get out before he did something else. Something awful. Fear leaped through him.

"Goodbye." He caught hold of the doorknob.

"You're really going?"

"Yes."

Her eyes were bright and wide. For a moment she stood facing him. Then she turned away. "Good night. I'll see you tomorrow."

Carl hesitated. "I —"

"Good night."

"I'll see you in the morning. At breakfast. We can talk then. All right? Tomorrow morning. Thanks a lot for the wine. Good night."

Suddenly Barbara's face twitched. She stiffened, rigid. "*Wait*."

Carl waited, puzzled.

"Did you hear it?"

Carl shook his head. "No. What?"

"Listen!"

They listened. Carl could hear nothing except his own breathing. His fingers tightened around the knob. He wanted to go. "Barbara —"

And then he heard it.

Outside the building someone was coming up the porch steps. The sound came again, distant, faint. A dragging sound. Slow steps, someone going up step by step, far below them, climbing slowly and ponderously.

"Somebody's down there," Carl said.

"Shhhh!"

The person was inside the building, now. Time passed, endless time. Then the person moved across the corridor to the inside stairs.

"He's coming up."

Barbara's face was strangely hard. Her eyes had narrowed. "Yes. He's coming up."

"Who is it? Is it Verne?" Carl spoke almost in a whisper. What was the matter with Barbara? She was rigid, hard. Her face was bleak. Like stone. "Is it Verne?" he said again.

She did not answer. The person had reached the top of the

stairs. He was coming down the hall, walking slowly, a little way at a time, his steps heavy and uneven.

"Is he carrying something?" Carl asked.

"He is."

The steps came closer. The person halted, just outside the door. Carl strained, listening. He could hear breathing. Short, thick breathing, like an animal.

Barbara crossed to the door. Carl stepped back. She grabbed hold of the knob, pulling the door open wide.

In the middle of the hall stood Verne Tildon. He stood strangely, his hands shoved way down in his pockets, rocking back and forth. His glasses were on wrong, far out on his nose. He was gazing at them over his glasses. His shirt tail was out. His tie was loose. The top buttons of his shirt were unfastened.

What was the matter? Carl moved back. What was he doing out in the hall? Verne rocked back and forth, on his heels, gazing first at Carl, then at Barbara. His gaze was dim and vacant. He seemed to sag, as if all the stuffing inside him were settling. He smiled strangely, a complex, enigmatic smile.

"Well," Verne said. "How are you?" He came slowly into the room. "What's the matter? Cat got your tongues?"

There was silence.

"Or perhaps I should say, cats got your tongue?" Verne cleared his throat. "Or perhaps — "

"All right," Barbara said sharply. She closed the door after him. "Sit down."

"Thank you." Verne bowed deeply. "Thank you." He looked uncertainly around the room.

"Over there." Barbara indicated a chair.

"Thank you." Verne walked unsteadily over to it. He sat down heavily, with a whoosh of air. "I hope that you don't mind a visitor coming to see you so late."

Barbara said nothing.

"What time is it?" Carl looked around for a clock. "Is it getting late?"

He made a move toward the door, clutching his brown paper package.

"Don't go," Barbara said quietly.

"No. Don't go. Stay." Verne belched suddenly, his eyes filming over. "Please stay."

Carl put the manuscript down on the dresser. He walked over and stood uncertainly by Barbara.

In the straight chair, Verne Tildon gazed silently up at them, his arms resting on the chair arms. No one spoke. At last Verne sighed. He removed his glasses, and bringing out a handkerchief he began to clean the lenses, slowly and carefully, getting each speck of dust off. He put the handkerchief back in his pocket and adjusted his glasses on his nose. He crossed his legs, leaning back in the chair and looking up at them, smiling distantly, pleasantly.

"What's been happening?" he said.

They did not answer. Carl looked down unhappily at him, not knowing what to say. Barbara walked over to the dresser and took a cigarette from the package. She lit up and returned to the bed.

"Well, Verne?" She sat down. "What brings you here so late?"

Verne frowned, concentrating. "Springtime."

"Oh?"

"Overcome by the smell of springtime, the budding of blossoms, and the unfolding of the little plants —" He paused. "I set out." He smiled, touching his finger tips together. Like an ancient, benevolent teacher, Carl thought. Old. Too old. Nodding and murmuring in senility. He felt a vague sadness, looking down at the man in the chair.

"Go on," Barbara said crisply.

"So I gathered myself up. And here I am."

Silence.

"After all, with all the plants and animals enjoying the bliss of each other's company, each other's willing company, it doesn't seem right for me to be lying in my cold room, between the cold sheets. Alone. All by myself."

They said nothing.

"What's the matter?" Verne looked up at them, raising an eyebrow. "I'm sorry if I'm casting a pall over things. You have a very nice room here, Barbara. You missed your calling. You should have been an interior decorator. You would have been great. Too bad you strayed from your path. Of course, I realize this display is not a usual event. I realize that it is for special occasions, state functions and the like." He paused for a long time, considering. "You know, when the sun goes down it gets very dark."

They waited.

"Everything gets dark. Everything cools off. It gets cold. Cold and dark. It's not nice at all. You can't find your god damn way around anywhere when it's dark." He glanced up plaintively. "I had a hell of a time getting here. There isn't any light to see by."

His trousers were muddy at the knees. Bits of grass stuck out from the wool fibers.

"Easy to fall over things." He rubbed his chin slowly, meditating. The expression on his face had changed. The enigmatic smile was gone. He was frowning, frowning as if he were in violent pain. His eyebrows knitted together, jerking tight. His fingers pressed against each other, suddenly twisting.

"I fell." He bit his lip. "I fell."

He reached into his coat pocket and felt slowly around, staring down at the floor. He turned to the other pocket, rummaging for an endless time. Carl and Barbara watched helplessly.

"What is it?" Carl said.

"What are you looking for?" Barbara demanded.

Verne went on, searching silently. He lurched to his feet, stumbling. Carl caught his arm. Verne pulled away. He moved off from them to the other side of the room. There he stood, staring fixedly down, still searching through his pockets, again and again.

"I've left or lost my pipe," he said finally.

He looked up at them, his face drooping. Suddenly his features all seemed to melt and give way. He pushed his glasses up, wiping at his eyes.

"Want a cigarette?" Barbara said.

"I want my pipe."

Carl moved hesitantly toward him. "It's probably back in the room. You probably left it back there."

"Don't you suppose that's where it is?" Barbara said.

Verne shook his head.

"Come on," Carl said. "We can go over and get it."

"Carl will walk back with you," Barbara said. "How would that be?"

"I've lost it someplace," Verne said.

Carl and Barbara looked helplessly at each other. No one spoke. Verne went over and sat down on the bed. The springs sagged under him. He took off his glasses and put them in his coat pocket.

Carl went over and stood by him, not knowing what to do. "Come on," he said at last. "Let's go look for it. Maybe you lost it on the way coming over."

Verne set his mouth, grim and stubborn.

"Don't you want to go look for it?" Carl said.

Verne said nothing. His small lined face was rigid.

"For God's sake, Verne," Barbara said. "Well, we can all go and look for it."

"Forget the god damn pipe!" Verne stuck his chin out angrily. Then he rubbed his forehead wearily. "Let it go. Forget about it. I gave my lighter away, anyhow. Now they're both gone."

"Don't you—"

"Forget it!"

Barbara stood with her arms folded, smoking. At last she put her cigarette out and got another from the pack on the dresser. She held the pack out to Verne.

"Cigarette?"

"I want my pipe."

Barbara struck a match, lighting her cigarette. She slid the pack into the pocket of her blouse and folded her arms again.

Carl motioned to her, toward the door to the hall. The two of them went outside the room. Carl closed the door behind them. He caught a glimpse of Verne, still sitting on the bed, small and wan, staring ahead of him.

"What'll we do?" Carl said in a low voice.

Barbara shrugged. "This has happened before. He'll be all right by tomorrow."

"Is he—is he going to stay *here*?"

"I guess he thinks so."

"But he can't!"

Barbara considered. "No. He can't."

"Then what'll we do? We have to get him back."

"Back?"

"To his own room."

"I wouldn't worry."

"What do you mean? Why not?"

"He'll pass out pretty soon and then you can carry him back. It's happened before."

"You don't seem very worried."

"Sorry. I—"

"What's going on out there?" Verne bellowed suddenly, through the door.

"We better go back in," Barbara said. She opened the door. Verne had put his glasses back on. He glared belligerently as they entered the room.

"Where did you go?"

"Out in the hall."

"Why?"

"No reason."

Verne grunted. He was silent for a time. "Well?" he said suddenly. "How have you two been getting along?"

"Fine," Carl said.

"That's good. What have you been doing?"

"We've been listening to Carl's treatise," Barbara said.

"That's nice."

"But we've finished that. Carl was about to go."

"Why don't we go back together?" Carl said to Verne. "We can walk back to the dorm together."

"Oh, there must be something to do here," Verne said.

"It isn't that. It's getting late."

"What were you doing when I came in?"

"Barbara had fallen asleep."

"It's annoying when they do that."

Carl frowned. "Oh?"

"You'll find out. Shows an improper lack of interest."

"It does?"

"One of the many pitfalls in this world. There are many." Verne's voice was thick, the words muffled. He droned on, frowning intently, concentrating on each word. "Many pitfalls. Sometimes they fall asleep. Sometimes they get sick on the rug. Sometimes they break things. Sometimes they just get up and walk out."

"That's the best," Barbara said.

Verne raised his eyes. "What?"

"That's the best idea. When they walk out."

"Then they have to pay their own bus fare the rest of the way home."

"It's worth it." Barbara was pale. She stubbed her cigarette out harshly. "Maybe you better go on back to your own room."

Verne blinked. "Why?"

"Yes, let's go," Carl said quickly. "Come on."

"Don't you people want to talk? What's the matter with you? Carl likes to talk. He was telling me. Nothing in the world better than a good talk."

"Carl, take him back with you," Barbara said. Her voice was hard. She opened the door to the hall.

"For Christ's sake!" Verne said irritably. "What's the matter with you?"

"I think we better go." Carl reached for his arm, but Verne pulled away.

"Don't be unsociable," Verne murmured.

"It's her room."

"But we're old friends. Did you know that? Barbara and I are old friends. It's not right to toss an old friend out like this. In the middle of the night."

"I think we should go," Carl said.

"You do? Are you perhaps an authority?" Verne's voice was drowsy. "I'm astonished." He belched suddenly, his mouth falling open, his eyes staring glassily. "I beg your pardon. As I was saying. Carl, you don't seem to realize that I have your best interests at heart."

"You do?"

"So don't hurry me. We both have your best interests at heart. You should pay attention." Verne raised his finger slowly. "All kinds of things you ought to know for your own good. Do you?"

"Do I what?"

"Somebody has to explain them to you. It might as well be me. After all, the father always passes on everything to his son."

"Come on," Carl said. "Let's go."

"Don't rush me." Verne set his lips grimly. "I don't like to be rushed. I have something to tell you. A very important thing. You should listen to me. Sit down and we'll have a talk. It's important that we talk. I have worked out a treatise to speak to you."

"A treatise?"

"An ethical system of philosophy. A very great approach. One of the most valuable sets of approaches in the world. I've gone over it in my mind a number of times to make certain that it surpasses all the others. All of the others who came before. Kant. Spinoza. Whoever it is that came before. Lots of them came before. An endless number of them. Each with his five dollars. Only with this you won't need five dollars."

Verne's voice droned off into an indistinct murmur.

"You should have let me tell you before. I told you I wanted to talk to you. Maybe it's better. Now it's all worked out. In order. You can't go wrong. It never fails. You may have to make little changes. That's where the creative element comes in. The art. From time to time. But not big changes."

"I don't understand," Carl murmured.

"Some like music, for instance. Some don't. For the ones who like music you should have a phonograph. And albums of records. Bach. Bartok. Stravinsky. And prints on the wall. Modigliani. Kandinsky. Some like to dance. A place is needed. A little dark place. Progressive combo in one corner. Quiet. Not too many people. You have to find what they like."

Verne swung his head around, searching them out. "What's the matter? Why are you two looking at me?"

"Let's go," Carl said.

"Let me finish. You make changes. Small changes. It varies. You have to work that out yourself. But I teach you the basic system. Sure-fire. Never fails. It has to be learned sometime. Learn it now. I know she'll be glad to cooperate. Will you cooperate, Barbara? I know she will. I know." His voice trailed off. "I know."

"Get out of here," Barbara whispered.

Verne blinked. "Get out?" His head turned slowly until he was looking in Carl's direction. "You see? Now it's too late. Sponsor has withdrawn her offer. That's too bad. I tried to help you. But you wouldn't listen while you had the chance. Now it's too late. You should have let me talk to you. This is a good place to start. I'm sorry. As good as any there are. Good place for a young man."

"Something's going to happen," Barbara said tightly.

"Happen? It's already happened. One came today. I had a long talk with him. Nice little fellow. Like a snake. Iron. Iron and blood. Nice little guy." All at once he roused himself. His face became hard. He fixed his gaze on Carl. "You know what I came here for? I came here to warn you. Something very important."

"Warn me?"

"To warn you not to. It's not safe. I've been thinking it over."

"What do you mean?"

"It's bad. Forget the whole thing. Let's go. We'll go back. It's not safe." Verne had risen to his feet. "Carl, I want to tell you more about her. I was just about your age. Ellen. Came from a good family in the Middle West. Golden hair. Hot little bitch. Be careful. They'll destroy you. There won't be anything left of you. Once they get hold of you they'll eat you up. I know. They'll use you up. You better come away. If she lets you in she'll never let you out."

Carl's face had gone sickly white. He moved unsteadily toward Verne.

Barbara screamed. Carl grabbed hold of Verne. He dragged him across the room to the door, his face a dull mask.

"Carl!" Barbara ran in front of him. Carl pushed her out of the way with his shoulder. He kicked the door open. Verne's head sagged. He collapsed, limp and dangling, like a bundle of rags. His glasses fell to the floor.

Carl threw him out into the hall. Verne crashed against the floor, his arms out, one of his shoes flying off. For a moment he sat, his head bowed against his chest. Then he settled slowly, slumping down, like a rag doll that had been tossed away.

"Oh my God," Barbara said.

Carl slammed the door. He turned toward her, his face distorted, trembling from head to foot. "He had no right to talk that way. To say those things about you. I shouldn't have done it. But he shouldn't have said those things about you."

Barbara covered her eyes, pressing her hands into her face. She shuddered. "We — we better see if he's hurt." She picked up Verne's glasses, kneeling down unsteadily.

"Did they break?"

"No. Open the door."

Carl opened the hall door. Verne lay stretched out on the floor. He did not stir.

"Is he all right?" Carl said.

Barbara bent down, examining him. "Yes. He's all right. Passed out. He'll be all right. We better get him back to his room."

20

BETWEEN THEM THEY got Verne to his feet. He mumbled something they did not understand. They half carried, half dragged him down the hall to the stairs, down the stairs onto the porch. The night was cold and dark. Stars shone, scattered above them in the sky.

"I'm sorry," Carl said, pausing to get back his breath. "I know I shouldn't have done it. I don't do things like that. I don't know what happened to me. But he shouldn't have said those things."

"He'll be all right."

"In a way he had it coming to him. He was very insulting. Don't you think so? I wouldn't have done it if I hadn't been on edge."

"Let's go."

With Verne between them they made their way along the path. The air was thin and sharp. Carl took a deep breath, filling his lungs. "It's nice. The night air. I like it when it's this way. Clean and cold. I hope he'll be all right. I hope I didn't break anything. Do you think he'll be all right?"

Barbara did not answer. Between them, Verne had begun to stir a little. He grunted, trying to pull back. Carl held on tight to him.

"Don't let him fall," Barbara said.

"Maybe we'll find his pipe. He probably lost it along the way someplace. Don't you think?"

"I don't know."

They reached the men's dormitory without finding Verne's pipe. Verne had passed out again. Carl carried him up the stairs to the second floor, Barbara following behind. By the time he had put him down on his bed Carl was gasping and panting.

"Gosh." Carl stepped back from the bed. "What a job. I'm glad that's over."

Verne lay sprawled out on the bed, his mouth open, his body limp and loose. They could hear him breathing.

"What should we do?" Carl asked. "Will he sleep for a while? Should we do anything else?"

"Cover him with a blanket."

Carl got the top blanket over Verne. He pushed a pillow under Verne's head. "How will that be? There's not any chance of him smothering, is there?"

"No." Barbara wandered around the room. The room smelled of John Jamison. She bent over the waste basket, reaching down into it.

"What is it?"

Barbara pulled out the John Jamison bottle. It was almost empty. There was a little in the bottom. She put the bottle on the dresser. "I can almost understand it, now."

"What do you mean?"

"That's good stuff."

Carl nodded. He was still looking at Verne lying on the bed, under the blanket. "It's certainly an unfortunate thing, isn't it? A person with such a keen mind as he has. We shouldn't treat it as a moral crime, the way they used to, though. It's more an illness."

"I guess it is."

"I understand they can do things for it these days. Psychoanalysis, health farms, or creative therapy of some sort. They're making great strides."

Barbara said nothing. The room was silent except for Verne's heavy breathing. Carl moved around uneasily. After a while he removed Verne's tie and pulled his collar open. Verne stirred, snorting and grunting. Like an animal. Carl stepped back from the bed.

"It's too bad," he murmured. "I wish we could do something. But I guess we can't."

"No. He'll come to. Sometime tomorrow. This has happened before. He'll recover."

"It's certainly a shame."

Barbara moved to the door. "Coming?"

Carl hesitated. "I —"

"You left your manuscript. It's still back in the room."

"That's right. I did forget it. I'll go back with you and pick it up."

"Let's go, then." Barbara went out into the hall. Carl followed after her.

Barbara's room was frigid. They had left the door open and the night air had come in. Barbara closed the door after them. "I have an electric heater. I'll plug it in."

She got the heater from the closet and attached it to the wall socket. In a few minutes the elements were glowing warmly. Some of the chill left the room.

Carl stood in front of the heater, rubbing his hands together. "That feels good. It's a cold night."

Barbara sat down, lighting a cigarette. She sat smoking, leaning back on the bed, watching Carl in front of the little heater. "Yes. It is cold."

"I feel a lot better already. Isn't it strange how slight changes in the temperature affect your whole mood? I never feel right when I'm cold. Or damp. When I'm damp, or I have a headache or indigestion or some little pain, I never can think straight. My mind won't function right at all."

Barbara nodded.

"It shows how you can't escape the physical. Just when you start thinking you have a soul something comes along that disagrees with your stomach, and in a few minutes you find yourself faced with the fact that without your stomach you wouldn't be able to exist. We're as much a part of the physical as the mental. Sometimes I even think more so. If I had my choice I'd retain my physical over my mental part. Isn't that strange? You're not supposed to feel that way. You're supposed to believe your soul is wonderful and your body is wicked. Right?"

"Yes."

"I guess that's because of centuries of Christian teaching. It was the early Church people who advanced the concept of duality in the human being. The body of unworthy material and the pure spirit. They saw man as broken up in two parts, two conflicting parts. The body dragged the soul down into sin. The soul was lucky when it managed to get away from the body."

Barbara said nothing.

"It's an idea that's quite persuasive. It follows us around everywhere. Even the most advanced Westerners automatically accept the Christian duality. Like Freud. He assumed the unconscious was evil because it was associated with body instincts and passions. That's following right along in the Christian spirit."

Carl waited for Barbara to say something. She was gazing past him, cigarette smoke drifting around her. The room was beginning to become comfortably warm. By his feet the little electric heater glowed and simmered.

"But actually there's no reason why we should accept the Christian dichotomy. The concept of the innate depravity of man's natural instincts, his bodily needs. Eating, sleeping, reproduction. All natural functions. Spinoza demonstrated that. He advanced the concept of man as a whole, a single entity of body and mind working as a unit, together. Neither part bad. He pointed out that no one had ever seen a body without a mind, or a mind working without a body. We know them only together. So how could we talk about them as if they were distinct things? He had an interesting thought there, don't you agree? Doesn't that sound like a realistic appraisal?"

"It sounds all right."

"It's a monistic concept. Supplanting the dualism of the Christians." Carl babbled on, faster and faster, his words running together. He could not seem to stop. In a remote, detached way he wondered about it. Why was he going on so? What was the matter with him? But on he went, in a frenzy of theory and interpretation. His mind raced wildly, embracing whole vast concepts at one fell swoop. The mysteries of the universe dissolved around him, showering their secrets in his lap. He was drowning in an ocean of perceptions. All the while Barbara said nothing. She sat smoking silently, staring ahead, into the half-darkness of the room.

At last Carl slowed down to a stop. He threw himself down in a chair, exhausted. All at once he was completely worn out. His mind was vacant. Empty.

"Is it true?" Barbara said. "They're here?"

Carl stirred. "They?"

"The yuks."

"Verne says one came. He talked to him today."

Barbara put her cigarette out and lit another. She leaned back again, against the wall, her arms folded, smoke drifting up.

"What are you thinking about?" Carl asked.

"Nothing."

"Nothing at all?"

"About my life."

"You sound so unhappy."

"I took the wrong path. That god damn Verne Tildon was responsible."

"Oh?"

"I don't want to talk about it. You saw him tonight. You saw how he is. He wanted me to be that way."

"He did?"

"Of course. He wanted me to live like that. With him. I was something to satisfy his physical needs. Something he could pick up and use when he felt like it."

Barbara leaped to her feet and crossed the room to the heater. She yanked the plug out.

"It's too damn hot in here."

Carl nodded.

"What a stupid thing to look back on. It was years ago. Everything is so damn stupid." She raised the shade and stared out the window at the night. "So they're here. Well, they can have everything. Why they want it I don't know. A dirty, empty ruin. They're welcome to it." She put her fingers against the glass. "It's cold outside."

Carl got to his feet. "Cold and late."

Barbara turned from the window. "Cold and late. You know, we have many things in common. You make me feel better. I feel better being with you."

Carl flushed with pleasure. "I'm glad."

Barbara paced back and forth. "I'll be quite ready to turn things over to them. They can take it all. Dirty, cold, barren old place. How do we leave here? Is there a car? How do we get away?"

"Ed Forester left us a truck. Verne knows where it is. It's in one of the sheds someplace."

"We'll leave together. When we get in India we can take the

same train. The two of us. We can go all the way back to the States together. The same train, the same boat. What do you say? Do you want to do that?"

"That would be fine."

"Yes. Yes, it would be fine. It's a long way. A long way to go. It's a cruel world, Carl. A little warmth won't do any harm."

Carl agreed.

Barbara turned suddenly toward him. "You don't have to if you don't want to. You don't have to go back with me."

"I'd like to."

"It'll be a long trip."

"I really would like to."

"All right. We'll go back together."

Carl was pleased. "We can talk. We'll be able to talk about things on the way."

"Is that what it means to you?"

Carl hesitated. "Why, I —"

"Just talking? Nothing more than that?"

Carl twisted in embarrassment. "Of course it's more than that. Naturally. That goes without saying."

Neither of them spoke. The room was silent. With the heater unplugged the room began to grow cold again. The night air was coming back, seeping through the cracks in the walls, under the window, under the door. Carl was cold and tired. He moved toward the door. He felt numb. So many things had happened so quickly.

"I should be going back to my room. I'll see you at breakfast tomorrow. I hate to go." He lingered. "I hope he's still asleep. Maybe I'll move my bed to the far end of the dorm. It smells. It reeks."

"They'll be here soon. You won't have to stand it much longer."

"That's right. Any time now, I suppose." He took hold of the doorknob.

"Stay a while longer," Barbara said.

Carl hesitated. He wanted very much to go back to his room and throw himself into bed. "It's so late."

"What are you going to do?"

"Go to bed."

Barbara nodded. Her face was expressionless. He waited a moment and then opened the door.

"Good night."

"Good night, Carl."

Carl smiled. She did not smile back. Was she mad at him? He was too exhausted to think about it. "Well, I guess I'll see you tomorrow."

He went slowly down the hall, his hands deep in his pockets. Cold night air blew around him. The hall was bleak and dim. Deserted. He came to the top of the stairs and started down, holding onto the banister.

Behind him there was a sound. He looked back.

Barbara was standing in the corridor, at the door of her room, outlined in the light. She was watching him.

"What is it?" He came back a little way.

"You forgot your book."

Foolish embarrassment flooded over him. "Oh. I did, didn't I?" He hurried back, along the hall toward her. "That's what I came over for."

Barbara stepped aside. Carl entered the room, looking around.

"Where is it?"

"On the dresser."

Carl found the brown paper package lying where he had put it. He picked it up in his hands and stood holding it. The room was silent. Barbara came in from the hall and walked over to the window.

"Thanks for reminding me," Carl said. He sat down on the edge of the bed, his manuscript in his lap. He ran his fingers over the rough paper, smoothing it down with automatic care. After a while he got to his feet again. He moved toward the door. "Well, I guess I —"

"Don't leave."

"But I —"

"I don't want you to go." Barbara did not look at him. Her voice was thin and hard. A sharp command. He sat down awkwardly, the bed springs sagging and groaning under him. Tiredness seeped over him. Why did she want him to stay? What for?

He laid his manuscript down on the floor. He was too tired to understand. Perhaps later on, in the morning, when he had time to think it all over, when he could fit everything together into one picture —

He leaned back, resting against the wall. He closed his eyes. Barbara stood at the window staring out, her arms folded. Carl yawned. Soon he would go, when it was all right to go. After a while. His body was like lead. He seemed to be sinking down into the bed. Like lead that had been dropped in the ocean. Down and down. He sighed, stretching out.

He must have dozed. All at once it was later.

He opened his eyes. He was stiff and cold. His head ached. Barbara was no longer standing at the window. She was sitting on the bed by him, close by. She was doing something very rapidly and silently, bending over, her hands moving. What was she doing?

He stirred, lifting up a little.

She was taking off her sandals. She unfastened her sandals and put them over in the corner, by the end of the bed. She stood up and unbuttoned her blouse. She slipped her blouse from her and hung it over the back of a chair. She unzipped her slacks. She stepped out of them and folded them into the seat of the chair.

Carl must have made a sound. Suddenly she turned, looking intently down at him. Her face was full of hunger. Full of avid desire.

He was astonished. The astonishment gave way to shock. She was gazing down at him, twitching with naked yearning, her body taut and rigid. Was he dreaming?

"What — what time is it?"

"Two o'clock."

"Two o'clock! Good Lord. I should go."

She said nothing. She stood in front of him in her underclothes, her body hard and pale. Some of the wild hunger had faded from her face. Her face was cold, sharp. It frightened him. Fear moved through him, gaining force.

"I have to go." He struggled to get to his feet.

"Really?"

"Yes. It's late."

Barbara was silent. At last she spoke. Her voice was calm, detached. As if she were far away, remote from him. Lost in thought. "You know," she said, "You and I are the only ones here. For miles around. I've been thinking about it. Except for Verne, of course. But he's asleep."

The room was very still. Outside the window the night was cold. He could hear the night wind moving through the trees, stirring the branches together. There was no other sound. Wind and silence. Cold darkness. It was the truth. They were the only ones alive for endless miles. The brittle frozen coldness was all around them.

"Are you afraid?" Barbara said.

"No."

"You shouldn't be. You see, it's only that I want you so. But I wonder how you feel."

He did not know how to answer.

"You *are* afraid."

"No."

"Carl, do you want to go? You may, if you want."

He shook his head.

"Do you want to stay here?"

"I —" He hesitated. "I guess so. I think so." His heart was pounding, pounding so loudly that he could hardly speak. He got to his feet and walked around the room, touching things, examining a print on the wall, the cover of a book. He took a book from the bookcase and opened it.

Finally he put the book back. His mouth and lips were dry. He moistened them with his tongue. "Could — could we talk for a while?"

Barbara did not answer.

"Couldn't we talk?"

"Carl, why do you want to leave?"

"I don't know."

"It's cold and barren outside. Don't you want to stay here where it's warm? Don't you want to be warm?"

"Sure. Yes, of course."

She was watching him intently. In her underclothes she seemed even more naked than when he had seen her in the water, in the little artificial lake. There were goose-pimples up and down her legs, on her thighs and arms.

"Don't you want to be with me?"

"Yes. It's very nice here."

Barbara took her cigarettes from her blouse. She dropped the blouse back down on the chair and lit a match. Carl watched her smoking and staring past him. Abruptly she stubbed the cigarette out against the ashtray on the table. She reached behind her, unhooking the bra. She laid the bra over her blouse on the chair. "Carl?"

"Yes."

"Why won't you look at me?"

"I don't know."

"Please look at me."

Carl looked. She had taken off all her clothes and was standing completely naked in the center of the room. Her body was pale. She was shivering in the cold. He could see her flesh ripple.

Carl looked away again. Presently there was a creaking sound. "Carl?"

"Yes."

"Don't you want to come to me?"

He turned. She was lying on the bed, her naked legs raised, her arms at her sides. She was waiting for him, staring up at the ceiling.

"I —" He stood helplessly, twisting.

"Don't you want me?"

"Yes. But I —"

"That time at the lake. When you saw me. You weren't afraid then, were you? You were glad. I know. You didn't run away. I could tell."

Carl picked up his manuscript from the floor. He crossed toward the door. "I don't want to be foolish in front of you. There are so many things I don't know. Do we have to, now? Can't we wait? Later —"

She rose quickly from the bed, coming toward him. "But I want you now, Carl."

He could hear her breathing rapidly. Harsh, quick sounds. She slipped between him and the door, her breasts rising and falling.

"But I don't know what to do!"

"I'll show you."

"Couldn't we — wait?"

She shook her head. In the darkness outside the window the night wind rose, blowing through the trees. They could hear it moving, brushing the tree branches against the side of the building.

"Hear the wind," Barbara said.

"Yes."

Barbara reached out to the lamp. She snapped it off. The room was in darkness. Carl felt his heart begin to beat hard, slow booming beats, like an echoing thing far down in a vault. It was painful. He could hardly breathe. He was shaking all over, from cold and fear. In the darkness he could see nothing. Where was she? Where had she gone?

Her hand touched his arm. Then she was around him, warm and breathing, her body like fire. It burned him, the insistent pressure, pushing and beating against him. She was tearing at him, straining and clawing. He staggered.

She crowded him against the edge of the bed. He sat down heavily, the springs groaning under him. Now she was above him, filling the darkness, leaning over him. He slid away, struggling to his feet. He was weak with fear.

"Barbara — "

She was moving someplace in the darkness. He strained to hear. His arm touched something, the edge of the table. The ashtray fell to the floor, clinking.

She came quickly, grabbing for him. She was completely silent. There was no sound. Like a dream. Carl pulled away. Her nails left streaks of pain along his arms.

Again he could hear her breathing, panting in the cold darkness. He sensed her very near, almost by him. He put up his hands —

She caught hold of him, hard little arms tight around him.

Panting, breathing, silently working, she unfastened his clothes, tugging them away from him. Her unceasing, relentless fingers ripped his shirt loose, buttons flying.

He shoved her away. And was caught, swept up in a tide of flesh that engulfed him completely. He choked, gasping frantically for breath. Suddenly her teeth sank into his neck, biting into his muscles. He shoved and she let go.

Carl stepped back. He wavered, his arms out. He fell slowly, sprawling down, outstretched onto the bed. Before he could get up she was on him, pressing him back. He was helpless. Her arms were like steel.

For a moment she hung in the darkness above him, holding him down. Carl braced himself, crying out in pain. Then silently, soundlessly, she descended over him, flowing onto him, a crushing, inexorable weight.

Her breath hissed in his face. Her knees dug into him. He lay back, gasping, a sightless, weak thing lost in the darkness. The darkness and the clinging weight shuddered against him, turning into warmth, glowing and smouldering around him.

He was surrounded by warmth. A restless warmth that moved unceasingly, flowing back and forth, on and on. His eyes closed. His body relaxed. He ceased to struggle.

The motion picked him up. He was carried away, swept into the warm tide that plucked and pulled at him. Sweeping and lashing around him, scalding hot.

Finally, he slept.

Later, when much time had passed, time that was lost in the unknowable, the unthinkable, and the day was making itself ready to appear, Carl heard a sound.

He opened his eyes, lifting up suddenly in the bed, alert. Beside him the sleeping woman lay unmoving. She did not stir.

Carl listened. Far off, the sound came again. It was like thunder, a firm constant motion, a rumbling, steady and insistent. It made the building shake. It made everything in the room rattle and vibrate. Carl sat, listening intently, fully awake. Gray light was beginning to filter under the shades into the room.

The sound was coming nearer. It was moving, moving along, closer and closer. Toward them.

At last Carl sank back in the bed. He closed his eyes. He knew what the sound was. But he did not care. He was too exhausted. He was drained, left empty. He would care later, perhaps. Later it would mean a great deal.

But now he was too tired to worry or think about it. Trucks were on the road, moving along the highway, trucks and motorcycles. An endless procession hurrying through the early hours of the morning. Men bent over their handlebars, goggles and helmets, men in uniforms bumping up and down.

But at this moment it did not matter. Perhaps in some dim, distant time he would care and be interested, and worry. But now he did not feel concerned.

He sank back, farther and farther, into the soft bed. Beside him the woman stirred a little.

Carl returned to sleep.

EPILOGUE

THE YOUNG SOLDIER got off his motorcycle and stumped over. He was short and heavy, loaded down with equipment. His back bulged with a metal case, a rifle, a flashlight, tools, and many small lumpy objects wrapped up and tied together. He wore the parts of several uniforms, the shirt too large for him, the cap much too small. His legs were wound with cloth.

Carl and Barbara and Verne watched silently. The young soldier came up to them and stopped in front of them. He bowed slightly, keeping his eyes on them. His face was flat and featureless, like a dish. He reached into his shirt pocket and brought out his papers.

"The others are following. They will be here in a few minutes."

"We're all ready to leave," Verne said. "Our stuff is packed in the truck."

"Good." The young soldier bowed slightly again and turned to go back to his motorcycle.

Carl ran up to him and walked along beside him. "You don't mind if I talk to you, do you? Can I ask you a couple of things?"

The young soldier glanced at him and nodded.

"What do you think of the place? All these buildings and machinery. You know, we've been here a long time. It feels strange to leave."

The young soldier nodded noncommittally. He stopped at his motorcycle, looking around. The office building reared up at the edge of the road.

"That's our office. Where we do all our paper work. Do you want to come inside and see it? The records are still stored there. In the closet. We didn't take anything away. Everything is left for you. It's no good to us. I guess you'll want to set up your headquarters there."

The young soldier nodded. He crossed the road and started up the steps. Carl followed him, up the steps and into the office.

"Kind of a gloomy day," Carl said.

The young soldier wandered around the office. He stopped at the desk, examining the typewriter and all the papers scattered around. He opened the drawer and peered into it.

"You can clean all that out," Carl said. "You'll probably want to throw most of it away."

"Yes." The young soldier pulled the chair back and sat down at the desk. He stared impassively up at Carl. Carl began to feel a little uneasy. What was he thinking? It was impossible to tell. The man's face was perfectly blank. Presently his gaze moved from Carl to what Carl held gripped in his hand.

Carl looked down. "This? This is a treatise. A treatise on ethics. Philosophy."

The young soldier continued to gaze at the brown paper wrapped package in Carl's hand.

"Are you interested in such things?" Carl asked. He looked out the window. Verne was backing the truck out of the shed, onto the road. "I have to be going in a minute. He's getting the truck out. I don't want to be left behind. There won't be any other way to get out of here."

The young soldier said nothing.

Carl moved away from the window. "I've always wanted to talk to one of you people. There are things I want to know. I've been trying to find them out. Working them out in my mind. But I can't seem to get all of the answers. I can't seem to get them straight."

The soldier was watching him.

"I've been thinking a long time. Maybe you can help me. Maybe you know. Can I ask you?"

The soldier nodded.

"You people believe in force. Don't you? Don't you believe in force?" Carl rubbed his eyes, shaking his head wearily. "I'll be going in a minute. You know about such things. Force. Violence. Are things like that right? How can you know? You use force. You use ruthless force to get what you want. To get things done. You think they have to be done. You're completely ruthless about it. You let nothing stand in your way. You destroy everything in your way because it has to be done. Isn't that so? Isn't that what you do?"

Outside, beyond the office, the truck horn sounded harshly. Carl jumped a little. He moved toward the desk.

"But what if you're wrong? How can you be sure? Is there some way to tell? Maybe you can give me the answer. Is a person right in using force? He thinks he's doing the right thing. But maybe he's wrong. How is he to know? How do you know you're right? Maybe you're wrong. You destroy everybody who stands in your way. Maybe you're destroying too much. Maybe you're making a mistake. How do you know? *Do* you know? Is there some way to tell?"

The young soldier said nothing.

"Can't you tell me?" Carl asked.

Still the young soldier said nothing. He sat at the desk silently, his face bland and expressionless. Carl began to become angry.

"I'd like to know how you can be so sure you're doing the right thing. I'd like to see what proof you have. Can't you tell me in so many words? What do you go on? Where's your sanction? How can you be certain you're doing the right thing?"

The young soldier sat for a moment. He reached out his hand and touched Carl's manuscript.

"Do you want to see it?" Carl held it out. But the young soldier shook his head. "I don't understand."

The young soldier reached into his shirt. He brought out a little paperback book, shabby and worn, creased and folded again and again. He opened it, spreading it out on the table, smoothing the corners. He made a motion to Carl to come over. Carl came over beside him, looking down at the book. The characters were Chinese.

Tracing the words with his fingers the young soldier translated, slowly and haltingly.

"You oppressed peoples of the world! Arise! You have nothing to lose but your age-old bondage that has held you down. That has made slaves of you and taken what is yours. A new spirit is marching. Come out of your farms, from your land, from your shops. Join with us as we march through the world, crushing all those who oppose us. All the imperialists. All the reactionaries. All the blood-suckers who have drunk the people's blood. The world must be cleaned. The world must be seared clean. The face of the earth must be burned clean of the maggots and pests who have eaten and fed on the people. They must be cut into bits, tramped on, spat on, brought to their knees. From country to country, land to land, the — "

The young solder paused, looking up at Carl. His face was bland, and crafty. He watched Carl to see how he was reacting. He pushed the book around to Carl, turning the pages.

Carl laid down his manuscript and picked up the book. On the next page was a picture, a drawing in bright colors. Two men and two women, broad-faced, smiling, in native costumes. Leaning against a tractor.

The young soldier watched Carl, hopeful and alert. He smiled at Carl, pointing to the book.

Carl pushed the book back to him. "Thank you," he murmured. "Thanks."

He picked up his manuscript and moved toward the door. The young soldier began to fold his paper-backed book up again. Carefully, he restored it to his shirt. He was still smiling as Carl opened the door and went slowly down the steps, onto the road. Verne had brought the truck around. He waved to Carl.

"Come on! We're going."

Carl walked slowly toward the truck. The fog drifted and eddied around him. It had not lifted yet. The towers and buildings were vague and ghostly, lost in the gray murk. Verne snapped on the headlights of the truck as Carl came up to the door.

"Let's go," Verne said impatiently. He pushed the door open. Barbara moved over for Carl.

Carl got into the truck, his brown paper package gripped tightly against him.

"All right." He leaned back, closing the door. "I'm ready to go."

"It's a good thing," Barbara said. "We have a long way to go."

"I know," Carl said. "I know."

AFTERWORD

WALKING IN AN AGORAPHOBIC'S WONDERLAND

WHEN WAS *Gather Yourselves Together* written? No one knows for sure, but two of Philip K. Dick's biographers, Lawrence Sutin and Gregg Rickman, assert that *Gather* is Dick's first surviving novel. Sutin dates it between 1949 and 1950, while Rickman's only assertion is that Dick must have finished it before joining the Scott Meredith Agency in 1952. Andy Watson (publisher, WCS Books) and I exchanged voluminous electronic mail hashing out this question. Andy believes that *Voices from the Street,* a much cruder novel (and the only remaining unpublished Philip K. Dick novel manuscript), was written first; an opinion shared by Paul Williams. I'm inclined to side with Sutin and Rickman, whose circumstantial evidence for *Gather* being first I find more compelling. However, Andy suggests (and I'm inclined to agree) that *Gather* may have been polished up at some later date.

So, if we figure *Gather* as written between 1949 and 1951 (just to cover all the bases), what and where was Phil Dick at the time? He was living in Berkeley, working at Art Music. He had already been married (and divorced) once, and was probably seeing Kleo Apostolides, whom he wed in June of 1950. In the fall of 1949, he tried attending the University of California at Berkeley (and lasted about two months).

Gregg Rickman, in particular, details Dick's agoraphobia at the time, something he would overcome later in life. But during this period Dick had great difficulty eating in public; he stuck to one particular table at one particular restaurant near Art Music, in an almost compulsive fashion. Since childhood he had suffered from a psychological difficulty in swallowing (Rickman refers to this as "conversion dysphagia" or "globus hysteria"). Dick was also still exploring his sexuality and his relationships with women — relationships highly colored by both the experience of his mother and the idea of his twin sister (she died only days after their shared birthday).

The China of *Gather* is not the "real China," but a Disneyland for agoraphobics, an early version of the post-Apocalypse worlds of novels like *Do Androids Dream of Electric Sheep?* and *Dr. Bloodmoney*. This may have been Dick's idea of Paradise at the time; a nearly limitless world to explore, where all the creature comforts are still intact and there are "no deeds to do or promises to keep." None, because there's no one to answer to except one's self (or, as Verne says, "Rules and mores don't mean a thing anymore. There's no one here but us"). A clean slate.

One of the more telling and touching aspects of this "paradise" is the description of the kitchen in Chapter 4. Here's all this food, more than anyone could eat in a lifetime, and an ideal place to eat it: the "civilized" world is gone, and Carl/Dick doesn't have to worry about his dysphagia. (Also consider Dick's poverty during this period: a time when he and Kleo were buying and eating horsemeat from the Lucky Dog Pet Shop.)

Buried in *Gather* is also a Garden of Eden allusion: Barbara and Teddy are the Eves, aggressive seducers dangling the apple of their sexuality before Carl and Verne. Though Dick never clearly states it, the novel implies that Verne wound up in China, exiled from his normal life, as an escape from Teddy. And when Carl finally takes a bite of Barbara's apple, we've reached the climax of the novel: after that, nothing remains but the final expulsion from the symbolic paradise.

Carl Fitter is clearly an analogue of Phil Dick (or at least the Dick of that period). There's no room here for a detailed exploration of Phil Dick's childhood (the interested reader should try Gregg Rickman's *To the High Castle / Philip K. Dick: A Life 1928–1962*, published by Fragments West, or Lawrence Sutin's *Divine Invasions* from Harmony Books), but it's important to understand that much of Carl Fitter's flashback (Chapters 14–16) can be read directly as autobiography: the life in the East, the relationship with his mother, the separation from his father at an early age, the brief college career.

While Carl Fitter is, without argument, Phil Dick, the case for Barbara Mahler as Kleo Apostolides is much less clear, the parallels much less explicit. I still think, though, that Barbara's character is based heavily on Kleo — or at least, Dick's view of Kleo at that time. Note, particularly, that Carl is constantly afraid of alienating Barbara, and how he places her on a pedestal, reads to her from his "philosophy," and treats her as an intellectual equal: a recurring theme in Dick's relationships.

The character of Teddy would seem to have a much more obvious basis: Dick's imaginary friend "Teddy," and his possible later use of "Teddy" as a pseudonym for some of his youthful writings. But it's hard for me to imagine Dick making his imaginary friend, possibly another manifestation of his longing for his dead twin, into the psychotic Hell-bitch that the Teddy of *Gather* turns into. I think he may have been working out some of his feelings about his disastrous first marriage, and Teddy represents Dick's view of his first wife — a view tinged with a great deal of bitterness, and probably not completely accurate.

Verne Tildon is very probably Dick's first character based on his Art Music boss and long-time role model, Herb Hollis. Carl's obvious admiration for Verne, and his final break with Verne, prefigure Dick's admiration for, and eventual break with, Hollis. And the Hollis character template is central to some of Dick's best work (such as the Glen Runciter in *Ubik* and Leo Bulero in *The Three Stigmata of Palmer Eldritch*), as well as a recurring motif in his mainstream work. I think Verne Tildon is also based partially on another Art Music employee, Vince Lusby, who arranged for Dick to lose his virginity (and seems to have shared Verne's fondness for jazz).

In the end, *Gather Yourselves Together* is much more successful as a historical document than as a novel. *Gather* shows us just how early some of Dick's themes and tropes began to develop. Though it doesn't come close to the tear-your-heart-out intensity of Dick's best work, it remains, I think, a valuable addition to the man's work, and an invaluable window into his life.

Dwight Brown
Austin, Texas